# SEARCHING

# FOR

# AMERICA

*A Novel of Survival in a Nation Without Laws*

# R. THOMAS ROE

# Searching for America

A Novel of Survival in a Nation Without Laws

by R. Thomas Roe

Signalman Publishing   2011
www.signalmanpublishing.com
email: info@signalmanpublishing.com
Kissimmee, Florida

Publisher's Note:
This is a work of fiction. Names, characters, places, and incidents are either the product of the author's imagination or are used fictitiously, and any resemblance to actual persons, living or dead, business establishments, events, or locales is entirely coincidental.

Interior layout and design by John McClure

ISBN:
978-1-935991-07-6 (paperback)
978-1-935991-08-3 (ebook)

Library of Congress Control Number: 2011927932

Cover design by Duncan Long
www.duncanlong.com

Other books by R. Thomas Roe

*The Gaelic Letters*

*Palm Beach Gold*

*When plunder becomes a way of life for a group of men living together in society, they create for themselves in the course of time a legal system that authorizes it and a moral code that glorifies it.*

— Frédéric Bastiat, 1848

# Chapter One

Melbourne, Florida

Stuart was running as fast as he could. It was pitch dark but he was familiar with the path from the house to the shoreline of the Indian River. He was staying low to avoid the bullets that were screaming past him. At least two of the men were firing at them and the bullets were coming way too close. If they could get into the brush that ran alongside the river, they might have a chance. Chris, his wife, was right behind him and he could hear her breathing hard. "Chris, we're almost there."

The next sound he heard he knew was one or more bullets slamming into his wife. He heard the air rush out of her lungs and she tried to speak but she never finished the word before she crumpled to the ground. He stopped, looked back and fired two shots at the dark silhouettes of his attackers. His shots missed but they momentarily stopped the chase as the two men sought cover and that gave him time to quickly check his wife. He only needed a moments glance to see that she had suffered a fatal head as well as a chest wound. There was no pulse and both wounds were massive. His attackers were again on the move towards him and there was nothing he could do for her. He fired again and ran for his life. Stuart dove for cover behind the nearest shrubs and made his way down to the river bank. He found the canoe and pushed it out into the water. He jumped in and began to paddle furiously to get away from the shoreline and the two men who were not far behind him. The sky was overcast with no sign of moon or stars and there was no artificial light coming from either shore to illuminate him or his canoe. He made it some distance from shore and when he looked back, he saw his attackers had reached the river bank and were pointing in his general direction. He tried to crouch down in the canoe and continue to paddle away from the shore. The current and a steady breeze from the west were taking him farther away from the shore and deeper into the darkness.

Stuart knew he would be safe soon, but not soon enough. The force of the bullet that struck him in his right shoulder threw him forward and almost out of the canoe. There was little pain but he realized that his right arm was numb and not functioning. Using only his left arm, Stuart did his best to maneuver the canoe towards the opposite shore of the barrier island that lay some fifty yards away. He realized that he was losing a lot of blood. His shirt was soaked and he was wondering if he would pass out before he reached what he hoped was safety. When the bottom of the canoe began bumping the shoreline, Stuart stepped out and almost fell. He knew he was losing it. He held onto the canoe to steady himself and made his way towards the beach just a few feet away. As he looked up towards the grass along the shoreline, Stuart realized he was looking at a black man holding a rifle aimed right at him. Stuart's only thought was that his luck had finally run out. His vision was tunneling down and he was barely able to stumble a few feet up the river bank before he collapsed.

# Chapter Two

When Stuart awoke, he was lying in a room, alone, with a splint on his right arm and bandages around his shoulder. He was in considerable pain and very thirsty but he was too weak to call for water. In time a woman that he did not recognize came into the room and began taking his pulse. She saw that he had gained consciousness and smiled at him. "Well, it looks like our visitor is waking up." Stuart tried to speak but the words would not come. After a while he was able to ask her where he was. She only replied that he was safe and that he had to get his rest. She then left the room and Stuart again went into a deep sleep which he did frequently for the following days during the early part of his recovery. Stuart learned that he had been found by two residents of the condominium complex that were guarding the buildings and one of the men recognized him. They had brought him to their complex where he was under the very limited care that was available from one of the resident nurses. As Stuart slowly regained his health and his memory of the events surrounding his injury, he recalled seeing the black man with the rifle pointed at him. He wondered if he had been shot again by whoever that person was. In time he concluded that he had been shot just the one time when he was in the boat and that was by one of the men who killed his wife. Stuart was curious as to who the two men were and wanted to thank them for saving his life. As soon as he was able to move around a bit, he would find them and thank them for bringing him to the clinic.

Apparently the bullet that struck him in the shoulder shattered and then split apart with the larger portion going through the humorous bone of his upper right arm. The clinic staff did their best to reset the bone in the upper arm and concentrated on stopping the bleeding from the shoulder wound.

He sorely needed a blood transfusion but the facilities for that did not exist. There was still little or no power available to supply the refrigeration needed for donated blood, nor was the necessary testing and transfusion equipment available. After that the only thing they could do was to see if he was going to recover. In the process, the pain from the bullet wound, particularly in the arm was very severe and made it difficult for Stuart to get his rest. As Stuart convalesced in the makeshift clinic where he had been taken, he was becoming very aware that the life he had known for so many years was now ended. As the song went, it was a new day and he would have to make the best of it.

# Chapter Three

During the following weeks, Stuart was slowly on the mend. At first the pain from his injuries occupied his thoughts but as weeks passed and the pain lessened, Stuart began considering his current situation. He had lost his home, his wife and any semblance of a semi-normal life. He was angry, but in time he realized his anger was misplaced. Here he was an adult bitching about something he had done nothing to prevent. At first he was confused as to who should be the target of his anger. Stuart had always been somewhat apolitical. He voted but that was about it. He was never particularly interested in politics. He was, like the rest of the country, living his life from paycheck to paycheck. His life had focused around his schooling, work, recreation and home life. National affairs were not high on his radar. He considered the politicians of both parties in slightly higher regard than buffoons. President Turner was no better than the last one. Stuart had been aware that the nation had been declining in gross domestic product while debt was expanding at a rapid rate and that living the good life was becoming more difficult to achieve. Those were reasons he and his wife, Chris, had decided not to have children. Also, crime was increasing exponentially and Stuart had even purchased a firearm in recent years for the protection of his home. Stuart had always criticized reliance on guns for protection as a bit senseless but after his neighbor's home had been invaded by three young men who terrorized his family, he decided he should have one.

His knowledge of what was going on in the country had increased somewhat over the past few years as conditions continued to deteriorate. He was reading more on current events primarily from internet blogs and some of the less biased newspapers. The government was making it more and more difficult for "radical opinions", as the government referred to opinions critical of what they were doing, to be voiced. This did get Stuart's attention as he admired individualist traits particularly in historic figures although his own life was quite devoid of those attributes. Stuart worked for the government and abided by their dictates both in his personal life and in his professional duties as an attorney. He had been raised by very liberal parents who were both now deceased. He was careful with his personal life to keep it out of the spotlight of his employers and he never voiced a controversial comment outside of his home and very seldom there as well. He did not feel totally secure in his own home from the intrusions of government. His legal services for the State related primarily to paper shuffling. He worked in the area of property management which was increasingly burdensome as the State continued to take over more property, commercial and private. The inability of people to pay mortgages or rent contributed to this growth and Stuart was constantly involved in taking possession, custody and control of one piece of property or another. He had also benefited from this task in one respect as he had been residing in what had been a privately owned home located on the shore of the Indian River taken over at the pleasure of the State. State employees at a certain pay level were granted free rent of private residences and Stuart who managed such properties saw that he was properly qualified to receive one.

This last year in particular was a transitional phase for Stuart. In years past, he had drifted along as a social liberal but recently, he began to take notice of what was happening in the country and was increasingly concerned and critical of the government. The last two administrations had led to greatly increased spending and resulting national debt. The Turner administration had dwarfed the national debt they inherited and had gone on a spending spree that made no sense to anyone with any understanding of economics. The money that was spent by the government was supposedly for liberal causes but nothing ever seemed to change for anyone's benefit other than the declining value of the dollar. What amazed Stuart was that so few people apparently had any understanding of economics and assumed that the government could just print the money it was passing out.

The Turner administration appeared to be hell bent on spending the country into bankruptcy. Nothing else made any sense with respect to what they were doing. They were printing money and spending it lavishly on projects benefiting special interests or more benefits for the non-producers of the country. It was only in the last year or so that Stuart finally realized that the reason Turner was able to spend money the country did not have and could not afford was because over half of the population had no investment in the country whatsoever. They paid no taxes, they sucked up the benefits, they demanded more and they supported Turner whole heartedly, apparently for his empty promises. With minimal effort, Turner had the support of over 50% of the voters. The increased debt was backed only by increased loans from foreign countries. That source of funds soon dried up when the lenders realized they had little chance of recovering their money. After the government was no longer able to borrow funds, they resorted to printing massive amounts of money that was backed by nothing. There was no mention in the public press or news media that these printed dollars had only fractional value which was one reason they no longer printed the one dollar bill. It was not worth the printing or material cost to print that bill. The coins that still existed were being hoarded if they contained any silver or other valuable metal. Gold prices for gold dollars and other gold coins soared to unbelievable price levels.

Meanwhile the producers, those who created jobs, created profits, provided innovation, were taxed to the hilt and scoffed at by the administration. The media was complicit in the ongoing destruction of the fiscal life of the country by their turning a blind eye to what the administration was doing. The media stars and starlets were amply rewarded and feted by Turner and his cronies by being placed in the limelight, present at all State functions, along with the Hollywood elite, elevated by their money to positions of respect they did not deserve, traveling on Air Force One to various events across and out of the country, wined and dined at White House dinners and beyond a doubt financially benefited for their services with insider information if not outright cash payments. Meanwhile the pundits, playwrights, movie producers, writers and their parade of pandering stars took every opportunity to destroy the faith that was the foundation of the Republic and had sustained it throughout difficult times. Laughing at the very word, Christianity, as though it were some sop for non-thinking people. Stuart was not religious but had high regard for the faith that had lasted over two thousand years, was the foundation of our country and provided a solid foundation of morality especially for the few youth of the country that were so exposed.

Meanwhile the few critics of the New America that remained, that had the guts to speak out and print what was going on were relegated to the backwoods of the communications world. The FCC had gradually applied the pressure, questioning their rights to have the required licenses, serving them with violation notices for any and all possible infractions. The IRS and the other alphabet soup bureaucracies were likewise landing on their backs at every opportunity. Critical spokesmen were chided, laughed at, and pictured as clowns by the media following the techniques of Walter Kritchak, the author of his best seller, "How to Destroy the Opposition by Character Assassination".

Only the very few, the most dedicated, remained at their task of trying to tell the uninterested public just what was going on. The public was likewise complicit in the occurrence of the eventual fiscal and governmental collapse. They were investing wildly in one scheme after another. Bribes were frequent and the bribe takers were more frequent. There was little sign of any national morality any longer. Lying, cheating, theft, and fraud were rampant. Those that lacked the opportunity for the high buck crimes resorted to burglary, assault, murder, kidnapping, rape and home invasions as the source for their entertainment and financial needs. For the younger set, drugs and sex provided the main sources of entertainment. There seemed to be a massive paralysis of the brain that had overtaken a large segment of the public in its head long spiral into the abyss. It was only a minority that seemed to give a damn about what was happening. This Stuart attributed to the lack of any real education in the schools for the past fifty or more years.

Eventually, after decades of overspending and wasteful spending, the national debt produced an intolerable inflation followed by the government's inability to pay its debts. Pension payments fell into default; the dollar lost value and eventually lost all value. Unemployment immediately soared to unbelievable heights. Stores began closing; services were no longer available as no one had any form of money that had value. Food shelves in markets were cleaned out. Food was no longer available. The utilities, water, electric and sewer were no longer functioning properly. Barter became the new medium. Then the riots began with gangs roving into formerly affluent suburbs ripping open doors and taking whatever they found, including the young daughters and in some cases the young boys. Anyone who opposed them was slaughtered. The police no longer responded. They had left for safer pastures. The military had disbanded. President Turner had seen to that a few years prior. He did not want a strong military that could possibly throw him out of office. He had seen that happen too many times in other countries. He replaced them with the Federal Security Police, "His boys". He could trust them to do what he wanted done.

# Chapter Four

S tuart had taken his job with the Housing Administration seriously until the last year when his awareness of what was going on in government alerted him to the fact that the end was drawing near. He had been storing food, water and ammunition for his gun and the other necessities for survival that he would need when the end came. Unfortunately, when the thugs began beating on his front door, he had left with only his nine millimeter Glock pistol and his wife. Now he had lost even his wife and he had no idea what happened to his Glock.

Stuart blamed Turner and the crooks in his administration more than the thugs that were immediately responsible for the loss of his wife. The thugs were just ignorant animals on the hunt for food and whatever else they could find in his house. Turner knew what he was doing. The public had always had a long memory when it came to politicians that were failures. The last three or more presidents were all failures. Turner was only the last failure. Turner could have been great. He had the brains to be great but that was all. With the collapse of the government and the anarchy that followed, Stuart was convinced that the United States of America as we all knew it was a thing of the past. It would be a long time before the country had another president and it sure as hell wouldn't be another Turner.

The day finally came when Stuart knew his recovery in the clinic had progressed to the point that he could get up and start moving around again. He still had some numbness in his right shoulder and arm but he had been told by the physician that treated him that in time that should hopefully disappear.

Stuart inquired of the nurses as to who the fellows were that had rescued him. He recognized the name of one, Ross Perry, who was a black fellow that had served in the Army Reserve with Stuart for a short period of time. Perry had a legendary reputation as a special forces guru with considerable combat experience. Stuart was surprised to learn that it was Perry that he saw shortly before losing consciousness on the beach. He did not recognize him then but that was not surprising. Stuart could not recall his arrival on the beach other than faintly remembering that he saw a black man pointing a rifle at him. The other fellow was Andy Moss and Stuart recalled him when he heard the name. He had done some work with Moss in the state office. He told the nurses that he would like to thank the men in person if they had a minute to stop by the clinic. They assured him they would tell the men to come by.

Stuart's rescuers did stop by the clinic and Stuart offered his good hand to the men and told them how much he appreciated what they had done for him. Their response was that they were out looking for volunteers to help defend the condominium and Stuart looked like a good candidate. Perry quipped, "Besides, you have some good military training in your background. Gave it to you myself."

"Ross, you did do that and I thank you for it. I will definitely repay both of you fellows before I am out of here."

"Forget the 'out of here', Stuart. There is no other place to go and we already have a room arranged for you. We also have a job for you when you are all mended up. We need some good smart young men in our group and you can help us there."

"Ross, I will be there and thank you guys again. This has been a life's lesson for me. I'll be there to help with the lifting."

The room in the complex that had been arranged for Stuart appeared to have been a one room studio apartment with most of the furniture now gone except for a bed. Stuart was not complaining. He knew he was very fortunate to be given a place to stay in what appeared to be a somewhat organized and safe complex on the beach.

Perry and Moss were not long time close friends of Stuart but the relationship was sufficiently strong enough for the men to see that he had potential for their group and should receive the necessary care and protection that was available to permit him to recover from his wounds. Ross Perry had known Stuart for the years Stuart had served in the Army Reserve and the two had developed a friendship and mutual respect from that experience. In their conversations in the clinic, Moss and Perry informed him that he was in the Bayside Condominium complex located in Indian Harbour Beach just across the Indian River from Melbourne. The complex fronted what was formerly Highway A1A, the beachfront road along the Atlantic Ocean. Stuart was familiar with the condominium as friends of his had lived there in years past. Moss told Stuart that they had set up a minimal security system with 24 hour guards on the property and so far had been able to repel thieves and burglars who were constantly on the prowl on the island as elsewhere. He added that the attacks had been increasing in frequency and the day would soon come when they would have to upgrade their security. Before the two men left after that first meeting, Perry added, "Get well, buddy. We are going to need you soon. We didn't haul you in here for the hell of it."

Stuart laughed and responded, "Ross, believe me, I want to help. I'll be up and around pretty soon. I'm feeling better every day and I owe you guys a bunch. Thank God you pulled me into your clinic. Just super people working in here. I am very grateful for what you all have done. I'll be there when you need someone. I have nothing else to do you know."

"Yes. That's where we're all at. We can use your help, believe me."

During his long convalescence, Stuart's view of the world had changed considerably. He had experienced a life changing event and it was leaving him a much different person than he was a year ago. When he was laying in his bed recuperating, his first thoughts dealt with how the attack on his home, his wife and himself was so utterly unfair. He was angry at the attackers and wanted to get back at them. His thoughts revolved around just how he would get them for what they had done. The longer he pondered his loss and who was to blame, the more he realized that he was also to blame for not becoming involved in what was happening to the nation, the culture and the life style that he had enjoyed and benefited from. The three thugs were not the sole cause of his problems; they were only the most visible cause. Turner, his co-conspirators and the beneficiaries of the public largesse were the real culprits. The mass of the American public permitted those parties to destroy what had once been a great nation and Stuart was to blame along with them. He resolved that he would regain his strength and devote the remainder of his life to rebuilding the shattered remains of his country maybe not back to the full extent of nationhood that it had once occupied but at least to a reasonable facsimile thereof. Others had to be of like opinion with him and he would find those people and together they would recreate the New America. He was of the opinion he had already met two of those people. Stuart had many things to do and he wanted to get started.

Stuart knew Ross Perry had served on active duty as a Ranger and as a Green Beret. Later Perry served in a staff position with the Reserve and when Stuart had joined the Reserve just a few years prior to the collapse he began serving alongside Perry. The two became friends over time. These were difficult times for the military. The budgets were being severely cut and new equipment was in very short supply. The disintegration of the military was the result of a long term plan of many politicians who wanted absolute control over it to prevent the military from interfering with what they were doing.

The bureaucracy feared the military as a potential source of trouble for their long term ambitions and they had good reason to do so. Early on in the national disintegration process, many in the public sector looked upon the military as the savior for those interested in preserving the nation. Those opposed to the military as a force of the future did the dismantling slowly. Senior officers known to have contempt for how the government was operating were very slowly transferred into positions of no or limited authority. Officers that could be depended upon by the government were advanced to senior rank. Before the more responsible members of the public were aware of what was going on, the military was no longer a viable force to protect the union. In time, the Federal Security Police occupied most if not all of the military bases and enjoyed the largesse of the defense budget.

# Chapter Five

This morning, Stuart lay in his bed thinking about the situation they were in and the problems that they faced in their fight for survival. The Beach had been the home for the Space Center and Patrick Air Force Base and was still populated mostly by the engineers and military personnel that had worked for those two agencies as well as supporting engineering companies. Stuart knew he was in the best location he could be in under the circumstances. There was no law and order on the mainland and the only restraint on roving gangs was that of armed citizens protecting themselves and banding together to form defense teams. Fortunately the river separated the island from the far more dangerous mainland and the island residents were somewhat better organized, better educated and not as accessible to the roving gangs as the mainland residents.

This morning Stuart thought about the meeting of the members of the apartment complex the evening before last. It had gone on into the late hours with virtually everyone who lived in the complex trying to figure out what they were going to do. A substantial number still looked towards Washington as the answer to their problems. This produced laughter from the majority present and soon such suggestions were no longer made. A number were in favor of leaving the area which was Stuart's long range plan, but for the time being, as he told them, they had to plan on staying on the island in order to protect themselves and plan and prepare for the future. After much discussion most of those attending the meeting appeared to agree with Stuart's view.

From what little news Stuart was able to receive, he understood that globally, the world was in a state of chaos. The problems in the United States had taken the same course as those in the rest of the so called developed countries of the world and all were in a state of anarchy. The country appeared to have lost any semblance of control politically and was increasingly coming under the control of renegade bands of hoodlums.

The Hispanics in the southwest, bolstered by the influx of people coming up from Mexico and Central America, had successfully reclaimed that part of the country as far north as the southern half of Colorado and Utah as their own. They were also in control of large portions of California, extending from what had been the southern border to just south of San Francisco. They were attempting to reclaim Texas but were running into strong resistance in the northern and eastern sections from well armed, native Texans who were not willing to part with title to their land. Urban gangs of Blacks and Muslims generally controlled the states bordering the Great Lakes areas. Other urban centers in the east and south were being torn apart by ethnic conflicts of one kind or another. There was little information coming from the Midwestern states or the Northwest and Stuart assumed they were having the same difficulties the rest of the country was experiencing.

As Stuart became better organized in his new home, he began to consider what form of political structure it would take to make this group sufficiently effective to survive the trials and tribulations they would be facing. He had always respected the constitutional form of government that was viewed so highly in the former United States of America. At least, historically and in the abstract. With respect to the complex residents that Stuart now found himself living with, he was rapidly coming to the conclusion that democratic principles were not going to work at least during the rebuilding phase. Strong leadership had to be employed or this group of people would, along with all other similar groups, be casualties of the times. Most people he had observed appeared to be wandering around blindly looking for someone to tell them what to do.

During the years prior to Stuart fleeing for his life from his home in Melbourne, he had acquired an appreciation of the politics of the founders of the country and their political beliefs. He had read on his own the writings of Jefferson, Madison and Hamilton, men who were totally ignored in his school curriculum. There had been no study of the Bill of Rights at any time in Stuart's education and when he read over the Bill of Rights and thought about what it all meant, he began to understand why the government chose to leave that subject out of public school curriculums. He had read the Constitution many times and could see little if any similarity with the American government as it existed in the years prior to the collapse. The office of the President had assumed awesome power and operated primarily without restraint issuing executive orders that more properly should have been handled by Congress. There was little if any judicial restraint as the courts had been staffed by judges solidly in the pocket of the liberal executive administrations.

In the complex where Stuart now resided, there were a total of six buildings with thirty two housing units in each building with a total resident population maximum of approximately five hundred people. Some of the residents had evacuated as the political situation deteriorated so there was room for at least an additional one hundred or more people should the need arise. There was a wall around the complex and some of the residents had placed concertina wire on the top of the wall but when Stuart first moved in, there was no guard at the front gate or on the walls. Back then, everyone assumed that there was nothing of interest worth stealing in the complex. That did not last long as, in time, anything was fair game for a growing populace that had absolutely nothing. As crime increased, Stuart, Ross Perry, Andy Moss and a number of others in the complex discussed the situation and concluded that there were approximately 200 somewhat able bodied men and women that could be organized into a Defense Team. Most had their own weapons ranging from small caliber pistols to semi-automatic AK-47's and Mini 14's and they could well form the nucleus of a self Defense Team.

Stuart and Perry were soon busy organizing, training and equipping a number of men to serve as the complex security team. It had been obvious to Stuart watching Perry work with the men in their training exercises that he, Perry, was the right man for the job. He was a natural leader and knew military training and tactics. The men in the defense unit all respected Perry. His reputation as a dedicated military man was well known by everyone on the island.

The catalyst that brought the need for organization of the complex to the forefront occurred a short time later when a large group of armed street thugs took over many of the units in one of the buildings. They raped a number of the women as well as some of the children. The residents of the complex were cowering in fear for their lives and very few were offering any resistance to the intruders. As soon as Stuart and Perry became aware of the intrusion, they were able to locate and assemble twenty of their men who were sufficiently trained and well armed to carry off the expected assault on the uninvited guests. Stuart and Perry assembled the men in the complex administration building so that they could prepare plans and brief the men for the anticipated action.

While they were meeting, four of the thugs entered their building on the ground floor. They had been spotted approaching the building by one of the residents so that Stuart and his group were prepared for them when they came through the doorway. Not wanting to alert the remaining gang members, Stuart cautioned his companions to allow the foursome to enter the office area and to proceed with their objective which was apparently to search for food and valuables. After they were well inside the building and had separated into pairs, they were apprehended, with no shots having been fired. Each was bound and taken aside for questioning by Stuart and Ross Perry. At first their attitude was one of contempt, but when they realized they stood a good chance of being killed, they became more cooperative. They explained where in the dorm their companions were located, their number and the type of weapons they were carrying. When Stuart and Perry were of the opinion that they had obtained all of the information that they were going to receive from their prisoners, they left them bound and gagged under the watchful eye of John Barnes who was Perry's number two man in the security team and a former member of the Melbourne

Police Force.

It was estimated that approximately 18 to 20 insurgents were in the dorm and were busy filling up on the food and liquor taken from the residents that they had evicted or killed. The more they drank, the more they could be heard across the courtyard. There was an occasional scream from a resident who had fallen under their control followed shortly thereafter by sounds of gunfire.

After a lengthy period of silence and under cover of darkness, Stuart, Perry and twenty of the Security Team members hacked their watches and loaded up with stun grenades from supplies provided by Barnes.

After Stuart had made his way to the occupied dorm, he could hear muffled voices, slurred words and sounds of people moving around in the rooms, but little else. As the second hand came up on 12, Stuart and the others, on both sides of the dorm building hurled concussion grenades into the rooms, blowing out windows and shredding wall board. With the occupants of the rooms momentarily disabled by the force of the blast, other Security Team members broke down doors and entered the rooms spraying the intruders with automatic rifle fire. A few shots were fired in reply but within thirty seconds it was all over.

The remaining members of the Defense Team searched all rooms looking for any stragglers that were not in with the main group. Two were found and they were quickly dispatched with a burst of automatic fire. A few more were found wounded but still alive in the rooms they had occupied with their comrades. They were likewise finished off and the residents of the formerly occupied dorm were told to clean up the mess and take care of the bodies. Surprisingly, especially after what had happened to them, some of the dorm residents expressed distaste at the way in which the intruders had been dealt with by the armed residents.

Irene Covington, a matronly woman who lived in an adjoining dorm criticized the methods used by the Defense Team, arguing that they were all becoming the sort of animals they were running from. Stuart let her speak her piece and then told all the residents to get moving on cleaning up the mess. The group quickly responded with Irene Covington taking charge of detailing the work groups. A number of the residents of the occupied dorm had been killed or suffered injuries of one type or another. All of the injured residents were immediately sent to the medical clinic where Stuart had been treated when he was found on the beach.

As Stuart was returning to the administration building, he heard rifle fire from the area where Barnes had secured the four prisoners. One of the Defense Team members informed him that John Barnes, in his frustration at continuously fending off attacks from these street punks, had taken care of the prisoners in the administration building who he said were trying to escape. As a result of their injuries, they would not need any further care. All of the intruders had now been killed.

Stuart was somewhat concerned about the reaction of the residents to what Irene Covington had said about how they had disposed of men who more than likely would have surrendered if given the chance.

The following day, Stuart was walking with Ross Perry on the grounds of the complex when he was confronted by Irene Covington. "Well, I've been looking for you; if you have a few minutes, I would like to speak with you."

Stuart knew what was coming and told Perry that he would meet with him later. Stuart suggested they go to the office that he had taken over in the administration building and Irene readily agreed. She did not want to get into the middle of a conversation with Stuart that she had been mulling over since the previous day and then be interrupted by others.

Stuart closed the door to his office so that the two could have some privacy to discuss the topic that was obvious to both. Irene immediately went to the point. "You know what I am concerned about. I want stability in my life just like you do, but I think we may have a problem with respect to the methods that we use to obtain it. I don't think it's necessary that we begin acting like animals around here to protect ourselves from the other animals in the neighborhood. We should be above that. There are other, more humane ways, of dealing with people that are out to harm us than to kill them in cold blood."

Stuart took a moment to respond and also to try and figure out the woman sitting across from him. He could tell that there was no lack of self assurance with this one and that she was quite used to getting her way. She was not shy about letting her opinions be known as he had already found out. Furthermore, she spoke at a volume level that was a couple of decibels above that of comfortable conversation which Stuart figured was one of her methods of trying to intimidate people. He would have to give some thought as to how he was going to deal with her in the future.

For the moment, Stuart had no intention of further ruffling her feathers. "Irene, I think we both want the same thing. What we have to do first is to protect ourselves from the thugs that surround us so that we can build the society that we both want." Stuart emphasized that at this point in time, security is paramount.

After a period of time, it was clear to Stuart that they could sit there all day long discussing endless possibilities and she would still not be satisfied. He finally closed off the discussion and told her he had nothing further to say on the subject.

When they parted, Irene commented that she knew Stuart was trying to do what was right and she hoped that they could work together in the future towards an amicable resolution. Stuart was not so sure.

Stuart took the lead in calling a general meeting for the purpose of setting up a formal organization to deal with all of the problems that were rapidly coming to the forefront, including: the matter of setting up a full time Defense Team, allocation of scarce food supplies, the lack of an organized, well staffed, medical facility and, in general, an administrative body to oversee the basic needs of their small community.

The acting Defense Team was functioning well, so far, but it needed more equipment and more members. The Team was short staffed on troop requirements for patrols, guard duties, and other military requirements. After the incident involving the firefight in the complex itself, everyone Stuart spoke with enthusiastically supported the idea and interest in the meeting was universal. Stuart had his supporters post notices of the meeting, which was scheduled for the following evening, on the complex bulletin boards. He also arranged for a security detail to man the perimeter of the complex during the meeting so that roving bands did not take advantage of the situation.

When the time came for the meeting, virtually everyone that still resided in the Bayside complex was present. The support for the full time, 24/7, Defense Team was unanimous. In view of the fact that Stuart and Perry had led the residents in throwing the intruders out of the complex and had initiated the idea of the Defense Team, they were looked upon as the leaders in charge. Stuart had anticipated that this might occur and immediately told Perry that he was more qualified to manage the team. A number of the residents such as Barnes, were former military or law enforcement personnel and Stuart suggested Perry utilize these people for his staff, all of whom eagerly accepted their assignment.

At the organizational meeting which Stuart conducted, he proceeded to the first item on the agenda which was the need to organize administratively to provide for the basic needs of all who lived there. Food and water supplies, medical care, sanitation facilities and a myriad of other needs all demanded immediate attention. The Association also needed leadership administratively and Stuart suggested that volunteers were needed. Stuart was already involved in administration in an executive capacity and what was needed was a person with extensive administrative experience to oversee the entire operation. Three men and two women stepped forward indicating their willingness to assist.

An elderly gentleman, Anders Jensen, who was known to virtually everyone in the complex, was the unanimous favorite to be the overall administrator of the complex and responsible for dealing with the basic infrastructure needs of the community. Stuart knew Anders from conversations the two had during Stuart's convalescence and the two men were in general agreement on management methods. Anders possessed vast experience in community administration, working his entire lifetime in various capacities in Melbourne city government. Furthermore, he was not a political bureaucrat and had never run for public office. He believed in limited participation in the decision making process and immediately focused on Stuart as a key member of any policy group that might be required.

After a brief voting session, Anders was elected to the position of Association President and immediately took the podium detailing what had to be done. He reiterated what everyone knew that the country was in a state of total chaos and that they had to establish their own self governing board to serve for the foreseeable future. Anders suggested he proceed first with drafting a charter under which their Association would operate and lay out a set of rules and regulations guiding the Association and the members that lived under the protection of the Association.

There was some grumbling among the residents with the notion that a very select few would again be controlling their lives, but a clear majority saw the absolute necessity of establishing basic rules of conduct in view of the anarchy surrounding them.

The members of the policy board that Anders appointed were Stuart, Ross Perry, Andy Moss and John Barnes with Stuart functioning more as a Chief Executive Officer overseeing all functions and reporting to Anders. From Stuart's point of view, it appeared Anders was the right man for the job and as Stuart listened to his remarks, he couldn't believe his good fortune to have this person in charge rather than some of the others. The organization of the complex had not gone without problems. There were those that had no interest in participating or contributing. Some that expected county, state or federal leadership to appear at any moment and there were those that were part of the problem and were suspected of being involved with gangs that were terrorizing adjoining complexes and in some cases their immediate neighbors. The latter category of problem tenants was taken care of immediately by Anders Jensen. They were evicted from the complex and thrown out the front gate with nothing but the clothes they wore. In some cases, this resulted in the breakup of families and

Anders advised that anyone who wished to accompany the exiles could do so. As before, Anders received complaints from a number of residents and again, he stood his ground, stating that their very survival depended upon the discipline of the group. Anyone who threatened that discipline was a threat to the group and would have to go. With few exceptions, the residents were in agreement on that point.

After the meeting and the vote installing the two in key positions, Anders came over to Stuart's office in the administration building to discuss what needed to be done. As he entered the office, Stuart was engaged in a conversation with Perry and Barnes about the problem created by the great variety of weapons with which the Defense Team was equipped. Barnes had been tasked as the supply officer and was responsible for finding or procuring ammunition which was difficult enough without having to look for twenty different types. Both Perry and Barnes excused themselves so that Stuart and Anders could talk.

Anders and Stuart had discussed their situation a number of times both before Stuart was released from the clinic and afterwards. It was apparent to both that their political views were quite similar. Both believed in a strong executive approach to community organization particularly when they were existing in an unstable society. Anders commenced the discussion this morning, "I think we are off to a good start, Stuart. The meeting went quite well. What did you think?"

"I agree, Anders. I have given our little group here a lot of thought over the past month or two that I have been here. I might add, this has been a growing up experience for me. When I landed on your beach from that narrow escape on the mainland, I was still the naive jackass that I had been most of my life. As I came to in the clinic and started to think about where I was and what our situation was, I began a rather intense…involuntary sort of…metamorphosis shedding my previous lack of interest in the world around me to become a person much more aware of the problems we were about to be facing. This is a little hard for me to explain. I'm a fairly smart guy but I can't believe I lived so many years just assuming everything would be turning out all right. I was aware of the problems superficially but assumed others far more knowledgeable than me would be taking care of them. I am talking about the piling up of debt, the growing inflation, the increased unemployment and the growing crime. As I laid in that bed, I told myself we have a lot to do and I hope we have the people here to start doing it. I believe we have."

"Interesting, Stuart. I think you are being a bit hard on yourself because we were all a bit naive. Every damn one of us. Myself included and I worked right in the administrative offices. Where do you think we can go with our group and what are your long term goals if you have that worked out?"

"Anders, I don't know where or how we can move on and improve our situation. That is what we have to do. We have to figure that one out. I hope that we can organize, protect ourselves in the process, prepare our necessary defenses and then we are going to have to think about where to go from here. It is obvious that we can't survive here on the island. Not enough food. Not enough water. We are going to have to find a more hospitable place to live, hopefully with hospitable neighbors if such exist. From what I hear, they are hard to find. To get there we are going to need strong, centralized leadership. I have concluded that the democratic form of government does not work in this situation. Maybe at some time in the future but for the present I believe we have to run this operation a bit like a tight ship. Any comments on that?"

"My thoughts as well, Stuart. These people, from what I've seen, need a strong leadership and a firm but fair hand. I think you and I can give them that."

As the two men talked, it was apparent to both that their views meshed on virtually every aspect of the government of their small community. Anders told Stuart that he wanted his involvement with organizing the board in addition to his duties with the Defense Team.

Stuart smiled and told Anders that Ross Perry knew a lot more about running the Defense Team than he would ever know. "I would be glad to work on organizing the board and getting more involved in the governmental issues that we face. Frankly, that is more along the line of work I am somewhat familiar with. I would also enjoy working with you as I think we see pretty much eye to eye."

Anders shook Stuart's hand and said, "Great. Let's look at this as a partnership and let's get this organization up and running. We can then decide just what in hell we are going to do with it. I have noticed that your management style is quite a bit like mine. See what has to be done and do it before people ask too many questions."

Stuart smiled and then laughed. "Took the words right out of my mouth, Anders. We will have time to listen to questions later. I agree, now is not the time."

Stuart was more than willing to participate as he believed the survival prospects of the Bayside complex residents were deteriorating daily. He agreed to meet with Anders as time permitted to discuss the charter and other administrative appointments. Stuart's first concern was turning the duties he had been performing for the Defense Team over to Perry. He met with Perry shortly after speaking with Anders and Perry was only too pleased to be the Officer in Charge of Defense issues.

Perry's first action was to divide the group into two sections, each headed by a person with law enforcement or military experience and each section to be responsible for staffing a twelve hour guard shift around the complex.

Ross Perry assumed responsibility for overall management and training of all team members with John Barnes serving as Section A leader and Andy Moss, also formerly with the Melbourne Police Force, in charge of Section B. Stuart would have preferred someone else serving in Barnes place as John Barnes had already demonstrated a talent for solving supply problems and coming up with scarce materials. That, at the present time, was more valuable than being a section leader and Stuart resolved that he would have to talk to Perry about finding a suitable replacement for him on down the road.

# Chapter Six

The day after Anders and Stuart had their discussion; Anders again called on Stuart at his office in the company of a young woman. Stuart was alone in the office at the time and told the two to come in and take a chair. Anders introduced the woman as Sarah Taves and explained that she came to Anders' office to volunteer to serve in any capacity. She had compiled a resume which Anders handed to Stuart to look over. He took a moment to read the resume which detailed years of experience with the Department of the Navy working in intelligence as well as communications. Her educational background was equally impressive with a Masters Degree in Mathematics from MIT.

When Stuart had finished looking over the resume, he questioned her on her activities since leaving the Navy which included a short stint with NASA at the Cape doing photographic analysis. While he was conversing with her, he noted that she had a confident air about her but it was not an 'in your face' type of confidence. She was an attractive woman whose age Stuart estimated at around the mid forties. Stuart noticed that Anders had the look of the cat that had just found the canary. It was obvious that he favored the woman as the next addition to the administrative staff.

Stuart decided to move on to the real issues. "Sarah, you have indicated an interest in working with us, in what capacity do you think you would be most effective?"

Sarah had anticipated the question and without hesitation, she replied, "In time, if not right away, you are going to need to know what is going on around you. I'm talking about what is happening not only over on the mainland but across the state and across the country. That is where I can be of service. You will need intelligence information and a communications system that will provide that information as well as provide communications with other complexes, organizations, municipalities, whatever and wherever they might be. I can provide that. I will need equipment that I presently do not have, but now is the time to get working on getting the equipment and setting up the systems. I also know other people, not only in this complex, but others that would come and work with me in setting up the program. I think such a program is not only invaluable, it is essential."

"Sarah, what are your thoughts regarding the future of this country? I am just curious as to what you see in store for us or not in store for us."

"Stuart, I am not optimistic. We have all seen this coming for a very long time and the fact that the nation did not respond at all until all semblance of order was lost is an indication of how difficult it will be to establish order. I fully expected reasonable citizens to unite and take charge long before this but nothing happened. It was as if no one cared what happened."

"I gave it a lot of thought, Sarah, while I was convalescing from a bullet wound to the shoulder and I concluded that we all just let it happen. I think we are all at fault and the sooner we all realize that, the sooner we can get to work and fix the problems. I was one naïve son-of-a-bitch for an awful long time as I think back on it. It was like I was born again, politically speaking, when I landed on this island after escaping the mainland. I deeply regret my lack of interest in what was happening to the country but I am sure many other people fall into that category as well."

Sarah nodded, "Yes. I have thought that as well. I was in the military most of that time and of course we were under restraints that the general public was not but we could certainly have done more but by the time we really needed to act, our leadership was pretty much neutered. I'm sure you saw that as well."

"Yes Sarah, and it was through the intentional acts of our national leadership that the military was rendered ineffective. Someday we may be able to look into that further. What do you see as the form of our organization that you would like to see it assume?"

"I am a fan of the American Constitution and our Bill of Rights and I would like to move in that direction. I don't know how practical that is right at this moment, but I would like to see that as our eventual objective."

"Sarah, I agree. Not right now but some day in the future. Right now our members and most likely people across the country need someone telling them what to do. It's amazing, I didn't realize how much of a fan I was of our original form of government as I was when I realized we had lost it. I want it back."

"Let's work for that, Stuart."

"I agree."

Stuart was sold and clearly, even without further discussion, so was Anders. "Give us a minute privately if you would Sarah. Just wait in the lobby area and we will be right with you."

After she had left the office, Anders smiled and looked at Stuart. "Well, are you as impressed as I am? I totally agree with her vision of what we need and I think we have struck gold."

Stuart nodded in agreement. "I'm with you. You never really know until the cook serves the dinner, but I like what she has to say. Let's bring her in."

When Sarah was back in the room, Stuart let Anders do the talking as the Chief Administrator. "Sarah, we would be pleased to have you with us in our organization. We like what you have to offer. The three shook hands on the arrangement and then Stuart called John Barnes into the office to introduce him to Sarah as the Chief of Intelligence and Communications. He further instructed Barnes to sit down with Sarah and find out what it was that she needed to get her organization up and operating. He also told Barnes to get some men together to construct whatever facility Sarah needed in the administration building for her offices. The more Stuart thought about what Sarah had offered to provide the organization, the more he wanted it in place immediately.

# Chapter Seven

At the next Defense Team meeting, names of all volunteers were taken and due to the lack of communication facilities, it was decided that the manual fire siren from the Bayside complex fire house would be used for a general recall of the Defense Team to the assembly point. Plans were also made to canvas the general membership of the Association for additional materials. No one wanted to permanently give up their own weapons, ammunition, food and survival gear and they parted with these now priceless items only with the strongest assurances of the entire group that they would be returned at any time upon demand. A number of dissenters refused to part with their semi-automatic rifles regardless of the assurances and, while this was somewhat understandable to Stuart, something had to be done as the weapons were sorely needed for the general defense of the complex. Stuart's solution was to issue a mandate that owners of the automatic weapons had to either join and participate as members of the Defense Team or give up their weapons for others to use. This created some dissent but it was a decision that received the general support of the residents. Virtually everyone possessing such weapons then joined up with the Team rather than surrender their weapons to others. Another very sensitive possession guarded fiercely by their owners was that of bulk food stores comprised mostly of MRE, or Meals Ready to Eat, stores. Some of the complex residents had seen fit to store boxes of MRE's sufficient to provide meals for their owners for periods of years. The food stores were guaranteed to be safe in protected storage for time periods up to twenty-five years. The owners of these food supplies saw no reason to provide food for people that lacked the foresight to see to their own survival. An agreement was reached whereby the owners of MRE food stores were allowed to retain one half of their personal supply of food while participating in the complex communal food allocation.

A roster for the security guards was posted on the complex bulletin boards so that the volunteers knew who was assigned to what post and when. The section leaders made it a point to run a check of the outposts to ensure that they were all manned during the course of the evening. Another roster was posted for those Defense Team members assigned the following day for construction of perimeter defenses. It was not considered safe to have the residents handling tasks outside of the complex walls as marauding gangs, primarily coming over from the mainland, were very active and thick brush and melaleuca trees came up to within fifty yards of the walls on two sides of the square shaped complex. An abandoned housing area abutted one side and a small occupied, but unorganized and lightly defended, residential complex was approximately one hundred yards from the other wall. In consequence, three sides of the complex were very vulnerable to attack while the fourth offered little better protection.

Perry suggested that well fortified sentry outposts with four man teams be posted at least fifty to one hundred yards out from the walls. This meant that the brush and trees had to be cleared back at least another fifty yards from the present line and this was a lot of work for the men. Stuart approved the project and had Barnes get to work trying to locate the necessary power equipment, tractors and fuel for the job. John Barnes had contacts throughout the beach area and operated like the classic supply sergeant in the Army. He would trade items back and forth with others, in this very informal network. As the need arose he was constantly tasking Perry for armed security details to accompany his men out to pick up equipment, parts or fuel. In time, he usually came up with whatever was needed which was always a surprise for Stuart as everything was in very scarce supply and it was difficult to get anyone to part with anything. In a short period of time, Barnes had Sarah's office equipped with most everything she needed to be up and operating including global radio equipment provided by Robert Thomas, one of the residents with a somewhat colorful background who had contacts on the mainland that could provide him with almost anything of value. Barnes had also been able to restore power to the administration building with high output capacity generators. Due to the limitations on fuel availability, the generators were operated only from 9:00 a.m. to 9:00 p.m.

As for construction of guard posts and gun emplacements in the complex and immediately outside of the walls, work teams from the resident population had to be requisitioned through Anders. Again there were the usual grumblers, but by this time Anders and Stuart were being recognized by most residents as running the show and everyone followed their orders quite well.

Following a meeting with the Defense Team staff, Stuart was leaving the building when he found Anders Jensen in the main assembly room in deep conversation with five or six people that Stuart recognized as men and women that had, in the past, been active in matters involving the Bayside complex. Anders waved him over and he sat and listened as the group discussed the charter, what form of an organization they would take, what powers would be granted to those running the Association, and a number of related issues. It was clear from listening to this small group of five or six people that there was not going to be unanimity with respect to organization of the Association. It seemed that most of the group was for granting only very specific powers to the Association officers while the minority saw the need for broad powers permitting rapid action.

That meeting broke up with little resolved and Stuart could discern from the look on Anders face that he was not pleased with the results elicited in what was apparently an informal opinion poll discussing the proposed charter for the Association. When the others had left, Anders commented to Stuart, "These people just don't seem to understand that we are in a very precarious position and can't screw around with debates. Our food stocks are virtually nonexistent and our water tanks are about bone dry. Everyone anticipated trouble and stocked up with everything they thought they would need, but no one thought it would go on for so long."

Stuart agreed as he had as well lost all of his provisions which were in the house on the mainland and he was existing on the charity of others and what Barnes could obtain through his sources. Everyone had been living on canned food for the past two months and it was obvious that they had no more than a month or two of supplies left. The two talked well on into the night discussing the organization of the Association and what would be needed to survive.

Both men restated their long held beliefs that when their very survival was at stake, they needed an effective, centralized, form of leadership. Stuart commented: "This is not the time for us to pass out ballots to all the members of the Association on every problem that presents itself. We have to take decisive steps now or we will be in bad shape sooner rather than later. Anders, I believe we have to start lowering the boom on some of these people. In the future, I suggest we drop discussions on political charters for our operation. We just make the decisions and pass out the orders. If we run into a problem, then we revise it. All this talk is a waste of time. First of all, this weapons issue is a real headache. We need to standardize and I'm not sure how we do that other than subject all apartments to a mandatory search for weapons, ammo and also for food supplies. That would raise hackles all over the place but we damn well may have to do that in order to survive."

Anders nodded. "I totally agree, Stuart. I've wanted to do that for some time but, no doubt about it, all hell will break loose when we try it. We are going to have to wait for the right opportunity. That will come along soon, I'm sure. When the situation gets bad enough, then people will begin to realize more drastic measures are necessary. I can just see Irene storming in here right now as soon as we post that notice."

Anders thought about this for a moment. "You saw and heard the arguments against even a simple organization of the Association. These people are fed up with anything that remotely resembles a government. They see the need for it, but they don't want it. In the future, I'm just going to lay it out and anyone that doesn't like it can start looking for the front gate. No more mister nice guy."

# Chapter Eight

As the night progressed, Stuart and Anders discussed various possibilities as to what could be written into the charter. They concluded that it should contain a number of basic provisions necessary for the effective management that the times demanded. With certain, yet to be defined prerequisites, the Association president should be elected by a majority of "qualified electors". Fortunately, that had already taken place. The president should be subject to recall but only by a vote of two thirds of the "qualified electors". Defining "qualified" would be interesting. Furthermore, there should be an executive council with limited overview authority as well as overview of any punishments meted out by the executive department for infractions of rules or regulations. This overview provision was again considered as a sop to the majority of the residents who were suspicious of any form of organization with rule making authority. All five of the council members serving until one or more was removed and replaced by a two thirds vote of the members of the Association. The president would generally run the show until replaced or recalled. Stuart, as operating executive officer of the Association, would report only to the president. His removal would require a four-fifths vote of the entire council or by order of the president. The result of this arrangement would give permanence and great control to the president and the executive officer. There would be some griping about this provision which would be criticized as a power grab but the leadership would have to insist upon it without change. It was necessary to deal with serious current problems.

A four fifths vote of the executive council would be needed to countermand a policy order of the president. The council had no review authority of operating decisions of Anders or Stuart. Both Stuart and Anders recognized that conditions did not permit lengthy discussions of issues by the general membership. Pure democratic rule was, at least for the time being, placed on hold. As they headed out of the meeting room, they decided they would present this plan to the members at the next meeting scheduled for the following week. The plan as laid out gave them virtual authority to act as they saw fit and anyone that wanted to fight their proposals had some very high hills to climb.

They also discussed the need to stack the executive council with people that would be sympathetic to their general goals so that they did not have that group looking over their shoulders every time they made a policy decision. As they left the building, Anders stopped and shook Stuart's hand, thanking him for his support. Stuart replied with, "Don't thank me yet. This is going to be a hard sell and we are going to have to work like hell to pull in every vote we can to put this one through. I suggest we have some of our more trustworthy supporters leading the cheers for our proposals at the meeting."

In the time since Stuart had been taken in at the Bayside complex, incursions by renegade gangs or individuals had been increasing in strength and frequency. Had Stuart and Perry not taken action to organize a security team, surely someone else would have stepped forward. The street gangs had become bolder in their pursuits as their hunger for food and treasure became more difficult to satisfy.

When Stuart first arrived, there was an occasional forced entry into an apartment unit by one or two individuals but in recent months, before Stuart set up the team, such incursions had become almost common. A total of seven residents had been fatally injured in the last three months in gun battles with intruders and one resident in an adjoining apartment unit was killed by stray gun fire. These attacks were primarily responsible for making the residents hesitant to turn over their weapons to the Defense Team. All of the attacks had occurred under cover of darkness and the attackers were now coming in sufficient numbers to overcome single or small groups of defenders. The price of such attacks was also costly to the attackers in lives lost which was the only reason why they did not occur more often. Nevertheless, both Stuart and Anders realized that until the residents had total confidence that they were safe in their apartments, there would be no transfer of weapons to the Defense Team. For that reason, the residents had to be convinced of the fact that Defense Team guards were on guard on the perimeter of the complex, 24/7, and not drinking coffee in the administration building.

Within the past year, travel outside of the complex had become extremely dangerous particularly at night. The fact that the complex was on the beach rather than on the mainland afforded the residents a far better chance of survival and more freedom to move about provided they traveled in numbers , were vigilant and were well armed. The administration's acquisition of weapons had been limited to rifles, particularly semi-automatic rifles and not to pistols and shotguns. Most residents continued to possess pistols and shotguns after many automatic weapons had been taken over by the Defense Team and always carried them especially when outside of the perimeter of the complex.

There were only three bridges leading from the mainland and two of these had been blown in recent months to prevent access to the beach area. The problem was that at night, renegade gangs would slip over by boat, under cover of darkness, and hide their boats in the mangroves. They would sometimes operate out of the mangroves for days at a time before returning to their mainland haunts. Consequently, excursions out of the Bayside complex even during the day were fraught with danger. There was talk of establishing a 'beach-wide defense force' which Stuart was all for but thus far other complexes had not yet indicated a similar interest. He had also been told by travelers that had stayed the night in the complex that well armed groups, in great numbers, with more ambitious plans were steadily moving up from South Florida. These were well organized forces, equipped and led by Cuban interests who would be moving north faster were it not for the infighting that was taking place among their own community. There were also groups of armed gangs heading north, apparently evacuating the Cuban controlled south Florida area. Both of these very sizeable forces posed threats to anyone in their path.

Stuart was of the opinion that in the not too distant future, one or more of these groups would eventually overwhelm the unorganized resistance posed by the local Defense Teams and would, in time, control all of South Florida and portions of the East Coast. The center of Florida, north of Orlando, was more easily defended from these invading troops by reason of the terrain and the nature of the population. This was historic red neck territory which extended all the way north through Georgia and west through Alabama and into Mississippi. The old time residents of these regions were well armed, well prepared, organized and ready to fight.

In the years before the collapse of the government, relations between the races had continuously disintegrated for as long as Stuart could remember. In years past, the government had come out with one program after another with the avowed purpose of improving relations. Invariably, the government programs would have the opposite effect of causing antagonism, claims of favoritism, and further claims of discrimination against one part of the population or another. The last two administrations were famous for playing off one group of people against another for their own purposes.

In the recent census, if that could be believed, the White population of the United States was reported as 47%; the Black population was reported as 17%; Hispanic at 24%, and Asian at 12%. In the last five to ten years, Stuart was of the opinion that, as a result of failed government social policies, these racial groups, with exceptions, wanted little to do with one another. The population on the beach, in contrast to the mainland part of Melbourne, was mostly White while the population of the older portions of Melbourne was primarily Black. Hispanics, including the Cubans, in Florida were primarily in the south, particularly in the Miami area, where they were the majority race.

There was no question that since the collapse of the government, the population of the United States, or what was formerly the United States, was organizing itself primarily along racial lines. The Blacks did not appear, from the information available to Stuart, to be combining forces with any other racial group. Nor were the Hispanics. The Asians, in many cases, were joining with White groups, particularly in certain areas of the country where their numbers did not appear to support an organization of their own.

There were reports of atrocities related to racially incited violence coming from all across the country. It was considered suicidal for a White to venture into the inner city anywhere in the country. It was likewise unwise for a Black to go unescorted into a White bastion. There were occasional stories of individual bravery by citizens of either race rising up to defend or rescue the unwary traveler who inadvertently found himself in the wrong neighborhood. Unfortunately, such stories were the rare exception compared to the flood of reports of barbarity that Stuart heard on Sarah's short wave radio.

For the occasional Black, Hispanic or Asian remaining on the beach, his or her ethnic background remained a problem to be overcome. There were Whites on the beach who looked upon such people with suspicion as being a threat to their well being. There was a certain amount of conflict of opinion in the various complexes on how to deal with people of other races. Some were for sending the non-whites off the beach and back to the mainland. These people were a distinct minority and their views were disregarded by the others. Stuart was of the opinion that race was to be completely ignored and conduct was the guideline to be measured. There were a number of whites on the beach that Stuart would gladly send over to the mainland before he would ever send any of the non-whites that he was acquainted with.

As time went on, there was an occasional request for admission from someone either from another complex or one who had traveled to the area. Such requests now went to the Administration Staff for handling and in rare cases, the person or family was admitted. The general policy was that if the person requesting admission had resources or skills that would benefit the complex, then they should be admitted provided there was space available. There was some turnover in the Bayside complex occasioned by reason of departures, an occasional expulsion or by reason of losses sustained in gunfights, ill health or otherwise. As a result with the passing of time, space did become available.

The following morning as Stuart walked over to the admin building, Andy Moss with some of the B Team people were setting up concrete barricades at the entry gate in order to control access of vehicles to the compound. Moss was cross checking the layout with drawings he was carrying and shouting out orders to the team members. The men were having difficulty complying with all of his orders which were tumbling out in rapid succession. He yelled out a greeting to Stuart but immediately turned his attention back to his work, barking out instructions on exactly how to place the barricades. Stuart was pleased to see that Ross Perry had most of his team out filling and placing sand bags around the guard posts on either side of the entry way. His men were smiling as they looked over at those working for Moss. It was obvious that they were pleased that their supervisor was Perry and not Andy Moss, who was considered by some as too controlling. Some of the women residents were busy hauling and placing metal tire spikes in the entry way. These had been made that morning in the machine shop using fencing from the swimming pool. Such luxuries as swimming pools were no longer needed particularly since the pool water had been secured as a scarce item subject to rationing. The pool was now referred to as the "Reservoir" and a funneling apparatus gathering rain water from roof line gutters kept it filled especially since controls on water usage had been established.

Sarah Taves came out of the administration building just as Stuart was about to enter. "Well, Stuart, looks like you've started something here. I haven't seen this group so upbeat in a number of years. I like it. This place needed someone to come in and kick ass. It was about time."

Stuart had not had occasion to spend any time talking with her since she joined the administration, other than to say hello. From what he had heard thus far, his impressions of her remained unchanged. He had seen her setting up her offices in the administration building and she seemed to get a lot done in very little time. "Sarah, it was just something that had to be done. If we didn't do it who in hell was going to. I think we have a good core group to work with now and hopefully we can get something done. Anyway what are you up to this morning?"

Sarah shook her head, "I don't think I slept at all last night. I thought of all the things I should be doing and how to go about doing them and where to find the things we need to do them with. The more I thought about it, the more ideas I came up with and soon it was time to get up and get going. Anyway, I think we're making progress."

Stuart turned to enter the office and waved her on in. "Sarah, if you have a minute, come on into the office. I would like to cover a few items with you." Stuart held the door and the two walked on into the administration building. Anders Jensen was hurrying around with a sheaf of papers in his hand as a former secretary from the State Residence Office was trying her best to keep up with him. He had apparently requisitioned a secretary to assist him and that was fine with Stuart. It was time for people to take charge of the situation and get the job done instead of hiding in their separate apartments as they had all been doing until the management staff changed all of that. Stuart had a good feeling about the people that had stepped forward to volunteer for the work that needed to be done.

Stuart and Sarah sat down in Stuart's office that was formerly the Bayside complex caretaker's office in years past. The furniture was sparse but it was sufficient for the task at hand. Stuart had wanted to discuss with Sarah something that he had thought about at length in the middle of the night when he was unable to sleep. He had been lying in his dorm thinking of everything that needed to be accomplished, as Sarah had said that she had done. He could only assume that all the others who volunteered had the same problem sleeping with everything that needed to be done.

Stuart explained to Sarah that the defense of the complex appeared to be in good hands and that the organizational needs seemed to be in equally good hands. What was needed was information on where we go from here. Stuart laid out to Sarah his view of the situation that they were in, including his opinion that all of South Florida was existing on borrowed time. They would eventually have to go elsewhere but where that was, he had no idea. He was also in the dark as to how they would go wherever they would go and what they would need to get there. An additional problem along the same line was that they needed to establish communication with other complexes and organizations on the beach for the purpose of exchanging information as well as resources. Stuart figured that in view of her prior experience in Navy Intelligence, she was about as well prepared as anyone in the complex to assume what was essentially an intelligence gathering function for the survival of the 500 some residents of Bayside. She would also have to assume some of the tasks of a diplomat in arranging the transfer of resources among the organized complexes. He was now interested in her thoughts on what he had to say.

Sarah was visibly impressed by his insight into their situation and his analysis of what had to be done for their survival. She had the same thoughts well before she became part of the management team at Bayside. Stuart's concerns confirmed her view of what needed to be done for their future survival.

Sarah paused and then spoke. "Stuart, I have been giving that a lot of thought. My staff and I agree where we go from here is the elephant in the closet. We are already evaluating various safe areas around the country that we are able to study. We are getting weather data, climatology, crop growth and the present state of stability around the country. The sooner we get into this full time, the better off we will be. I have some ideas and maybe we should also get Anders in on this."

As the two of them stood up to get Anders, he rapped on the door and entered the room. Stuart looked up and said, "You saved us a trip. We were just going in to see you."

Anders sat back attentively and listened as Stuart went over the assignment that he had just discussed with Sarah.

When Stuart was finished, Anders paused for just a moment and then said that he was in full agreement. "The sooner, the better. Our supplies are dwindling rapidly. We are going to have to make some rapid changes in how we have been operating." Anders went on to say that he had met with and discussed a staff position with Robert Thomas who had been a successful independent businessman in times past before that became, as the Department of Equalization called it, "self profiting". Thomas had fought the government as long as he could to sustain his privately owned fishing fleet, but after the government had taxed his company out of business, he entered into an arrangement with the Department of Equalization whereby he acted as the managing agent of the government in the operation of what was formerly his business. The Equalization Department, unfortunately, also assigned to him a dozen additional staff personnel to assist him in running now half the business that he formerly handled by himself. The income to be produced was assigned to also cover the added costs of the additional staff. In a short period of time, the business could no longer sustain itself and the government concluded that Robert was not fit for the task at hand. A committee of three, totally unfamiliar with commercial fishing, was assigned in his place and as a result, the business was totally defunct within three months. In the meantime, Robert had become very active in the black market and was soon doing better financially than he ever had in the fishing business.

When the black markets first began, as commodities became harder and harder to obtain through the government controlled economy, the government cracked down hard on persons found profiting outside the 'legal' market. As time went on, the government seemed to realize that in order to maintain control over the citizenry; the black markets would have to be tolerated at least to some extent. Consequently, at the time of the collapse, black marketers, such as Robert Thomas were operating fairly openly with no interference from the authorities.

It was the black marketers in many communities that established some semblance of order with their security forces following the collapse of the local governments. They did so in order to protect their businesses and in many cases had the best armed Militias to carry out the task. Robert Thomas had continued his organization from the complex and many of the men that volunteered for the Defense Teams came from his operation.

Stuart had some questions about the motivation and allegiance of Robert Thomas but had nothing negative to say about him. Thomas was known as a person who always did what he said he would do and that was obviously the reason Anders had selected him to be on his staff. Time would tell if Robert Thomas would be satisfied acting as a staff person rather than the guy running the show. In the meantime, Stuart would give him the benefit of the doubt.

Anders commented that he was getting a great deal of assistance from Thomas on meeting their looming food shortage but it was obvious they had to look to the future and other venues for their survival. He agreed that Sarah was the person for the job.

Sarah said she would discuss the matter further with her staff and be back with them with specifics in the near future. She agreed this project had great importance for their long term survival. Sarah went about her business and Stuart and Anders discussed the format of the meeting planned for that evening to conclude the organizational matters that were briefly discussed at the last meeting. The matter of the executive council was discussed and the two men reviewed the list of residents who would be most qualified to fill the positions and who, most importantly, would not become thorns in the side of Anders and Stuart in the management of complex matters. It was further arranged between the two for trusted associates to bring motions from the floor, subject to a voice vote, for the appointment of those meeting the approval of Stuart and Anders. This having been taken care of, basic rules of conduct in the complex were discussed and decided upon for presentation at the meeting.

Both Stuart and Anders considered it wise not to proceed too hastily with their pet political views regarding the organization until they had matters more firmly in hand. They both felt that for their own survival as well as that of the group, control of the Association was going to have to be limited to themselves at least until the country was somewhat stabilized and they were living in a more hospitable environment.

As the risks of injury or death from attacks increased, communication and travel between the organized groups on the beach decreased. Occasionally well guarded units would travel from one complex to another if the particular need that they wished to satisfy justified the exposure to attack. In time, these became less frequent with increased use of Ham radio or CB communication. Many of these communications involved trading food and material goods among the complexes. Some of the organizations had water desalinization facilities but lacked material goods or armaments. Bayside had an excess of material goods, but a shortage of food and water.

Trades could be arranged if communication and methods of delivery were available. Stuart and Anders discussed the need for establishing these relationships and the importance of utilizing the limited Ham and CB communications more effectively. It was decided between the two that Sarah should conduct an inventory to determine what communication resources were available in the complex. Stuart located Sarah working with Barnes' supply staff conducting their own inventory of critical items that were in short supply. The two sat in the supply room office and Stuart went over the conversation that he and Anders had regarding the need to establish better communications with adjoining complexes.

Sarah let him finish and then brought out a notebook filled with entries. "I hope you don't mind, but I've been working on that. Let me get my notes together and I can go over what I have found out. I have a couple of more people to talk with and I can be in your office in an hour with a status report if that's OK with you."

Stuart was in his office preparing notes for the next meeting when Sarah walked in carrying a clip board. "Well Sarah, what have we got here?"

Going over her notes as she responded, "Did you know that we have five, yes five, certified, licensed, not that such are required anymore, radio operators among our residents. Furthermore, we have two fully equipped

Ham radio stations lacking only generating power to make them fully operational and they are about to be connected to our power source as we speak. Not only that, besides the complex generating equipment which, as we all know, is already grossly overloaded, we have in excess of twenty portable generators, each of which is easily capable of powering the radio equipment. The Bayside radio station is presently operating and we are in the process of determining all beach radio facilities that are in operation. We have made contact with four that all claim to be operating under the auspices of their own established organizations. Two of which seem to be more highly organized than the other two, but at this point, who knows. I have a meeting, by radio of course, set up for tomorrow at 10:00 a.m. between their principals and you, and or Anders, whichever you choose. I consider this a significant first start as one of the complexes involved has their own desalinization equipment and they apparently have no water shortage problems whatsoever. I thought you would be interested in that."

"Awesome." Stuart thought for a moment. "I wonder what sort of arrangement they might be interested in that would, among other things, solve our water problems?"

Sarah immediately responded. "Frankly, Stuart, having seen the response that we had to the Defense Team request and the experience level that we have in military and police matters, not to mention the extent of our military stores, we may be in a very good bargaining position with our defense force. We can put close to 200 well armed men and women on the street and there are very few organizations on the beach that could come up with a fraction of that."

Stuart was aware that Perry, Moss and Barnes had been working with all of the Defense Team members on combat training tactics and maintenance of equipment. Combat teams were organized by squads of ten men and women with an assigned squad leader who had previous military and preferably, combat experience. Fortunately, there was a sufficient pool of former military retired men and women living in the complex to staff all squad leader positions and that would be of considerable assistance to the three men in forging an effective military force.

Attempts were being made to standardize weapons at least by squad so that men and women fighting alongside each other were using the same munitions. There were not enough AR20 rifles to equip each member of the Defense team, but there were a sufficient number to equip five squads of the more experienced members.

Four units were equipped with fully automatic rifles varying from modified mini 14s to AR15s and AK47s. At least each unit was commonly outfitted with a particular type of semi-automatic rifle and rifles were being machined daily to bring them all up to fully automatic status. These four units could also claim considerable experience among their ranks and could be counted on to be effective fighting units. Of the remaining eleven squads, two were assigned as medical units and were staffed with experienced medical technicians including paramedics, trained nurses, doctor's assistants and two physicians serving as medical commanders.

Four of the remaining units were assigned to supply and logistics duties. The remaining five units had little or no military experience and were temporarily assigned cadre duty, staffing guard posts and providing administrative services for the Defense Team while they underwent an intensive military training program.

Within the walls on the west side of the complex was an open field that had already been converted into a tactics training area with a hazard course and assault targets including an automobile hulk and an old shed. These practice targets were in use at all hours of the day and night but that was not a problem as due to the shortage of live ammunition, all firing was simulated. As Stuart observed the units in their work, he was impressed by their good discipline and high morale. The instructors all had extensive combat training with the Army Rangers, Special Forces, or one of the special combat units of the other services.

Protected guard posts were constructed fifty to one hundred yards or so from the complex walls at sufficient intervals to provide visual coverage from post to post around the complex. Each post was staffed by four experienced guards, all equipped with automatic weapons as well as night vision equipment. When all of the posts were constructed, the complex residents began resting more comfortably through the night knowing that if any problems developed, everyone would have adequate warning.

# Chapter Nine

Two nights after the defenses had been extended, a small group of intruders came out of the mangroves apparently intending to bypass Bayside and move farther into the island. When the intruders were challenged by one of the patrols, they opened fire with their weapons and were immediately cut down by the patrol and fire from two guard posts. Their bodies, after being stripped of ammunition and weapons, were hauled back into the mangroves by a patrol the following day and laid across their secured rubber raft as a continuing message to any who tried to follow.

The confidence level of the Defense Team was growing daily. On the afternoon of the scheduled meeting, Stuart and Anders met with their staff and discussed the plans for the meeting. Certain policies had to be discussed and both Stuart and Anders felt that sufficient progress had been made in the organization of the complex that they should now begin to lay out some of the ground rules. The residents had to understand that in order for the Association to be successful, all the residents were going to have to observe some basic rules and regulations. This would involve giving up some of their individual rights that had heretofore gone unchallenged. Among those rights was their ownership of basic resources such as food, water, weapons and ammunition. The complex must become the owner of all basic necessities and material items required for the common good. At some future date, the residents would be compensated if that was possible or the items would be returned if needs changed. As food supplies were being confiscated by the complex, arrangements were made for communal meals to provide for the residents. A dietician was appointed to ensure sufficient caloric intake was provided at minimal levels to extend the limited food inventories.

Crimes committed by residents against other residents or against the administration of the complex would be dealt with severely, including expulsion. These and other policies were discussed in detail by all of the staff including Anders, Stuart, Sarah, Perry, Moss, Barnes, Thomas and others. All heartily agreed that without a strong central organization and discipline in the complex, they would not make it. It was further decided that anyone that did not wish to reside in the complex under those conditions would be provided a minimal supply of food and water and allowed to leave. For every five leaving under those circumstances, an older weapon and limited rounds of ammunition would be provided if available.

After the policy discussions were concluded, the group all sat in silence and pondered their situation. They all seemed to realize that they had crossed a threshold in their organization and they were no longer a group of individuals wandering aimlessly, trying to make it on their own, rather they were a cohesive group with a purpose and with, what appeared to be, good direction. After a brief silence, Anders thanked them all for their support and concluded the staff meeting.

That evening, the residents eagerly crowded into the administration building meeting room and were busy talking among themselves as Anders, Stuart, Sarah and the other staff members took their respective places up on the stage. It appeared that everyone in the complex was in attendance with the exception of those manning the guard posts and on patrol. Anders stepped up to the podium and as he did so the residents stopped talking among themselves and directed their attention to the Association President. After a moment of quiet, Anders proceeded by laying out the agenda for the meeting.

All members of the administrative staff were then introduced with a brief explanation as to their duties and to whom they were to report. These appointments seemed to receive the approval of the residents and Anders moved on with a report on the level of preparedness achieved by the Defense Teams. This produced a round of applause from the residents who deeply appreciated the sacrifices and risks assumed by those who were bearing arms in defense of the complex. Following those items, Anders proceeded with the more controversial items on the agenda. Without softening the blow, Anders began by laying out the proposed charter that had been agreed upon by all members of the administrative staff: The president to serve until removal by two thirds vote of the residents; the president to have executive authority in all matters, administrative, rule making and judicial, subject to review by the executive council; the president to have full authority with respect to all discretionary operating matter decisions; members of the executive council to serve until removal by two thirds vote of the residents; removal elections to be held only once every two years by petition of one third of the residents; and Stuart and the administrative staff, including the commanders of the Defense Teams to report only to the president.

As Anders went through the proposed charter provisions, there was absolute silence in the auditorium. Finally as he finished and looked up from his notes at the residents, Irene Covington stood up and waited for Anders to recognize her. He nodded to her and she looked around at the residents as if to seek support for what she was about to say. "It seems that you have saved all of us a considerable amount of time by deciding what form of Association we are going to live under for the foreseeable future. It seems to me that these are very important issues that may more properly have been brought before the Association residents for comment and input. I suggest that before we adopt your proposed charter, that we have a study commission comprised of a cross section of the residents to discuss and decide exactly what form of government we wish to have, if any. There were nods of approval from some to the residents and Irene went on. "I move that such a study commission be appointed and that all wishing to serve on the commission so indicate."

Anders had anticipated such a response, particularly from Irene Covington, and was well prepared. "Irene, I agree totally with your suggestion and believe me, we would not have moved as quickly as we did were it not for the situation that we found ourselves in when we took stock of our reserves and the total lack of defenses available to the complex. We concluded that we do not have the luxury at this time of discussing issues that in normal times we would certainly discuss. We have food and water reserves that will last us no longer than four weeks. We are informed that better equipped aggressive forces, in greater numbers than we have dealt with in the past, are right now moving north and may be in our vicinity within the following weeks. We have moved fast in all respects. That includes with the establishment of our Defense Teams, with inventorying our resources, gathering intelligence data on our adversaries and on those that may be of assistance to us. Last, but not least, we have moved fast with respect to our structure of organization and the rules under which we must operate. I believe that all of you realize the tenuous situation that we are in and I ask for your cooperation and support, as well as your trust during these difficult times. We are confident that the day will come when we can do just what you have requested. The administrative staff has discussed this very issue at length and we have concluded that the charter that I have reviewed for you is the best vehicle at this time to extricate us, with a minimum loss of life and property, from the situation that we are in."

Applause began in various sections of the auditorium and rapidly spread throughout as the residents, with few exceptions, looked at one another, nodding approval. A hand was raised from the back of the room and when recognized, the speaker moved for adoption of the charter as stated. There was loud support from a few of the members which was picked up by what appeared to be the majority of attendees and Anders brought the gavel down and announced, "The motion is carried and the charter is passed as read." Stuart and Anders looked at each other trying not to smile. Irene Covington looked about her and finding little if any support for her proposal, took her seat. Anders moved on to the next item on the agenda which was the nomination and appointment of the executive council. Nominations came from the floor quickly, from the same areas where the applause had been initiated and in no time, five names had been submitted. As soon as the fifth name was proposed, a motion came from the floor that the nominations be closed and a voice vote be taken affirming the appointment of the five.

Anders brought the five proposed council members to the front of the auditorium and taking the microphone, stated, "All in favor of the appointment of these five individuals to serve as the Association executive council, please say 'aye'." Again, the ayes came from various sections of the auditorium and quickly spread throughout. The five nominees were all well known in the complex and were all apparently fit for the task so that there would not have been any particular controversy with respect to any one of them. The five were Perry, Barnes, Moss, Thomas and Beth Sloan. Stuart and Sarah were considered members of the executive. Irene Covington sat in her chair with a puzzled look on her face. It had become apparent to her that Anders, and most likely Stuart, had orchestrated the entire process and she had not realized it until it was too late.

Anders had moved on to the next item on the agenda which involved the necessity for the Association to assume ownership of all food stuffs, weapons, ammunition, communications equipment, tools, machinery, and other listed items that would be necessary for the general welfare of the residents. There was a certain amount of grumbling among the attendees as the items were named but most were silent, probably assuming that their particular possessions would not be discovered and consequently, not appropriated.

Anders dashed their hopes with his next statement which was to the effect that a complex wide inventory inspection of all residential areas would be taken in the following weeks. Records would be kept of what items were confiscated from which residents for possible return if some miracle happened that would allow for that to happen. The residents were now silent and listening attentively. They were all beginning to realize that Anders and the new governing body meant business and were not playing games. The agenda items that followed were potentially more controversial, but by now the attendees, with very few exceptions, were a bit overwhelmed by the changes in their lives and were putting up no vocal resistance.

Rules of conduct and the punishment to be exacted were read. Anders also announced that punishment would be handled by the administrative staff and would swiftly follow any breach of conduct. Hoarding of scarce resources and theft would be severely punished and could lead to banishment from the complex. This brought a murmur from the residents as they all realized that banishment could well mean death. Anders then announced that there would be monthly meetings to resolve problems and discuss future plans. He implied that the staff had been discussing long range plans for survival but did not go into any details. Anders concluded the meeting with the request that anyone wishing to participate in administration of the complex or assistance on any of the various projects to make themselves known.

The residents stood up and were soon involved in loud conversation throughout the auditorium. Irene Covington, without hesitation, made her way up to the podium and approached Anders. "Well, you fellows did a good job of ramroding your program through. I hope you do everything else as well."

Anders smiled at her and replied, "Irene, I have no idea what you are talking about, but I did want to talk with you. We may have a job for you if you are interested in working with us."

This took her back a bit as she assumed they would be quite content was she to just disappear from the scene. "Exactly what did you have in mind?"

Anders could see the look of disbelief written all over her face. "Irene, you brought up an important issue regarding the prisoner situation some time ago and we still have not figured out how to deal with that. Why don't you take the responsibility of coming up with a policy proposal that you could present to the executive council. If it is something that we could live with, I am sure that it would be adopted. You could appoint a staff to assist you on that project and we could assign you an office in the administrative building for you to operate out of. Are you interested?"

Anders could tell by the look on her face that she saw all sorts of potential in his suggestion. Anders was aware that Irene, by being in the administrative building, would have immediate access to what was going on in the complex. On the other hand, she would also be where Anders could keep an eye on her. In time, possibly she could become an ally. Time would tell.

As Stuart was leaving the building, one of the new council women, Beth Sloan, approached him about setting up a day care center for the complex children to free up the mothers to assist on other projects. Stuart agreed heartily and noted that there was ample space available in the administration building for such a facility. He would talk with Anders about reserving the space in the morning and knowing that Anders would approve the project, he suggested that Beth proceed with her idea. Stuart was heartened to see the vast majority of the residents getting involved in Association matters as most had been in a state of depression for some time, apparently overwhelmed by the futility of their situation.

As Stuart continued talking with her, he discovered that she had been a school teacher and the thought came to him that their organization needed to think about the children and how they were to be, not only cared for, but educated. Stuart brought up the possibility of establishing some sort of school for the children. Beth Sloan said that she had been thinking about that and had spoken with other women in the complex who were teachers or who had taught in the past.

Stuart and Beth continued talking as they strolled back to the dormitory building, deeply involved in conversation discussing how the school could be set up, what materials were available, where the school would be, the students, and so forth. When they parted, Stuart told Beth to lay out a plan for the operation of the school, how it would be set up, and, in particular, how to deal with the existing situation where many older children did not have the benefit of any education whatsoever. Some did and some did not depending upon whether their parents were interested or not. That was not going to be a problem.

# Chapter Ten

Months had passed since the charter was adopted and the executive council was appointed. Progress had been made in the organization of the complex, but it had not gone without problems. Barnes had been able to secure additional stores of ammunition from former associates in the police departments of Melbourne and Orlando. Apparently, weapons stores had been secreted by some of the people living in another complex, The Osprey, at the time the government was collapsing and the hidden stores were used as bargaining chips by those who knew of their locations. Barnes was able to obtain large quantities of ammunition for the AR20s, flares, anti tank missiles with launchers, grenades, and a number of AR20 rifles with extended rapid fire capability. The trade off that Barnes had arranged, and that was approved by Anders and Stuart, was that Bayside would provide protection to the Osprey people who had no effective defensive force of their own. The population of the Osprey organization, which was located on the ocean side of the beach about one mile from Bayside, was approximately two hundred and fifty men, women and a few children. Generally an older group of people most of whom had been retired when the collapse came. Barnes was also able to obtain an agreement from the president of Osprey that they would provide twenty able bodied men and women for training under the direction of the Bayside Defense Team.

Once trained, the twenty men and women would serve as a security detail for The Osprey and in time of need, as part of the Association Defense Team. This would bring the number of personnel under arms in the Association to two hundred and fifty which was a substantial force.

Sarah Taves had made great strides in getting her intelligence unit up and operating. She had built a staff of five men and women, three of whom had intelligence experience in the Army or Air Force and two of whom were administrative clerks in the Army. She had moved the radio communications facility to an office adjoining her own so that news from the outside, by way of Ham or other radio was immediately channeled to the intelligence section for review. She conducted a daily briefing of intelligence data for administrative staff including Anders, Stuart and the leaders of the Defense Team, Perry, Moss and Barnes.

Barnes was no longer involved directly with the Defense Teams rather had by this time assumed the responsibilities of a logistics, or supply officer, being responsible for obtaining, securing and allocating equipment for the teams. He had become a bit of a tyrant in carrying out his duties, but it was apparent that was necessary in order to protect and ration those scarce resources between competing interests. He was also in the process of setting up a fabrication shop for the repair and building of required equipment as well as a weapons shop for the conversion of weapons from semi-automatic to fully automatic. Barnes was also working quietly with some of the chemists in one of the outlying buildings to develop ammunition and explosives to supply the Defense Teams.

Sarah had established good communications with a number of radio operators on the beach which led to a high degree of cooperation among the better led beach side complexes. It was her work that eventually led to Barnes being able to obtain the military hardware that was so difficult to come by these days. Her contacts also brought about an agreement with Oceanside complex to provide Bayside with potable water supplies from Oceanside's desalinization equipment. The tradeoff was that Bayside had technical expertise which was necessary to keep the equipment operating. Bayside also had a well equipped machine shop, thanks to Barnes, for the repair and replacement of parts necessary for the operation of the desalinization equipment.

From Sarah's briefings, it was apparent that there were a number of well organized islands of humanity across the country that were under the control of various groups ranging from ultra conservative, militia style organizations to highly organized criminal bands. The least functional areas included the upper east coast and the west coast. That was an assumption based on the fact that very few reports seemed to be coming from those areas. Nowhere in the country was there anything resembling what had formerly been known as the United States of America.

The government that had previously been located in Washington, D.C. had totally disappeared. There was nothing seen or heard of any of the national political figures that had been so prominently displayed in the press and on television. No one seemed to know the whereabouts of President Turner since the collapse and most everyone assumed that he had been killed in the riots that followed in the Washington, D.C. area.

According to some who witnessed the carnage, all of the capital buildings and many of the national monuments no longer existed. The entire area was taken over by thugs and rampaging, uncontrolled, angry mobs who slew anyone that appeared to be involved with the government or had worked with any of the businesses located in the capital. Some who escaped later after the bloodbath reported that people were dying of starvation in the streets.

A very authoritarian trend had taken place across the entire country with good and bad results depending upon who was running the show. Racism and religious prejudice were very much a part of many of the controlling leadership factions. A number of groups did not permit Blacks or Hispanics and some did not permit Whites. Certain groups in particular the Muslim groups, were anti-Semitic and were ostracizing anyone believed or suspected of being Jewish. On the other hand, some areas were totally under the control of Jewish organizations and a number did not permit access to anyone that was not Jewish.

There was little, if any, travel being conducted across the country due to the dangers involved. Travel outside of one's own protected area meant exposure to uncontrolled renegade gangs or, most likely, to accidental entry into areas controlled by persons or factions with violently opposing political or religious views.

Underlying the more apparent dangers was the subtle risk of exposing oneself to the unknown in a world of scarce resources. Food and water were hard to come by and were not willingly shared by those in possession without receiving something in return of equal or greater value. The principal items of barter were now food, water, weapons and ammunition. Any travel that could be considered at all safe was being done by armed convoy on carefully chosen routes. These convoys had to provide their own food, fuel and defenses and in view of the threats that existed along the way, they had to have ample supplies of everything. The convoys were also looked upon by renegade units along the way as sources of materials, fuel and additional armaments and consequently were under threat of constant attack by one group or another.

There were some aircraft still in existence, but little available fuel and very few safe places for the aircraft to fly. There was also the problem that many people wanted to go somewhere else and the very limited number of aircraft in existence did not provide much of a travel option. Some of the larger, more organized groups, particularly in the west, did utilize aircraft to some extent for the purpose of obtaining scarce materials. It was known that some flights were taking place among some of the western settlements and very occasionally even out of the country. Where they could be going, no one could guess as the entire world was in a chaotic state. As far as rail transportation was concerned, that was virtually nonexistent as the rail beds had been destroyed in many sections of the country by opportunists who ripped up the tracks and ties to sell or barter for construction or fuel purposes.

Sarah had set up a number of meetings between Anders and the leaders of other organized groups on the Beach. Some of these were face to face meetings and some by radio net. Stuart had sat in on most of the meetings and had the opportunity to meet members of other complexes that were involved with responsibilities similar to his. As a result of these meetings and radio communications, the beginnings of a cohesive beach wide organization had been established. Bayside was well ahead of any other group on the beach and consequently, they took the lead in establishing a more formal relationship among the interested parties.

Stuart and Anders laid out plans to form a defensive Alliance with those groups within a reasonable geographic area that would permit access and assistance if need be. They reasoned that such a reasonable distance would extend down to the southernmost bridge and north to what used to be the community of Cocoa Beach. North of there was Cape Canaveral, with the old Space Center, now a deserted area with overgrown concrete launch pads.

The limits of the Control Zone, as they referred to it, was determined by the physical layout and area of the zone which would lend itself to defense by a force the size of that which Stuart and Anders believed they would have available. The zone was bounded on the west by the Indian River, formerly referred to as the Intracoastal Waterway and on the east by the Atlantic Ocean. The southern boundary would be the most difficult to defend due to its width, with the north fairly easily defended as the island there was no more than a half a mile wide. The zone comprised a somewhat rectangular piece of land which was approximately twenty miles long and a half mile wide at the top and one mile wide at the bottom.

With the assistance of Sarah, a meeting of the principals of all organized groups within the zone was set up in what had been the Radisson Hotel on the Atlantic side of the beach. All members of the Bayside Defense Teams were placed on duty to provide security for the meeting. In view of the fact that security involved placing units all along the length of the zone, other volunteers from the participating groups had to be called upon. A total security force of over five hundred was raised and while many of these security personnel were fairly well trained and equipped, they were not used to working in concert with relatively large numbers of personnel. Some problems developed, particularly with respect to the matter of who would be in charge of the defensive units, but in time, most participants recognized the Bayside group as most capable of assuming that responsibility.

The additional forces from neighboring complexes were spread among the active Bayside Defense Team members with the understanding that the Bayside personnel would be guiding their actions. Perry was the overall commander of the troops with Moss in charge of the northernmost sector and Barnes handling the southern sector. The southern sector was supplemented with a heavier concentration of available troops as that was considered the most vulnerable. Barricades were set up in that area and gun emplacements were heavily manned in what had been the area surrounding the old highway 192 bridge leading over to Melbourne. The bridge had been blown months before to make access from the mainland more difficult.

Some organizations from south of the established control zone wished to participate as they recognized the potential of the proposed Alliance. They were allowed to attend, but for the time being were not considered active participants primarily due to the need to draw the line at some point. There were approximately one hundred men and women in attendance at the meeting representing over ten thousand men, women and children in the various complexes and housing areas. For the most part, they and their people had been fending for themselves since the total collapse of the government and had been scavenging food and material goods from whatever source was available. In many cases, they had been stealing and plundering from one another so that consequently, there was not a high level of trust existing among them.

One of the first tasks involved in organizing the meeting was for Ross Perry to lead a number of the troops over to the Radisson Hotel to clean it out. They found out that quite a few separate gangs of five to ten members had set up camps inside the hotel. Perry offered all of them safe passage out of the hotel and this seemed to work with most but there were some that offered resistance. When they saw what they were up against, they soon decided to cooperate and agreed to leave. Obviously the building was a mess and that turned out to be the larger problem. Perry selected the gang members that had refused to leave and used them as the cleaning crew. They finally got down to work after force had been applied to some of the less cooperative members who finally saw the light. The hotel rooms were completely trashed which was not the issue. The primary problem was the accumulation of filth and waste from months of habitation by human animals. After basic sanitation procedures were applied to the first three floors and windows opened on all floors, the decision was made that the building was in satisfactory condition for the two or three hour meeting. There was not going to be any food service so after the stench was removed, the large conference room was ready.

Anders was aware of the fragile relationship that existed among those in attendance and knew that he was going to have difficulty in bringing all of these people together in one cohesive unit. He and Stuart had discussed at length exactly how they would approach those in attendance with their proposal that they all work together. They had decided that Anders should, in effect, grab the bull by the horns right from the start. At the appointed time for the meeting and with an impressive lineup of armed Defense Team guards, in formation, behind him, Anders approached the podium. Conversation in the hall died down and when it was perfectly still, Anders introduced himself. He then proceeded to tell them of the necessity that their survival depended on them all working together. "If you think you can do it on your own, you are sadly mistaken."

Anders went on and outlined the initial steps in his proposal for a mutual Defense Alliance among the participating complexes. Participating groups would be assessed a percentage of their overall population to conscript a certain number of able bodied men and women to the Alliance Defense Force. Not all would be trained for combat duty, as a certain number would be needed for administrative purposes, medical duty, or other non combat roles.

Anders explained that the Bayside military staff would be in charge of the Alliance Defense Force at least until personnel from other organizations were recognized as qualified for the task at hand. Anders pointed out the experience level of those in charge of the Bayside military effort and the successes of the teams. Since being committed to the defense of the complex, the Bayside teams had been involved in one hundred seven fire fights involving over fifty attackers at any one time. While the attackers had sustained heavy losses, there had only been three fatalities among Bayside personnel. None of the attacks had been successful even though, for the most part, they were aimed directly at the complex or neighboring complexes.

Anders went on, explaining the growth and effectiveness of their intelligence and communication operation. Laying out in brief form the condition of the rest of the country as it was then known to be. This was of considerable interest to the audience as very few had any idea as to what was happening in other parts of the country. Anders alluded to the fact that the Bayside Staff was also looking into long term survival prospects and plans. He did not go into the details of what he was referring to, but he let the audience know that the Defense Alliance was only the initial step in achieving some form of safe future. This peaked their interest as anyone with reasonable mental skills knew that their long term survival depended on major changes in their present situation.

Anders laid out some of the principles that Bayside operated under and that Anders considered crucial to the effectiveness of the Alliance. Weaponry had to be considered a scarce resource and controlled by the governing agencies. In this case and initially, Bayside logistics personnel would be in charge of inventorying, maintaining and storing all weapons and ammunition. This, again, brought on grumbling from many in the hall which Anders fully expected, but without hesitation he went on to explain that most of these activities would take place in complexes of Alliance members and very few weapons would leave their areas but that it was essential to ensure that all Alliance members were equally defended rather than to have one area with an excess of arms and ammunition while a fellow Alliance member was unprotected. When he further advised them that no weapons would be taken from a condominium unless and until security was firmly in place for that condo, the grumbling then seemed to soften.

Anders further expanded on the need for a working Alliance among the residents on the island. He argued the strength they would have in the numbers of people involved in the Alliance and the benefits that would transpire. "If we all work together, we can survive. If we don't, we may not survive. We need you and you need us. Let's join together and make this work."

Applause began in the back of the hall where some of Robert Thomas' people were seated and rapidly spread through the hall. Eventually, everyone in the hall was standing, clapping and cheering for Anders as well as for the idea of a united Alliance. It was clear that while some were not in agreement with the idea of giving up control of their individual weapons, an overwhelming number of those in attendance understood the need for the concept and agreed with it.

Irene Covington had been sitting in the back of the hall taking in the entire proceeding. This time she was a bit better prepared for the events taking place and had chosen her seat in the rear of the auditorium so she could observe what was going on. Irene smiled as she noted the men that were leading clapping and making the floor nominations. All of them were clearly in the camp of Anders or Stuart. She would have to be better organized the next time she wanted to challenge either one of them on important policy issues. Possibly she and her like minded friends could adopt some of the tactics that seemed to succeed for Anders and Stuart.

# Chapter Eleven

Anders came up with a proposal to build a marina on the Indian River side of the island immediately next to the Bayside complex and have Robert Thomas manage it. Thomas had been active in the fishing business in years past, before his black market days, and there was great need for that at this time when food supplies were becoming more difficult to obtain with each passing day. There was a natural boat harbor that was close to the complex which could be defended with the construction of guard posts, towers, and hardened bunkers. Anders assigned to Thomas the responsibility for building and managing the marina and fishing fleet for the purpose of developing an additional food source for the Association as well as for the proposed Alliance.

Thomas was allocated men and supplies necessary to secure and build the marina and was given the green light to use men from the Moss Defense Team to requisition boats from the mainland adequate for the task of conducting a large scale fishing operation. Thomas also brought out the fact that there would be a collateral need for higher powered, faster, well armed boats to provide protection for the slower, less maneuverable, fishing fleet, particularly when they were traversing the cut to the ocean. Thomas immediately proceeded to set up his fishing fleet and within one week had obtained four cigarette boats and seven fishing trawlers. All of the boats were in need of repair including extensive maintenance and parts replacement.

Thomas was able to find a number of marine mechanics living in the complex who were only too eager to get back to work on diesel engines, hydraulic systems and boat electrical problems. All of the acquired boats were pulled out of the water, on ramps, and their hulls were being scraped for repainting, while the mechanics were deep in their hulls, disassembling engine and system parts for cleaning, lubrication and in some cases for removal and replacement.

During this repair work on the boats, the activity along the beach attracted the attention of persons along the mainland and not many days passed before a party of approximately ten or more made a night time raid, apparently hoping to make off with one or more of the cigarette boats that they had observed being repaired. They did not land directly at the partially constructed marina; rather they beached their rafts some distance north, hoping to come down to the marina through the brush and mangroves. Unfortunately for them, they had been observed well before they left their boats and the team members had figured out what they were up to and what their route of travel would most likely be. The intruders were allowed to proceed, without interruption, to an area just to the north of the marina where the dry land funneled down to a narrow, barren strip, with the Indian River on their right When they had reached the middle of the strip, crouching down to avoid detection, B Team members fired flares over them and then opened up with automatic rifle fire and grenades. Hardly a shot was fired in return and under the light of additional flares, their bodies could be seen strewn around the path they had been taking.

In the middle of the group, one lone gunman stood up with his arms raised casting an eerie shadow against the glowing light of the descending flares. There was complete silence from the Defense Team as they awaited the decision of their unit commander on what to do about the lone survivor of their initial salvo. Not receiving an order to fire, a five man squad warily approached the sole remaining trespasser as their fellow team members continued to fire flares to illuminate the area. While one of the team members brought the prisoner back to the marina area, the others checked the ten bodies, lying on the ground, for signs of life.

Two were found alive but were mortally wounded and would not survive for long. These were put away with pistol shots to the head by the squad leader. That was not the decision of the squad leader, rather had been the determined policy by Anders and Stuart for dealing with prisoners who from reasonable observation at the scene by the squad leader, would most likely not survive with the limited medical care available. Stuart took the position that operational decisions, of which this was clearly one, were not appealable, only the more substantial governmental issues, such as decisions that had a direct impact on each and every resident in the Association.

In time the respective limits of power in the Association structure would be worked out. Stuart let Irene know, when she complained about shooting the two survivors, that, as far as he was concerned, the decision was final.

The prisoner that had been taken in the aborted attack on the marina was returned to the administrative building for questioning by Stuart, Moss and Barnes. He was young around twenty years of age, very ill kept, extremely thin, and very frightened by what he had seen happen to his companions. He was seated in what had been turned into an interrogation room with a bare wooden chair located in the center of the room and other chairs placed in a semi circle around it. A single bare light bulb, located directly over the single chair, illuminated the room. There were no windows in the room and no other furniture or decorations on the bare walls. At first the prisoner was uncommunicative, not providing any information as to where he was from or how he and his companions had obtained the sophisticated AR20 automatic rifles that they were carrying. With two of the bodies, the team members had found automatic grenade launchers which were the first Barnes had seen in a number of years, other than those in the possession of the Association. What concerned Barnes and the others was that the launchers were all Russian made.

After a series of questions had gone unanswered by the prisoner, Barnes, who had been standing behind him, told him in Spanish that if he didn't start cooperating, he would go into the same pit as his buddies. The prisoner turned around to look at Barnes and replied in fluent Spanish that he spoke no or little English and had no idea what was requested of him. As it turned out, he was Cuban and had been in Florida for only a few months. He had been conscripted, in Cuba, into a group led by one, Paco Morales.

In return, he was provided a very basic allowance of food, clothing and shelter. Morales had a highly disciplined group of men under his command numbering around two thousand under arms with an additional number of support personnel. His was just one of a number of Cuban groups active in South Florida, but, according to the prisoner, Carlos Moran, his was the best led and best disciplined of all.

The troops under Morales' command came from the Cuban areas of South Florida, primarily Miami, with the majority having come to Florida from Cuba following the collapse of the American government. The Cuban government was continuing to function on a very limited basis as it had since the death of Castro shortly after the turn of the century. Various political groups were in sharp competition for control of the reins of government with the Morales Group, followers of the Cuban National Socialist Party, leading the pack. Morales was not the head of the party, Carlos explained, but he was in the upper echelon and was assigned to south Florida to conduct military operations and to secure the area for the CNSP. The other Cuban groups operating in South Florida had the same objective, but for competing political interests.

The Cuban Liberation Party, comprised mostly of American born Cubans, was the primary opposing force to the CNSP and was strongest in the Miami and Tampa areas. Thus far, the two groups had gained virtual control of the population along the east and west coast of Florida from the Keys to just south of the Tampa-Melbourne line with small force expeditions extending up to Daytona Beach. These were primarily reconnaissance outfits as was the unit that Carlos was assigned to. The group that he landed on the beach with was only a small part of a larger Recon group which was presently located in north Melbourne. They were to regroup the following day and return to the Vero Beach area and rejoin their main contingent.

Carlos stated that they had run into little resistance in their trip north, with the exception of small bands of poorly armed renegades who quickly fled into the night when they realized they had crawled into a hornets' nest of well armed, well disciplined Cubans. Following the interrogation, Carlos, who had been very cooperative throughout, was made comfortable, well fed and secured under guard until the Defense Team decided what to do with him. In the meantime, they wanted to treat him well as there was a general feeling in the group that he could be of use to them.

Irene Covington was allowed to interview the prisoner, by interpreter, for a twofold purpose. To allay any fears that the prisoner might have regarding his future and to show Irene Covington that the Defense Team was treating its prisoners humanely. Irene had submitted no proposals to the executive committee regarding treatment of prisoners rather had indicated to Stuart that she preferred for the time being to act as an observer any time a prisoner was taken to ensure he was well treated.

Stuart felt strongly that Carlos could be of use to the Association as a conduit to communicate with what appeared to be their primary immediate threat, the Morales Group. Stuart saw all of south Florida, including the Melbourne area, as eventually falling under the control of Hispanic interests of one form or another. Stuart would rather deal with a disciplined group any day, rather than with an unpredictable unorganized mob. Whatever transpired, he did not believe that they would be able to stay much longer in the area that they presently occupied. For that reason, he was considering the possibility that they might negotiate some quid pro quo arrangement with the Morales group that might benefit their future plans, whatever they may be. Stuart tended to believe that Carlos had been telling them the truth as to the aspirations of the Cubans, what the limits of their interests were, and the quality of their leadership.

In the meantime, the various members of the Alliance had submitted the names of their chosen delegates to represent their interests in the Assembly, the representative organization. The meeting was again held in what remained of the Radisson on the beach, again in the same conference room as the organization meeting. Anders began the meeting with a layout of the agenda and then had Sarah Taves present an intelligence briefing based on the information obtained from Carlos and from other sources.

Based on the rate of progress of the Morales group in its trek northward in Florida, Sarah was of the opinion that they would be in the Melbourne area, in significant force, within one month. They could obviously be there much sooner, but it was their practice to take an area, by force if necessary, and then to establish a controlling government, using locals as often as possible, secured by a small armed force. While this was taking place, the main force would be used to secure the area, ferret out any resistance, and assist in restarting basic services. She stated that from the information available, it appeared that the group was very well equipped, with some armored vehicles, late style automatic weapons, including standard issue AR20 rifles, shoulder fired Russian missiles for tanks and hardened defenses, all in the hands of well trained, disciplined combat veterans estimated to number over six thousand in number. There was complete silence in the hall as the audience absorbed what she had just said. Sarah went on, "I will now turn the briefing over to Stuart, the acting executive officer of the Alliance."

Stuart took the podium and motioned to an assistant to turn on the overhead projector. He first presented a slide of the estimated strength of the Morales combat force, the next slide showed the number of trained combat forces presently available to the Alliance. The number of friendly combat experienced forces available was approximately one third that of the assumed attacking force.

Stuart went on to explain that while the Defense Force numbers were not particularly impressive, being one third of the estimated attacking force, there was an additional force in training that brought the defensive troop numbers roughly to parity.

Then Anders took over and explained the preparations that would be required. He produced a chart with each member organization listed, the population of adult males and females and the number of conscripts expected to be produced from each one. Again there was mumbling heard throughout the hall.

Anders pressed on and stated in a clear, firm voice that the conscripts were expected to present themselves for training at the assigned areas, depicted on the chart no later than twelve noon the following day. For the time being, Bayside personnel would be in charge of conducting all training at all of the training sites. Each conscript was to bring with him personal items necessary to sustain himself at the training site for the ensuing month. Food and shelter would be provided at the sites. All sites were abandoned educational facilities which could quickly be converted into dormitories and had ample open spaces for drilling, tactics training and physical fitness programs. Member organizations were tasked to provide food, food service and maintenance personnel, administrative assistants, training materials, hardware and a list of the basic items necessary to get the training facilities up and operating. These were to be in place by noon the following day together with labor teams to prepare the sites.

When Anders finished, there was some shaking of heads and comments coming from the audience that they would not be able to assemble all of the men and materials requested in the time allowed. Anders stood at the podium for a minute or two, allowing the grumbling to continue and he then called for quiet. Waiting until there was not a single whisper being passed, Anders told the assembled group, "you have a choice, right now, of working with us or walking out of this hall. I don't want to waste my time, the time of my staff or the time of any one of you who are willing to make the same sacrifices that we are willing to make. There is the door. If you or the organization that you represent cannot or will not provide the men or materials we have told you that we expect from you, then leave right now. We have work to do and we are going to start after a five minute break. I expect that everyone that remains is going to stay for the long haul. As for the rest, good luck. We will resume in five minutes."

Loud discussion followed as Anders departed the podium. Stuart approached him, grabbed him by the arm and told him he was in full agreement with the way that he had handled the representatives. "Let's filter out the dead wood right now."

Anders nodded in agreement, not saying anything. Stuart could tell that he was incensed that with the life and death situation they were in, a number in the hall were not willing to do what clearly had to be done.

The Osprey representative commented to Stuart, "Screw 'em. Let 'em fend for themselves."

After the meeting resumed, there were three or four of the original group that were no longer present. Anders took roll and noted the absence of three men who represented groups on the south side of the zone. They were the ones who had the most to benefit from the Alliance as they were in the most vulnerable area, but if that was their choice, so be it. Anders continued the meeting with the following days schedule and locations of assembly points. Stuart was relieved that the losses to the Alliance were so minimal.

# Chapter Twelve

S tuart's work schedule during the past months was stretched at both ends. He was continuing to be very involved in organizing and upgrading the Bayside complex and was now the apparent choice to provide the overall administration of the Alliance Defense effort. He was also very involved with virtually all important policy decisions affecting both Bayside and the proposed Alliance organization. Anders used him for much more than just a sounding board for his own ideas. He relied on his judgment and for his opinions on touchy issues of which there were very many. On the down side, Stuart was working eighteen hours a day or more but so far he was bearing up quite well. In a sense, he thrived on the challenge and for the first time in his life, he thoroughly enjoyed the work in which he was involved. He enthusiastically threw himself into the challenge that he faced. He made it a point to get sufficient rest and food to carry out his heavy work load. He was throwing all of his intellectual skills, energy and personal drive into what he viewed as the fight of his life. He saw that what he, Anders, Sarah and the others were working for was most likely very similar to what others fighting for the survival of their country had seen in years past.

Stuart had been disappointed to say the least at the reception that he and Anders and others in the Bayside group had been receiving from some of the other condo organizations on the island. He saw a definite need for redefining their goals for survival by an addition of morale building programs to instill desire and a willingness to sacrifice in order to achieve success. They had to get their members and associate organizations to want to pitch in on the work, to sacrifice when that was needed, and to be willing to fight for the success of the organization, not just for themselves. He would have to give that further thought and would talk to Anders about it. Anders would have some ideas there as he was obviously becoming frustrated at the lack of incentive on the part of many of the people on the island.

Stuart laid out a temporary Alliance Defense Team Staff, with Ross Perry serving as the Chief of Operations. Below him he placed Andy Moss and some of the more experienced former military personnel from Bayside. The positions were announced as temporary pending review of nominees from among their new associate organizations. Stuart was confident that there was an undiscovered pool of military and law enforcement personnel that was lying untapped in the various groups. He did not wish to offend anyone by appointing Bayside personnel to all of the important posts.

John Barnes' duties as the Logistics Officer had been increased to now include the Alliance requirements. This was a huge expansion in his responsibilities and he increased his staff to deal with the greater work load. His first task was to determine what military assets were available and he set about assigning teams to conduct inventories at the new member's locations. It was the old problem all over again, with people not wanting to part with their personal stores of weapons, ammunition and materials that had military value, be it radios, knapsacks, ground positioning locators or whatever.

Robert Thomas had suggested to Barnes that it would help if they made the military operation more attractive to their Bayside members and other condo members by working on building 'esprit de corps' in the military organization. Thomas' initial suggestion was to come up with a more attractive uniform, than the present use of plain brown coveralls, complete with a beret with a flash of color. Shoulder patches would also look good. Thomas added that it might present a more imposing appearing force to some of the "scumballs so intent on harming us."

Barnes replied, "Just where in hell would we get these uniforms may I ask?"

Thomas laughed. "I can get the materials and we could put some of these sewing ladies to work. Have someone design a decent uniform, nothing overly fancy, and I will get the material for you. You will notice a definite increase in interest in the military program, including recruits wanting to join, trust me. I know this business."

Barnes laughed but said that he would talk to Stuart about it. "I'll let you know what he says."

The day following the meeting, Barnes had his teams preparing for the arrival of the new trainees. Alliance conscripts were to begin arriving at the training sites within a few hours and weapons and materials would be needed within a day or two for training. The first couple of days after their arrival would be devoted to administrative matters such as determining the experience of the recruits, assigning them to billets and to squad leaders for training. Some determination would have to be made as to their physical fitness and suitability for combat or support roles. All of this impacted on Barnes task. He was also to oversee the accumulation of food service equipment, housing accommodations, and all of the other materials needed to provide for the influx of personnel expected at the training sites. In order to meet the needs of his assignment, Barnes delegated his work out to his ever expanding staff with an apparent ease that Stuart found amazing in view of the complexity of his task.

With the additional responsibilities assigned to Sarah by reason of the Alliance organization, she had searched out experienced intelligence people from the new member complexes. She had known a few from prior years and had mentioned them to Stuart in the past as potential staff members and immediately following the Alliance meeting had brought them into her organization.

Stuart also wanted to talk with Sarah concerning the matter of Carlos but he wanted to do so with Anders as well, so the two headed towards Anders office. Sitting down with Anders, Stuart brought up the fact that Carlos and his associates had been expected to return and meet their companions on the mainland by now. Something should be done immediately to use Carlos as a messenger and send him back to the mainland to communicate with the Morales group leaders.

The problem was what should be the message sent with Carlos. Both Sarah and Anders waited for Stuart to go on, as they figured that he must have something in mind. Stuart proceeded, "Possibly we can offer some form of trade off to the Morales Group whereby they get what they want and we get what we want." Both Sarah and Anders waited expectantly for Stuart to say what trade off he had in mind. After a pause, Stuart continued, "We can't stay on this narrow strip of land forever. We've got Robert Thomas scouring the ocean floor for fish that we need to feed our people. Within two months, all we will have to eat will be the fish that Robert finds for us. How long is that going to continue? Others will get the same idea and soon there won't be enough to go around. The Morales Group wants to take over this area. At least we believe they do. We won't be able to stop them in the long run."

Stuart went on, "I suggest we offer them a bargain. They don't want to waste men and materials fighting us. We work a deal. They stay off our back for a few months and we leave. They give us protection through their controlled areas and we head north or west or wherever. I don't know where, we would have to set it up so that we have some insurance when we left our positions that they wouldn't double cross us. I haven't figured that one out yet, but we should be able to work that out."

Anders and Sarah were silent for a moment and then Anders spoke up. "I think you're right. I've had the same thoughts. I suggest we send Carlos back with a message, in writing, from you or me speaking on behalf of the Bayside interests or better yet, on behalf of the Alliance. Our offer to work with the Cubans can be left purposely vague pending further negotiations. What do you say, Sarah?"

Sarah had been silent, but now nodded in agreement. "I don't think we have much of a choice. I say send Carlos back and the sooner the better so that they have time to give us an indication of what they are going to do before it is too late."

Stuart drafted up the dispatch to Paco Morales offering to enter into discussions that would be mutually beneficial to both their causes.

Stuart implied, without stating so specifically, that a well fortified base of operations could be made available to the Morales Group provided satisfactory arrangements could be made to provide for the safe departure of those in the Alliance Group.

Carlos was then brought in to Stuart's office and provided the sealed letter with instructions that it was to be given only to Paco Morales personally. Stuart then, by prearrangement with Ross Perry, had a tour set up so that Carlos could view well trained combat troops, comprised solely of Bayside personnel, in tactics training. All of the troops carrying the latest model weapons, with support vehicles standing by, maneuvering in and around well fortified bunkers. Carlos was visibly impressed and the efforts made to give the appearance of a well prepared, well equipped, disciplined military force standing ready to defend their homeland, appeared to be successful.

Stuart instructed Carlos that he was expecting a reply to his communication and suggested that Carlos return with a representative of the Morales Group who was authorized to speak on behalf of Paco Morales and to enter into an agreement with the Alliance Staff. Carlos was shown the well fortified marina, which was to be used as a meeting point, and provided with maps of the entry from the ocean, into the Indian River and up to the Marina. The channel to the ocean was narrow and Carlos was warned that only three vessels, with light armament would be permitted access from the ocean. Radio frequencies were likewise arranged so that they could announce their presence outside the channel entrance prior to entry.

Carlos was noncommittal throughout the briefing by Stuart, but when Stuart had concluded his instructions, Carlos told him that he believed Morales would respond to his letter. Carlos was then escorted to the Melbourne side of the Indian River by Moss' troops and was kept under observation, to ensure his safe passage on land, until he again contacted the remainder of his company. All Stuart could do now was to wait for a response from Morales. In the meantime, he would continue to fortify the beach areas in the event his attempt at negotiation failed.

At the group staff meeting, Stuart explained the problems that had come up in the course of training the recruits, especially from adjoining complexes and the policies that had been adopted in order to resolve the disciplinary problems. A number of the Representatives objected strenuously to some of the more punitive measures. Stuart, at this point, could have cared less. He had concluded before the meeting that about one third to one half of the Alliance member groups were not worth the trouble of having around. They were along strictly for the ride and had thus far contributed little or nothing to the Alliance concept and he, as well as Anders, was for putting them to the test.

Stuart listened to the complaints and arguments of the objectors for a few minutes and then stated that it was the decided policy of the staff that the level of discipline described was necessary and anyone that did not agree with the staff decision should separate from the Alliance immediately and take their personnel with them because the policy was in effect at midnight on that very day. Anyone remaining in the training facilities at that time was presumed to be under the new rules. Following the meeting, the resignations began to come in. All in all, seven complexes departed the Alliance and, without exception, they were non-contributing, non-cooperating, complainers that Stuart was happy to see leave the group.

As a result of the recent departures from the Alliance, Stuart, Perry, Moss and Barnes had to again redraw the zone of defense that they had previously drawn up. The southern border of the zone was moved north approximately one mile. The area that was removed from the zone was the site of four of the complexes that had left the Alliance.

In the following week Stuart and his staff continued to consolidate the Alliance organization, strengthen the defenses and increase the readiness level of the military force. With the withdrawals of the complexes following the publication of the new disciplinary rules, the total available troop strength of the Alliance had declined to roughly fifteen hundred men and women, of whom approximately six hundred were considered fully combat ready. Sarah estimated that they had at the most, four weeks of available training time remaining before they would possibly be challenged by the Cuban groups. Stuart was advised by Perry and Moss that the conscripts would be at acceptable combat skill levels by that time provided they had the necessary weapons. If they were not, they would be receiving on the job training.

Barnes took the opportunity to mention Robert Thomas' suggestion regarding uniforms for the military personnel to Stuart. Stuart had a number of serious problems to contend with involving much different matters and Barnes did not expect a favorable response from Stuart but the longer Stuart took to reply, he began to think that there was some interest there.

Finally Stuart spoke. "Not a bad idea. Have someone come up with a military appearing, simple, uniform with some military patches and, yes, a beret, dark blue with a green or yellow unit designation." Stuart laughed. "Have Robert Thomas work on the design. Crazy, but it just might work wonders. If he can get the material, we have lost nothing."

Now Barnes laughed. "I thought you might hit me if I mentioned that as I know you are busier than hell right now. But there is no doubt we need some good ideas in the area of military operations. I will talk to Thomas today."

The various complexes that remained in the Alliance had, after a few weeks of working with the Bayside administration team, realized the benefits to be obtained from combining their resources and working together. Their confidence level in Anders, as well as Stuart and other visible staff personnel, such as Sarah, had increased many fold. An additional benefit was that a number of highly skilled, experienced people with technical and professional training stepped forward to offer their services.

Jack Nix had served for years with the Army Special Forces and had been working with a select group of men from the Meadowbrook complex at the time the Alliance was formed. They were all seasoned military veterans with Ranger or Special Forces experience with all around skills in munitions, communications, evasive tactics, survival training, basic medicine, and other talents that resulted in their being a very valuable special assignment unit, should the need for such arise in the future. Stuart assigned them special billeting and training facilities and advised Nix that the unit would likely be called upon to serve as a long range reconnaissance unit within the next two or three months. In the meantime, they should train for the expected assignment and to see Barnes for any special equipment that they might need. In their new role, they should be prepared to survive in an unfriendly environment for long periods of time without resupply or other assistance from the Alliance. Nix assured Stuart that they would be ready when called upon.

Following the inventories conducted among the various new complexes of the Alliance, the Staff concluded that they had weapons and ammunition available for little over half of the personnel assigned to the Alliance Defense Team. In the meantime, training would have to be conducted using wooden guns and all firing would be simulated. In the meantime, steps would have to be taken immediately to find additional weapons or come up with other solutions.

Following the regular Staff Meeting where Alliance organizational efforts had again been reported and discussed, Anders waved to Stuart and Sarah to follow him to his office. When they entered, Anders closed the door and motioned for them to have a chair. When they were seated, Anders went on; "we are getting things pretty well squared away with our new friends. Now, let's discuss just where in hell we go from here. Sarah, have you made any progress on the where and how' questions that we laid on you some time ago?"

Without any hesitation, Sarah replied, "We have obtained a considerable amount of information by way of radio communications with other organizations around the country and from interviews with people familiar with the locations that are of interest to us at this point. I would suggest that we prepare a briefing just for a very select group so that we provide the information in as organized a fashion as we can. Before we do that, we should first discuss and decide how many people we are talking about that may be resettling and what is the timetable for departing. These two questions will impact where we can go and how we will get there." Sarah directed the questions at Stuart as well as Anders.

Anders responded first. "That is difficult to answer, and I can only speculate at this time. The population of our present Alliance residents is approximately five thousand of which approximately twenty five hundred to three thousand maximum would even discuss such a journey and resettlement. Of that group, I would estimate only a maximum of one or more thousand would really go. A more likely figure might be five hundred. That is a complete wag on my part and I don't think we would know until we actually left as to just how many would go. As to when, I would say in the early spring we would depart so that we could travel in good weather and hopefully have time to prepare for winter wherever it is that we are going to be. Those are my thoughts."

Sarah directed her attention at Stuart and he paused, nodded, and said, "I would agree with Anders' thoughts on that. I would think the very maximum number might be between five hundred and a thousand that would actually leave this area and go and that would be assuming that we had a place to go that appeared to be worth the risks inherent in such a journey. I would just add that I would think there are advantages in having a large group, but there are also advantages in having a small group which can be moved more quickly and with less supply problems. I think that when the time comes, we should lay out our plan with all of the warts and sores showing so that we don't end up selling something that we cannot provide. I don't want to listen to a bunch of 'bellyachers' crying about not having enough to eat or whatever. I've had it with those people. Time wise, I agree with Anders. Leave at the end of our winter so that we can be in place during the summer."

Sarah agreed with the estimates and opinions of both men and suggested that for the time being and present planning that they assume their departing group would total approximately one thousand people max. For her briefing, she would assume that number and an estimated departure date of March the first that gave them four months to prepare for the trip. She had already organized her intelligence group into specialized units with specific tasks including a unit of four people working solely on travel methods, supply needs, and routes. Routes had been limited to objectives in the northwestern part of the country as that was where the safe havens appeared to be from the information gathered thus far. Another unit was gathering information on risk assessment in the route areas, focusing on threats posed by organized or semi organized political groups or gangs. The assumption would have to be made that the Association would be the target of threat activity from individuals and small groups all along the route but that it should be able to defend itself against whatever risks that involved. The other, larger threats would have to be avoided or, in some manner, neutralized.

It was also decided that John Barnes should be brought into the picture to begin storing up the immense quantity of materials that would be needed for the trip. That also required the participation of Perry to begin considering the defense force that would accompany the group. From the time when talk began about the possibility of leaving the area, it had always been assumed that the original Bayside Defense Team would be with the travelers. That was clearly no longer the case with the Defense Team now merged with members from other complexes. There would obviously be no shortage of security forces for the trip and in fact, the opposite could well be the case. Perry would have to handle that problem.

When Sarah, Anders and Stuart concluded their meeting, it was decided that a very confidential gathering of Anders, Stuart, Sarah, Perry, Thomas, Nix and Barnes would be scheduled later that week to lay out the specifics of the departure. Sarah would start the meeting with an in depth briefing of routes, threats, en route resources, methods of travel available and other intelligence data that her people had been compiling. Stuart would provide a report on the anticipated available defense resources from which the Defense Team would be selected and Anders would provide the departure dates and general plan for the trip. The three swore to maintain strict secrecy on the plan and concluded the meeting.

Since the conversation that Stuart and Beth Sloan had discussing the need for establishing formal schooling for the children of the Association, Beth Sloan had been heavily involved in organizing a teaching staff, locating materials and finding class rooms. She took up Stuart's offer and set up an office in the administration building, near the day care center, and it soon became a beehive of activity as teachers were selected from among numerous volunteers who had come to Beth offering their services. As she soon found out, there were a number of highly qualified, educated men and women in the complex who were eager to help out either on a full or part time basis. Beth set up a staff to assist her in administering the school and among those that were ever present at the meetings of volunteers was Irene Covington. It soon became clear to Beth that Irene's primary interest in the education of the Associations children was not to teach, rather it was to determine what was to be taught and by whom. Irene had also expanded her staff in the administration building and their activities were not limited to the matter of protecting the rights of prisoners as was her original assignment.

Irene's other problem for Beth was her somewhat abrasive manner and her irritating habit of being present whenever a major decision regarding the children's schooling was made. Irene would give her two cents worth just prior to decision time. After this happened on a few occasions, Beth suggested that Irene be made part of the process as she was apparently not going to go away and her ideas were, in general, well thought out. A number had, in fact, been accepted by the group. After that, Irene tempered her manner somewhat and Beth found herself admiring her for her talents rather than disliking her for her personal traits. Irene, likewise, found Beth to be an able administrator, and the two developed a very compatible working relationship.

# Chapter Thirteen

After the initial organizational matters were taken care of and the teaching staff lined up, the matter of what would be taught became the next hurdle to overcome. Beth had no idea when she started that the curriculum would become the hot topic that it did among the parents as well as the school staff. There had been little if any serious disagreement among the staff members up to that point. As she soon found out, there were as many totally separate, strongly held, opinions regarding course materials as there were members on the staff. It was clear that most, if not all, of the staff members had participated solely for the purpose of ensuring that their concept regarding what was to be taught to the children would, in the end, be adopted.

After the third day of continuous wrangling, she cornered Stuart in his office to get his input on how to handle the problem. She knew he had problems of his own that he had to worry about; nevertheless, she was at her wits end trying to figure out how to resolve the deadlock among the teachers over the curriculum.

Beth explained her problem to him in its entirety and finished with a plea, "Just what in the hell do I do now?"

Stuart paused and then replied, "Beth, you know more about the teaching business than I do. I think you first have to ask yourself what you want to have when you are done teaching them. For openers, all, or most all parents want their children to learn discipline. I am not talking about whipping kids; I am talking about teaching kids to learn to work for results. Personally, I would stick with the basic subjects. No controversy involved in reading, writing and mathematics. I agree with you that history must be a part of the basic curriculum but I would limit that for the time being to American History. Now, what I would do right off the bat is, I would let them all know that you run the show and this is the program. You have to let them know that right away or you are going to have nothing but trouble. Talking time is over. What are they going to do about it? Nothing. Anders will back you up, believe me. I will guarantee that."

Beth listened without comment. Finally she said, "You're right" and that was the end of the discussion.

Stuart's office was close to the lounge that Anders had appropriated for his own purposes and both of the men found that they increasingly spent more of their waking hours in their offices passing out orders to the various staff people that worked for them. Many a night, one or both of the men spent the night on the couch in their offices rather than take the time making their way back to their own quarters. After a few weeks of following this schedule, the two found themselves one night as the only occupants of the administration building other than the late guard shift that patrolled all of the complex buildings.

Stuart was about to leave for his apartment when Anders called him into his office. "Join me for a drink before you leave, Stuart. You deserve a break." Stuart was not aware that Anders or anyone still had any hard liquor around as it had become a scarce commodity well before Stuart had become involved with the Association. Apparently Anders had kept a private stock as many of the residents had. It had just become such an invitation for thieves that those who did have a supply of liquor on hand soon found it advisable to get rid of it as word sooner or later got out as to their private stock and they would lose not only their liquor but whatever else they had that was worth taking.

Whatever the explanation, Stuart was not about to inquire and was ready for a good drink if one was to be made available. Stuart went into Anders office and made himself comfortable on Anders couch as Anders poured the two of them a drink from the quart bottle of Bacardi Rum that Stuart noticed was still almost full. There was no ice to cool the drink, but Stuart could have cared less. He held the glass up to his mouth, but before tasting, he let the aroma of the rum come to him and remind him of times long gone. He had always enjoyed a drink of fine rum, particularly when he was on the ocean, in his boat or at a waterfront restaurant. There was something about rum that he associated with the ocean, ocean breezes and moon lit nights. It wasn't a matter of romance, it was a matter of beauty and rum went with the beauty, majesty and power of the ocean. He had taken a sip of the rum and could almost hear the sound of the waves when his thoughts were interrupted by Anders voice. He wasn't sure what Anders had said and apologized for not being attentive.

Anders laughed; he knew what the problem was. They were both virtually exhausted from burning the candle at both ends. "No problem, Stuart. I'm wiped out myself and can't remember what I did this morning. We have to take care of ourselves though because I don't think there is anyone else in the Association that would fill your shoes or mine. In the future, make sure you kick back and get your rest. We need you for what has to be done."

Anders had somewhat slurred the last few words and Stuart figured that this was not Anders first drink of the evening. That did not concern Stuart as Anders was not the drinking type and this was a much needed break for both of them. Stuart thought about what he had said and commented. "Anders, we need both of us. You know, this is the first job I have ever had that I must say, I really enjoy. I must be nuts. I've been thinking about what put us in this situation. It wasn't only Turner or prior administrations, it was everyone's fault. We just did not meet the challenge of our own system of government. Our democratic system succeeds only if basic assumptions are satisfied. It presumes an educated, involved, knowledgeable electorate. We have failed every one of those premises. Our educational system did not educate. It was more of a day care center than a school system. Our people did not participate in the process. They knew little if anything about government, economics, the judiciary, or social policy. That was also the fault of our educational system and our so called Free Press. The media since the middle of the last century has absolutely sucked. 'Worthless'.

They were a tool of the government and were in the end virtually taken over by the government and became their spokesman. What really pissed me off about the media was their elitist, damned attitude. It got to the point that I couldn't stand to listen to them bla bla on their TV shows. What jackasses. Our justice system collapsed long before the government went under. When I realized what our judicial system was supposed to do compared to what it was doing, I was ashamed to be a lawyer. You notice, I don't tell people I was a lawyer. I don't know for sure what system would be best for whatever organization we end up establishing or joining. I am and always have been a constitutionalist but with some modifications to deal with present day problems. For now, in the situation that we are in, I am of the opinion that we should maintain tight control of the Association and the Alliance. When we have ourselves set up safely somewhere else and we can look at rebuilding our lives somewhat securely without an immediate threat from someone or something, then I would be for turning over control of the Association to a representative group under a system similar to what we had in the early years of our nation but with better controls. But, before we do that, I think we should give considerable thought to the structure of that group and learn from the past. From my limited understanding of history, our former American system was very successful until the bureaucracy went completely out of control. I would suggest that we set up a study group comprised of a very select number of trained professionals and academics to come up with proposals for the future government of our Association with the thought in mind that we could well become a much larger organization than we are today. In the process, we have to ensure that the tendency of government of any kind to grow is curtailed. If any deficiencies were present in the former system, the one that was most destructive and the part that grew the fastest and was least responsive to the will of the electorate were the administrative agencies. We must never again fall into that trap. Anders, are you aware that if you were alleged to have violated a regulation of one of the alphabet soup bureaucracies, your hearing was before an employee of that agency and the prosecutor was an employee of that agency as well? When you lost, which you would, your appeal had to go to the Court of Appeals. How many people could afford to do that? Ridiculous asinine theft of our rights by the bureaucracy."

Stuart then laughed. "My God, that rum does get me going. Yes, I am pissed at what has happened to this great country. Feels good to get it off my chest."

Anders poured another glass of rum for the two of them and only commented, "I know. I'm in the same place, Stuart."

Stuart observed that the bottle was now half empty. Anders eyes were reddened and half closed. He looked haggard and exhausted but he was still interested in the conversation and wanted to go on. "Yes, I agree. But we have to be careful that we don't work our ass off and bring all of these people to the Promised Land just to turn over the Association to another group of ambitious bureaucratic types who will just destroy everything we have worked for. We can't let that happen. We have to see this thing through or the hell with it."

"I agree, Anders, we can have a study group, but we keep tabs on what they do and control just how important they become. They only report to you and me and we divide the areas of study among them so that none of them see the entire picture until we want them to see it. That way we are totally in charge until we are ready to give up the reins. Sometimes it takes a dictator to create an acceptable form of democracy. These are the times."

Anders eyes were almost closed but he was able to direct them at Stuart as he issued his final statement on the subject, "Set it up. Find the people. We'll talk about it tomorrow. As he finished the last sentence, Stuart could see that he was sound asleep. Stuart made him comfortable on the couch, laid a blanket over him, turned out the light and began to close the door when he remembered the rum bottle sitting on Anders desk. He returned to the desk and was placing the bottle in the lower cabinet drawer when he noticed a stamped shipping date that was just barely two years old. On closer examination, he saw that the rum was bottled in Mexico and, from his own experience he knew that this particular Bacardi Rum, Añejo, was not sold in this country. Obviously Robert Thomas had managed to find the rum somewhere. He placed the bottle in the desk cabinet, closed the door and left the office.

# Chapter Fourteen

Even though anarchy reigned in the country, you could still find almost anything if you worked at it. That reminded Stuart of the task at hand and the weapons shortage problem that they had to solve soon in order to equip the new members of the Alliance Defense Team. His thoughts were focused on where to find the equipment as he made his way back to his apartment. As he drifted off to sleep, he thought about the study group and what he would do in the morning to get that up and operating. There were a number of what he considered 'intellectuals' in the Association and they would find that task right up their alley.

He had two or three individuals in mind, and one in particular, that would be perfect for the job. He would have Irene Covington spread so thin, she wouldn't have time to sleep anymore. That was not his primary purpose in picking her for the task, but it was one consideration. She was also ably qualified to serve on the study group and certainly her interests lay in that area.

While Stuart thought of Irene as a gadfly and somewhat of a nuisance in the operation of the Association, he also was beginning to develop a certain amount of respect for her. This may also have been the result of Beth Sloan's lobbying on Irene's behalf.

The following morning, as Stuart entered his office, he found Barnes and Perry waiting to meet with him. Stuart closed the door to his office as he entered as it was obvious to him that the two had something of importance to discuss and that called for privacy. Perry waited for Stuart to sit down and then proceeded. "Stuart, we have less than half of our Alliance Defense Team equipped with suitable weapons. We have around one third of the force that has no weapons at all and another significant number that are marginally equipped at best. We have to do something soon and Barnes here may have a viable solution. Go ahead, Barnes."

Barnes cleared his throat and began. "When I was on the force," referring to the Melbourne Police Department, "just as the department and the rest of city government was in the process of disintegrating and the military base here on the beach was evacuating, I was told that a large store of weapons which had been on the base was being moved to a secret location. The weapons belonged to the Federal Security guys. That was at the time when everyone knew everything was going down the shitter and apparently a few of the more responsible types in the Security Force wanted to make sure that the weapon and ammo stores didn't get into the wrong hands. I don't know where they were moved to, or if in fact they were moved and stored. I did have a friend who seemed to be aware of what was going on then and I think we could locate the guy if he's still alive. It might be worth a shot."

Stuart was very interested in what Barnes had to say and told him to continue with everything he knew about the matter. Barnes went on and explained that his source for the story was another detective on the force whom Barnes knew that now lived in a secluded area well north of Melbourne. The detective worked with the Federal Security Police and had some involvement with the security of the weapons on the base. The Federal Police were always concerned, according to Barnes that the military would glom onto the weapons because they were state of the art and the military personnel were still operating with the older AR15 models.

Barnes had been to the detective's home on one or two occasions and was sure that he could find it if he had to. It was entirely possible that he was still up there and, as Barnes understood the story, the detective was involved in the transfer and secreting of the weapons, so he should be able to direct them to the cache if it was still there and if he was willing to do so. Again, Barnes cautioned that his information was limited and it might be worthwhile to follow up on or, on the other hand, maybe the stockpile had already been found by someone else. Stuart questioned him regarding the stockpile of weapons, how large a cache, what type of weapons and so on. Barnes had no specific information, but understood that it consisted mostly of AR20 rifles, presumably hundreds or thousands of those as the cache was the regional storage area for the Federal Security Police and they had to number over a hundred thousand for the Southeast Region.

In the years just prior to the collapse, it seemed like everyone was a Federal Agent. Any weapons stored by the Federal Security Police would be kept at a military base because that was probably the safest place around. State and local police stations were being overrun with increasing frequency at that time so they were out of the question as a storage area. Most likely the weapons were no longer on the base as looters had cleaned everything out as soon as base security fell apart. But if they were buried and secreted somewhere on the base, they could still be there. The detective, who Barnes was friendly with, resided in an area that was approximately a hundred miles north and west of their Control Zone. Stuart sent a message for Nix to report to his office and also had Sarah come in to see if she could provide assistance. Sarah did have a Ham radio contact in the area and she told Stuart that she would attempt to make contact with him as soon as she got back to her office. Stuart also had her get information together on what was known regarding the threat areas between their control zone and the objective, one hundred miles to the north and in from the coast approximately ten miles. She left his office with the promise that she would have the requested information within the hour. In the meantime, Nix came in and Stuart brought him up to date on what they might need. Nix assured him that a small squad of his men would be able to get through but it might be less risky if they went north by water and then inland at a lightly inhabited spot. That made good sense to Stuart and Robert Thomas' cigarette boats could be put to good use transporting the men up the coast. It sounded considerably less risky than trying to go overland.

Stuart had his office contact Thomas, Perry and Barnes and had them come in while Nix was still there. The three came right over and when they had been briefed on what was involved, Robert Thomas assured everyone that he could get the required team up there and back safely. What happened while they were ashore would have to be Nix's job.

At about that time, Sarah returned to Stuart's office with information on travel to the objective as well as a considerable amount of information on the objective area itself, including maps and some aerial photographs from government land surveys. She had not been able to make contact with the radio operator in the immediate area but expected to do so before the end of the day. That particular operator was usually on frequency in the evenings and she expected they would be able to communicate with him then.

Sarah mentioned that there was some boat traffic in the area believed to be involved with the drug trade. Thomas was confident that these could be eluded as he had two boats that had been heavily modified with powerful turbocharged twin diesel engines and were equipped with radar for night and weather travel. They were perfect for this assignment. He also had GPS available that he could install in the boats for pin-point navigation. Thomas assured Stuart that he would be ready for the mission just as soon as they wanted to go.

A final preplanning meeting was held and it was decided that two boats would make the trip, one as a backup in case of a mechanical or other problem. Nix would be in charge of the shore party and Thomas would be in charge of the mission while it was operating on the ocean. Barnes would accompany the group as he was somewhat familiar with the land layout around the farm where the detective was living before the collapse and personally knew the party they were interested in. Travel up the coast would be conducted under cover of darkness. The party consisting of ten men would be landed shortly after midnight and they should be in the vicinity of their objective by first light. Hopefully, they would return with their man or with information by the following morning. The assumption being that they would not be able to leave their objective until that following evening with a return to the Control Zone sometime in the early morning hours.

The land team would also be equipped with GPS equipment for use in navigating to their objective and for finding the boat on their return to the coast. They would also carry ample stores of weapons, ammunition, grenades, flares, maps and survival gear. All of Nix's men were experienced Special Forces or Ranger personnel. With the method of travel selected and the experience of the men on the mission, Stuart was more concerned about finding the person they were seeking than the threats they might encounter. Sarah did make contact with the Ham radio operator in the target vicinity and according to that source, the target individual was believed to still be in the area, but that roving bands of lightly armed thugs were a constant threat and travel through the area was considered by the locals to be dangerous. There was also the ever present risk of being fired on by law abiding, but nervous, residents. The distance to be covered from the drop off point to the objective was less than ten miles.

Stuart gave the final go ahead for the operation for departure when weather conditions permitted. He left that decision up to Robert Thomas and Jack Nix with the instruction that he be kept advised as to the planned departure.

Among her other activities, Sarah had set up a weather office which took reports from radio stations on the Ham net and with her assigned meteorologists, forecast weather maps were prepared which proved to be reasonably accurate. Based on that data and the moon phase, the mission was expected to be launched within the next two or three days. In view of the fact that this was the first military action taken outside of the control zone, Stuart considered it a matter that should be briefed to Anders. Consequently, he had Sarah prepare briefing slides depicting the mission, possible threats, personnel, armament, water craft and other details to bring Anders and those involved in the operation up to date on what was taking place. Anders attended the briefing and afterwards was asked for comments. He had nothing other to say than they appeared to have staffed the matter quite well and that he did appreciate being informed of major actions before they had taken place, if at all possible. Stuart assured him that would be his policy. Along that line, Stuart also advised Anders that the Alliance forces would begin sending patrols out to the mainland within the next few days or weeks to determine conditions and to detect any sign of impending attacks by the Cubans or others on their position. These would be frequent and at any given time, there would be one or more of such patrols operating somewhere on the mainland.

# Chapter Fifteen

Irene Covington had raised an issue regarding "Alliance Courts...and just who the hell set those up?" This question was directed at Stuart as he walked into the admin building. Stuart was not aware that any such courts had been set up but assumed Anders must have set them up in accordance with one of their many conversations and he thought he had better get more information on this before others asked him as well. When Stuart inquired of Anders' secretary concerning the matter of the Alliance Courts, Mary McClarty gave him a copy of the directive announcing their existence. The announcement generally restated what his assumption had been concerning the need for and purpose of the Court. There were to be a number of Courts impaneled, depending upon the extent of the need and each Court would be staffed by five people, preferably with legal experience. The panels would be selected by the Administration and would serve at the pleasure of the Administration, meaning individual members thereof could be replaced whenever Anders felt like it. Punishment meted out by the courts could range from verbal sanctions to incarceration or even banishment from the Association and from the Control Zone.

Corporal punishment was authorized for severe cases as was hard labor for those sent to the disciplinary yard. There was no mention of any appellate procedures or avenues for those found guilty to pursue with the clear implication that, once found guilty they would endure their punishment unless the Court or the Administration changed its mind. The members of the first Court were given and Stuart recognized their names as tough minded, very conservative men.

This would undoubtedly offend a number of the women of the Association, that no women were on the Court, and that would confirm, somewhat, the view of many women that Anders was of the opinion that they belonged at home taking care of children. After Stuart finished reading over the directive, Anders was watching him.

"Well, what do you think?"

"Interesting. I've already had one complaint from guess who and I'm sure we will have many more. Pretty tough bunch of judges but maybe that's what we need right now. Also, what do you have in mind for corporal punishment. I see it is not defined."

"My answer to that would be anything needed to do the job up to and including a good whipping. I would think that would be limited to the more severe cases and not to be applied for minor offenses. Other than that, maybe leaving it blank is more effective than defining it."

"You may have a point there."

Anders went on, "I agreed with your comments the other night that we should put these people to the test now and get rid of the crybabies as you called them. I want to pull everyone out of the woodwork that is going to be a thorn in our side. Wait until we lay the whip on somebody's brat's rear end. That will really bring them out. In the meantime, we have a little over three months to get our act together or we are going to have to wait another year to bail out of here. I don't think we have another year so that gives us the three months. I expect a reaction to this directive and I will provide a brief explanation of the need for this in a follow-on policy statement. After that, we assume that everyone that continues to complain and bitch is asking to be left behind and we plan accordingly. We've got too many people to take care of anyway and this is a good way to get rid of some that we don't need."

Stuart pondered Anders' remarks for a moment, nodded and said, "Totally agree, Anders. Get rid of the dead weight." As he walked back to his office, he thought about the courts and figured that there would be many people bitching over the selection of conservative judges. So be it. Anders was right, better to hit them hard now than to have to deal with them on the journey out of here.

Stuart was in a deep sleep and was dreaming that someone was pounding on his apartment door when he realized that the noise was not a dream. Someone was pounding on his door. He roused himself and made his way through the apartment in the dark trying his best to maintain his balance and not trip over anything. The duty officer apologized for waking him, but advised him that the radar had picked up two targets approaching the shoreline, and Perry had instructed the D.O. to alert Stuart. In his semi-awake state, Stuart did not immediately take in the import of the report, but then began to realize that the targets were most likely Thomas' two cigarette boats returning with Nix, Barnes and their support team. He hurriedly dressed and ran over to the administration building where Perry and a number of the Defense Team staff were huddled around the radar repeater watching the progress of the vessels.

"How far out are they?" Stuart directed his question at Ross Perry who responded that they should be coming up the river and into the dock in just a few minutes. He also advised Stuart that they had not had any radio contact with the boats, so there was no word on the success of the mission or the possibility of casualties. Stuart instructed the duty officer to have medical personnel ready for any emergency treatment that might be necessary but Perry had already taken care of this. The medical team had been alerted and were awaiting the arrival of the boats. Stuart left the office and ran down to the Marina where he found Andy Moss and his staff busy preparing for the arrival of the men. As Stuart peered into the darkness towards the entry to the river from the ocean, he could faintly make out what appeared to be the wake of a boat off in the distance. They all waited anxiously as the boats themselves finally came into view and they could identify some of the figures that were standing about the cabin. Stuart saw Nix and Barnes and both men appeared to have suffered no harm on the mission. Everyone on the dock was counting the men on the boats and, as they neared the dock, it appeared that most, if not all men on the mission had been accounted for. The families of some of the men began gathering, having been notified that the boats were returning. As they recognized their husband, brother, or son they shouted their name and waved to the approaching boats. The cigarette boats each roared into their separate slips. Expertly handled by their pilots and with a burst of reverse thrust, came to a stop next to the mooring posts attended by marina personnel. The boats were quickly secured and after the engines were shut down, the crew disembarked. On Stuart's orders, they were immediately hustled off to the debriefing room in the administration building. Sarah Taves' intelligence people had first access to the security team that accompanied Nix and Barnes. The latter two, with Robert Thomas, were hustled directly into Stuart's office to be debriefed by Stuart, Perry and Sarah. Barnes was the senior officer on the mission and he spoke for those on the mission except for matters within the special knowledge of Nix and Thomas. He deferred to Robert Thomas to cover the trip north which was described as generally unremarkable with no particular problems. They had seen some other boats on the trip north, but they were all in the distance and Thomas questioned that their smaller cigarette boats were ever observed.

There was some difficulty in locating a landing site on the shoreline free of obstructions. After running up and down the coastline and using the night vision goggles, they finally located a suitable spot. After some delay, rubber rafts were deployed and the ground party was sent to the beach in the rafts. Thomas and his crews stayed with their boats and took them up the coast to an uninhabited portion of the beach where they anchored at a safe distance out from the shore until the pickup time. At no time did they observe anyone along the shore where they were anchored. Even though there appeared to be a beach road running along the shoreline, no one passed down the road from either direction. It was totally quiet. Other than the waves striking the shoreline, they heard nothing.

Nix took over the narrative of their trip at that point. They arrived on the shore without mishap and secreted their rafts in the bushes after ensuring that their arrival had gone unobserved. They crossed over the road that Thomas had described which ran north and south along the beach. There were, what appeared to be, abandoned homes or huts along the road, but there was no sign that any of them were inhabited. As they later found out, some of them were. They located the road that they were to follow to the west which was almost directly at the point where they had been disembarked by Thomas. They noted their GPS coordinates so that they would be able to find their way back and then proceeded to the west along the roadway. The information that Sarah had provided proved relatively accurate with respect to the buildings located where indicated on the route maps and also her briefing to the effect that few people lived along the road they were traveling to the west. Sarah's information was based on pre-collapse data but from what Nix observed, it was still valid. They had departed the beach area at around midnight and reached their objective by half past two in the morning. They had taken their time because they did not want to stumble into anyone and furthermore, they had to neutralize a number of dogs that were in the area. They did this by firing a sedative with a co2 gun that put them out for a short period of time, but not so long that their owners would be aware that something was amiss. They saw no one traveling along the roadway nor did they see any sign of life in any of the homes or huts that they passed by. Relatively few of the homes and buildings appeared to have been burned or damaged and they saw no sign of dead bodies lying around such as the patrols reported seeing with great frequency in the Melbourne area. As they proceeded westward along the road, in the dark with only the starlight guiding their way, they began to relax having followed one another at safe intervals without encountering any problems. As the lead man rounded a corner and came upon a road intersection, he cautioned those behind to slow down and disperse while he reconnoitered the area. He returned a short time later and reported that the store buildings appeared to have been burned out and that, "There's a damned corpse hanging from the lamp post at the intersection. Scared the shit out of me. I didn't see it until I about walked right into it." He figured that it had been there for some time as there was little flesh remaining on the body. The men then split into two groups, one on each side of the roadway, each man spread at least twenty feet behind the one in front, and they made their way through the crossroad. That was the only time on the trip that there was some concern that they could be in danger.

The detective, Mark Campbell, lived in a secluded area, on a county dirt road that was off the road that they had been following. It had been some time since Barnes had been to the place and at first he was a bit confused as to where to turn off the road that they were on. Fortunately he finally recognized the remains of a gasoline station that he had once utilized and then got his bearings back. They traveled down the county road for a mile or two and then took a seldom used dirt road through a heavily wooded area until they could make out the dim outlines of structures. They appeared to have found their target.

# Chapter Sixteen

It was a few minutes after three in the morning when they found their target. They considered it wise at that point to await the light of day and see who or what if anything was in the buildings. Again, they didn't want to barge into something until they were reasonably sure as to what they were getting into.

Nix assigned team personnel to stand watch with instructions to keep a close watch with the night vision goggles. He was to be awakened if there was a sign of any activity. The men tried to make themselves as comfortable as possible and soon they were fast asleep. Nix was awakened by the man on watch at around six in the morning who was motioning for him to take a look in the direction he was pointing. It was still quite dark out, but Nix could barely make out two men heading towards an outbuilding from what appeared to be the residence on the property. There was a dog following the men which was of some concern to Nix, but the animal did not appear to be picking up any of their scent. Nix told the trooper to get the sedative gun ready in case he did. The two men and the dog went into the barn and Nix took the opportunity to waken Barnes so that he could see if he recognized either of the men as Campbell. The three waited for someone to come out of the barn and also kept a sharp lookout to see if others were present in the house. No lights were on in the house and occasionally a light could be seen reflecting on the windows in the barn. Nix assumed it was from a lantern rather than from an electric light. Most likely, they had no electricity on the property unless they ran a generator and Nix did not hear one running. After a while the three came out of the barn and as the light was now much better than when they went in, their features were more discernible.

Barnes tapped Nix on the arm and whispered that Campbell was the taller of the two men. He did not know who the other man was. Again, not knowing what the situation was, Barnes did not want to disclose their presence until they had more information. They discussed the matter and decided that they would continue observing the house and the surrounding area until later in the morning and if it looked safe, they would make contact at that time. In the meantime, Nix dispatched two patrols of two men each to reconnoiter the area and report back in one hour. In the meantime, they continued to watch the house.

The only occupants of the house appeared to be the two men that they had initially observed and they had a number of further opportunities to observe them as they passed from the house back and forth to the barn. The patrols returned and reported that they saw nothing out of the ordinary and from all appearances, the two men were busy with what appeared to be a small farm. They had to put the dog down temporarily as he appeared to be following their scent at one point. There were some animals penned up behind the barn, including a couple of cows and goats and they had about a hundred acres of vegetable crop land that appeared to be under tillage.

It was decided that Barnes would approach the farm from the access road and would call out to Campbell as he came up the road to the residence. The other men would remain hidden in the brush and would be prepared to render assistance to Barnes should he need it. At the appointed time, Barnes backtracked to the entry road and the others took up positions. The occupants of the house were last seen entering the barn and were presumed to still be there. Nix had positioned men on the backside of the farm to report any movements in that area.

As Barnes made his way up the road, he began shouting for Campbell which brought an immediate reaction from the, now awakened, dog who began barking and running down the road to meet Barnes. There was some concern that the dog might present a threat but that was soon dispelled as he came up to Barnes, wagging his tail and trotting alongside Barnes as he made his way up the road.

Hearing the barking of the dog and possibly the shouts of Barnes, the two men came out of the barn and stood looking down the roadway.

In time, the one identified as Campbell, let out a yell, "Well, I'll be a son of a bitch. What the hell are you doing here?"

Barnes approached Campbell and the two men shook hands and slapped each other on the back. Nix could not hear what was being said, but after a brief conversation, Barnes looked in the direction of their position and waved the men on in.

Stuart, Perry, Taves and the others in the room listened intently as Barnes continued to tell them what had transpired on the mission. Campbell was surprised, to say the least, that Barnes had made the trip up to his farm and informed Barnes, Nix and the others, that they were lucky to find him there at that time as he had just arrived a couple of days ago and was departing the following day for the Georgia area. Campbell wondered what had brought the group to his place, and at that time Barnes suggested they find someplace where they could sit and talk so that he could explain everything to Campbell. Nix, Barnes, Campbell and the, as of yet, unidentified man went into the house where they sat down in the living room while Campbell provided them with water and some bread that appeared to be fairly fresh.

Barnes began by stating that it would be best if they each identified themselves so everyone would know who they were talking with. He explained his position, briefly, with the Association and generally what his duties were. Nix did the same. At that point, Campbell said that he and his companion, Roy Yates, were both affiliated with a somewhat similar group operating in Georgia and that he, Campbell, was down at his old farm to see if it was still there. Campbell had turned the place temporarily over to a neighbor who, along with others in the vicinity, was protecting it and in return they could have any crop produced on the place.

That was all the information that Campbell provided and he then directed his attention at Barnes as if to ask and just what are you doing up here. Barnes had the distinct impression that Campbell was holding back on his organization that he referred to, but that could be dealt with later. In the meantime, Barnes went ahead with the purpose of their mission which was to see if Campbell could give them any information on the supposedly secreted arms cache of the Federal Security Police.

When Barnes had finished, he and Nix waited for Campbell to respond and the latter merely looked over at his companion, Yates, and said, "Do you want to handle this or do you want me to handle it?"

Yates, who hadn't said anything up to this point, now took over. "This is a very touchy subject and pardon me if we seem like we are holding back on some matters that might be of interest to you guys. Let me say for openers that Mark and I both continue to work for an organization that has a great interest in those weapons and, in fact, considers itself the rightful owner of them. Yes, the Federal Security Police are still around and we are still associated with their organization. It's just that things have changed a bit. We no longer get paid and we no longer fly around in their fleet of executive aircraft. Seems like they don't have them anymore." Yates chuckled a bit at this and went on. "I will tell you as much as I think I can, as I gather from Mark's reception of you fellows that he considers you to be reliable and responsible and I will proceed on the basis of that assumption."

Yates proceeded to explain that when the government began to fall apart, a number of agencies in the government disintegrated. Not the Federal Security Police. They had contingency plans in effect for just such an eventuality and from everything Yates had seen, the plans were executed flawlessly. The Southeast Region had taken a fallback position in Georgia that was stocked with the support requirements necessary to handle the estimated one hundred thousand personnel that could be expected to arrive. The only slip up in the plan was that no one expected the government to collapse as rapidly as it, in fact, did. Consequently, many of those expected to travel to the Macon, Georgia area were unable to do so at the time they elected to leave their various posts.

"You know how difficult or impossible it is to travel anymore. From here, we can only go up to Georgia in armored vehicles with a security escort or we would never make it. As a consequence, the so called 'gathering of troops' never took place." Yates continued to explain that as a result, the number at the fall back positions was at this time still only a fraction of those expected to arrive. Furthermore, arms caches, such as the one Barnes and Nix were inquiring about, had not been delivered to the Georgia Base before the method of delivery became a problem. The cache was still secreted in the Melbourne area and FSP leadership was trying to figure out how to get it up to Georgia. "That's sort of where we are at the moment and the matter is still being worked on up in Georgia." Yates then paused, shrugged his shoulders and looked to Barnes for comment or questions.

It was clear to Barnes at that point that Campbell, who had said little up to this point, and Yates were not about to tell them where the cache was because their own organization wanted it themselves. After a long pause, while he tried to put his thoughts together, carefully considering his words, Barnes made a suggestion that possibly their mutual problems could be solved if everyone worked together. He then paused and waited for Yates, or Campbell, to take the bait and hopefully make a proposal. Yates then inquired as to what exactly Barnes had in mind. Barnes acknowledged that anything in excess of a thousand AR20 rifles, ammo and accessory items would not be needed. This brought a chuckle from both Campbell and Yates but Barnes could tell he had made his point.

Yates then suggested that possibly a few hundred rifles might be suitable consideration for delivering the weapons up to Savannah. Barnes came back with an offer to do just that for five hundred rifles, ten thousand rounds of ammunition, hand held missile launchers and two hundred missiles, subject to approval of his employers.

Roy Yates thought about that for a moment and responded, "We all have employers. We'll pass that on to ours and see what they have to say about it. That's all we can do. When would you do this if we can work this out?"

Barnes thought about that for a moment and replied, "That depends on a lot of unknowns that we don't have the facts on right now, but, unless there are some big surprises here, we could possibly deliver in thirty days assuming the weapons themselves are reasonably accessible."

Yates smiled at Campbell and told the men to sit tight as he and Campbell left the room and walked over to the barn. After approximately thirty minutes, they came back and told the two that they might have a deal. Yates explained that there were approximately fifty thousand rifles together with tons of ammunition, missile launchers, missiles, flares and other assorted items of military equipment.

Barnes was stunned at the size of the cache and expressed doubt at that point that they would be able to deliver that quantity of weapons up to Savannah and that he would have to confirm on that point before they finalized any agreement.

Campbell then took charge of handling the details of the transaction and prefaced his comments with the statement that both sides of the bargain were going to have to trust each other to some extent. Campbell had known Barnes for many years in law enforcement and stated that he trusted him implicitly and if Barnes said he would do something, Campbell believed him. Barnes replied that he had the same degree of trust in Campbell and would rely on his word if it got down to that. All of the details of the transaction were worked out with the exception of the location of the weapons. That would be taken care of last when all other problems were resolved.

Barnes brought up the matter of communications and how that would be handled. Yates inquired as to what radio equipment they had and if they had qualified radio technicians available. When Barnes assured him they did, Yates waved the matter off and commented, "No problem."

Yates told Barnes to follow him into the barn. There, just inside the entry, was a sophisticated radio package that had apparently been in use for some time at the farm. Yates disconnected a small electronic device that was attached to the transmitting apparatus and handed it to Barnes. "Tell your radio guy to use this scrambler on all incoming and outgoing transmissions from our people. If it is not hooked up and properly in use, you will receive nothing from us and we will receive nothing from you. No one, I repeat no one, can intercept anything that passes through the scrambler." Yates then gave Barnes frequencies to communicate on as well as the times the FSP station was operating.

The four men returned to the house and continued talking well into the afternoon. Yates and Campbell were not very talkative when it came to the specifics of their group until well into the afternoon when they loosened up a bit. There were times when Barnes even questioned the existence of the group or the so called bases, but he could only assume, for the moment, that he was being told the truth. These doubts were brushed aside when Yates came out with a bombshell just as they were preparing to leave for the trip back to the coast. The leader of their group in Georgia was, none other than, the former President of the defunct United States, Frank Turner. Barnes and Nix were stunned at this information as both assumed he and all of his staff had been killed in the bloody riots that shook the capital. Yates chuckled as he explained that he was with Turner in the capital when matters were getting shaky.

They had their contingency plans well laid out with various options available for whatever problem arose. There was, of course, the publicized contingency plan whereby the President, the Cabinet and other Administration heads would go to a secured area where they would continue to operate the government for the good of the people. That plan was flushed in a heartbeat when Turner and his staff realized their good came well ahead of that of the people and, as Yates put it, "They decided to get their butts out of there ASAP." Not many people were aware that Turner was alive and well but he was and he was busy trying to get things moving again. This time though, he was going to get them moving his way without the interference of Congress. That's what Yates and Campbell were involved with and that's what the FSP was doing. "I don't know what he's got in mind but right now, I'm jumping on his train because it looks like the best one around." Yates let out a hearty laugh as he looked at Campbell who appeared to be in full agreement.

Barnes winced as he thought of Turner back in any kind of saddle. He had pandered to every self serving interest in what was left of the economy to feather his own nest and filled every high paying post with his incompetent cronies and family members thereby creating an obedient, ineffective administration that propelled an already failing government in a downward spiral to total collapse. Apparently what he had in mind was to enslave a portion of the country through the use of force rather than through the intimidating fear of bureaucratic administrative investigations by an overreaching government. His style may have been forced to change, but not his purpose.

Barnes assured the two men that they would receive a communication within the next few days and after that, they all relaxed, rested and waited for dark before beginning their trek back to the pickup point. Yates had told them that they would meet little if any difficulty in arriving safely at the beach because this particular area was under FSP watch and was considered off limits by any hoodlums in the vicinity. Some had tried and learned the hard way as their bones still swung in the breeze on the lamp posts. Now faded messages nailed to the posts, signed by the FSP, advised readers not to try removing the bodies or they would join them. A chill went through Barnes as Yates chuckled at this bit of macabre humor.

The trip back to the beach and joining up with Thomas had gone without a hitch and again no one was seen other than the lonely sentinel hanging from the post. Apparently the FSP was highly respected or at least feared in this area. When he had finished his report, Barnes handed the electronic scrambling device to Sarah and also gave her the list of frequencies and times that Yates had provided.

Stuart commented that a number of decisions would have to be made soon regarding the matter of delivery of the weapons to the FSP He didn't have to voice his concern about providing arms to the Federal Security Police who were hated and feared by virtually every rational thinking person before the collapse not to mention after the collapse when, all over the country, the FSP had run roughshod over men, women and children standing in their way as they grabbed anything of value, jewelry, bank funds, gold supplies, food stocks, or whatever, for their own use.

Stuart pondered the matter for a moment or two and then commented "We will have a response by tomorrow. In the meantime, I want you, Perry and Thomas, to let me know if and how you could transport fifty thousand rifles and the other items, as requested, should we decide to agree to deliver them. I will get together with Anders and Sarah and we will have a decision by noon tomorrow on whether or not we will deliver. That may present other problems."

It was clear from the look on the faces of Perry and Thomas that such a delivery would present a challenge in view of the other activities going on in the Association. Nevertheless, both acknowledged the order and said they would have a response in the morning. Stuart then told the men to get some rest as they all had a busy day coming up. As the others left the room, Stuart told Sarah to meet with him at Anders' office first thing in the morning so that they could figure out how to deal with the FSP request. It was already three a.m. in the morning as Stuart looked at his watch. "Let's get together at eight. That'll give us a little sleep."

Sarah responded, "No problem. See you then," and left the room.

Stuart was in his office by seven, not being able to sleep thinking about how or if they would handle the weapons delivery. He was of the opinion that they should not assist the FSP, or Turner in any fashion, but was very concerned that the Association might suffer as a result. That thought was countered by the realization that the FSP had never kept its word on anything anyway so what the hell was the sense in dealing with them as if they were a respected and honorable governmental agency. Stuart chuckled to himself at that thought.

It was some twenty years prior that all of the arrogant, bureaucratic government police agencies had been merged and lumped together into the Federal Security Police and it seemed as though the most insolent, obnoxious agents had been propelled to the top of the organization. They had a history of bullying all whom they dealt with, giving only lip service to any so called rights of the accused. Stuart could not stomach the thought of assisting them in any respect regardless of the cost. He had come to his office early so that he could organize his thoughts before the meeting with Anders and Sarah. He was fairly certain they would be of a like mind, but if they were not, he wanted to be prepared. He figured that from the report that Barnes had given them, it sounded as though the FSP was not yet operating in strength and were also in need of weapons. They may not, as of yet, be a viable threat to anyone for a number of months, or even a year or more, during which time the Association could carry out its plan to leave the area. The weapons may also present a bargaining tool with the Cubans who presumably were interested only in South Florida and who already had virtual control of that area without the weapons. On the other hand, the weapons were apparently either within the Control Zone or close by as Yates and Campbell seemed to indicate. Stuart considered the possibility that the Association could attempt to locate and take control of the weapons to supply its own needs and for use as bargaining chips. Weapons were more valuable than gold when it came to bargaining power. One problem that would have to be dealt with soon was the point made by Barnes that Campbell was basing his cooperation with the Association on his trust of Barnes. Something would have to be done so that Barnes was not seen as double crossing his lifelong friend, Campbell. That could create big problems for not only Barnes, but also for the Association.

Anders was in his office, again surrounded by staff waiting to discuss various matters, when Stuart walked in. Anders looked up from his cluttered desk. "What's up? I hear the boys returned safe and sound." Stuart nodded and told Anders that Sarah would be there shortly to discuss some items of interest. That was a code term that Stuart and Anders had established when they wished to discuss something in private. Anders took the clue and told everyone to leave for a few minutes. He would call them back when he had finished with Stuart and Sarah. Just then Sarah entered the room and, shutting the door, Stuart proceeded to brief Anders on the main points of

Barnes report of the night before.

When he had finished, he summarized the issues that they needed to resolve. The principle issue being that of deciding whether or not they would participate in delivering the weapons to the FSP. Anders was silent for a moment and then asked Stuart and Sarah for their opinions on the subject. Sarah deferred to Stuart and he proceeded to voice his thoughts as he had formulated them in his office. Anders listened attentively and when Stuart had finished, Anders thought for a moment, looked up and said, "I totally agree. I don't want to help a single one of those bastards, much less deliver fifty thousand rifles so those sons a bitches can take over this country again. Especially with that bastard Turner up there. He's the sorriest excuse for a president this country ever had and we've had some sorry ones. Sarah, what's your take on this?"

"Couldn't agree more, gentlemen. I had my fill of them in the Navy. I have nothing to add other than possibly some insight into how we deal with them if we don't deliver."

The two men looked at one another, and then Anders said, "Go ahead. That's the next problem. Give us your thoughts."

Sarah continued, "According to the information that we are receiving from the Georgia area, and I had my staff check this out immediately after Barnes gave us his report, the FSP is known to be in and around Macon, down at the old Air Force Base, but that appears to be it. They have not extended their organization beyond the environs of that area. At this time they are very quiet up there and our sources believe they are strictly in the organizing phase. They have not been operating in strength and their combat troop strength, while sizeable for that area, is estimated at no more than five thousand men under arms. Their zone of influence, while covering a vast area, including northern parts of Florida, is somewhat isolated. From the information that we have right now, there are other groups that we should be more concerned about in the immediate future than the FSP. On the other hand, in the long term, they are clearly going to be someone to be reckoned with."

Anders sat back, looked at Sarah and Stuart and said, "Fine. Then it's decided. We don't cooperate with them. Let them make the move. We are preparing for an attack anyway, might as well be them. Frankly, I don't think they will. I've always thought they were a bunch of bullying cowards that only used their muscle when they had little fear that their victim would actually fight back. Furthermore, they must know this area is in the target area of the Cubans who could kick the shit out of the FSP even with their fifty thousand AR20s."

Stuart then brought out his thoughts on how they would deal with other problems that could develop from their failure to work with the FSP. He would have to talk with Barnes about his semi commitment to Campbell. He would also talk with Perry about beginning a careful search of the area with metal detectors and other equipment to see if they could locate the arsenal of weapons the FSP was after. Sarah said that, to be on the safe side, she would detail some of her staff to keep a good eye on the FSP to detect any movement of their people or any change in their operation that could signal problems for the Association. Anders told the two of them to keep him informed of any significant events along those lines and to keep moving on the departure plans. Stuart and Sarah left the room as Anders was shouting for his staff to "Come on back in. Let's get rolling, folks. We've got work to do."

As Stuart hurried back to his office, he remembered that the meeting that he had scheduled a few days ago was set to start in a few minutes. He had almost forgotten about it with all of the activities that had taken place in the last day or two.

# Chapter Seventeen

The four men and one woman, being Irene Covington, all arrived at the appointed time. Stuart had not told them what the study group was for, but as all in the group were very familiar with one another and their academic credentials, they had assumed that it had something to do with research or study of some project for the Association. As they entered the building, they were making idle chatter and laughing among themselves about events that had been occurring in the community. Stuart came in the conference room when they had all taken their seats and closed the door. The group sat silent as they waited, somewhat nervously, to find out just what the purpose of their get together was. Irene Covington pulled out her notepad, pencil and sat back waiting for Stuart to proceed.

"Well, I suppose you all wonder why I asked you to come in. Anders and I have come up with a project that I believe all of you will have great interest in working on. At least that is what I would assume. I have mentioned this group to no one and I want it understood that whatever transpires here or in any undertaking involving your group is to be kept in the strictest confidence. Hopefully the day will come when your work, whatever it involves, will be discussed openly. Until then, mums the word."

Stuart waited for the import of his words to sink into the group and all nodded that they would keep the business that they were undertaking secret. Stuart went on. "You have all been selected because you have extensive professional and educational experience, training and insight into the matters that we may want your assistance on. You may feel that others in the Association, or elsewhere, would be of value to this group. If so, let me know and I will take it up with Anders. For the present, you are the group and you will be reporting to me in connection with any projects and for any support that you may need in carrying out the project."

Stuart then explained the purpose of the initial project for the study group which was to lay out a charter for the government of the Association at such time as their situation permitted. Stuart accentuated the last two words knowing full well that Irene Covington was of the opinion that their situation permitted a more representative form of government now and any further delay in setting it up was not necessary. Stuart was aware that others in the Association had similar views and he addressed them to the group. "Within the next few months, it is entirely possible that most, if not all, of the Association members may be leaving this area for a more hospitable environment." Stuart observed the look of surprise and concern on all except for Irene Covington. "That is a matter to be kept in the strictest confidence. Suffice to say for the moment that our situation in our present location is tenuous. We are running out of food and water and we anticipate conflict with a vastly superior force within months, if not sooner. We are at the present time studying alternative locations and hope to present the information to the Association within the month. For the present, in view of the fluid situation we are in, we will maintain the present organizational structure and methods of operating. When we are situated elsewhere and are not operating in an emergency status, we would like to have alternative governing structures available for review, so that we can all, and I stress all, decide how we want to live. It may well be that in our new environment, these matters may be moot. We may be absorbed into an existing structure that we find acceptable. We may also, on the other hand, continue to be operating in a stress filled environment where rapid decisions are necessary, in which case, the present structure may be continued for some time." With that last comment, Irene Covington visibly frowned to express her displeasure. Stuart continued, "So be it. In the meantime, we want to intelligently explore alternatives."

Irene Covington spoke up. "I take it that what you want is a final product or products. Are you intending to participate yourself, or is Anders?"

Stuart thought a moment and replied; "I will sit in from time to time and observe progress of the group. I may make suggestions based upon my experience in the management of our group if I feel that would be helpful. Otherwise, I will be a silent partner so to speak. Anders may occupy the same status. I want you to fully understand that your product goes to no one other than to Anders and me. It may well be that it never goes farther. If that is a problem for any of you, now is the time to bow out."

Irene again frowned, but she had no intention of leaving a group that could potentially be writing the articles of government for their Association. Some of the men in the group spoke of the need for research materials, books, computers, a place to meet and store their materials, desks, chairs and all of the other items that would be needed. Stuart assured him that these had already been procured and that space had been allocated in the administration building for the group. The allocated space was in the upper floor of the building, in a corner and was relatively soundproof, but Stuart had taken additional steps to ensure that eves droppers would not be able to overhear the discussions.

A substantial library of governmental materials had been procured by Nix's team two weeks prior in a raid on the mainland. Fortunately, the thugs and human refuse in control of the city had little interest in books and reading materials and had left the government library in disarray but relatively unscathed except for damage done when bookcases and an occasional wall was destroyed. Using maps of the building provided by former employees, Nix and his team, accompanied by a former employee as a guide, made their way into the city in the dark of night. They had to make half a dozen forays into the government library in order to carry away the materials that they were after.

The materials that were obtained were, for the most part, collections of historical materials that had not been available for the reading enjoyment of the citizens in the days the government was still operating. They were maintained in a special library for the use of government researchers only and included writings by Rousseau, Plutarch, Blackstone, Tacitus,

Machiavelli, eighteenth century French and English writers that Stuart had never heard of, and a sizeable collection of writings by American political figures, including Jefferson, Hamilton, Madison, John Adams and others. Revolutionary writings of Paine, Burke, the Federalist Papers, Anti-Federalist Papers, numerous political essays and journals, the combined total of which virtually filled the conference room that had been set aside for the study group.

After Stuart had concluded his explanation of the purpose of the group and news regarding the possibility of a move to another area of the country, he inquired if there was anyone that was not interested in working on the project. No one spoke and, on the contrary, each commented that they would be more than interested to offer their services and hoped that they would be up to the project.

With that taken care of, Stuart told the group to follow him. All five followed Stuart as he proceeded up the back steps of the administration building and made his way to the rear of the upper floor of the structure. A guard, seated at a chair adjacent to a door at the end of the hallway, nodded at Stuart and removing a key, unlocked the door. Stuart proceeded into a room that was filled with book cases of reading materials along the walls, from floor to ceiling, with computer equipped desks spaced around the room and a long conference table and chairs off to the side. There were no windows in the room, but there was adequate lighting provided by fluorescents hanging from the ceilings.

The five walked into the room in stunned silence. They were totally unaware of the wealth of material that had been obtained and placed in the shelves for their use and benefit. All five had extensive academic backgrounds. All had Masters Degrees and four had Doctorate Degrees in History, Government or the Social Sciences. The materials that had been placed in the shelves and organized alphabetically, by author, had not been available in publicly accessible libraries since around the early years of the twenty-first century. The former government had considered much, if not all, of the material in the room as subversive and, to use their phrase,

"Prejudicial to the established form of government."

The committee members stood in awe as they searched the shelves and realized they were looking at a treasure trove of political literature. One could tell, by the way they turned the pages of the books and journals, the tremendous reverence for the documents that they were holding. Stuart gave each of them a key to the room and a special pass card with their photograph on the card. He instructed them that they had access to the room twenty four hours of the day, seven days a week and if they needed anything further, to inform only him. Irene Covington inquired as to whether or not there were any ground rules they were to follow or any timetables to be met. Stuart assured her that they had complete freedom in how they carried out their project and as far as a timetable was concerned, there was none. He did state that no materials or notes were to leave the room. He ended by saying that he would check with them from time to time. Stuart left them as they were familiarizing themselves with the wealth of reading materials.

# Chapter Eighteen

It had been over twelve hours since Barnes had returned from his mission north to meet with Campbell and Stuart was still pondering as to how to deal with the assurances given to Campbell by Barnes. There was no sense in antagonizing people unless it was absolutely necessary. No sense in making more enemies than one already had. That had always been one of Stuart's principles of life and he believed it applied to this case as well. Campbell had not actually been an employee of the FSP, rather had been detailed to them by the Melbourne Police Force and consequently, Stuart was of the opinion, that Campbell's status might provide an opportunity to resolve the matter. He sent out word for Barnes to come to his office and within minutes, Barnes was coming through the door. Stuart motioned for him to sit down as he walked around his desk and shut his office door. Stuart went right to the point. "John, we have a bit of a problem. We have decided that we are not going to work with the FSP. We are not going to deliver their weapons to them. We are not going to help them obtain the weapons and furthermore, we may even want to keep the weapons ourselves in the event that we can find them." Stuart waited for Barnes to digest his words.

After thinking for a moment or two, Barnes replied, "Whoa. I can't throw a screw into Campbell. He could get killed for this. I told him we wouldn't cross him."

Stuart expected that response and followed with, "I agree, John. We don't want to cross Campbell for a number of reasons. The question is how do we deal with it. That's what you and I are going to figure out. For starters, we can tell them we can't physically deliver the weapons. We don't have the resources and, in truth, we would be hard pressed to do the job, furthermore it would be a hell of a risky trip to haul that load up to Georgia. But, we have to be careful, because we do not intend to help them even if they come up with the freight haulers. We have no interest in helping the FSP get back into power. That is our position now and I don't see it changing." Barnes nodded in agreement. He had no more love for the FSP than anyone in the Association but that was not the issue. Stuart continued, "Now, back to how do we deal with Campbell. Have you ever thought that maybe he would prefer working with us instead of the FSP? That would solve the problem."

Barnes sat back in the chair with a troubled look on his face. "I don't know. He was close to a number of guys in the FSP and I don't know what his commitments or connections are there. He may not have any choice. Let me think about it. In any event, I trust we are not publicizing any of this just yet. I owe that to Campbell."

Stuart nodded and replied, "Agreed. We won't do anything further on this until you give me your input. But, we have to respond to them, with something soon, so get back to me ASAP."

Barnes assured him that he would be back that afternoon with something; he just wanted some time to think. Shortly after noon, Barnes returned to Stuart's office and seeing him coming down the hall, Stuart walked over to the door and closed it as Barnes entered. Neither man said a word as Stuart walked around his desk and sat down. Barnes was already seated as he began talking. "This is how I think it should go down. We have the scrambler and the frequencies to talk with Campbell. The FSP in Macon can listen in on these communications, so we can't get too candid with what we say. I suggest that I return to the beach landing site, with an adequate support crew of Nix's men in case things are not friendly on our return. I meet with Campbell at the beach. No walking ten miles through unknown country. I tell him that we cannot deliver the goods because we do not have the transportation resources, boats, or whatever. I then suggest, impliedly or whatever, that he and Yates, if he's there, join our group. That way, we aren't telling them to get screwed. We just don't have the horses to do the job. They can go elsewhere. They haven't told us where the goods are so what is their loss. Furthermore, they may decide to join up with us. I don't know Yates, but he seems to be a reasonable guy and I will vouch for Campbell. What do you think?"

Stuart had arrived at the same plan himself, but wanted Barnes to come up with it first because it involved some risks to Barnes in making the trip. He waited a polite few seconds and then agreed with Barnes proposal. He gave Barnes the authority to handle the radio communication to Campbell and to set up the operation with Thomas and Nix, but to keep Stuart informed as to his progress. Within a few hours, Barnes was back in Stuart's office reporting that he had communicated, via the scrambler, with Campbell and a meeting was set up for midnight three days from then.

Stuart wished him well and told him to proceed. Stuart then called Perry and Thomas in and told them not to spend any more time researching the delivery method, because they were not going to deliver the weapons to the FSP Stuart didn't have to explain the reason as both men were apparently in full agreement with the decision.

Anders had set up the exodus meeting for that evening in the secure conference room adjacent to his office after being assured by Sarah that her briefing was ready to go. The day before, he and Stuart had gone over the list of those they felt should be in attendance and the only slight disagreement had involved Robert Thomas whom Stuart did not consider a necessary party at this time.

Stuart continued to harbor some distrust of Thomas and questioned that his motives were in line with those of the Association. He had always considered Thomas as being more interested in taking care of himself than in watching out for the good of members of the group. Anders, having known Thomas for a number of years, was more confident of his character and in the end, Stuart deferred out of respect for his friend and, in many respects, his mentor. The two men laid out the format of the meeting with Anders explaining the purpose of the meeting, followed by Stuart handling administrative matters, then Sarah Taves with her briefing covering not only the research by her staff regarding appropriate alternative venues but also the latest on the Cuban forces in the area.

Perry's Security Team was positioned at the conference room access doors and the room was set up with the projection equipment, map stands, drawing board and podium for the speakers. All was in readiness when the first attendees arrived. At the scheduled time for the meeting all that had been requested to attend were in their seats waiting with much anticipation to hear whatever it was that generated this sort of activity. Perry, Moss, Nix, Barnes, Mary McClarty, Anders' administrative assistant, Beth Sloan, Robert Thomas and of course, Anders, Stuart and Sarah were all present.

Anders nodded to the security guard who closed and locked the door. He then stepped up to the podium and as was his style, took his time laying out his notes and occasionally looking up to observe those awaiting his words. When he was absolutely certain that he had the attention of those seated in the room, he proceeded. "I will get right to the point. You are here at this meeting because you are the key people in our Association and I want you to know what it is that you may be called upon to participate in within the next few months."

Anders went on to explain to his now very attentive audience that he, Stuart and Sarah had been working for some time on a very sensitive project that must not yet be publicized to the other residents of the Association or the Alliance as such publication could be dangerously disruptive to the well being of their group to say the least. "Sarah will be giving you more detailed information on the status of the current threats, human and environmental, to our continued existence in our present location. Suffice it to say that we have been exploring not the possibility but the high probability that we will be leaving this area, hopefully as an organized group, to an area of the country where it will not only be safer for us to live out our lives but which will also provide adequate food, water and shelter for a group our size."

Anders and Stuart had decided well before the meeting that they would, from the start, run the show in laying out the plans for the exodus. They would staff all necessary research projects and obtain the best information available to assist them in arriving at their decisions but they would not turn decision making authority over to any groups including the group in attendance at this meeting. Anders and Stuart both believed that the more cooks in the kitchen, the more problems they would have to deal with and the more arguments they would have to resolve. Sarah was aware of their policy in this regard and was in agreement with it. They would take suggestions, but they would lead the way.

Anders finished his remarks with a statement that would make it clear to those attending just who was running the show. "We have been staffing this project through Sarah Taves' office for some time. We have a number of alternative locations in mind and we are going to go over them tonight. We welcome your suggestions but our purpose in having you attend this meeting is primarily to let you know what is being considered and secondly we want you to prepare your particular area of responsibility for the tasks that lie ahead. Some or all of you will have particular problems that are going to impact other operational areas. We want to anticipate those problems so that when the time comes, we can resolve them. Stuart has a few words and then we will hear from Sarah."

Stuart took over the podium and reminded everyone that the information being discussed was highly confidential. It could destroy the Alliance which was still in the formative stages and furthermore, there were undoubtedly many people, possibly half of the residents of the Association and the Alliance that would, under no circumstances, leave the area. Should these people get wind of any plans for the key staff organizers of the Association to leave, there could be real trouble for everyone. Stuart told the group that in time "The residents would have to be informed of the plans, but not until this group, you people, and those you manage, have your troops in line, prepared to go, prepared to handle any sort of organized, armed or unarmed resistance that might occur."

Stuart told them that they had a difficult job as they had to prepare for the move without appearing to be preparing for a move. They would have to come up with a cover story and, "We have one provided for you. Sarah will brief you on that as well. Now before I turn this over to Sarah, I want to know where everyone stands on this issue, at least to this point, based on what you have heard so far. Assuming that we do proceed with this move within the next three months and it is going to be a very difficult and dangerous move, to say the least, is there anyone of you that is not willing to go along with us on this endeavor." Stuart waited and looked around the room. Robert Thomas shifted around in his chair and appeared uncomfortable, but said nothing.

Stuart said, "Very well" and moved away from the podium as Sarah stepped forward. One of her assistants took the chair by the overhead projector and placed the first slide in the mount. All of the men present were fully aware of the resources that Sarah had available to her as they had all listened to her intelligence briefings in Anders conference room many times. They knew that she had an extensive operating radio network that covered the country that provided her with a wealth of information from her many sources. They now listened attentively as Sarah proceeded with what to them could be her most interesting briefing. Her first slide was a topographical map of the continental United States with different areas of the country shown in various colors. Sarah paused for a moment to give everyone the opportunity to view the map and note the location of the distinguishing colors. She then went on with her briefing.

"As Anders has stated, we have been researching alternative locations in the continental United States where we may find a suitable environment in which to take up residence. From our various sources of information, we have discovered that such safe havens are very hard to find. I have colored in red, areas of the country that are considered generally unsafe. Obviously there are specific locations in the red areas that are protected by smaller, armed groups that are relatively safe but, in general, the red areas are not considered suitable by our research staff. You will note that the red areas cover most of the east coast and the lower half of the west coast from San Francisco south. The red area extends across most of the southwest as well as westward from the east coast along the industrial beltway of the great lakes region to west of Chicago. There are also pockets of red areas which are located all across the country in what were formerly heavy metropolitan areas. Atlanta, St. Louis, Denver, and all of the other areas you see on the map." Sarah again paused to let her audience study the map in view of her remarks. She then went on.

"The yellow areas are considered questionable for safety and for environmental hazard. The latter term we apply to geographic areas that are not considered suitable for habitation or for the production of food. You will note that a good portion of what is not colored red in the eastern United States, we have colored yellow. The reason for this is that our sources tell us that there is considerable racial and civil strife in these areas rendering them questionably safe. The yellow areas in the west have been so designated primarily because they are not suitable environmentally although, again, there are certain areas not considered to be safe due to civil strife and are colored yellow for that reason. Now the very limited areas that we have colored green are considered to be generally safe and capable of sustaining a group our size with adequate food and water supplies and the necessary resources to provide adequate shelter during the less hospitable times of the year. You will note that there is a substantial part of the country that has no color coding. We do not have adequate information to assign a color to those areas or the information that we have from those areas is not validated."

Again Sarah stood back from the screen to let her comments sink in to the now mesmerized audience. No one had yet asked a question or said a word as they were all taking in the information that she was providing to them. Sarah continued, "We have obviously concentrated our research into the areas depicted in green and we have had numerous communications by our radio system with groups and individuals residing in these areas. Some are friendlier than others. Some would welcome our move to their areas because they need more people for their own protection and survival and others feel that they already have too many people to take care of and do not want any others coming in. Nevertheless, most of the groups that we have communicated with seem to have reasonably stable, fairly operated and organized structures that we feel that we could work with. Again, without being there and seeing what they have and how they are organized, we cannot deal in absolutes, but we have taken great pains to verify as much of the information as we can through independent sources and following this procedure, we have located three areas in particular that we are reasonably confident would be a good location for us to consider as our next home."

Sarah went on to explain the criteria that was used in the selection process. The first was area security which included stability of the area as well as how defensible the area would be if the need arose. The second factor was productivity of the land and forests. Thirdly, the potential for future growth and expansion. Balancing all of these factors, Sarah and her research staff had concluded by use of a grading system that three areas had ranked first, second and third among all possibilities. Sarah then identified the second and third ranked areas as being in Wyoming and Idaho. The first ranked area was in Montana. Sarah described the three areas using finer scale maps and explained the defining features that placed the Montana area in a higher standing than the other two.

The number one ranking area consisted of a long valley, approximately one hundred miles in length, through which a river ran from north to south. Both sides of the valley were lined with high mountain ranges which closed together in narrow passes at both the north and south ends. The physical features of the area placed it number one in security. It was presently fairly unpopulated due to its remote location however Sarah did have communication with ranchers in the valley who indicated that they would be interested, under the 'right circumstances' for a stable, well organized group their size to take up residence there. The ranchers had been somewhat impressed with the degree of organization as well as the policies of the Association and advised Sarah that they would welcome further negotiations.

Sarah suggested that the ranch community in the valley was undoubtedly concerned about their own security and more than likely were willing to give up part of their lands as a tradeoff for the security and the technical expertise that the Association could provide. There had been some minor incursions into the valley by small bandit groups but these had been repelled with little difficulty by hurriedly organized groups of men from the various ranches and the small community that was in the center of the valley. Sarah estimated the population of the valley, based on old demographic studies, to be approximately two to three hundred including the residents of the town. The Association would make a significant addition to the population of the valley but this did not seem to concern her radio contacts. Sarah went on with the specifics that she knew would be of considerable interest to her audience.

"The valley has historically had high productivity in agricultural products. Water supply is ample for both human and livestock consumption as well as for irrigation. Cattle and livestock in general, have good grazing grounds, substantial hay and feed production, and a surprisingly mild winter which have made the area ideal for beef, sheep, pig and poultry farming. You may wonder what we know about farming. Well, let me tell you. We have many people in our Association who do know a great deal about farming and we have contacted them confidentially and organized them into a Farm Management Group to lay out plans and management methods so that when our Association does arrive, hopefully in this area, we will be prepared to go right to work and produce the crops and meat supplies that we are going to need to feed our people."

Sarah then addressed the issue that by that time was on everyone's mind. Just how were they going to get there? There was no longer anything remotely resembling safe travel from city to city on highways and interstate roads. Airlines no longer existed. Rail travel was a thing of the past. Gasoline for automobiles, buses or trucks was scarce to nonexistent. Diesel fuel was even harder to obtain. Robert Thomas was down to a maximum of six months of diesel fuel for his boats provided he did not increase his usage. Sarah emphasized the seriousness of the transport issue. "How do we move our resident population to the new site? That is the most difficult question and the one that gives us the greatest concern from the point of view of security and provisioning. We are working on the fuel issue as we speak and are hopeful that we will be able to resolve it. We have to carry all of our expendables with us no matter how we travel. We have to protect our people and our supplies from the many threats along the route. Ross Perry will be in charge of security along the route responsible for all Association troops including the men and women presently assigned to Marina defense under the command of Robert Thomas. Thomas will continue to report directly to Stuart on the journey and will assume other responsibilities."

At this comment, Thomas took particular notice, wondering what they had in mind for him. He was not overly excited about leaving the Melbourne area and the ocean to take up a life on the farm. This was going to be a tough decision and he would just wait to hear what they had in store for him, job wise. Sarah continued, "Jack Nix, and his men, will handle reconnaissance along the route and will report to Ross Perry who will have overall responsibility for security during the trip."

Stuart knew this would please Perry as the latter was a little offended by the operating independence that Nix had arranged for himself in the Association. Nix, on the other hand, as Stuart noted, gave no indication that the arrangement would be a problem for him. Stuart had included the proviso that Nix's men stayed with Nix to ensure that Perry did not try to break up the team. He made a mental note to see that Perry did not stifle the freedom of action that made Nix's group the effective specialized combat force that it was. They could ill afford petty jealousies and Stuart would see that they did not have that problem. Stuart directed his attention back to Sarah as she continued her briefing.

"Let me say this regarding the route. We have been studying the potential routes for some time. The first qualifier in the study is by what means are we traveling. We have concluded that with all of the equipment, supplies, basic personal items, weapons, ammunition, medical equipment and the basics necessary to sustain our people on the journey, we will need to travel by road, using truck transport vehicles. Some of the travel may well be on foot, particularly depending upon how many people are making the trip. Based upon our present estimates of how many would be willing and capable of going, we figure approximately five hundred people would be traveling. Obviously, only those people can take this journey that are physically and mentally able to withstand the rigors involved. We have included that in our estimate. That selection process alone will present problems. Should we be correct in our estimate of the number of people and no more, most of the travelers, if not all, could be accommodated in the trucks. A larger group would necessitate travel by foot and this would in turn increase the amount of supplies necessary for the trip. Approximately 12 to 15 diesel truck transports will be provided by our logistics people under John Barnes."

This was clearly news to Barnes and he let out a long sigh as he was already loaded down with supply problems with the needs created by the Alliance. Stuart was aware that Barnes had only a few operating trucks at his disposal and these were in poor condition but there were a number of suitable candidates in various stages of disrepair abandoned around the control zone that could be rehabilitated. Stuart smiled as he thought to himself that Barnes would have the trucks ready when the time came because he was just that kind of guy. He would bitch a lot, but the trucks would be ready.

Sarah went on as the men in the room absorbed her every word. "We do believe that we can map out a route that will bypass the major threat areas. Needless to say, we must anticipate the need for defensive measures all along the route. Our Intelligence unit can provide a wealth of information on the route structure including regional instability, bridges, known road damage, anticipated detours for threats of various kinds. We are presently preparing detailed route maps for the use of the travel guides leading the way. These men will also receive detailed briefings prior to departure. I should also add that we will keep our intelligence operation functioning along the route, continuing to gather information as it comes in which may necessitate changes on a day to day basis. As far as fuel is concerned, we are presently planning to have two additional diesel trucks to carry fuel and replacement parts although we may revise this and spread the inflammables out further. We figure that we will need ten thousand gallons of diesel fuel and two thousand gallons of gasoline for support and defense force vehicles. We are assigning the task of acquiring the fuel to Jack Nix."

Sarah glanced over at Nix who was rolling his eyes back as he pondered the enormity of the task. Diesel fuel was as scarce as black diamonds in South Florida. Everyone wanted it and no one produced it anymore. Nix was wondering just where in hell would he ever find that quantity of fuel and how would he transport it if he did find it. At that point, his assignment appeared to be an impossible task.

"Jack, I have good news and bad news for you. We know where the fuel is. That is the good news. The bad news is that it is well protected and getting it out will take some doing. Perry will be tasked to provide the men required for the mission over and above the men in your unit. You will be the overall mission commander. My staff will give you all of the known data on the storage sites at the conclusion of this meeting. Ross, you should also attend that briefing so that you are aware of the requirements that may be laid on you. Nix, you will be given all of the support that you need and you will need plenty."

Ross Perry nodded in agreement with the assignment, but Stuart could tell that he did not like it that Nix was the mission commander. Stuart and Sarah had discussed the assignment at length and in view of its apparent difficulty, they both felt that Nix had more operational special combat experience than Perry and was, in general, more qualified to tackle what appeared to be a very difficult mission. Stuart had no doubt that Perry's ego was bruised but he also knew Perry would do what he was asked to do and do it well.

Sarah then covered the estimated time that the trip would take assuming the departure date was the first of March. She explained that the estimate included delays occasioned by mechanical difficulties, threat suppression, and detours resulting from road conditions or threat avoidance, weather and other unknown causes. The estimate was also based on eight hours of movement at an average speed of ten miles per hour for those times that the convoy was actually underway. Based on these, hopefully conservative, estimates, Sarah's staff had concluded that the trip would take at least two months time to reach the objective.

Sarah indicated that she had about concluded her briefing except for the matter of a cover story for the activity that all of the operating departments would generate in preparing for the move. "We need a cover story for all of you to use and it should protect all of the anticipated activity that this business will generate. Food production is sorely needed for the beach residents. Unfortunately, the soil is not suitable for agricultural products. There are areas to the north that are suitable for growing crops and supporting livestock. We can kill two birds with one stone by activating a plan to take over crop land to the north and inland between Daytona and St. Augustine. Our preparations that will be visible will be explained as being for that purpose. Ross Perry's staff can draft up a military plan to take over the area. It may well be that we may even activate the plan for the benefit of those staying should they be interested in occupying the area. It is presently relatively uninhabited and should be suitable for farming. Not ideal, but suitable. Better than the sand we are standing on which will produce absolutely nothing." The men chuckled knowing full well that the Control Zone was not capable of producing anything edible.

"That's the cover story. You should be able to explain most, if not all, of your activities under that canopy of cover. Good luck." At that point, Sarah turned the meeting over to Stuart.

Stuart approached the podium and as he set down his notes, he observed that the somewhat carefree attitude that normally attended staff meetings was absent. That was very understandable. Everyone in the room was very interested in what was being said. "A couple of very sensitive matters that I think you should be aware of. We have sent a message to the Cuban leader, Paco Morales for the purpose of inviting negotiations regarding our departure. We don't want to have to fight our way out of here and we assume they don't want to have to fight us to take over this area if they don't have to. Now that all presents problems for the many people that will not be making the trip with us. All I can say to that is that Morales or someone will eventually take over this area and from what we know of Morales, we could be leaving our fellow residents in much worse hands. The reports that we get from areas that the Cubans have taken over are generally favorable. As for our message to Morales, we have had no response as of yet to our invitation to talk and if and when we do, we will let you know. In the meantime, we have to prepare for the worst and assume that we may be under attack within the coming month or so. You are to prepare accordingly. One more item along that line, we have taken over control of a quantity of weapons from our residents and some from the Alliance. Should we leave, we will have to give back weapons to people who surrendered their own weapons to us. We are presently trying to figure out how to replace those weapons as we will need them for our journey. Just one more problem."

Stuart went over his notes while those in the room considered the import of his comments. He again looked up from his notes and continued. "Regarding the target location that we have termed, for security reasons, 'Safe Valley', this is what we intend to do in the next few days or weeks. Thus far we have received a green light on joining them on their land. We have not covered all of the details and that is what we have to do now. We will set up a negotiation meeting with the principals in 'Safe Valley' to determine if there is a meeting of the minds on what we intend to do and how they intend to deal with us when we arrive in their area. We are going to send an emissary to 'Safe Valley' to inspect the area and conduct the negotiations on behalf of the Association. I should say on behalf of the Alliance, but that is a bit debatable. We have arranged for an aircraft to make a nonstop flight to 'Safe Valley' carrying one passenger. I have elected to make the trip on behalf of the Association. Anders has agreed. I anticipate that I will stay in 'Safe Valley' until negotiations are completed or until we reach a deadlock at which time I will return to this area. I am leaving the day after tomorrow. No one, other than those in this room, must know where I have gone or why I have gone." Again, Stuart paused to let the words sink in. When he figured they had received the message, he continued. "Sarah will be responsible for all of my operational duties. Whatever she says will be considered as coming from me. I trust you will all give her your full cooperation."

Stuart went on with his comments. "You all know the timetable. Prepare the operational units that you are responsible for to handle tasks that you may assume will come your way as a result of the journey. We will task you further as time goes on to handle additional responsibilities, so plan on that also. Robert Thomas, we won't be needing boats where we are going, but we will be needing heavy machinery, maintenance, and many of the activities that you have handled so well right here. You will receive your changed assignment shortly. It will be a challenge fit for your talents and I believe you will be pleased. In the meantime, continue with your fishing fleet. We have to eat until we leave and we will need to store up on food supplies for the trip. Also Robert, I am sure that Barnes could use maintenance help with his new trucking company. Continue with your search for good mechanics. We can use them and any others you have on your staff to get that trucking fleet in good operating condition."

Stuart turned to John Barnes and continued, "John, you and Robert get together and organize a maintenance team to tackle the job of getting those trucks going. We don't want any breakdowns once we're on the road." Stuart could tell that Thomas was generally pleased with what sounded like his new assignment.

Up to that point, Thomas was more than curious as to just what use, if any, they intended to make of him in what was clearly a land operation. He would miss the water and the boats, but as he leaned back in his chair, he told himself that nothing lasts forever anyway. Should be interesting, he told himself.

Sarah motioned to Jack Nix and Ross Perry to follow her for the special briefing on the fuel storage mission. As they left the room, headed for Sarah's office, Anders grabbed Stuart's arm and gave him a big grin as he said, "Well, we're off and running. We've got a lot of work to do and a lot of planning. Good luck on your trip to Montana. Take care of yourself and if you don't like what you see, get the hell out of there."

Stuart nodded and smiled, "I have no intention of doing anything stupid. I'm more concerned about the trip out and back than I am about the visit to the valley. Sarah has me convinced that I will be well received. The real risk is in the travel. She has lined up a single engine aircraft that is specially equipped with extra tanks to make the flight. She tells me that the pilot is in the business of doing this and takes reservations over the single side band from around the country. According to her, he has many successful trips under his belt so hopefully, he will have at least one more. We had to pay him a wad so he'd better be good."

Anders was aware of the cost as he had to sign the release for the funds. The pilot wanted only gold, but in the end settled for payment in equal amounts of one ounce gold Krugerrands and American dollars, the latter of which were still useful currency in many places in the country. People still traded in dollars, more out of habit than anything else because the U.S. Treasury had been defunct now for quite some time.

# Chapter Nineteen

Over one hundred students had signed up to attend the school that Beth Sloan had organized with the help of Irene Covington and the other members of the school staff. Various tests were introduced to determine the student's particular skill level and to assign him or her into the proper Primary or Secondary Class. The organization of the classes had gone smoothly until the parents were informed as to the particular class assignment for their son or daughter. Some were pleased. Some were not overly interested. Some were infuriated that their offspring had not been assigned to a higher level class. They took it as a personal insult that their child was the oldest in the class and in one case, the oldest by four years.

Under the former government, students spent a significant amount of their time learning the ropes on filling out applications for the various social support programs that the government offered. These had formerly been called welfare programs until that title fell into disrepute. A student graduating from High School in the days before the collapse of the government, could be assumed to be able to count to one hundred and in about half of the cases, read and understand simple four to six letter words. Everyone that attended the High School system for four years graduated, regardless of achievement, as there were no skill tests used after about the year 2015. They were considered discriminatory.

In view of the fact that private schools were outlawed after 2015 as also being discriminatory, most of the children upon reaching maturity were basically unskilled automatons trained only to observe government edicts and policies. As public education continued to deteriorate, the Government Education Office never stopped touting the less than credible national test scores which were soaring ever higher into the ozone layer.

The results of the deteriorated educational system were reflected in the decline of research and development that occurred in the United States in the first quarter of the century. There were other reasons for the decline and finally the total absence of this necessary tool for progress including the destructive tax system that virtually destroyed private incentive in the business world. But, by far, the most destructive factor, in the opinion of older, truly educated Americans, was the charade being passed off as a school system.

When classes in Bayside commenced, a number of problems developed as could be expected, particularly in the primary classrooms. The most serious problem related to discipline. A few of these kids had been brought before the Alliance Courts. One of the boys, aged fourteen and appearing even older, was assigned to the Primary Two classes. He had very minimally tested above the primary entry level, having learned something in his fourteen years, and made it clear to the teacher and the students that he was running the classroom. The teacher, Kate Nolan, worked with him for days, trying to establish a level of rapport that was not destructive of the educational process for the other students. After days of total class disruption, Kate had no alternative but to call for security to take him to detention and schedule a hearing.

At the hearing, as the teacher explained the problem to the Alliance Court Judge, the student now restrained by a security officer, yelled out, "Shut up bitch." The room became totally silent as the Judge stepped out from behind the bench and walked up to the sneering youth. "Well now. That's pretty tough talk. Let me explain something to you, son. You are in the wrong place at the wrong time to be pulling that stuff. Now, let's hear you apologize to Miss Nolan."

"Dream on, Jerk. My old man's FSP. Screw with me and you'll be pushing a broo…"

He never got the last word fully out as the flat of the Judges hand made a loud smack as it came in contact with the boy's cheek. The youth reeled backwards, held up by the security guard as he took another flat hand on the other cheek. Both blows landed in a fraction of a second which made a significant impression on the boy. What followed made a greater impression. "Gag him and we'll have sentencing." The security guard ripped off a piece of duct tape and slapped it across the mouth of the now wide-eyed youth, cuffed him and dragged him in front of the bench. "Well, punk, welcome to the detention center. If you had kept your mouth shut, you would most likely have gone to the youth camp, which is a lot more fun than where you're going. Now seeing as how you are such a tough guy, you will get tough guy treatment. Let's see how you like thirty days there. Let me warn you. Don't mouth off to anyone there. Not to the guards and not to your fellow vacationers. It is very unhealthy to do that. Now while you are there, I want you to think of what you are going to say to Miss Nolan here, in this room, in thirty days and it better be sweet or you will go back. Keep that in mind and by the way, around here, we think the FSP sucks. I wouldn't wave that label around. Get the punk out of here."

Kate Nolan was a bit in shock at what had taken place. She had been a teacher in the Government School system for years and this was a total reverse of her experience there. She did not quite know what to make of what she had seen. The Judge looked over at her and seeing the surprised look on her face, shaking his head, he commented, "Things are different now. We don't have time to listen to that crap anymore. We do what we have to do to get the job done. If we don't clamp down on this kid today, he'll be worse tomorrow. You did the right thing by reporting him. If you hadn't, your other students would have suffered. Those guys over there are tough, but they are not sadists. So don't worry about the kid. He will be well taken care of. Next case."

Kate left the room in a daze, determined to try even harder on the next discipline problem to prevent a reoccurrence of another hearing. She also thought about what the Judge had said and she had to agree. Nothing was perfect but this was a hell of a lot better than what she had before.

# Chapter Twenty

Sarah had given Jack Nix and Ross Perry access to all of the materials that she had obtained relating to their assignment to appropriate ten thousand gallons of diesel fuel and two thousand gallons of gasoline. The gasoline was not going to be the big problem. Diesel fuel was the particularly scarce item. Sarah had learned that a fuel tanker, carrying diesel fuel, was located in the harbor at Jacksonville and according to her sources, the tanker was apparently loaded with fuel as the ship was floating at her water line. Empty vessels floated with a substantial portion of their hull showing. The tanker had been in service operating between Freeport in the Bahamas and Jacksonville prior to the collapse. It was currently in the possession of a well armed group that was selling the fuel in relatively small quantities for exorbitant prices. Sarah was informed that the group consisted of approximately thirty to fifty individuals who ran a marketing operation selling scarce items such as fuel and food to anyone with enough gold or script to pay their prices. They were well armed and had repelled a number of attempts by individuals and groups to obtain their merchandise free of charge. The vessel was chained to the pier at the commercial wharf in Jacksonville and was under heavy guard but, as Sarah noted, the guards were primarily guarding against an assault from the adjoining landmass and not from the water.

As she passed the materials, including aerial photos, still photographs of the vessel, and other items to the two men, she said, "Take a look at this and let me know if you need anything else. I do have a good source there."

Nix saw the photograph of the tanker which showed two or three guards standing on the dock holding what appeared to be AR20 automatic rifles. "How in the hell did you get a hold of these photos? I take it they are fairly recent?"

Sarah laughed. "They were taken two days ago and transmitted by radio. Our computer equipment enhances the transmitted digital data to produce a photograph with as much detail, or more, as one taken using regular photographic equipment. My source is with a group holed up in a complex on the north side of the bay across from the commercial docks and she took this image, I don't want to call it a photograph, with a digital camera and transmitted the data to our staff for processing. We can get more of these when the need arises, just let me know."

Nix whistled. "Great. We will want updated photos prior to whatever we end up doing here. This is most interesting."

Sarah replied, "Have fun" as she left the two men pouring over the photos, maps, water navigation charts, tanker schematic diagrams and other items that she had collected for their review. Both men were intently involved in their study of the documents, photos and charts.

Perry commented, "Yes, this is going to be very interesting." Nix looked up at him and chuckled.

Nix and Perry were both amazed at the wealth of information that Sarah had accumulated for them. There were current tide charts that were printed up on computer paper which must have been prepared by Sarah's staff as there was no longer any governmental agency producing these figures. The water navigational charts were those most recently published by the Government Charting Office and although they were six years old, and channel dredging had stopped over four years ago, they were far better than nothing. With the Subsurface Visualization Equipment on Thomas' cigarette boats, charts were not as important as they used to be. More than likely, they would be able to find their way through the harbor entrance using SVE if a channel, in fact, still existed.

Nix was studying the Enhanced Global Positioning System, EGPS, data that was included in the packet of materials and commented to Perry that Sarah had somehow obtained the coordinates for the exact location of the vessel, right down to the latitude and longitude of the pilings to which the vessel was secured by chains. The thickness of the chain links was also provided, being estimated at between three and five inches. Perry was not familiar with the accuracy of EGPS, but Nix was as they had used it in special operations when he was in the Army. The system was rated as accurate within one meter and the beauty of EGPS was that it was a self sustaining system, not requiring land based support.

Very handy in view of the fact government support for navigation systems no longer existed. This apparently was accomplished by the use of computers on board the satellites that periodically reconfigured the data being transmitted thus sustaining its accuracy. Solar batteries provided the power source and the entire satellite system was estimated to have a one hundred year maintenance free life in orbit which would hopefully last until a national government could again be reestablished in what had been the United States of America, or at least a significant portion of the former nation.

As Nix read through the materials and studied the aerial photographs of the harbor, he commented that they would have to bring Thomas in as he was obviously a key element in the success of the operation. Perry suggested that they first figure out the general line of attack to take possession of the vessel and when they had that figured out, they could bring Thomas in to support their basic plan. Nix agreed with that and the two men began pondering how the mission would be run. It was obviously going to be difficult to bring sufficient force into the harbor without being detected, release the vessel, tow it out of the harbor at obviously a very slow rate of speed and make it safely back to the Control Zone. Possibly there could be another way to accomplish the mission.

The two men continued discussing alternatives late into the night and when they left the intelligence section conference room, they could hear the radio equipment and computers humming as the intel night shift continued their ongoing task of gathering information for the Association.

Stuart had Perry send Detention inmates over to the old military airfield with equipment to upgrade the runway to allow for seven thousand feet of useable surface. The airfield had not been used for a number of years and the concrete had broken up in spots and portions of the strip were overgrown with weeds, grass and drifted over with sand. The contract pilot had advised Sarah, by radio, that he would need seven thousand feet in view of his heavy takeoff weight which was over allowable limits and would also need 300 gallons of aviation grade gasoline. The request presented problems as no one had any knowledge as to where that grade of fuel could be obtained, but Sarah advised him that they did have lower octane automobile gasoline and possibly their chemists would be able to raise the octane level to meet the requirements of the pilot.

The pilot, Hans Frick, had been through this before with other customers as most stores of avgas around the country had been vandalized or used as heating fuels by people trying to survive. Automobile gasoline, while very difficult to find, was in more plentiful supply. It could usually be bought, but for a very high price. Frick told Sarah to have a chemist available who was familiar with fuels, fuel additives and octane ratings, and he would reconnect that evening. Sarah had her staff locate two men with the credentials Frick had specified, in fact more than he had asked for as they were former NASA propulsion engineers, both with extensive backgrounds in chemistry. Sarah turned the microphone over to them and they took down the information that Frick gave them and nodded to one another as though the request would not present any particular problem. When they had concluded, they assured Sarah that they would be able to upgrade the octane rating provided Sarah had the fuel. She had already taken care of that so that was one more problem solved. The pickup was scheduled for the following night and Sarah had coordinated the estimated time of arrival of the aircraft with the contacts in 'Safe Valley'.

The pilot figured the flight would take twelve hours from take off to landing provided they did not have any serious weather problems. Sarah had her people preparing weather data from contacts around the country who radioed basic weather information, including barometric readings, winds, temperature, and other data and told Frick that she would have a flight briefing prepared for him prior to departure.

Stuart, Sarah and Anders had been in conference since the Staff meeting when they announced Stuart's planned visit to 'Safe Valley'. All three wanted to ensure that Stuart was fully prepared to conduct the negotiations on behalf of the Association so that all bases were covered with their new neighbors before the Association departed their present, somewhat safe, sanctuary. The influx of new residents to the Valley would undoubtedly cause some disruption and friction with those currently residing there.

Stuart, Anders and Sarah all wanted to make sure that every potential problem was fully explained in advance so that antagonisms did not develop once they were there. They were also fully aware that, no matter how careful they were to spell out all of the forthcoming inconveniences to their hosts, there would still be many among the current valley residents who would not welcome their presence. That should also be discussed. On the flip side, the Association residents that would be expected to be making the trip could make a substantial contribution to the quality of life of the Valley. There were engineers, teachers, scientists, three medical doctors, and a number of other professionals, technicians and trades people in their group that could be expected to be a valuable addition to the present Valley population that consisted primarily of ranchers, farmers and laborers. That, and the rather sophisticated defense force of the Association, was the prime selling point that Stuart would have in his favor. Further, Anders and Sarah stressed to Stuart, in many respects the Association had as much or more to offer to their new neighbors than they would receive and Stuart was cautioned not to sell the Association short in the trade offs.

Stuart spent most of the time prior to the departure pouring over the information on the Valley that Sarah had obtained from her various sources. Stuart was sure by noon of the day of departure that he would be more familiar with their area than they were. He also had profiles on the principal parties running the show in the Valley. They were all ranchers and had employed many of the Valley residents prior to the collapse and continued to run the show after the collapse. They had set up their own economic structure, using paper script printed by the local print shop that was used to pay for services rendered or goods purchased. The local tool shop was providing replacement machinery parts and they had established a communications network throughout the Valley using CB radio. An amplifier had been set up in the small village in the center of the valley extending the normally short CB range up and down the valley, encompassing most of the residents.

All residents in the valley had been informed as to Stuart's anticipated arrival and the purpose of the visit. The principals had visited local meeting sites in the valley and discussed at length the proposed additional residents and, as could be expected, some were in favor and some were against, but the majority realized the necessity of improving their very limited defense force. Sooner or later, they would be facing a problem that they could not defend against and it would be better to have what appeared to be a well organized, disciplined and goal oriented group join them than to be overrun by a group of opportunistic anarchists that were already roaming too close to the borders of their valley. Many continued to question the wisdom of opening their doors to the visitors from the south, but, hopefully, the man that was coming to visit them could answer some of their questions.

# Chapter Twenty-One

Robert Thomas expertly maneuvered the twin diesel turbocharged cigarette boat out of the slip while Nix's men checked over their weapons and ammunition. Barnes was sitting in the copilot's chair going over notes that he had apparently prepared for his meeting with Campbell and Yates. Nix was not along on the trip as he was tied up with Perry working on his fuel retrieval assignment. Thomas figured he would be involved in that before long as there were no fuel tankers or storage tanks within walking distance of the control zone and that left just one mode of transportation, his boats. As he pushed the throttles up on the engines he felt the guttural power of the twin four fifties come to life, lifting the bow of the boat up out of the water and quickly dropping it down again as the boat planed on the flat bay water. It wouldn't be quite this smooth on the open ocean but it looked relatively calm as he had viewed it from the beach front.

The moon was just coming up and as he rounded the bend at the channel entrance, he could see the ocean reflected in the moon's rays extending out to infinity. About five miles out, he would pick up the gulf stream and that would add a few knots to his progress unless it was too rough. If that was the case, he would go north on a course that kept him out of the stream and closer to shore. With the wind out of the south as it was now, the stream should be relatively calm but one thing about the stream that he had learned was that you could never predict exactly what it would do. As they moved out of the channel and into the open sea, the swells began to build up a bit, not too high, but high enough to send some spray over the bow and onto the windshield of the boat. They had placed the canvas cover over the cockpit and ran it back to aft of the passenger seating area. Thomas looked back at the passengers and he could tell at a glance which ones would be 'barking at the whales' and which would be lulled to sleep by the monotonous rhythm of the boat rolling over the gentle swells of the ocean.

The plan was to stay offshore at the drop off point until they received the light signal from Campbell giving the all clear. Barnes would then be taken by skiff over the reef to the shoreline with some protection consisting of ten of Nix's best men. Barnes figured he would need no longer than one or two hours with Campbell and Yates during which time Thomas was to cut engines, drift and check in by VHF radio every hour.

The trip north was uneventful and sea conditions were favorable giving them a fairly smooth ride. Every now and then Thomas would check behind him to ensure that the backup boat was in sight. Even though a double engine failure was extremely rare on a boat of this type, Thomas didn't want to be one of the very few who had the experience. The second boat also had a contingent of ten of Nix's men to provide added support in the event problems developed on shore.

Many in the Association considered Thomas somewhat of a cowboy in the sense that he usually did things his own way, still in all, he was fairly conservative when it came to protecting his own skin. He was as ready to take a risk as any other man in the Association but he was nobody's fool and if there was a way to reduce a particular risk, he would find it and take advantage of it. He had demanded the backup boat and the extra contingent of men even though some in Stuart's staff considered that to be a waste of valuable and scarce diesel fuel. He had won the point when he told them that if they wanted to, they could drive the boat, without the backup, and he would take over their duties, safely sitting in the staff room, adding up inventory figures for the ten or so hours they would be out on the ocean.

Stuart had not been present at that meeting as he was busy preparing for his trip north. If he had been, Thomas knew he would back him up. As he thought about Stuart, Thomas looked at his watch and figured Stuart would be departing within an hour or so or could even be departing at this very time. He scanned the skies to the southwest back towards the Control

Zone, but couldn't make out anything against the backdrop of a starry sky. As he thought about it, he concluded that the pilot would not have his running lights on anyway. No need for that and it would only increase the risk. It appeared to be good weather for the flight as it was here for the boat trip north.

As they rolled along the swells, the minutes passed by uneventfully as they proceeded to the north. They were riding about three miles off shore and occasionally could see signs of activity along the beach as they moved up the coastline. Lights here and there or fires burning along the shoreline; most likely for warmth as it was cool even here in Florida. It was still winter time and the temperature at night could dip down into the thirties or forties. About every ten miles or so, they would pass what had been a city or larger community. They went past Daytona Beach, or what was left of it. The blacked out buildings against the starlit background, with an occasional structure burning, and no sign of people anywhere, gave the oceanfront city the appearance of a ghost town. Thomas knew, from his experience with Melbourne, that people were there. The hunters and the hunted. He could smell the city this far out from the shoreline. The acrid smell of burning rubber and the haze from the smoke reached out to the men in the passing boats and reminded all of them of the violence that reigned in this city and in most across the country.

The smell of the city brought the men out of their lethargy and they checked their watches noting that they were close to their objective. The men rechecked their weapons again and wiped their ammo clips until they shined to ensure they would function should the need arise. The AR20s were designed never to jam but they didn't want to find out that was not exactly true. The men checked each other over, pulling on straps, checking grenade packs, ammo clips, radio gear, EGPS equipment, and all of the sundry war making tools that they had brought with them for the mission. Hopefully they would not need any of it, but one never knew.

Thomas proceeded up the coast, watching the EGPS nav gear as he came closer to the latitude of the drop off point. When he was just south of a point abeam the target, he pulled back on the throttles and the bow of the boat again came up as it slowed down and mushed into the swells. He turned towards the shoreline and turned on his depth equipment. He was still well out to sea and the signals from the depth meter would not yet reach the five or six thousand feet down to the bottom of the ocean. He knew he had no problem until he was within a half mile or so from the beach. Then he would have to be very careful as the ocean floor came up a vertical wall and then leveled off at about a hundred feet. From that point on, the sea bed could change from one hundred feet to four feet with little or no warning. He would proceed slowly then to within a quarter mile of the shore where he would have to drop his passengers off to make the rest of the trip in the rubber skiff.

As he glided slowly towards the blacked out shoreline, still a mile off according to his radar, he could make out what appeared to be a signal light coming from what should be the target area. "Barnes, take a look over there and tell me, is that your boy." Barnes stood up in the cockpit, holding onto the console to steady himself as he peered into the blackness ahead of him. He could tell where the shoreline was as it was blacker than the dark sky in the background. As he searched the shoreline, first one way and then another, he caught sight of a light off to the right of where he had been looking. He concentrated on the flashes and made out three longs followed by a long, a short and a long, spelling out OK. That was the signal Campbell was to give for them to come ashore. "OK, Mac, you can drop us off anytime."

Thomas continued running on into the shoreline at slow speed, watching the depth meter and turning on the Subsurface Visualization Equipment so that they didn't run headlong into a coral head or part of the reef that came closer to the surface than the seabed. The SVE would read out about fifty feet ahead of the boat which at his slow speed gave Thomas time to react if a hazard came into view. He maneuvered the boat in as far as he felt comfortable and brought the throttles into idle. The crew lowered the dingy over the side as Barnes and his support team clambered into the smaller boat. As a final act before cutting loose, the crewman on the skiff double checked the EGPS coordinates to ensure that they matched those on Thomas' boat. They did, right to the hundredth of a degree and starting the engine, they shoved off into the black towards the beach.

The crewman brought the skiff between the outcropping rocks lining the shoreline to a smooth stop on the white sand of the beach. Campbell and Yates were waiting for them, having been able to observe them as they proceeded to the shoreline. There were three other men standing well behind Campbell and Yates who appeared to be armed with automatic weapons. Barnes was not alarmed at this as he expected that his two hosts would have some protection in their ten mile journey to the beach. Nix's team clambered out of the boat and pulled the rubber skiff up on the shore while Barnes shook hands and greeted his former companion.

The men exchanged pleasantries and then Campbell suggested they go over to a small hut on the other side of the beach road where they had built a fire and had coffee brewing. That sounded good to Barnes as it had turned very cool and he wanted to be able to concentrate as much as possible on the negotiations that were to follow. The three men entered the hut which had been heated in anticipation of the meeting. There was no one inside, other than themselves, but coffee was brewing on a wood burning stove and Barnes could see and feel the red hot coals and flames through the glass door on the stove which was a welcome sight after the chilling ride to the beach. Yates poured coffee for the three of them while Campbell and Barnes continued their light chatter discussing the possible whereabouts of former associates on the Police force.

After they were all seated and it was time to get down to business, Barnes turned to the issues that had brought them there. "I will get right to the point. Unfortunately, we are not going to be able to deliver the weapons and ammo. We have been trying to figure out a way to do the job but quite frankly, we don't have the resources to do it safely and by that I mean to do it successfully. We have considered hauling the load by truck, which is not feasible in view of the fact that most of the bridges are down between our

Control Zone and this area, not to mention Savannah. We have considered hauling it by barge, but we need tugs and we don't have those. Our final consideration is that no matter how it would be done, it would be risky and we don't want to have to tell the FSP, sorry folks, but we dropped all of your goods in the ocean. We have enough problems of our own. Now, before you comment, let me say that our entire staff hassled this out ad infinitum and they are not about to change their minds. We would like the weapons we would receive out of the deal, but we can take care of ourselves the way it is. Sorry guys."

Campbell was taken aback by the announcement and Barnes could tell that Yates was somewhat irritated that the Association was not assisting them on this project. Campbell spoke first. "What if we sent a boat down from Savannah that could carry the load. Would you people support us at Melbourne." Barnes assumed that would come up and he had discussed that eventuality with Stuart and Anders. The plan was not to commit to anything, but to offer to carry any proposals back to the Association for their consideration. Barnes was to delay on any commitment one way or the other and steer the discussion over to the issue of Campbell and Yates joining up with them. Barnes feigned some interest in Campbell's suggestion and told the two men he would have to discuss that with the principals in the Association. That was not well received, as Barnes anticipated, and he followed up with the explanation that the Association had some problems in the past as a result of assisting a neighboring group in a project which ended up causing problems with other neighboring groups and they had sworn off getting involved in such matters in the future unless their very survival depended upon it.

Yates was angered by the lack of progress and finally spoke up. "Well, what if your very survival depended upon you working with us."

Barnes turned red, stood up and facing Yates, replied, "Just what the hell does that mean."

Campbell then stood between the two and told them both to sit down, "C'mon guys, we all have problems. Let's see if we can't work things out.

Yates is just pissed because we are having a hell of time figuring out how to pick up those weapons. We should have done this long ago when things weren't as bad as they are now." Yates, still scowling and apparently quite angry sat back down without saying a word.

Barnes figured that was as good a time as any to get into the real purpose of his mission and directing his words primarily at Campbell, he forged ahead. "Look, we want the guns. I am not totally sure what you fellows are after. I'm not talking about the FSP, I think I know what they want. I'm talking about the two of you. Mark, I know you weren't FSP but Roy, I don't really know your background. I assume you were not FSP and if I'm wrong, I apologize. By the way, Roy, I'm sorry if I pissed you off. Remember, I'm a messenger. I didn't determine the message so lets you and I work together and maybe we can come to a good solution here."

Yates softened a bit with that and apologized, in turn, to Barnes for flying off the handle. "No problem, Roy, I did too."

Barnes continued; "Now let's talk some business. I'll get right to the point and please don't take offense at what I have to say. How tight are you guys with the FSP? We need guys like you in our group and it's not just for the guns." Yates began to speak, but Barnes stopped him and said, "No, Roy, hear me out. I'll listen to anything you guys have to say on any topic relevant to what we are all doing here but first hear me out. I don't know you that well, Roy, but I assume if Mark can stand you, our group probably could also." Barnes smiled at Yates as he made the remark and Yates appeared to take it well. "We have a great group of people in our Association with some very good ideas."

Barnes went into some detail on how the Association was organized, the Defense Force, the intelligence unit, the logistics group, the justice system, school system and the management structure that ran the Association. Barnes did not discuss the plan to leave the Florida area for safer quarters elsewhere, but he did allude to the fact that they were studying plans for their future well being. He let it go at that and the two men did not inquire as to what that meant.

Barnes finished with a proposal that the two men come with them and check out the Association. If they liked what they saw, they could consider joining up. "If not, we'll haul you back here and you can go on with your lives. One more thing, this is confidential. No one will know about this conversation or any visit you make to check us out. You will not be identified to anyone other than our key staff people and I can vouch for them. This is strictly between the three of us. Now, sorry if I offended you by this suggestion, but I think you both could work out well with our group. If you have any interest in what I have had to say, I would like to hear it."

Yates and Campbell looked at one another and Campbell spoke up first. "We aren't locked into the FSP. I've known Roy since we were in the Police Academy in Denver. His Association with the FSP is through my contacts so, no, we aren't locked into the FSP one way or another. They have been fairly good to us and we don't want to piss them off because they tend to spank hard when they get pissed off, but we are, like most people today, trying to save our ass by jumping on the best bus in town. Up to this point the FSP has been that bus." Campbell looked over at Yates for confirmation and Yates nodded in agreement. Campbell continued, "If we did what you suggest and I'm not saying we would, what about the weapons? We obviously know where they are but we don't want the FSP gunning for a couple of turncoats. This whole deal could really put us on the spot."

Barnes didn't want to go into the planned exodus from the Control Zone, with or without the weapons, but he did view that as a solution to the problem the two men, and most likely the Association, would face were they to take over the weapons sought by the FSP. Barnes looked at both men and said, "Let me say to both of you in response to that concern, which is a very valid concern and not only for you, but for my group. Obviously were you to work with us and we were to gain control of the weapons, under any conditions agreed upon between you and us, and I want to make that clear, we would be inviting problems with the FSP. I believe we have a solution to that problem, but I am not at liberty to divulge exactly what that is at this time. Should you visit with us at Melbourne, I believe we could go into more detail and I believe you would like what you hear. I will leave it at that."

The men continued talking for another hour, going into more detail on the Association, how it operated, the general makeup of the residents, supply problems, basic operating equipment that the Association had managed to accumulate and sundry other details that were of interest to Campbell and Yates in making up their minds as to what they were going to do. At the end of the discussion, they again said they would think it over and would communicate by radio within a few days as to their decision. They were nervous about word of this conversation getting back to the FSP and Barnes assured them, that under no circumstances would anyone other than the two or three key people in the Association and the three men here be aware of what was said. In the meantime, it was understood that Campbell and Yates would inform the principals in the FSP that the Association was not in a position to handle the delivery. The meeting was concluded on a friendly basis with Barnes and his support team returning by skiff to the parent boat as Campbell and Yates with their people, heading back to their farm. The trip back to the Control Zone was again uneventful with only a few fishing boats out on the ocean and a glimpse of a larger vessel or two far out in the stream.

When Barnes reached home base, he immediately met with Anders and Sarah, Stuart was on his way to Montana, and briefed them on the conversation with Campbell and Yates. After that, they all concluded that they would have to just sit and wait for a reply from the two men and deal with whatever followed. They now had to consider that no matter what their response, the Association could expect problems from the FSP attempting to retrieve their weapons. Hopefully they would be gone before that came to pass. There were only two months left before the expected departure date. It was the intention of Anders and Stuart to bring their anticipated move out into the open soon and that would present additional problems when all of the Alliance members got word of their plans. All physically able to make the move would be invited to come along so that would alleviate some of the tension. Furthermore, plans were being worked on to see that those staying were provided with access to food supplies and the necessary infrastructure and defensive weapons needed to survive.

The cover operation, 'North Farm', used to disguise the exodus buildup was also going along well. Word had been intentionally leaked out to the residents that all of the activity taking place, storing food and materials, the work on salvaging diesel tractors and trailers that were lying around the Control Zone and high level of staff activity were all related to the move to take over the agricultural area to the north. The staff had further decided that following the announcement of the move, the residents who were not going to make the trip would be canvassed regarding the land between Saint Augustine and Daytona to see if they were willing to make the effort to develop the area. If they were, the Defense Force would activate the plan, already prepared, to take control of approximately five thousand acres of what appeared in studies prepared by Sarah's staff to be fairly suited to the raising of crops as well as providing adequate access to supplies of fresh water and lumber. Those deciding to stay in Florida at North Farm would continue to have access to food supplies from fishing as the target area extended from the beach inland, and it was the intention of Anders and Stuart to leave all boating equipment and fishing supplies to those staying. Most of the maintenance equipment would go, but a basic inventory would remain with the boats.

During this period of increased activity other problems inherent in their situation continued. The incursions from the mainland were ever present but they came in larger groups than before and were better armed. Formerly, they came as individuals hoping to be able to steal a small boat, food or anything they could get their hands on. Now they came armed, in larger groups, intent upon a specific objective and usually with a plan for attaining their objective. Consequently the Defense Force had to upgrade their thinking to cope with the more sophisticated intrusions. There had been an attack on the marina by what initially appeared to be a fairly sizeable band of well armed men. The Marina defenders brought their reserves in to repel the attack and in doing so left a storehouse unguarded some distance from the docks. A separate group of insurgents moved into the storehouse and had it virtually emptied before the Marina troops realized that the initial attack had been nothing more than a diversion. Stuart and the Defense Team staff met after that episode and revised their defenses to adapt to the heightened level of intrusion.

# Chapter Twenty-Two

There had been many other problems in the Association that required resolution as the organization grew in numbers and in social development. Couples living together wished to have their union solemnized in some fashion and likewise, some couples wanted a permanent and final separation from one another. To handle these and the many related administrative problems that could be expected to arise in a community the size of that existing in the Control Zone, Anders appointed Jim McLeod as the Commissioner of Social Affairs. Stuart found the title somewhat amusing, but Anders stuck with it and that was what the sign said above the door in the office assigned to McLeod. The new Commissioner had been an attorney with the Government Justice Department prior to the collapse and was considered one of the few in that office gifted with a good understanding of human nature and willing to apply his understanding to cases at hand.

McLeod met his new responsibilities with enthusiasm. There had been many social problems that had developed by reason of the absence of any judicial authority to deal with the great variety of family problems that arise in any society. There was an immediate flood of cases coming to McLeod's office and he sought and received the assistance of many former practicing attorneys to act as his authorized representatives. In view of the fact that the former national government and all of its attendant financial apparatus had by now disappeared, greatly simplified the disposition of divorce cases in particular. The long and short of it was that there was no longer any property or income to fight over. The more difficult cases that remained dealt with matters of custody and control of minor offspring of the parties. These cases took most of McLeod's time and effort.

# Chapter Twenty-Three

Preparing for the trip to Montana had kept Stuart busy and, consequently, he had no time to worry about the risks involved until it was time to board the small plane for the trip across the country. Trying his best to appear at ease, he strapped himself into the small aircraft as Frick ran through his checklists and warmed up the engine. The weather in Melbourne was clear, although chilling down a bit. The weather en route, according to Sarah's meteorologist, was expected to be at least acceptable. There appeared to be a weather front midway on the trip, but the barometric pressure ranges they had received did not evidence particularly stormy weather. Weather at destination was expected to be clear with ceiling and visibility unlimited.

Stuart was somewhat uncomfortable in the small aircraft and was restricted to carrying a limited amount of baggage as there was no place to store anything. All available space appeared to have been assigned to fuel storage. A large rubber bladder tank occupied what would have been the rear seats in the aircraft and a similar tank occupied what had been the storage locker in the rear part of the fuselage. Normally the aircraft would not be able to fly such long distances without the addition of these tanks. The aircraft was very heavy for the take off and Hans reviewed his take off data a number of times to ensure that he had enough runway to get off the ground. He commented more than once that the cool weather was going to make the difference. Stuart's only reply to that was, "Well, that makes me feel just a hell of a lot better." Frick just looked at his passenger not quite sure what he had meant by the remark. In time he would get to know Stuart and realize that he did not enjoy traveling in an airplane. Frick delayed the departure for the temperature to fall even more as he was concerned that Stuart's baggage and their heavy fuel load well exceeded his allowable limits. When they did depart, they used up virtually the entire runway.

After he was able to relax, Stuart found the trip very interesting as they passed over rural areas, cities, and smaller communities. There were very few signs of functioning electrical power providing lighting for homes or buildings. These, if seen, were usually in small, isolated communities, far from metropolitan areas. They were undoubtedly little oases that had achieved a sufficient level of organization and discipline to establish, at least, the basics of a civilized society. Stuart thought about the problems they were probably dealing with which were the same ones the Association was confronted with on a daily basis. Hopefully, some day in the future, these separate communities could come together and again create a national structure. That was far down the road, if ever, and Stuart questioned that he would ever again see national unity in his lifetime.

The flight continued without incident and they lost sight of the ground for the last half of their trip as they passed over the cold front mentioned in their weather briefing. Frick explained to Stuart that they were flying at a high enough altitude so that they would not have a problem with icing. The temperature at their altitude was well below that which would permit the moisture to cling to the wings of the plane. Stuart was thankful for that as he had never been comfortable in an airplane. In the short time that he had known Frick, he had become quite confident of him as the pilot of the aircraft. Hans had the bearing of a professional as he poured over his charts and graphs and scanned the multitude of instruments in the cockpit, occasionally making adjustments as he saw fit. Frick also had an air of supreme confidence about him which put his passenger, Stuart, at ease. As time passed and the ground was obscured from view, Stuart fell into a deep sleep which continued until Frick woke him when it was time to begin the descent to the landing strip.

Frick had established radio communication with their hosts at the strip and was advised that they were experiencing light snow showers with overcast skies giving a ceiling of about five hundred feet above the strip. Not the good weather they were forecast to have. The report from the ground stated that the strip was well lighted and their hosts were awaiting their arrival. Frick made a remark about another weather briefing down the toilet as he set up his EGPS equipment for the approach to the airstrip. He had acquired the EGPS coordinates and runway heading data from Sarah together with a layout of surrounding terrain and had prepared the approach that he would use for the landing based on this data.

Having accurate approach data had been a concern of Frick's prior to his arrival in the Control Zone, but once having met with Sarah and her staff, his confidence level was raised. While he was at the administration building receiving his weather and intelligence briefing, he drew up the approach data, based on Sarah's information that he would insert into his on board computer for the instrument approach, should the weather at the destination not be as forecast. The EGPS computer system on the aircraft permitted him to create a computerized Initial Approach Point, or IAP, eight hundred feet above the ground, where he would begin his final descent for the landing. The course line from that point to the touchdown was graphically portrayed on his cockpit instruments indicating to him the corrections necessary to stay on the course line. The computer could fly the path to touchdown, but Frick preferred to do the job himself, at least from the IAP on in. As he passed over the IAP, Frick slowed the aircraft to permit extension of the landing gear and flaps. He was picking up some ice, but he assured Stuart that the temperature was too low for serious icing. He continued the descent, following his instruments, and occasionally scanning up to see if he could pick up any signs of the airfield. He saw nothing and noted that he was down to three hundred feet above the ground. His concern was rising as he detected what appeared to be some illumination coming through the falling snow. He continued his descent and slowed the aircraft to the minimum approach speed for his weight. He told Stuart to keep his eyes out ahead to see if he saw the runway. Stuart was leaning forward staring through the windscreen and shouted out that he could see a line of lights just as the aircraft passed through the one hundred foot mark. Frick looked up and saw the airfield lined with lights on either side. Fortunately, they had cleaned off the tarmac so that the black airstrip surface stood out in stark contrast to the white snow on either side. Frick made minimal corrections to his flight path and, moments later, was on the runway, bringing the aircraft to a stop. Stuart was breathing a sigh of relief, having heard the weather briefing and being aware that this was not quite the way it was supposed to be. They saw some vehicles parked over by a small building on the side of the strip and Frick taxied the aircraft over to the adjoining parking area and cut the engine. Stuart stepped out on the wing as three men walked over, raising their arms in greeting to the visitors.

# Chapter Twenty-Four

Captain Monty Wyatt and his patrol had stayed out four more days reconnoitering an area from Melbourne to north of Titusville. They would have stayed out longer, but Wyatt did not want to subject fifteen year old Tracy to any more hardships than she had already endured. For the first couple of days that she had been with them since being rescued in the firefight, she had spoken only a few words. Wyatt figured she was in shock from losing her family and tried to make her as comfortable as he could under the circumstances. She was undernourished and exhausted from the sparse conditions she had lived in with her parents in the basement of the remains of a building in what had been downtown old Melbourne. Wyatt could only imagine what she had been through before being rescued and he did not question her about it. Others in the complex were better equipped to deal with those matters than was he.

After two days of making their way north from Melbourne, usually under cover of darkness and resting in the daytime, Tracy began to take notice of her companions and to ask questions of Wyatt as to where they were going as well as the nature of their group. When they had made camp in some relatively safe location and Monty Wyatt had seen to it that Tracy was made as comfortable as possible, he would sit down with her and explain, as best he could, the makeup of the Association and the life they were leading on the Island. Tracy appeared fascinated by the descriptions that Wyatt provided of the people running the Association and the policies that they had put in effect for the benefit of the residents. It was clear that she had been living in fear for so long and without the basic necessities of life, that the accommodations and resources available to those on the Island, under the protection of the Association, seemed like a dream come true. Every now and then she would slip into a deep depression and go off by herself to the edge of their encampment. Wyatt told her that if she wanted to talk about anything at all, that he was there for her but he did not press the issue as he knew that she would eventually have to learn to deal with her loss herself. Fortunately for everyone in the patrol, they encountered little if any threats in the course of their movement to the north.

They had run into individuals or small groups of foragers who were looking for food or anything of value, but these people took one look at their weapons and took off in the opposite direction. Fortunately, Wyatt's team did not encounter any scouts or patrols from more organized groups although he was well aware that such threats were known to be in the area. That was the purpose of their patrol, to determine the presence and strength of such units. Wyatt would radio the results of their reconnaissance effort to the Intel Command Post every morning following their all night treks. They were to report any evidence of other forces operating in strength in the area, observations of operating motorized vehicles, road conditions, evidence of food or material resources, or any other sighting of significance. Wyatt made his regular report and included the fact that they had the fifteen year old Tracy in their custody and were bringing her back to the Island.

Wyatt knew that Perry would want a full report when they returned as there was a standing rule that patrols were not to pick up any refugees because they would just expose the patrol to additional risks, but to Wyatt, this situation was different. They could not have left the girl where they found her. She would have been dead, or worse, within the hour. Further, Wyatt discovered that the girl had no trouble keeping up with their normal pace and on more than one occasion had spotted people moving in the night shadows before any of the other patrol members saw them. By the third night after she had joined them, Tracy was preparing food at the campsite alongside the men. This had a positive effect on her general attitude and as time went on, she did not seem to be having the spells of depression that Wyatt had observed earlier.

By the fourth day, the patrol had begun an easterly trek, in the general direction of the town of Cocoa which was located across from the north end of the island. Their route would take them through what had been the business section of the small community of Cocoa as that was the route they would have to take to cross the bridge over to the island to the north of the Control Zone. They camped on the outskirts of the town after a night long trek through a relatively uninhabited area to the west of what had been Highway 95. After posting a guard and having something to eat, Wyatt sat back and pondered their situation. He anticipated the probability that they would, very likely, be involved in a firefight or two before they were able to get through the area and he spent some time with Tracy instructing her on how to conduct herself as they made their way through the area and what to do in the event they encountered trouble. Wyatt gave her his flak jacket which he knew Perry would totally object to and told her to stay close to him as they passed through the town. During the day, the guards reported little if any movement in the town but Wyatt knew that people would be there and, more than likely, they would not be friendly. He based that on other patrols they had run to the north out of the Control Zone where they had frequently received rifle fire from the Cocoa side of the Indian River.

As night fell, Wyatt noted that they were fortunate in that the full moon was obscured by cloud cover. Hopefully the overcast condition would last until they had transited the town. At approximately eleven o'clock, Wyatt sent out a scout to lead the way through the town. The remaining members of the patrol, led by Wyatt, followed at intervals. All equipment had been completely muffled so that the team proceeded noiselessly as they began to enter the town. Wyatt maintained contact with the lead scout by way of his helmet head set and would speak with him periodically to ensure their proper separation. They had to detour off the road they were following a number of times as the scout spotted movements of people in their path.

It was close to one in the morning before they reached what appeared to have been the business center of the town. Most of the buildings had been burned and debris littered the streets. Wyatt figured that this would be the area where they would most likely find any organized gang maintaining control of the town. His assumptions proved correct as the scout radioed back to him that there was a group of approximately a hundred armed men in the immediate vicinity of what appeared to have been a court house. The scout had no sooner observed the men than they began fanning out from the court house and taking up positions around the area, including very near to the location in which the scout was now hiding. It appeared they were anticipating some type of problem as they were fully armed and were setting up defensive positions in a very wide perimeter around the court house. When the scout warned Wyatt of their movements, he, and the others in the patrol, took refuge in the shell of a burned out building, again hiding in the basement. He could hear the boot steps and muffled voices of the armed men as they took up positions above them. After a while, all was silent. The scout reported that the lights in the court house were now extinguished and he could detect no movement anywhere.

Obviously something was taking place and Wyatt and his team had wandered into the middle of it. The scout was of the opinion, from what he observed that this was their base of operations. He also reported a number of motor vehicles, including two trucks, all of which appeared to be in operating condition. The finding of the armed group presented a real dilemma to Wyatt as the armed men had them virtually surrounded. The only saving feature to their situation was that they were within two hundred yards of the Indian River and the bridge they had hoped to cross was within sight. Their only other route back to the Island was through the city of Melbourne but in their present situation, that was not a viable option.

Wyatt figured that their present position was approximately ten miles from the Control Zone and, as he thought about their situation, he concluded that he was going to need some assistance in order to get back safely. He advised the scout to keep him posted and to stay out of sight while he called back to the Command Post. Within minutes Wyatt was in contact with Perry and he gave him a report as to their predicament. Following Stuart's established policy for such matters, Perry activated the Tactics Team and within thirty minutes of the first call, a plan to extricate the patrol had been drawn up. A twenty man squad of Nix's men would be dispatched in Thomas' boats and landed south of the bridge a distance of a half mile. They would set up a diversionary attack to hopefully draw the men away from the area of the court house and bridge. A second boat would be dispatched to pick up the patrol at a dock north of the bridge and Perry gave Wyatt the EGPS coordinates for the pickup point. The attack would be launched at 0300 hours and the pickup boat would be in position at 0315. Wyatt acknowledged the plan and confirmed the location of the particular dock on his map. He advised the scout of the plan and told him to keep his eyes open as the armed men apparently had plans of their own for someone else.

The patrol team members and Tracy tried to make themselves as comfortable as possible as they waited for the time to pass. There was not a sound coming from outside of the building they were hiding in and all sign of activity around the court house had ceased. According to the scout, there appeared to be a lone sentry standing at the door of the court house and occasionally a light could be observed inside. All of the armed men had by now secreted themselves in and around the buildings surrounding the court house and it was clear that they were waiting for someone to arrive. Wyatt could hear the crackle of an old style personnel radio in close proximity to his position and occasional bits of conversation that indicated visitors of some type were approaching the court house area. Wyatt stayed in radio contact with his scout and advised him of the imminent arrival and the possibility that there could be trouble of some kind. As the minutes passed, Wyatt looked at his watch and noted that they still had one hour and forty five minutes before the diversionary attack. Hopefully the business taking place above his position would be concluded by that time. As he looked about the dimly lit basement, he noted that Tracy appeared to be asleep on a bundle of newspapers in the corner.

The men in the patrol, having been alerted by Wyatt were awake, alert and prepared for any action that might ensue. As he checked his own gear, he began to hear what sounded like motor vehicles off in the distance. The noise became louder and soon there was the roar of what sounded like heavy machinery coming down the street in the direction of the court house. It was the same street that Wyatt and his squad had just come down and Wyatt was curious as to where they had come from and why they had not been observed previously by the patrol.

The scout had a better view of the source of the noise and reported to Wyatt that there were three armored personnel carriers. He was unable to tell if or how many personnel were aboard but reported that they had pulled in front of the court house and a number of men were getting out. Other men were coming out of the court house building and the two groups were greeting each other. Wyatt told the scout to use his Voice Amplifier and see if he could pick up any of the conversation. Wyatt was very curious as to who was operating such sophisticated military equipment this close to the Control Zone. He had the radio operator place a call back to the Command Post to apprise them of the situation.

The scout came back on frequency and informed Wyatt that the visitors were Cuban and the men in the court house were apparently some sort of organized local group that claimed to control this particular city and the surrounding area out to west of old highway 95. The spokesman of the Cuban group, who was apparently the leader, was politely informing the local leader that they, the Cubans, wished to utilize the area around the bridge for an operation that they were involved in. They wanted the cooperation of the local group, but the Cuban made it very clear that they would be taking possession of the area one way or another and it would be to everyone's benefit if it was done without the necessity of force. The local leader did not take kindly to the threatening remarks and told the Cuban so. Words were exchanged, but, as the scout reported, the 'local' was not putting up much resistance to the Cubans demands. He questioned that the Cubans would leave after their mission was accomplished and the

Cuban countered this with a question as to why they would want to stay where there were no resources and only burned out buildings.

Wyatt was reporting the scouts transmissions back to the Command Post as he was receiving them and by now Perry was handling the messages in the CP. Perry sounded very excited by the information that he was receiving from Wyatt and asked for a description of the Cuban leader if that was possible. Wyatt passed the request on to the scout and was advised that with the limited light, it was very difficult to describe the man, but he appeared to be of slender build, around six foot, mustache, around forty years of age and that was a wild guess, and he seemed to favor his left leg.

Perry passed a message to Wyatt that the diversionary attack and rescue of the patrol would be set back one hour to four and four fifteen. Morning light would not come until around seven so they would still have the benefit of darkness and Wyatt understood that Perry wanted the visitors to leave before they made their rescue move. Wyatt continued to pass on the conversations that the scout was picking up. The two groups apparently were in agreement regarding the temporary occupation of the area around the bridge which would begin in approximately four weeks and would last possibly another four to six weeks after that. The Cubans wanted the locals to withdraw completely from the center of the town and remove themselves to the outskirts pending completion of the Cuban mission. They would be placed back into their present positions when the Cubans had finished their business. The locals were not to interfere in any activities that might take place while the Cubans were in town. The local leader inquired as to what activities might be taking place and the Cuban leader told him that was none of his business, just to stay out of anything that might occur.

It was clear to Wyatt that the Cubans were planning some sort of combat mission. The question was, involving who. The men conferred for another half an hour, primarily on the logistics of moving the Cuban force into the town, the expected dates when the transfer of men and equipment would take place and how further radio communications between the two groups would take place. This last bit of information was considered most valuable and was immediately passed on to Perry in the Command Post. There was the possibility that the frequencies or transmissions would be scrambled somehow, but Wyatt knew from prior missions that Sarah Taves and her staff were proficient at deciphering such communications.

When the major points of the meeting had been taken care of, the Cubans again reentered their vehicles and departed back down the street from where they came. The local leaders continued talking in loud, angry voices on the steps of the court house and it was clear that they were incensed at the treatment they had received, but they were also aware of their inferior strength and were in no position to argue with their new guests. They continued arguing with one another as they reentered the building at which time the scout reported that he could no longer receive anything on his voice amplifier. The armed men that had been positioned around the court house square began coming out of their positions and walking over to the court house. Some of them had been close enough to the principals that they had overheard parts of the conversation and they passed on what they had heard to the others. As the men became aware of the Cuban demands, their voices were raised in anger with some calling for an attack on the Cubans if they tried to return. Others in the group were silent or counseled against getting into a hassle with the Cubans. They had heard of their military force and it far surpassed anything the locals could generate.

In time the men began to disperse to their various shelters as a cadre of guards was placed around the area to ensure the security of their operating base. The scout reported the various sentry positions and it was clear that the patrol was not going to get out of their hiding places without being observed. Wyatt had no doubt that the armed men in the group would be out in force within minutes of an alarm. He radioed back to the Command Post that the meeting had concluded, but that their situation still required the plan to extricate them. Perry assured him that the rescue mission was going ahead as planned and to be at the dock at the appointed time.

At three thirty in the morning, Wyatt gathered everyone in the basement around him as he showed them their present position on the map and the location of the pickup point on the map. He explained the route that they would take upon leaving the building and the precautionary measures they would use in order to arrive at the dock safely. Tracy, again, was to stay with Wyatt. They would pass by the position of the scout and he would join them there. They would not fire on anyone unless fired upon. They did not want to draw any attention to themselves until they were safely out of there. According to the scout, there were two or three sentries that were in a position to observe them when they left their building. If these sentries were not drawn out of position by the diversionary attack, they would have to be suppressed.

Wyatt gathered three of his best men around him and pointed out the sentry positions on the map. They were all in second story windows of burned out buildings and would be difficult to take out but Wyatt's plan called for the group to cross the street and move along the wall of the buildings underneath where the sentries were located making it difficult for Wyatt's squad to be observed. Wyatt's take out men were to stay on the far side of the street watching for any sign the sentries were taking action against the main part of the squad. If such action was noted, the take out men were to use their scoped and silencer equipped AR20s and remove the threat. Hopefully it would all be done quietly and not draw the attention of any of the locals. If all went as planned, the diversionary attack would draw the sentries out of their positions along with the other renegades down to the attack point, south of the court house. Perry had also made it clear to Wyatt and Wyatt passed this along to his men, they were not to kill or injure any of the local force unless it was absolutely necessary. It was not clear at this point who the locals were or whether or not the Association may wish to have further dealings with them at some future point in time. There was no sense in "pissing them off," as Perry stated.

The diversionary attack was going to be mostly a noise making affair with percussion grenades and no use of mortars, missiles or heavier weapons was planned unless it became necessary. It was to be quick, noisy and out of there. Wyatt figured that their route to the dock would take them eight minutes, moving with caution and not running into any problems. The plan was to leave the building at exactly four o five and that would give them an extra two minutes to get to the dock and board the boat. The diversion would end at the same time as they were getting on their own rescue boat and hopefully, they would all travel safely back to the Marina. At four o'clock, straight up, loud explosions were heard coming from the area south of the court house. Sentries were pointing to the south at the flashes of light in the sky and shouting to their companions that they were under attack. Men were running from buildings and from the court house, to the south, towards the river with their weapons at the ready. They were a fairly well organized group as they seemed to be forming into tactical squads with specific unit leaders who were yelling out commands to the men. Wyatt had positioned himself up the stairway leading out of the basement so that he could observe how they were reacting to the attack. The scout reported that two of the three sentries had left their positions and joined those running to the river.

The third scout had stayed in position and could be seen silhouetted in the burned out window frame of the building adjacent to Wyatt's position. Wyatt pointed him out to the man assigned and reminded him not to take him out unless it was absolutely necessary. The sentry was watching the activity and the reaction of his own troops and was not looking towards the building where the patrol was located. The problem was that the scout would not be able to leave his building without being seen if the sentry continued to be focused in that direction.

The 'take out' patrol member grabbed Wyatt's arm and suggested that he could put the sentry down without killing him. It was now four o' two and Wyatt told him he had three minutes to do the job. The squad member slowly, noiselessly, made his way across the street and into the building where the sentry was stationed. In less than two minutes, he was in the window where the sentry had been and was signaling to Wyatt that the job was done. At exactly four o five, Wyatt, Tracy and the squad members, amid all the commotion coming from the diversionary attack, departed the safety of their hiding place and made their way, in single file along the darkened building, picking up the scout as they passed his position, moving towards the area of the docks. They saw many men in the vicinity of the court house, but their attention was focused in the opposite direction and they were not spotted. They had to take shelter only one time on their way to the dock as additional men running towards the action, passed through their route of travel.

They saw no one in the area of the dock and as they ran out onto the concrete pier, they saw the cigarette boat lying in the shadows of the warehouse alongside the pier. The driver of the boat expertly positioned the boat by the stairway on the side of the pier and within minutes the entire squad and Tracy were safely in the boat and on their way back to the Marina. As they passed the diversionary attack target, they saw the other cigarette boat, outlined by the burning buildings, coming towards them at high speed. Both boats hugged the opposite shore as a hail of bullets fell short in the water behind them. Monty Wyatt covered Tracy with his arms as they made their way to safety towards the marina.

# Chapter Twenty-Five

Jack Nix and Ross Perry had spent hundreds of hours poring over the wealth of information provided to them by Sarah for the fuel mission. The obvious problem for them was how to get the tanker out of the harbor without suffering heavy losses of men and materials and most likely the target ship as well. The port area was heavily guarded as their later intelligence showed them and the armed guards controlling the ship were part of a large, well organized group of renegades that virtually controlled all of Jacksonville. They undoubtedly had the resources to defend one of their prize possessions and would not just sit back and watch the vessel disappear over the horizon. Both Nix and Perry had concluded that there was no reasonably safe way they would be able to take over the ship and pull it or drive it out of the harbor. There had to be another way of getting the fuel. After considering various alternatives that led nowhere, Nix voiced his conclusion that the only way they could do the job was if the guards did not know the fuel was being stolen. Perry looked at him with a quizzical look and asked, "Just how do you propose to do that?"

Nix replied, drumming his pencil as he stared out into space, obviously deep in thought. "I don't know, but I'll bet there is a way we could pull the fuel out of the hull, bag it and haul it away with nobody the wiser on the boat or on the wharf. What we do need right now is some help from people who know more about that stuff than we do."

Nix and Perry talked with Sarah about their need for technical assistance and they were soon put in touch with a former NASA technician with training and experience in laser welding techniques and a fuel tanker crewmember who had spent his lifetime crewing and maintaining tankers on the great lakes before retiring. Both men were cleared for access to mission materials by Sarah before they were briefed on the task at hand

and were made familiar with the limitations the target location presented as well as the security that would have to be penetrated. When they were on speed with the task at hand, the two technicians met with Perry and Nix in the intel briefing room and the four men got to work on figuring out how to accomplish the mission.

The tanker crewmember was familiar with the type of boat that was involved and proceeded to describe the general interior layout to the other three. Nix and Perry listened intently as the crewmember drew the general layout of the tanker, explaining that the fuel stored in the tanker was contained in approximately twenty separate compartments with their own transfer pumps operated independently from the bridge of the ship. Most likely, in view of the fact only small quantities of fuel were being removed at a time, the fuel was coming from just one or two compartments. The concern of those in charge of the ship and its cargo was primarily to maintain a reasonable center of balance or gravity for the vessel as the fuel was being offloaded. He went on to explain that the hull of the vessel, on the bottom, was usually three inch metal alloy plate and the storage tank structure was normally specified at one to two inch titanium for weight reduction and corrosion resistance.

The storage tanks in the vessel were supported by alloy frames that were integrated with the structure of the vessel itself. Nix questioned the man, in depth, regarding access to the fuel storage tanks from inside the vessel and was advised that all tanks were accessible by crewmembers but it was not common practice to do so unless maintenance was required. He doubted that with the vessel permanently tied up to the pier that anyone would be down on the narrow catwalks looking at the storage tanks. Virtually all of the crew activity on the boat would take place in the area of the engine room and the boiler room with some activity forward in the dry storage space at the front of the vessel. The mid section of the ship carried the fuel storage tanks and the fuel in each tank was accessible in the control room merely by selecting various transfer pumps. Nix also questioned the man as to how fuel could be taken out of the tanks without the knowledge of crewmembers on the vessel. The crewmember looked at him and chuckled as he stated that the only way that could be done, to his knowledge, was if it was drawn out the bottom of the ship in the dark of night.

Nix commented, more to himself than the others at the table, that that was exactly what he had in mind. In response to questions from Perry, the crewmember estimated the total full fuel capacity of the vessel at two hundred thousand gallons of fuel with approximately ten thousand in each storage tank.

Nix now turned his attention to the NASA engineer and began questioning him as to how the hull of the vessel could be penetrated without anyone being aware that it was occurring. The engineer explained that underwater metal work was not new and had been going on since the middle of the last century and had been significantly technically advanced in the years before the collapse of the government when most activities of that type ceased completely. There were men still around the area that were proficient in the art who had more firsthand knowledge of it than he did.

The engineer went on to explain that laser technology had advanced to the point where he was certain that the hull of the ship could be penetrated as it sat in the slip but that obviously measures would have to be taken to prevent the vessel from sinking. Nix suggested that a capsule be constructed that could be fastened to the bottom of the tanker that would permit one or two men to work inside as they removed the plate and further to act as a platform for the additional work they would have to perform to penetrate the storage tank. The engineer nodded, indicating that this was certainly possible and that the capsule could be made airtight and secured to the bottom of the vessel without the knowledge of the crewmembers working the ship. Nix could tell that the engineer was becoming more interested in the project as he added that a mechanism would have to be installed in the capsule to catch the fuel coming out of the storage tank once that was penetrated. After a bit, he said, "That is not a difficult problem."

The tanker crewmember, now seeing the potential of the plan, added that, "You also have to pump something into the fuel tank or pulling ten thousand gallons of diesel fuel out will be evident to the men on the boat as it begins to rise in the water. You could pump seawater into the hull of the ship and as long as it was being balanced by the fuel leaving, no one would be the wiser unless someone came down to inspect the tanks." Nix and Perry saw they now had the rapt attention of their two advisors. Nix went on, "The next question is how we remove the fuel from the harbor area. Obviously we have to run it into some type of tank or bladder that will not float to the surface. As I recall, fuel is lighter than seawater and will go to the surface. The depth of the water in the vicinity of the tanker is forty feet. What type of a container will do the job and can it be maneuvered in and out of the harbor without detection."

The four men, with their interest in the challenging project now peaked, worked on well into the night discussing the details of the plan. They concluded that a large bladder tank, or tanks, appropriately weighted as they took on the fuel could do the job. The tricky part was the weights and maneuvering the bladders out of the harbor. The engineer suggested that other engineers still in the area of the Control Zone be brought in on the project. He added that they would be more than eager to participate as they had not had a solid challenge like this in years. Nix delegated the engineering matters to the NASA man and assigned the tanker crewmember to him as well for technical assistance. He advised both that they were not to talk about this to anyone without first having that person or persons cleared by Sarah Taves' Intel Team. In the meantime, Nix and Perry would work on mission planning. The total number of men needed for the project would have to await the final engineering workup, but the general mission outline could begin.

Stuart was still in Montana when Anders was notified by Perry's Defense Team that they were picking up radar echoes out on the ocean, apparently heading for the channel entrance. Anders immediately thought of the instructions that were given to Carlos Moran for delivery to Paco Morales of the Cuban National Socialist Party.

Anders called Sarah and Perry into his office and instructed the Command Post to keep him informed as to the vessels progress. Perry had already sent armed vessels under Thomas out to check on the identity of the boats and had provided him with the radio frequencies that Moran was given when he left the Control Zone. Thomas was to notify Perry just as soon as he had made an identification of the boats. Anders' immediate concern related to the information brought back to the Control Zone by way of Captain Wyatt's patrol. He was deeply disturbed that they were being set up by the Cubans and questioned that the Cuban force at Cocoa was under the command of the CNSP. Perry had the same concerns as did Sarah, but she also suggested that the Cuban Liberation Party was also active nearby and they could be involved.

All three decided that they would deal cautiously with their visitors if in fact they were from the Morales Group. If they had not arrived at a consensus regarding the identity of the Cocoa group at the conclusion of the meeting with their visitors, it was decided that they would bring the matter out in the open and see how Morales or his envoys handled that. They were still deeply engrossed in their plans for the meeting when word came from Thomas that the boats were, indeed, those belonging to Morales. In keeping with the instructions, there were only three boats, all lightly armed and carrying a minimum complement of men. Thomas recognized Carlos Moran on the lead vessel and waved to him when he got his attention. Moran had made a favorable impression on those he was involved with when he was in the Control Zone and Thomas was glad to see that he was part of the negotiating team sent by the Cubans.

The Cuban boats followed Thomas to the Marina and pulled into slips assigned to them as the dock boys passed lines to the crewmembers to secure their vessels. Anders and his staff had decided that it would be best if they remained in the administration building and sent others down to greet the visitors on their behalf. The principals in the Cuban group appeared to be Carlos Moran who was acting primarily as the intermediary and three other older men who were obviously high ranking members of the Morales Group. They were an impressive team, saying little and acting in a very professional manner as they greeted their hosts. Andy Moss had been assigned to bring them to the administration building and to see to their needs while they were on the Island. He assured them that comfortable quarters had been provided for them and their crews and if they wished, they could first retire to those quarters before meeting with the leaders of the Association. The Cubans assured them that they were prepared to proceed with the meetings and Andy escorted them to the administration building. As they walked up to the Building the Cubans commented as to the cleanliness of the area and how well organized everything appeared to be. Moss could tell from the looks of surprise on their faces that they were not used to seeing a community of people with their lives so well under control as those living in the Association.

Anders had established tight security on the administration building and surrounding grounds and consequently there was no one else present in or around the building other than the principals involved and their own security guards. Anders greeted the men cordially and introduced Sarah as a member of his staff. The visitors all identified themselves and provided a brief description of their responsibilities in their own organization. Anders made notes as they spoke and was overall impressed by their businesslike manner and the way they, in general, handled themselves. They all spoke excellent English which indicated to Anders that they had obviously spent considerable time in the United States either before the collapse or after. After they were seated, Anders inquired as to the whereabouts of Carlos Moran who had apparently been with the party at the Marina. The visitor who appeared most junior in the pecking order explained that Carlos did not become involved in matters at this level and consequently had remained with the other Cubans at the Marina.

Perry was disappointed that Carlos was not present as he had said beforehand that he could read Carlos like a book and if any 'bullshit' was being passed out, he would be a good book to have around. Perry suggested that Carlos be called in as he was familiar with some of the physical features of the Association property that may be of interest to the Cuban emissaries and was further the one who delivered the invitation to negotiate. Not having a valid reason to exclude him, the leader nodded in assent and Carlos was soon joining the party at the table. Perry was seated directly across from Carlos where he could observe him as matters were being discussed.

Anders led off the discussions, again getting right to the point as was his style. He explained, briefly, the organization of the Association bringing out the fact that what he had to say in the course of the negotiations would be the official position of his group. He assumed that the leader of the Cuban party, now identified as Ernesto could likewise speak with authority on behalf of the Cuban National Socialist Party and Paco Morales. Ernesto assured him that he had full authority to speak on behalf of his organization and that Anders could rely on anything he had to say.

Anders then proceeded into the heart of the discussion. He explained that they intended to leave the island within two months for another location across country. They wished to accomplish that move with a minimum of difficulty and risk. That was why they were talking with the Morales Group. Anders went on that it was a well known fact that the Morales Group controlled extensive territories to the south of the Control Zone and would in time, more than likely, attempt to take control of Melbourne and the Island. The purpose of this meeting for the Association was to negotiate an agreement with the Cubans that was mutually beneficial and to prevent any bloodshed between the two groups.

The Cubans all nodded in agreement with the general purpose as explained by Anders and Ernesto assured Anders that the Cubans were of like mind. Ernesto, at this point, also interjected that the Morales Group did have interests in the Melbourne area as it was their intended purpose to expand their area of influence to a Tampa-Orlando-Melbourne line. Anders told him he appreciated his candor and that Anders would be speaking as frankly and candidly himself.

Anders discussed their proposed departure date and method of transportation as well as a general idea of the number of people leaving and the number that were expected not to leave. This was a matter of some importance to Anders as he wanted assurances from the Cubans that those staying would be treated well and not oppressed by the Cubans. Ernesto explained at some length the methods that they had used in taking over new territories and the fact that they had experienced few if any problems with the locals that came under their control. Sarah had done extensive intelligence on this subject and what Ernesto had to say conformed to the information Sarah had produced. Anders then brought up the matter of safe passage through all areas controlled by the CNSP and Ernesto assured him that would be the case. Other matters of a logistics nature were discussed at length.

The Cubans were very interested in what facilities were available in the Control Zone for water purification, sewage, housing, food resources, and other matters of a generally civic nature. They were also curious as to other forces operating in the area, whether organized or renegade groups. Anders handled the civic matters and Sarah Taves provided the data regarding intrusions into the Control Zone as well as a summary of Patrol reports submitted by Captain Wyatt and others relating to conditions on the mainland. She did not mention the matter of the Cubans in the Cocoa area. Anders would handle that later.

Up to this point in the meeting, Anders had been favorably impressed by their Cuban guests and was doubting that they were, in any manner, trying to set up the Association. During a break, Anders, Perry and Sarah got together in Anders office and discussed the matter of the Cuban activity in the Cocoa area. It was agreed that Anders would lay the cards out on the table and they could see what happened. As they were about to leave Ander's office, Perry commented, "None of them limp." Sarah and Anders both said that was one of the first things they had looked for as the Cubans had entered the conference room.

Sitting back at the table, Anders suggested that the Cubans assign a liaison officer to work with one of Anders staff people in taking care of the details of the transfer. He again brought out the fact that the leadership of the Association did not know what type of reaction they would receive from those not leaving for the new location. He finished by saying that he was fairly certain the entire business could be handled amicably but it was still up in the air. As they were about to finish up their business, Anders got their attention, saying, "We have one problem that we are very interested in resolving and that is we are aware of a Cuban military operation of some type currently taking place in the Cocoa area which is some ten to fifteen miles north of our Control Zone." As he said the words, Sarah and Perry intently watched the reaction of the Cubans. All of the Cubans in the room showed surprise and disbelief at the news.

Ernesto interrupted Anders with a series of questions, how many were involved, what type of equipment, where had they come from and many more. Before Anders could answer, Ernesto turned his attention to one of his companions and angrily asked, "What is this about?" The reply of, "I have no idea" did not satisfy Ernesto. "That is your job to know. I want a full report on this as soon as we return."

Ernesto again directed his attention towards Anders, asking a series of questions directed at further identification of the group, the size of the force and so on. Anders provided the information as he knew it and stated further that from the information the Association had regarding the Cubans in Cocoa, they were planning some sort of military exercise in the area and the only likely target that Anders could come up with was the Association complex. Ernesto calmed down a bit as he pondered the information that Anders had given to him. "It must be the CLP, the Cuban Liberation Party. I had no idea they were operating this far to the north. I will be frank, we are competing with them for South Florida and they are our number one enemy. I might add, they are ruthless in their military operations and you do not want to have them around. Also, I might add, you cannot trust them in any respect. We tried, through negotiations a few times, and got burned every time. Now we just shoot first and discuss later. That seems to get their respect."

Anders brought out that the Cuban leader in Cocoa had indicated that their military operation would commence in about four weeks and included a takeover of the Cocoa area presently held by a small armed local group whose politics were unknown. Anders added that the local group was not happy about the takeover which might be of future interest. He then mentioned the description of the Cuban leader including the matter of the limp. This brought an immediate reaction from Ernesto. "It is the CLP. That's Ricardo Ortega, the number three man in the organization. He handles military operations and his being there indicates that they have something of substance in mind. They have been operating primarily along the west coast of Florida, on the other side of the everglades aiming at the Tampa-St.Pete area. They must be looking at this area as an anchor to what they hope will be an east west line across Florida." Ernesto continued talking as he pondered the situation. "That doesn't make sense though. Their supply line would be strung out and vulnerable. They are not stupid. They must know we have an interest in this area and are planning on a quick strike when we least expect it and they will head back to the west."

Ernesto paused and then looked up at his two companions. "How do they know we are moving into this particular area?" He paused again. "We must have a mole in our operation." He thought about that and went on, "We'll feed the mole and maybe he will show his face." Ernesto looked at Anders as he continued. "We will pass the word in our organization that we are taking over this area in four weeks. We will position a force north of Melbourne and wait for our friends to make their way to what appears to be their launching point. We will then hit them from behind but we will need you to defend the other side of the Indian River. That should not be too difficult as they are not expecting any resistance in crossing the bridge. You should be able to hold the bridge without significant loss of life."

Anders mentioned that the Cocoa Cubans did have armored vehicles and presumably may have tanks. He also mentioned that the Association had anti tank weapons but Ernesto should be aware of what he was facing. Anders went on by saying the Association Defense Team could handle the mission and they may as well take care of this threat early on rather than face them en route during their trip out of the area. The CLP could also be interested in the resources the Association would be taking with them. Just to make sure that everyone in the room understood, Anders concluded by saying that whoever might try to attack them en route would pay a terrible price, successful or not.

It was agreed that a Cuban liaison officer would be assigned and sent to the Control Zone in the next day or so. Also, radio frequencies and scramblers were exchanged for future communications so that details of the transfer could be worked out. There was to be no mention of transfer dates as this information was considered too critical for transmission. When the basic negotiating matters had been covered sufficiently, the Cubans thanked their hosts, immediately boarded their boats and with an escort by Robert Thomas and a security force, departed the area.

# Chapter Twenty-Six

Stuart had received word by radio from Sarah regarding the meeting with the Cuban delegation. He was not provided all of the details but he was informed that matters were proceeding as planned. Stuart had been very busy since landing at the airport in Riverton, the only town of any size in the Valley and the site of the negotiations. After a brief rest in the quarters that he was to occupy for the next week, he met with the principal representatives of the Valley organization. The three men, who spoke on behalf of the Valley residents, were all ranchers from families that had been living in the area for generations.

After one or two days of general discussions, it became clear to Stuart that the one calling the shots was Matt Parker who ranched three thousand acres north of town. Parker was relatively quiet in the meetings, but whenever he made a suggestion, the others quickly adopted it without question. He was apparently a power in the community and as Stuart began to realize, for good reason. He was very intelligent, well read, a successful businessman, somewhere in his sixties, and didn't waste his time on anything that was not worthy of his attention.

Parker was very interested in the makeup of the proposed new residents and for good reason as their numbers would, if Stuart's estimates were correct, exceed the existing resident population of the Valley. Parker wanted to ensure that bringing that many people onto their land would not create more problems than it would solve. The initial discussions revolved around educating each other as to the resources that would be brought to the valley and the resources presently in place.

Stuart first explained the demographics of the residents of the Association that he expected would make the journey to Montana. He had been provided the data by Sarah and the figures were impressive. They included three medical doctors, all badly needed by the Valley residents, electricians, plumbers, carpenters, mechanics, teachers, and representatives of virtually every trade and profession imaginable. Of the three hundred adults expected to make the trip, two hundred and fifty had college degrees or the equivalent thereof. Seventy five had graduate level degrees and forty seven had doctorate degrees, mostly in engineering disciplines of one form or another. Three fourths of the men had served in the military and fifty-five had served to retirement. Stuart laid out the age groupings with the majority of the proposed residents in the twenty to fifty age group and very few in the over sixty group. Children and youths under twenty accounted for twenty percent.

Parker asked a number of questions relating to the general health of the group, their intentions with respect to their new life in the Valley, the organization of schools and medical facilities that would be needed to educate and provide care for them after they settled in the Valley.

Stuart had expected to deal with these issues and explained to Parker and the others that the Association had established an educational system and medical care for the members of the Association. He went on to explain that these organizations and the materials necessary for their continued operation would be brought with the Association residents when they made their move to Montana.

Parker did pick up on the weak point in Stuart's presentation which was that the Association had not yet been informed of the move and consequently, Stuart could not predict with absolute certainty who would make the trip and what assets they would be able to bring with them. Stuart addressed that issue with an explanation as to their present situation in Florida, the threats to their continued occupation and control of the island where they resided and the limited options available to them. Stuart estimated that more would want to make the trip than they would be able to support during transit and he was more concerned with how to deal with that problem than whether or not he would have volunteers for the journey. His explanation seemed to satisfy Parker and the others.

After Stuart had explained the resources that they would bring to the Valley, one of their representatives laid out the data relating to the Valley residents. The population figures that he gave were fairly close to those that Sarah had estimated. The present Valley population was 357 with over fifty percent in the over fifty age group. The less than twenty age group accounted for only seven percent and the forty to fifty age group made up thirty percent of the population. It was very apparent that the Valley was presently occupied by an aging population and the proposed influx of new residents should have a beneficial effect.

When the population figures had been exchanged between the two parties, Parker took over the discussion. "Based on your estimates of three to four hundred people coming to this area, we have, through some pretty tough negotiations with some of our residents, come up with a plot of land north of Riverton and along the River, that should be a good site for you all to take up residence. The land has only been used for cattle grazing, as that was the mainstay of the Valley before things went to hell...but just where are you going to ship beef off to nowadays without getting shot. The market is gone. I suppose it'll come back someday, but I'll be dead and buried when it does. In the meantime, all the farmers and ranchers are using their land to produce what we need here in the valley to exist. Food crops primarily with some of the guys providing fleece from their sheep farms for the woolen mill that we have set up here in Riverton. We even make our own clothes now. Unfortunately we can't raise cotton here... at least we haven't figured out how to do that with our climate, but wool seems to do the job... that and leather, of which we have a large supply. Anyway, we have land set aside consisting of twenty thousand acres of good crop and grazing land. That should amply provide for your people. We will also take steps to see that you have sufficient food supplies to see your people through to their first food crop and will also provide the farm animals that you all will need to provide for your other needs. We will teach your people how to farm, grow crops and care for farm animals. We will, in general, see that you are all provided for through the initial period of your getting settled."

Stuart did not expect this much assistance from the Valley residents and was heartened by what he was hearing and what he had seen since his arrival. The townspeople had all appeared friendly to him and they were apparently well aware of who he was and the purpose of his visit. A very few people appeared somewhat cold to him, but that was to be expected and they were in the distinct minority. Stuart was also impressed by the orderly appearance of the town. Public areas appeared to be kept clean and he saw no sign of graffiti which had become commonplace in public areas of Florida that he was familiar with. The Control Zone occupied by the Association residents was free of graffiti, but that was the result of a crackdown on the youthful offenders that put them on cleanup details for extended periods of time when they were apprehended. After a while, their supposed artwork had literally disappeared. Possibly the same scenario had taken place here in Riverton.

Stuart sat listening to Parker and absorbing the possibilities of what he was hearing. It was clear that Parker was not making his offer free of charge and that soon became apparent as Parker continued. "Now I am sure that you are pleased with what we are prepared to provide in order to make your move as comfortable as possible under the circumstances. Let me assure you that I had considerable difficulty in obtaining these generous concessions from the farmers and townsfolk living in the Valley. Some were easier to deal with than others, but all were a bit wary of opening our doors to complete strangers. In providing you with the resources to take up a new life, we expect certain benefits in return. Before I get to that, let me tell you a bit more about the organization we have set up in the Valley. I want to make certain that what we have is compatible with what you are experiencing or expecting. We are a very Christian community of people who are very involved with their families, their church and their community. I would have to say their focus is in that order, family, church, community. We have virtually no crime. We have established a police and defense force but we are aware that in time, with increasing unrest in areas outside of the Valley that what we have will not be adequate. We are by nature not familiar with or particularly interested in military matters. We expect your organization to generally conform to our sense of moral values and to provide the technical expertise to provide our people with a better standard of living than they presently enjoy. That means upgrading our electrical system, water system, plumbing system and the infrastructure needed to support a community of our size. We have 'made do' since the collapse of the government in all of these areas and quite frankly, we lack the technical, engineering experience and training to do the job properly. We have been interested in your group primarily for the defense assistance that you tell us you can provide and also for the high level of technical experience and training you possess. We are providing you with extensive valuable resources and we expect an organized extensive program of technical assistance in return. Before we finalize our commitment as I have laid it out to you, we want a formal, written reply laying out how your people will provide our community with the technical and I should add educational assistance that we so desperately need. We will review your proposal and we will then accept it as is, or with modifications, or will reject it as being too far off target."

Stuart thought for a moment before responding to get his thoughts in order. "I don't think that we will have any problem providing you with what you want and need. We have considered that from the get-go as we are a rather unique community in that we have a very high percentage of our population holding advanced degrees and great experience in areas that would provide any community with hard-to-find resources. We have always considered that our main selling point and we are prepared to utilize those resources to the fullest to improve the lives of residents of the area that we finally take on as our new home. We have organized our defense force primarily for our own benefit as we live in a very unstable part of the country and we are further going to have to travel through rough country in order to take up our new homes elsewhere. In the process we have built up a very sizeable, well trained and well supplied military force that would be the envy of most if not all communities such as yours." Stuart went on, explaining again the organization of the Association, the branches of their government and the services that they provided: The policing function, the court system, the juvenile system, youth homes, the educational system, the intelligence unit, and the executive council acting as the supreme authority over the management of the Association by Anders and Stuart. He also discussed briefly the work of the study group and their responsibilities in laying out a road map for future organization of the Association. Along that line, Stuart opened up the matter of what form of governing authority the Valley residents had in mind in view of the fact that there was no sign of an organized regional or national government coming into existence in the foreseeable future. Stuart suggested that this could well be the most important matter that should be discussed between the two parties.

Parker concurred and inquired as to what Stuart and his group had in mind. Stuart explained that for the present, a fairly tightly controlled management style seemed to be most effective in their presently somewhat precarious state. In time, it was generally thought by most people in the Association that they would take up a more representative form of government than the system under which they presently operated. That was one purpose of the study group, to come up with proposals for submission to the Association. Parker listened attentively as Stuart responded to his question and nodded in agreement when he had concluded.

Parker explained that the Valley residents had been involved with other challenges in their lives in the past few years than setting up a governmental organization and as a result Parker and the others in the room had taken it upon themselves to provide a very limited form of civic leadership when matters of community interest came about. So far that had sufficed and no one had complained. Obviously, in time something more formal would have to be established and from what Stuart had to say, it sounded as though their general objectives were similar.

Stuart was busy from morning to night, familiarizing himself with what the Valley had to offer.

Parker acted as Stuart's guide and Stuart found himself enjoying the company of this soft spoken rancher who, although successful, had endured a life of long days and hard work in the unforgiving Montana ranch land. Parker took Stuart to the land along the river that had been selected for the new residents. Stuart liked what he saw. The land was relatively flat on either side of the river and was elevated enough above the rapidly flowing stream to be safe from the dangers of spring flooding which was a problem in these areas with the heavy snow runoff in the mountains. The northern part of the proposed landsite consisted of woodlands which should provide ample lumber supplies for building the homes and structures that would be needed by the new residents. Pine, spruce, fir and cedar grew in great quantities in the woodland and could be floated down the river and milled on site.

Stuart also considered the possibility of using the river to generate electrical power, but with limited knowledge in such matters, he would leave that up to others. Stuart was not knowledgeable on soils and what made some fertile and others barren, but from what he could tell, the soil in the area appeared rich and black and corresponded in appearance to the soils on some of the farms in the areas that were said to be producing bountiful crops. He discussed with Parker the crops and other uses that could be made of the proposed Association land site. Parker explained to Stuart that the area was one of the most fruitful in what was formerly the entire State of Montana. He himself had concentrated on raising Angus and Hereford cattle for which the rangelands in the Valley were particularly well suited, but small farmers along the river running the length of the Valley had successfully raised good crops of wheat and barley, and using the river for irrigation, had raised sugar beets, potatoes and other crops for shipment to markets outside of the Valley.

There was no doubt that the natural layout of the Valley, with the river running through its entire length, would well provide for all of the new residents as well as those presently there. Parker went on to describe the other uses that could be made of the land, including cattle and sheep for beef, leather and wool, and dairy animals for milk production and other dairy products. As he continued to describe the wealth of natural resources in the area, Stuart watched him become visibly excited about what this area had to offer and Stuart was convinced in his own mind that the Valley could well provide for the needs of the Association residents. He liked what he saw and was very impressed with Parker and the others that he had met in the course of his visit.

Parker told Stuart that for years before the Collapse, the ranchers knew it was coming because in their business, they were so susceptible to the vagaries of the national economy that the ranchers watched it like a hawk. They saw how the national government was, piece by piece, destroying the economic stimulation that was the necessary ingredient in fueling the economy. The 1980s had been called the "Decade of Greed", but that was nothing compared to the huge profits taken by the "Robber Barons" of the 1990s who, Parker referred to as the "Imperial Elite" consisting of the political, corporate, media and entertainment moguls with multimillion dollar salaries, bonuses, stock deals and other benefits at the expense of a constantly declining and disappearing middle class. It was the middle class, Parker went on, that supported not only the cattle business, but virtually every other business in the country. The government bureaucracy was strangling the middle class small business operators and mid level executives, professionals, and trades people with high taxes and over regulation. The 1990s saw a decline in small business enterprises, but that was nothing compared to what happened in the next decade. The corporate crimes of the 1990s were overshadowed by a decade long apparent growth in the national economy.

Unfortunately, the growth of the economy in the 90s was really nothing more than a shell game. A true shell game, because there was nothing under the shell. National debt was increasing, inflation was increasing, personal net worth, in real terms, was declining, and all that was missing for a total collapse was an initiating cause. That occurred in the decades after the turn of the century when crop failure after crop failure hit the country at the same time as global economic depression. Then everything hit the wall with inflation out of control as the government was incapable of stopping the spending spree that it had been on for the previous fifty years. The Valley ranchers had ample time to prepare and were ready for the collapse when it hit. They had been growing and storing their own food crops for a number of years before the rest of the country realized what was happening. Cattle ranchers continued beef production, but on a much smaller scale. They were now also farmers growing crops for themselves and others, at first for others both in the Valley and outside to other markets. After a while, all production of food crops was for Valley residents only as they closed off contact with the outside world for their own protection. Some of the ranchers tried to continue solely as producers of beef, but they soon learned that times had changed and their cattle were now more valuable for their hides than for their beef.

During those transition years, the various Militia groups operating in Montana had grown in numbers and strength and there was the thought that in time, they would take over the entire state. It was a surprise to many that such did not occur. The various militia units were all led by men who were not willing to work with others or other groups to attain a greater good. They were invariably led by men who acted towards the achievement of a single purpose. Usually a purpose that was not commonly held by others and consequently one that did not lend itself to popular conversion necessary to create a massive movement. As a result, the various militia organizations that continued to exist through the economic collapse and the collapse of the government and to the present time did not present that great a threat to people such as those living in the valley because they were not able to generate a sufficient following to overcome the defenses Valley residents were able to present. Parker was not concerned with the threat that Militias presented, although they had to be watched because they were out there. Parker also commented that some of the Militia units that he had come in contact with were basically defense forces acting on behalf of a particular geographical area and were no more a threat to adjoining populations than was the Valley Police Force.

Parker was more concerned with what he saw coming in the future than what they were presently faced with. At some time in the future others, more persuasive with respect to their political or ideological views, would emerge and they would be able to generate mass followings with notions of expanding into the territories of others. These would be the ones that one should prepare for because they were sure to come. It was only a matter of time. Whenever a massive population as existed in this country was leaderless and suffering, sooner or later, out of the mire, would come false prophets to lead them to the Promised Land and they would follow. Parker had not discussed these thoughts with his fellow Valley residents because he questioned that they saw what was happening and what was eventually going to come. They would have to be led, over time, to a realization that a substantial growth in their organization was necessary for their survival. Stuart commented that he and Anders had followed much the same course and were actively involved in a sort of covert activity with the move to Montana which was clearly in the best interests of all, but would still be a very hard sell.

As they sat talking, Stuart, for the first time, considered the possibility that he could be instrumental in reestablishing a governmental structure that would encompass much more than one small community of people. He had always considered Bayside, then the Association and the Control Zone as organizations that would support his own personal survival. As he listened to Parker, it dawned on him that he could have a higher purpose than just saving his own skin.

Possibly Anders had a broader outlook that took in this notion of a national purpose. He would have to discuss this further with Anders when they had time to talk. He missed the talks he had with Anders in the past when they discussed political philosophies and social structures. These were topics that had been ignored in recent times and were only becoming relevant when there was an absence of any political governing structure.

On the day before they were to depart for Florida, Stuart sat down with

Hans to go over the details of the trip home. After Hans had detailed the route home and the weather expected en route, he told Stuart that he had thoroughly enjoyed his visit to the Valley. It was then that he mentioned to Stuart that he would be interested in settling in the area as he found the people very friendly and was of the opinion that the Valley could well provide for new people. Stuart told Hans that he could be very useful to the new community, particularly when they had a landing strip in the Valley but no pilots and no other aircraft. In his air transport operation, he had an arrangement with a radio facility in the Midwest that took all of the flight requests and served as his booking agent. He was not sure that he wanted to terminate that relationship and Stuart was not sure if that would present a problem or not. Both concluded they would have to give it further thought and they could talk about it when they returned to Florida.

The following morning, just as the black of night was being replaced by a grey dawn, Hans was giving the aircraft a final check and heating the engine for starting as Stuart bid his farewell to his hosts. He had particularly enjoyed his time spent with Parker and the two had established a kinship that would be valuable in easing the problems they would face in the marriage of their two communities. Hans had received the weather report prepared by Sarah from the ham operator in Riverton and there did not appear to be any significant systems to impede their journey. Tailwinds were expected to shave one to two hours from their time en route and this was welcome news to Stuart. Stuart gave Parker a final handshake and waved at the other Valley residents that he had been working with during his visit. As the aircraft lifted off into the sky and gained altitude, turning to the east and southeast, the sunshine coming over the mountain top warmed the interior of the cockpit and within minutes, Stuart was fast asleep.

As forecast, the weather en route was perfect for the flight. Stuart dozed off and on through the entire flight until shortly before they began their descent towards the Control Zone strip. Hans made a comment about Stuart being a real sack rat to which Stuart made no reply. He thought about it a minute and concluded that the trip had taken more out of him

than he had been aware. He had enjoyed the trip but it had been tiring.
He would relax a bit when he got home before he dove back into his job.
Unfortunately that wouldn't work out either.

# Chapter Twenty-Seven

Nix and Perry had assembled a team of twenty men for what they now called "Project Petrol". Robert Thomas had been brought in as the operation required the support of not only his boats, but also the assistance of his dive team. As Thomas was briefed on the project, it was clear to him that it was his divers who were being tasked with the difficult part of the operation. Transporting personnel to and from the target was the easy part. The difficult part was extracting the fuel from the vessel and removing it from the harbor without losing both those involved in that operation and the targeted fuel.

A number of engineers, formerly with NASA, had been rounded up and provided a security clearance by Sarah. They went to work immediately on designing and building a capsule that could be attached to the underside of the tanker and serve as a work station for the removal of the diesel fuel. Other engineers worked on the design of the bladder that would serve as the container for the fuel once it was removed from the tanker. In the meantime, Nix and Perry supervised the design phase and laid out the overall plans for the operation. Time was a factor and both Anders and Sarah were requesting status updates almost daily on the progress the two men were making. As the days passed, both Perry and Nix showed signs of stress from the building pressure to get the job done, particularly when they were not very confident that their plan would even work.

As time passed and the design engineers resolved one problem after another, the details of the operation began to take shape. The basic plan was to make contact with the tanker crew and set up a fuel buy. One of Thomas' boats would then enter the harbor at the appointed time, preferably under cover of darkness, towing a weighted, submerged bladder tank equipped with a beeper device. A second boat, explained as a security vessel, would be towing the work station capsule. Both of these towed objects would be released and sink to the bottom of the harbor approximately one hundred feet from the target vessel. After buying the fuel, the two boats would depart the harbor and return to the Control Zone.

The following evening, assuming weather was not a factor, five boats would be used to complete the operation. Under cover of darkness, divers, equipped with closed circuit rebreathers which did not emit air bubbles when in operation, would enter the water outside the harbor entrance and, using electric submersibles and homing devices, proceed to the capsule and bladder tank. Separate crews trained to perform their specific missions would proceed to either the capsule or the bladder tank and ready them for use.

A third team would connect the capsule to the bladder by way of a synthetic tube with valve attachments at either end. The capsule, with an opening at the top and a closeable hatch at the bottom, would be taken under the hull of the vessel using its own propulsion device. A separate suction pad conforming to the dimensions of the top of the capsule would first be attached and made secure to the underside of the tanker. The upper portion of the capsule would then be fitted to the suction pad and the lower hatch would remain open. Air pressure valves controlling air tanks in the capsule would then be opened forcing the water in the capsule out the open hatch at the bottom.

When the water level dropped down to the level of the hatch, the valves would be carefully monitored so that air bubbles did not boil out from the underside of the tanker and alert the crew. With the water level in the capsule stabilized just at or above the hatch level, the bottom hatch would be closed, making the capsule airtight. The two men in the capsule would then cut through the hull of the vessel using laser equipment and access the underside of the storage tanks.

Their next task would be to connect to the tankers diesel storage tank a length of eight inch diameter, double line, synthetic tubing. The purpose of the tubing was twofold. First, to contain the fuel as it was being removed from the storage tank and transport it to an exit valve in the side of the capsule leading to the bladder. Secondly, to provide a conduit for seawater to be pumped into the tank after the fuel was removed so that tanker control room quantity gauges did not show a change. The Diesel fuel would first be withdrawn from the tank and then seawater would be run into the tank in an equal quantity.

From the capsule, the intake fuel would be tubed over to the storage bladder under pressure from a fuel flow pump inside the capsule. As the bladder would fill, it would tend to rise as the fuel weighed less than the seawater, and according to the calculations of the engineers, the weighted bladder would rise no higher than ten feet below the surface, provided their weight calculations proved accurate. That was the desired position with respect to the water surface as it would be difficult to tow if at a deeper level and if it were any higher, it could possibly be detected by those on board the tanker.

The difficult task for the engineers was how to remove the plate and insert the tubing into the storage tank without filling the capsule with diesel fuel. They ran a number of tests in the lab, established in the administration building, and determined that the best way to accomplish the task was to connect a transparent funnel like device, again by suction, to the underside of the target tank with the narrow part of the funnel connecting to the eight inch diameter flexible tube. The upper, wider, part of the funnel had arm entry points to permit the capsule team to operate their laser equipment inside the transparent funnel which was kept visually clear by solvents. That way they could see what they were doing, and operate the laser gun inside the funnel. They would first drill a small hole in the tank to measure the thickness of the metal. They would then plug the hole and then adjust the laser unit to cut through the metal leaving a fraction of an inch of metal in place. After a circular cut was made in the bottom of the tank, they would attach a suction device to the circular cut and pull the metal out, leaving a hole in the tank that would quickly fill the funnel. They would then open the valve in the capsule and the fuel would then flow from the capsule to the holding bladder.

Assuming the operation would go as planned, the filled bladder would be reconnected to one of Thomas' boats, using the same tow line previously detached with the bladder, and silently pulled out of the harbor still under the cover of darkness. According to the engineers, it would take one hour and thirty seven minutes to connect the equipment and three hours to drill and drain a ten thousand gallon storage tank into the bladder. Assuming that the operation began at eleven p.m. local time, planned completion of the operation was set for four a.m., allowing some additional time for unforeseen problems. It was a tight schedule with considerable risk including a very short window of time for towing the filled bladder out of the harbor.

Tide schedules would be favorable for the scheduled date of the operation provided the times were met. Tides were to go slack shortly after 4 a.m., and would reverse at 5 a.m. Many things could go wrong in the meantime and that was the reason why five boats were being used in the plan. Two were to carry divers and equipment and the other three were loaded with defensive armament and troops should something go wrong.

It was a very risky operation and Nix, Perry and Thomas made that abundantly clear in their final briefing to Anders and Sarah. Anders gave final approval to the mission and it was set to commence the following evening. Andy Moss had assumed the primary role for managing the defense of the Control Zone with Perry being tied up on the fuel mission. Moss was kept quite busy with incursions into the zone continuing unabated with a growing sophistication of tactics and weaponry on the part of the unwanted visitors. The attacking parties were becoming more adept at using diversionary attacks to confuse the defensive forces.

The Control Zone defenses on the bridge running from Cocoa over to the beachside had been beefed up considerably following Wyatt's initial report of the Cuban force operating in the Cocoa area. The Cocoa group likewise appeared to have increased their security on the bridge in response to what they observed at the opposite end. There had been little if any communication between the forces occupying either end, but Anders had given specific instructions to the on- scene commander to maintain tight discipline over his men and not to antagonize the opposing security force. He anticipated that there was a good possibility that a deal, of sorts, might be worked out with the mainland group. Anders had also instructed Andy Moss that the Cocoa patrols, under Wyatt, were to gather information only and not to engage in combat with the mainland group unless it was absolutely necessary for their own safety. He did not want to anger anyone at this point until he had decided on their best course of action.

Anders had the Tactics Team preparing the plan for the Cuban operation which primarily involved defense of the bridge and beach areas adjacent to Cocoa assuming events went as anticipated. To play it safe, he instructed them to consider all contingencies including the possibility that Paco Morales and the Cuban National Socialist Force was the real party behind the Cuban Cocoa group. He was of the opinion that Morales could be trusted, but it was best to cover all bases.

Beth Sloan had the school system in full operation with one hundred and fifty full time students in primary and secondary grades, one through ten. Materials continued to be in short supply as was to be expected, but Beth had found a friend in Robert Thomas who proved adept as usual with obtaining scarce and hard to find items. His black market talents acquired in the final days of the old government continued to be of value in the Zone as he continued to maintain contact with some of his old sources on the mainland. Anders and others in the administration had mixed thoughts on Thomas' activities, but did not complain, particularly when Thomas would provide some rare commodity, such as Anders' rum. In any event, Thomas had been successful in locating a supply of writing materials, blackboards, projectors and other items necessary or useful in operating the school much to the delight of Beth and the teachers.

# Chapter Twenty-Eight

Monday morning, Kate, with some trepidation, sat in the courtroom awaiting the arrival of the Judge and her former student. In time, the student arrived in the company of an escort from the barracks and sat down on the bench assigned to those charged with various infractions of Zone rules. The clerk paged through the court schedule while those in the courtroom sat in nervous silence awaiting the appearance of the Judge. In time, the door to his chambers opened and the Judge stepped forward, wearing the traditional black robes of his office. The student and his escort immediately stood up as the Judge made his way to the raised dais and took a seat in the impressive leather upholstered chair that had been procured for him by Robert Thomas. The clerk announced the list of cases that would be heard that morning and those in attendance noted their appearance as their name was called. Third on the list was the student's case and Kate was required to sit nervously while the two cases in front of his were heard. They were minor matters requiring only a few words of chastisement from the Judge, much to the relief of Kate, and were disposed of rather quickly.

The clerk then called the Student's case and he rose immediately, with his escort from the disciplinary barracks, and approached the bench. The Judge leafed through his notes and frowned as he read the words laying out the prior incident in the courtroom. He then looked up and his eyes passed around the courtroom until they locked on Kate sitting towards the rear of the room. Glancing down at the notes and then up again at Kate, the Judges voice boomed out into the room, making Kate's heart race even faster than it had been.

"Miss Nolan would you please approach the bench."

Kate stood up and began walking towards the front of the room confident that her lack of composure was evident to everyone. The student maintained his position in front of the bench, directing his attention solely at the Judge. When Kate had taken her place in front of the Judge and alongside the student, Richard Chastain, the Judge then directed his attention to the barracks escort and requested his report. The escort read from a typed statement detailing the charges against the youth, his admission date to the facility, his record while at the barracks and the date of his return for hearing which was the current date. When he was finished, the Judge paused briefly and looking down at him, commented, "Interesting. Now, tell me in your own words, how has young Mr. Chastain done while he was a visitor in your facility? I ask that because the last time Mr. Chastain and I were together, he had a certain difficulty with politeness, particularly with respect to Ms. Nolan who has been kind enough to be with us again this morning."

Kate blushed at the reference by the Judge as the escort put away the report sheet in his file folder and spoke. "Your Honor, Mr. Chastain came into our facility in need of some... ah... I guess you could say... attention. He received the attention he sought from not only the counselors... but also from some of his new friends and fellow guests at the facility. Suffice it to say that after a period of approximately four or five days, Mr. Chastain adopted a new attitude about... not only the facility in whose care he had been placed, but also about life in general. Pursuant to the order of this Court and the specific request that Mr. Chastain learn how to act in polite society, efforts were concentrated in that direction. As a result of the efforts of those in the facility, I can state as a matter of fact that Mr. Chastain has become a model guest of the facility and is considered by those most knowledgeable in such matters to be one of the most polite, courteous visitors that we have ever had and it is the considered opinion of those in the facility that Mr. Chastain is ready to resume his role as an active, law abiding and very polite member of our society."

The Judge considered the escort's comments as he looked down on Chastain who continued to stand at rigid attention before the bench. The arrogance that the Judge recalled from his previous meeting with Chastain was nowhere in sight. Before him stood a most respectful, chastised, young man with closely clipped hair and impeccable prison garb assuming the posture of a well trained soldier about to graduate from boot camp. The Judge suppressed a smile as he absorbed the sight in front of him. Being a Judge had some rewards and this, apparently, was one of them.

"Well, Mr. Chastain, what do you have to say for yourself?"

"Your Honor, I will be the first to admit that when we last met, I had a real attitude problem. My stay in the disciplinary barracks was not fun, but I will say this, I learned a lot about myself that I guess I should have learned some time ago. In any event, I don't think you will see me again in your courtroom. I also wish to take this opportunity to apologize to Ms. Nolan as well as to the Court and those in attendance when I was last here. We all have to grow up. I just took a little longer than I should have."

The Judge was clearly moved by Chastain's words and paused briefly before responding. "Well... I believe you have had a learning experience and I believe you when you say you won't be back. Continue to learn from this experience and work with your teachers in the school. Your school is giving you a great opportunity that very few people in what is left of this country continue to enjoy. Make the most of it. If you have problems in dealing with life, remember there are people you can talk to such as Ms. Nolan here or, if you want, come and see me. You look like you have the raw materials to make it, so use what you have. Good luck to you. Ms. Nolan, do you have anything to say?"

"No I don't. It's good to have Richard back with us and I am sure he has learned from this experience."

The Court released Richard to Kate Nolan and as they walked back to the complex, Kate told him she was glad to have him back in the class and to work with her in the future in dealing with some of his problems rather than letting them get out of control and get him into trouble. Richard said little other than that he was glad to be "out of there", but Kate was confident that he had learned his lesson. As they parted company by the housing area, he again apologized to her for his prior behavior in class and in the courtroom. She made up her mind then that she would work doubly hard to get him back with his peer group class as that was a major reason why he had his problem in the first place.

The Alliance Court System had grown since its inception when two judges handled the entire schedule. Jim McLeod, the Commissioner for Social Affairs had taken quite a bit of the pressure off the system when he was appointed by Anders to handle the administrative hearings, disputes, divorces and marriage ceremonies. Most of the civil matters that were not able to be amicably resolved by the parties ended up in his hearing room for resolution. As a result, his work load had increased many fold and he was eventually in need of assistance as were the two Alliance Court Judges. In view of the fact that Stuart was an attorney, Anders delegated the supervision of the court system to him with authority to appoint as many judges as were needed so that such matters could proceed expeditiously. Stuart organized a judicial council comprised of residents who had legal experience. Either as attorneys or others with practical legal experience, such as court clerks, legal secretaries or others who were generally familiar with the judicial process.

As with all committees, the initial assignment of selecting competent men and women to serve as judges of the Alliance Court, in time, did not challenge the group sufficiently and they expanded their horizons to give consideration to the issue of the rights and privileges of those accused of crimes. When Stuart learned of this, he immediately reminded the committee of what their responsibilities entailed and what they did not entail. He did not want to revisit the judicial system of the past. Most of the committee members agreed with his view of criminal law and its basic purpose. A few of the more liberal members were of the opinion that rights of the accused were of considerable importance and should be honored by the Alliance Court. However, when advised to do so, they agreed to put their personal view on hold until their situation had stabilized. Stuart reminded them that considerable time would pass before that occurred. He had no intention of reinventing the endless appeals program of the former legal system.

# Chapter Twenty-Nine

Sarah knocked on Anders' door to get his attention as he sat at his desk pouring over the latest food inventory sheets. She could tell by the frown on his face that he did not find the figures pleasing. As she entered his office, Anders commented that they had better pack their bags soon because they were running out of virtually everything including food and adequate water supplies. As Sarah sat down in the chair in front of the desk, she replied, "In seven weeks we will be doing just that if we get the fuel. Let's hope Nix and Perry get the job done. The weather should be favorable to run the mission this evening and tomorrow night should be equally as good. Let's keep our fingers crossed. The only hitch could be off shore weather that we cannot get and that could bring rough seas that would close the inlet channel. That's the unknown risk that we have to accept. At least they would know if they had a problem there before they off loaded the divers. But, Anders, that is not why I am here. We received a message from our friends up north, Campbell and Yates. They want us to pick them up so that they can come down and look us over. Sounds like they are basically interested in working some sort of deal."

Anders sat back in his chair and commented that he wished Stuart was back as these little problems are cropping up. He paused and went on. "What are your thoughts Sarah on how we should handle this one?"

Sarah was prepared for the question as she knew Anders had been overwhelmed making decisions on everything from food problems, defense issues and right down to minor disciplinary matters.

"I would suggest that we assign Barnes to deal with them. They are going to want to learn about the Association and look us over. He can handle that. Before they, or we for that matter, make a decision regarding their coming on board, there will be some negotiations that will have to be handled. Barnes could take care of the preliminary matters and I would suggest that you or I handle the final agreement unless Stuart is back, in which case, he should take charge of that. By the way, he should be back in the next day or so according to our last communication.

Anders grinned with that news. "Thank God. I could use his help. OK, you talk with Barnes and make sure that he has all the details. He has been effective on this business up to this point and knows both of the men. Tell him not to commit to anything of consequence because, quite frankly, I think they need us about as much as we need them. We could use the equipment, especially for our trip north. I would like to know we are traveling with an adequate arsenal of weapons and without their assistance in that area, we will be marginally equipped. You run the show until Stuart gets back and he may want you to continue for all we know. I'll leave that up to you and Stuart. Anything else?"

Sarah said that was all she needed this visit and left Anders to his other problems.

Barnes was busy for the next day or two preparing for the visit by Campbell and Yates. He had decided to forego the trip with Robert Thomas to make the pickup as he would have plenty of time to talk to the two men and furthermore, he did not care for boat trips on the open ocean. The only hitch to the visit was that Thomas' boats were tied up on the fuel operation. Sarah had commented in her visit with Anders that off shore weather could hinder the operation and it had. They had tried to run a weather boat to check sea conditions in the Jacksonville area and the report that came back was negative. They had fought ever increasing swells right up to the Jacksonville area at which time it became apparent that onshore winds were causing huge swells to pile up at the harbor entrance. Thomas knew before he could even see the breaking rollers that there was no way his boats could make the entry way. The disappointed crew turned around and headed back to await more favorable weather. When they returned, Sarah passed the word that the fuel operation was the priority mission for the boats and they were not to be used for anything else until they ran the mission. Weather in the area was to remain favorable for the next few days and it was decided that a weather boat would be sent out the next day, or as soon thereafter as feasible, to check on the swells to see if they were diminishing. If they were down, the mission would go that following evening.

Frick flew over the length of the Control Zone to let everyone know they had returned and soon the oil cans were lit along the sides of the runway to guide them in. Frick lined the aircraft up with the centerline of the strip and brought the plane in for a smooth landing. As they taxied up to the parking area, Stuart saw Sarah and Anders waving to them. It was obvious that both Sarah and Anders had many questions to ask Stuart, but Anders suggested that they get together first thing in the morning so that Stuart could take a break and rest up from his trip. Frick raised an eyebrow at that as Stuart had, again, slept for most of the return trip.

Stuart agreed to meet in Anders office in the morning but took Anders and Sarah aside before departing the field and suggested to them that they take good care of Frick as he was interested in joining the Association and they could well use his talents. Sarah, with a bit of a grin on her face, assured Anders that she would handle that job. She had her eye on Frick from the time that she had first seen him climb down from his plane and didn't need anyone to tell her a second time to see what she could do to get him to stay. As she headed over to welcome Frick back, Anders chuckled and said, "Fine with me. She deserves it. I don't know what we would do without her." Stuart agreed and as the two continued talking, Anders suggested he head home and get some rest. Apparently it was showing as Stuart was tired from the trip and had not been asleep for most of trip back as Frick had assumed. He had been deep in thought contemplating everything that needed to be done to prepare for the move. That was assuming that there would be a move and that all negotiations between the parties were worked out successfully. Stuart took the cue from Anders and headed back to the dorm as they continued talking about administrative matters in general.

Stuart was back at work bright and early the morning after his return to Florida. He was still a bit groggy from the flight even though he had been able to catch a few winks on the flight back. He had gone through the stack of memos that were lying on his desk awaiting his return when Sarah and Anders came into the admin building. They had prepared an 'in briefing' for Stuart to bring him up to date on what had transpired since he had left for the Montana visit and their staff personnel were waiting in the briefing room for everyone to gather. As usual, Sarah began the briefing by running through intelligence reports prepared by her section laying out what had transpired across the country while Stuart was in Montana. Anders and Sarah brought Stuart up to date on the meeting with the Cubans and the plans for the Cocoa operation. Stuart agreed with both that they might as well deal with the western Cuban group while they had the support of Paco Morales and his troops. That would be better than taking them on without help from anyone while they were en route to Montana. Stuart also had some questions about the possibility of a connection between the two groups, but agreed they had no way of knowing and at this point, they had to assume that Morales and his men were on the up and up. To be safe, they would also prepare for the possibility that they were being tricked.

After the update briefing, Stuart called together a meeting between himself, Anders, Sarah, Perry, Nix, Monty Wyatt and the officer in charge of the Cocoa Bridge. When they all had gathered together in the administration building, Monty Wyatt briefed everyone on defensive preparations at the Cocoa Bridge. Wyatt had been running his patrols both north and south of the central part of Cocoa and had determined that the men controlling that area were not highly organized and not particularly disciplined. He found that security was lax, that their patrols were infrequent and careless in their methods. In running his patrols in the area surrounding Cocoa, he had made no direct contact and avoided any confrontation with the local force. On a number of occasions, his scouts reported to him that some of the Cocoa patrol members appeared to be intoxicated or on drugs.

The Cocoa group physically occupied an area in the center of Cocoa that encompassed approximately a four square mile area. They also ran patrols an additional five to ten miles out from the center of their zone where they appeared to be operating with little or no visible opposition. There were a few small independent gangs working the area as well, but they were not a threat to anyone and they seemed to scatter whenever the Cocoa patrols showed up. It seems the Cocoa group had matters well under control until the western Cubans showed up.

What made the Cubans become interested in Cocoa was still a mystery to Stuart and the others. Stuart was wondering if they had somehow become privy to the arms cache that was rumored to be in the area. Maybe they knew more than the Association did. The CNSP, or eastern Cuban group, apparently was not informed of the arms treasure that was secreted somewhere on the beach side. At least they had never indicated that they knew about it.

As time passed, and on orders from Anders, soldiers from the Cocoa side had been invited to come over for food or water. Politics were never discussed on these occasions per the instructions handed down through Perry and that was not a problem as the visitors were primarily interested in what was available on the beach, particularly food, water, housing and women. Apparently there were very few women in the Cocoa area for whatever reason. Wyatt commented that from what he could tell in his patrols, they had either been killed or had fled for their lives. The bridge Defense Team commander agreed with that comment as his opinion of the troops that he had seen come over from the other side was not high.

Anders absorbed the comments of the two men and after a brief parley with Stuart and Sarah reconvened the briefing. They had concluded that someone who ran the show in Cocoa had to have some intelligence and they had to get in contact with that person. Once they did make contact, they would then decide if the Cocoa organization was someone that they might be able to work with in connection with frustrating the efforts of the western Cubans, whatever their intentions might be. With that in mind, Anders drafted a message, with the input and agreement of Sarah and

Stuart, to the effect that he wished to send an emissary to meet with the Cocoa group to see if there could not be some tradeoffs that they could enter into that would be mutually beneficial. The suggested meeting place was the middle of the bridge. Only the principals were to be present and no weapons. That should be agreeable to both sides as the meeting would then be in full view of each parties own protecting troops and neither side would be particularly at risk. Anders figured Stuart would be the best person to handle the job of meeting the Cocoa people and he readily accepted the task when Anders suggested that. Sarah had the message prepared, sealed and delivered to Capt. Wyatt for transmittal. It would probably be a few days before a response was received and that would give Anders, Sarah and Stuart time to work out the details of the meeting.

To the surprise of all, Monty Wyatt returned the following day with a response from a Howard Stone who signed his letter as Cocoa CC. Perry recognized the letters as U.S. Military terminology for Commander. He more than likely had some involvement in times past with the military which was, in Anders mind, a plus. The letter suggested that they meet the following day at noon on the bridge as requested. He would be there with his number two in command. Anders, Stuart and Sarah had one final conference regarding how Stuart should deal with Mr. Stone while, at the same time, Wyatt met with Perry to discuss security for the meeting site. When all plans were laid, the matter was put aside until Stuart, Wyatt and the assigned security force departed for the meeting the following morning.

Stuart took Perry with him as they began walking towards the center of the bridge at the appointed time. Wyatt had his men stationed at the bridge head and along the banks of the River in the event that the meeting was a set up. As Stuart was walking, he could see two figures emerge from the other side and walk in their direction. He could also see their security troops taking up positions on the other bank. As Stuart approached the two men, he noted that they appeared to be in their mid to late thirties and both men were clean shaven and were smiling as they approached. From what Stuart could tell, they seemed to be in reasonably good health and physical condition. He had expected to meet somewhat scruffy appearing representatives and that is not what was coming towards him. As they met, the taller man of the two held out his hand and introduced himself as Howard Stone . The four men exchanged pleasantries and then got down to business. Stuart explained the general setup of the Association and their concern having learned from one of their patrols that there was, what appeared to be, a Cuban force in the area. Stone let Stuart go on without commenting one way or the other, merely nodding as though to indicate that he too was aware of their presence. Seeing that Stone was not opening up, Stuart got a bit more direct.

"I assume that you have an interest in not spending the rest of your life cutting sugar cane and I thought that we may have a common goal of protecting ourselves from anyone taking over our turf."

Stone was silent for a moment, clearly pondering the alternatives that he was facing. Taking the bait offered by Stuart or sticking with his commitment to work with a Cuban force that he well knew would cut him down in a heartbeat if he didn't cooperate. Stone tossed the ball back to Stuart with his response.

"I'm not sure we can stop them if they want to visit our properties. I don't want to go into what we have or don't have, but I will say, our tanks are not as good as what we know they have."

Stone said that with a smile and all four knew that Stone had no tanks whatsoever and the Cubans had a fair number. The banter continued back and forth for a time during which Stuart appraised his counterpart and concluded that he was a reasonable person to deal with. He found the reports of discipline problems with his troops a bit disconcerting and could not reconcile those reports with the person standing before him. Stone's associate was not cut of the same cloth however and that could account for the disparity. Possibly Stone ran the overall operation in the Cocoa area and his second in command managed the troops. Stuart decided to press on and get a bit more candid about the overall situation.

"There is a possibility that other forces in the area, who just happen to also be Cuban, might be interested in taking care of your problem. I should add that you might find the other group to be more amenable to your continued independent operation in the Cocoa area than I am told your visitors are likely to be. If you wish to explore that possibility, I may be able to make the appropriate arrangements."

This set Stone back a bit. "Interesting. How do we know that they won't harpoon us just as fast as the other group?"

Stuart had the same concern and admitted it. "We don't but frankly, I think it's the best game in town at the moment and I don't have any other suggestions."

Stuart and Stone talked for another hour or so as Stuart maneuvered Stone into concluding that the best course of action would be to see if they could not work a deal with Paco Morales. Stuart was not overly confident himself of the true objectives of Morales and his group, but, based on Sarah's information and other sources, the western Cubans presented a much greater risk to their health and well being. Stuart did not bring out that the leaders of the Association intended to leave the area within the coming weeks. He would have to do that at some time, but not yet. That was one more problem that they would have to put off for some future date. His not being entirely truthful to Stone did not bother him as he truly believed he was presenting Stone with good advice, even though he was not explaining all of the relevant facts. That could wait.

Before they parted, it was decided that Stuart would inform Morales of Stones willingness to cooperate in frustrating the objectives of the western Cuban group. Stuart had no doubt that Morales would work Stone's people into their plans and they might be willing to pay, in some fashion, for Stone's services. As they continued discussing the Cocoa group and how they might fit into the planned operation, Stuart's thoughts kept reverting to what he saw as a more difficult hurdle to overcome and that was how they were going to handle informing all members of the Alliance that they were about to bail out of Florida and head out to Montana with a good share of the resources they had collected over the past two years. That was going to require some real headwork on the part of everyone managing the move as many people that were staying, if not most, were going to think Stuart and the others were playing fast and easy with their very lives.

Back at the conference room, Stuart, Anders, Sarah and the staff all joined into the discussion on how and when to announce the move to Montana. Sarah mentioned that some of her staff had reported hearing rumors that such a move was in the works. Clearly something had to be done and done soon or they would have a real problem on their hands.

Stuart was adamant that the announcement should be made in the next few days as numerous people had been more than curious as to where he had gone during his absence and for what purpose. Anders agreed.

After further discussion, it was agreed that a full briefing of all Alliance personnel would be held in three days in the Conference Center. Notices were to be posted on the bulletin boards that all members were to be present for a very important announcement that would affect the future of all residents.

In the meantime, Sarah was to prepare all briefing materials and provide Anders, who was going to handle the meeting, with the format of the information to be conveyed. Stuart was to provide information relating to the site, explaining the facilities and resources that would be available once they arrived. Ross Perry was to brief the travel arrangements, with full explanation regarding the risks and hazards to be expected during the trip.

Finally, Anders would close with an offer, to those who did not wish to leave Florida, to provide them with adequate and somewhat safe facilities at North Farm. The area would require extensive development which would tax available resources and Anders was to warn those who were interested that they would have to participate actively or the project would not succeed. He also was to acknowledge that many may consider staying in the Control Zone and at that time, Sarah, Anders or Stuart was to brief everyone on the likelihood that the Cuban group, under Paco Morales, would possibly be taking over the territory. Sarah would provide what was known about Morales and the experiences of people in areas controlled by his group. The Alliance members were then to be told that they had three days to make their election known as to what their intentions were. They had the option of traveling to Montana, going to North Farm or staying in the Control Zone and accepting their chances. In the meantime, the staff was going ahead with preparing for the move to Montana while also preparing contingency plans for the other two alternatives which it was known some members would elect.

The three days before the member wide meeting passed rapidly with all staff members furiously trying to prepare the slides and briefing materials needed while at the same time fending off the questions of their friends and associates as to what was going on. As the time passed before the meeting, the rumors ran rampant with some of them more on target than others. Tensions were building in the community as some began to grumble that they were being sold out by Anders, Stuart and the others. As the meeting time grew near, the residents began flocking to the Conference Center in eager anticipation of what they were about to hear. It was standing room only in the hall when Anders approached the podium and arranged his papers as Sarah set up the projection equipment and slides. The conversation in the hall fell silent and you could hear a pin drop by the time Anders was ready to proceed.

Anders went right to the point. He explained that the resources of the Control Zone were very limited. He explained the time lines to depletion of food and water resources which were absolutely required for their continued stay on the island. This produced a murmuring in the crowd as there were always a few that were oblivious to the plight they were in. Waiting for the whispers to die down, he concluded this part of the briefing with a clear statement; "Our group cannot sustain itself in the Control Zone after December 1." He waited for the listeners to absorb this fact. The date was less than two months away. What began as a murmur in the crowd grew to a roar as everyone began talking loudly either to their immediate neighbor or shouting up at Anders.

Anders let it all sink in and then gaveled them to silence. When the room was again still, he went on. He explained the three options that they could all elect. He did not cover the fact that the Montana option was open to only around four to five hundred reasonably healthy residents. He would cross that bridge when he had to. Hopefully, those electing North Farm or to stay in the Control Zone would solve the problem for him. If there were a few extras, he would be able to handle them. If they all wanted to go, he had a real problem that might require some revisions of plans.

When Stuart took the podium he could not fathom preferring North Farm or staying in the Control Zone, under the Cubans, over the option of traveling to Montana. He provided the basic facts on what he had seen and heard while in the Valley. He covered the geographic limits and layout of the Valley and some of the more visible characteristics of the people and a description of how they lived. He explained what he saw as the benefits and opportunities offered by the Valley residents and what he saw as the contributions that the Alliance men and women could bring to the Valley. He concluded his remarks with some environmental details on Valley living, particularly the great temperature difference between that part of the country and what the Alliance residents were used to. He figured that would be a sufficient downer to keep out the least adventurous of the residents and solve some of his problems. When he finished, he silently hoped that he had not oversold or undersold the Montana project and as he took his chair next to Sarah, she assured him that he had laid it out just right.

If Stuart had any concerns about overselling the Montana project, he put his mind to rest after Ross Perry went into graphic detail on the risks and hardships associated with the trip west. Ross explained that it would be extremely physically demanding, requiring extensive walking at times, limited food, limited rest, and environmental threats from not only lightly armed renegades to well equipped and organized military Forces that controlled some of the areas they would be traveling through. When he finished, a murmur of voices again went through the Conference Center and it was obvious that many in the hall did not find the trip, as described, appealing.

Anders then took the podium and made the announcement that the Cuban National Socialists were negotiating with the Administration regarding an eventual takeover of the Control Zone. This brought an instant negative reaction from the listeners. Anders let that die down before he proceeded. "Let me assure you, this is not something that we want to happen. It is something that is going to happen. The C.N.S.P. is the most powerful military Force in Florida today, according to the information that we have. They are also one of the more liberal in their attitude towards the inhabitants of areas under their control. From what we know, they have done a very good job of providing for their people and they control sufficient land masses in South Florida so they do not have the food and water problems that we have been trying to deal with here on the beach."

Most in the audience accepted what he was saying. Anders went on and explained that information on each option would be made available at briefings beginning the following morning in the Conference Center. All questions would be answered at that time. "In the meantime and within the next three days, we need your decision on which of the three options you elect, Montana, North Farm or the Zone."

He thereupon summarily concluded the meeting even though most of the people in the room had numerous questions for everyone on the staff.

In the days that followed, life in the Zone was pandemonium. People were running from briefing to briefing trying to get as much information as possible to assist them in making up their minds as to what they were going to do. Anders had Sarah gathering some polling data to get an idea of what the trends were. At first, very few were interested in going to Montana, but as time passed, the numbers of those interested grew, until at the end of the three day period following the meeting, the polling data showed that about half were interested in making the trip. Obviously, many of those were not in the required physical condition to take on such a trip and Anders felt that the numbers were consequently quite workable. A greater problem was how to deal with the large number of people who had apparently made up their minds not to make the trip west. They were becoming increasingly nervous about their future with each passing minute. Small pockets of these residents, who now considered themselves basically disenfranchised, were beginning to take action to protect their own interests. Anders had anticipated such a reaction and had called upon Perry to double security at all locations where arms, ammunition, food and supplies were stored. Attempts to break in to storerooms had increased many fold since the meeting and as time passed, the size of such groups had been growing rapidly. The dissidents were becoming more vocal by the minute. It was apparent that something had to be done or there would be an active rebellion by a large, rapidly organizing part of the Zone.

All Defense Forces were placed on alert and meetings not sanctioned by the administration were prohibited. This produced a further outcry from the dissidents but it had to be done, at least temporarily, to prevent a further increase in the unrest that was occurring in the Zone. A meeting specifically for those not planning on making the move to Montana was scheduled for the following evening in the Conference Center. Anders had decided that he would handle the meeting himself without the assistance of anyone else on the staff. He had Perry arrange for maximum security to ensure that matters did not get out of hand. At the appointed time, the hall was filled with an angry crowd who were involved in intense conversation with one another voicing their criticisms of Anders and the Alliance Staff. The crowd had concluded in the past few days that the original Bayside residents had conspired to take over their resources for their own purposes, knowing all along that they would leave the zone when the opportunity arose. Many of these people had donated arms and resources for the use of the Alliance and, in many respects, they had a valid gripe.

Anders was aware of the legitimacy of some of their complaints and intended to address them. That was one purpose of the meeting. The other was that he wanted everyone to know that he was not going to tolerate any interference with what had to be done for the future well being of most, if not all of the residents. Anders gaveled the crowd to silence and dealt directly with the problem at hand. He first announced that no one was going to disrupt what had to be done for the good of all. That produced a murmur in the crowd which Anders quieted down with the use of the gavel. He had decided before the meeting that he was not going to plead with those attending the meeting. He was going to give it to them straight and if they could not handle that then so be it. He then went on by admonishing those who criticized his decisions to get their act together and take steps to prepare for their own futures before it was too late to do so because Anders and the Montana group were leaving and if those staying or going to North Farm did not organize and start thinking about their futures then they were in for some very difficult times.

Anders continued, explaining to the crowd that resources were being collected and assigned for use at North Farm. "Arms would be provided for the use of security in that area and that adequate supplies of AR20's and ammunition would be available to take care of your needs." That responded to the many complaints of those who had donated weapons to the Alliance for the Defense Force. This statement of Anders was based on the assumption that they would be able to obtain weapons through the assistance of Campbell and Yates. He was taking an optimistic view of that situation, but again, he would deal with that later. He also announced that they would be provided most, if not all of the marine equipment, including Robert Thomas' boats, engines and supplies. By this time, the audience was taking on a new attitude and listening intently. Anders continued, explaining the work that had to be done at North Farm: Laying out crop lands, getting seed in the ground, building shelters, defensive positions, schools, and the entire infrastructure necessary to make the area habitable and safe for those relocating there.

Anders figured that most of those not going to Montana would eventually elect to move to North Farm. There would be some that would stay in the Zone, but they would be a distinct minority.

Stuart had been sitting in the Hall listening and observing and as he walked out, feeling much better than when he had arrived, he commented to Sarah, another problem solved. Sarah nodded in agreement.

With time running out and so many squares to fill before the planned departure date, the staff was working long into the night in order to meet the time deadlines that Anders had established. Sarah's concern was focused on accomplishing Project Petrol, as she correctly viewed obtaining the fuel supply as essential to transporting the residents and their belongings safely to their new home in Montana. Stuart did not question that the oil mission was primary but he was also concerned that Campbell and Yates be transported down to the Control Zone soon so as to accommodate them in, hopefully, arriving at a decision to work with the Alliance in obtaining the needed weapons. It was finally agreed that one of the support boats for the oil mission would be detached and utilized for the pickup of the two men with the understanding that it could be called upon for support should the need arise. With that in mind, a squad of Jack Nix's troops would be on the boat not only for security on the pickup, but also to be available if needed at Jacksonville.

The Intelligence Section reported at the morning briefing that the weather reports coming in appeared to be favorable for dispatching the mission at any time over the next few days. A weather boat was sent out that evening to check the swells at the Jacksonville harbor entrance and reported back that they were down and would cause no problem for the mission. All other reports, including those of observers on the scene passing radio messages to the Zone, were favorable with no information casting a shadow on the planned operation. Robert Thomas had his mechanics going over every piece of equipment necessary for the mission with particular emphasis on the newly engineered and constructed devices that were to be used to extract the oil from the tanker and transport it to the container bag. The engineers were likewise hovering around their creations attentive as new mothers with their babies, tinkering with each separate component and discussing among themselves any potential problems that were likely to occur. Everyone knew the mission was not only very difficult in all respects, but also very dangerous. Jack Nix had his best men assigned to the support boats and had stores of pyrotechnics loaded into Thomas' boats to use in the event the mission ran into trouble.

The following morning after radio contact was used to establish the fuel buy at the Jacksonville dock, two boats were dispatched with the oil extraction chamber, bag, tubing and support equipment that would be dropped in the harbor for use either that night or very soon thereafter. The idea was that the gear would be towed into the harbor, and weighted so that it was well below the surface and then released some distance from the target tanker. Locator beacons and propulsion devices on the equipment would then be used to locate and propel the equipment to where it was needed. This part of the operation was not considered high risk as it had been tested and modified to the extent that Anders and Stuart could never tell when the boats were or were not towing the test vehicles. Likewise, the divers had become expert in operating the locator devices and finding the submerged equipment in the dark of night.

In the afternoon when the drop boats returned, they reported their part of the mission as a success. They had made the drop, then proceeded to the tanker and made the fuel buy. While the tanker crew was an arrogant, ignorant crowd to deal with, there had been no trouble. They were obviously under orders to make money and not cause problems. On the way out of the harbor, the drop boats had tuned into the locator beacon frequencies and reported that they were beeping, loud and clear.

That evening, as the boats were being finally loaded with men, their equipment and supplies, everyone was intently involved in checking their weapons and stores to ensure that everything would work as planned. The divers were going over their own gear and that of their partners to make sure they had no problem with anything that could be prevented beforehand. While the primary fuel mission crews were boarding and loading their supplies, the boat that was to pick up Campbell and Yates was already departing. They were to send a coded message back with a final check of the Jacksonville Harbor conditions to the four boats that would be an hour behind them. Regardless of the weather conditions at Jacksonville, the pickup boat was to proceed with its mission and bring back the two men. According to the schedule, the modified tanker tug boat would depart the Marina at midnight as it did not need to be in the harbor vicinity until around four in the morning. Stuart had been concerned about the tankers relatively slow speed which made it particularly vulnerable to attack from any other boats that happened to be in the area. Consequently, he had Perry assign a squad of men to the vessel and provided them with anti-tank missile launchers, capable of a four mile range with accuracy, in the event problems developed.

By nine in the evening all boats, except the tanker tugboat, had departed and Anders, Stuart and Sarah returned to the Intelligence Section to be on hand should any adverse radio reports come in. There had been no transmittal of information to anyone regarding the oil mission to preclude knowledge of the raiding party's plans. The observers in the Jacksonville area had been requested to send daily updates of activity on the docks so that there would not be any increased level of activity as the date of the actual mission drew near. Sarah had complete confidence in her informants in the Jacksonville area, but one could not be too careful, particularly when they were involved in as difficult and dangerous a mission as this one appeared to be.

At eleven thirty the pickup boat sent a message that, decoded, gave the final green light for the mission. By this time, the Intelligence Section radio room was getting crowded with Perry, Sarah, Stuart, Anders and the staff intently listening to the crackling radio for any information on how 'Project Petrol' was going. Stuart had also invited the NASA engineers and the tanker crewmember advisor to the radio room so that, if need be, their assistance could be called upon should a problem develop.

The minutes dragged by slowly with all eyes watching the clock as Stuart explained the planned time sequences that they all hoped were being met. Sarah and Stuart were more familiar than the rest with the narrow window of opportunity that the raiders were working with to get the oil bag out of the harbor before the tide turned against them. Once the tide turned, it would be virtually impossible to propel the large, weighted bag with its ten thousand gallons of diesel fuel out of the harbor without detection. A secure radio had been installed on the control boat so that messages could be transmitted from the site to the Intelligence Section. The control boat was outside of the harbor entrance some two or three miles depending upon visibility conditions and other boat traffic in the area so their knowledge of exactly what was going on was rather limited. Nonetheless, if trouble developed, they would be able to determine that. They were also instructed not to transmit any messages unless the situation dictated or unless all cover was blown. The fact that the radio was silent was somewhat reassuring. The minutes turned into hours and nothing came across either radio receiver which, while unnerving, was also somewhat comforting. By four thirty in the morning, most in the room were either drifting off to sleep or pacing nervously from one end of the room to the other.

Perry was now beginning to keep an eye out towards the ocean in hopes of catching some reflection on the water, but this night was particularly dark in the absence of any moonlight. The mission had been timed during a new moon or the phase of the moon when the face was obscured by shadow to hide the raiding party in darkness. As it turned out, the sky in the Jacksonville area was also covered by a thin overcast which provided complete darkness at all times the men were in the area. As they all later learned, it was so dark on the sea that night that the pickup boat containing Campbell and Yates almost collided with the control boat which was then sitting some two miles outside of the harbor entrance. By seven thirty in the morning, as the sun was beginning to rise in the east, making the breaking swell crests visible to the naked eye, Perry yelled out that he could see a boat coming from the north. Those sound asleep staggered to their feet as the others rushed to the window to see if they could determine the success or failure of the mission just by looking at the white speck in the water making its way to the south and the inlet to the river.

The residents in the Control Zone close to the Administration building and the Marina had observed the heightened level of activity over the past two days and were more than curious as to what was going on. When they observed the boats leaving the harbor area, loaded down with men and equipment, they knew that some military operation was taking place. That was not particularly unusual in the day to day happenings in the Zone as military operations were almost a daily activity with the instability that reigned supreme across the water in Melbourne and in other adjoining built up areas.

To the north of the Zone, Captain Wyatt and his men continued their far ranging patrols which had the effect of countering small unit incursions into the zone. They were assisted by high tech monitoring devices that transmitted warnings of an unauthorized entry into the security area. Furthermore, since relations had been established with the paramilitary group that controlled the Cocoa area, incursions across the river from their sector virtually ceased. Now trespassers had two security points to cross in order to enter the Zone through Cocoa.

Since Stuart had met with the leaders of the Cocoa group, there was sort of an unwritten agreement that no one from either side would do anything to irritate the other and that included maintaining border security. There would be no problems at least until there was a decision made as to whether or not Paco Morales would accept Howard Stone's offer to work with them against the western Cuban group. The offer had been sent to Morales over two weeks ago and thus far, there had been no response. Stuart was becoming a bit concerned as to what was transpiring, particularly with the time drawing nearer for the planned incursion by the western Cuban force. It was about that time that word came by way of the Intelligence Sections radio net that Carlos Moran would be arriving within a day or so to respond to prior messages and to act as the liaison for the transfer of control of the Zone to the Morales people. As it so happened, Carlos arrived at about the same time as the boats were returning from the fuel mission in Jacksonville.

The first boat to return brought the divers, as well as Yates and Campbell, back ahead of the others. That way, news of the operation would get back and the other boats, with their support troops, would come back with, and protect, the slower fuel laden tug boat. As soon as the first boat touched shore, the senior officer on board, Capt. Kessler, was hustled up to the briefing room where Anders, Stuart, Sarah and the others anxiously awaited word of the success of the mission.

Capt. Kessler's first words brought smiles to everyone's face. The mission was a complete success. When we left the area, there was absolutely no indication that they knew we had even been there. All of the equipment worked just the way it had in the water off the Zone. We were worried about cutting through the tanker hull because that was something that we could not duplicate with certainty here, but it went just like it did when we ran the tests in the tank. The steel plate on the bottom of the vessel actually cut through quicker than did our test metal. We did have some problems getting into the actual fuel tank inside the vessel, but we had expected that and we had constructed worst case scenarios in our test tank to train the men to handle virtually any type of construction that we could expect to encounter."

Kessler then directed his attention at the tanker crewmember who had advised the men on what they might encounter in the support mechanism for the actual fuel tank. "You couldn't have done a better job of laying out the structure supporting the tank if you had given us a photograph. It was virtually identical to your description. You were also very accurate on the tank locations. We entered the bottom of the vessel where you suggested and entered the ship just forward of the center of one of the tanks. We did have a problem or two getting around a support beam with our laser equipment, but again, we anticipated that and had practiced that so many times that this was just one more time."

Kessler went on with a detailed report regarding the mechanisms for withdrawing the fuel and transporting it to the container bag. The actual time to fill the bag with the ten thousand gallons of fuel had been slightly less than estimated which worked out very well as the men were very concerned about the tide changes. All in the room listened intently as Kessler continued his report and they all breathed a sigh of relief knowing that this very high risk mission had gone so well. It was a great confidence builder in their own estimate of their organization to know that they could carry off such a difficult task with such success. When Kessler had concluded, Anders congratulated him and the men and women that worked on the operation, either those directly involved or those who worked behind the scenes, preparing for the mission. He specifically complimented the engineers who had designed and built the complicated apparatus needed to withdraw the fuel from the tanker and replace it with sea water. It was entirely possible that the tanker operators would never know that they had a substantial quantity of fuel oil taken from them without their knowledge. When Anders had concluded his remarks, he suggested that everyone, including the staff get some rest. They were still well behind schedule in preparing for their move and they had no time to waste, even on their successes.

Roy Yates and Mark Campbell had come in with the first boat and were not fully aware of what all of the activity involved. The crew of the pickup boat had silently done their job making the pickup and was well trained to maintain security at all times unless instructed otherwise. John Barnes had not made the trip as he was kept very busy with heightened security in the Zone and besides, he spent most of his time on boats, bent over the rail, as he said, "barking at the whales". Yates and Campbell were greeted by Barnes upon their arrival, but he immediately thereafter turned them over to one of his staff to take them to their assigned quarters so that they could change and rest up. Barnes had been up all night with everyone else in the Admin staff anxiously waiting for news of the oil mission and he, like the others, needed to get some sleep before dealing with his two guests. He advised the assigned staff member to take the two men on a lengthy tour of the facility, with the exception of security sections, such as the Intelligence

Section, and he would get together with them later in the day. With that, he attended the briefing by Captain Kessler and then to his quarters for some rest.

Yates and Campbell were impressed by what they were seeing on the visit to the Zone. They were a bit confused by the activity, but they concluded that some sort of military operation had just been conducted and it had apparently gone off successfully which further impressed them. They toured the Zone facilities, including the dorms, the school, cafeteria, judicial section and the administration building, at least the sections that were open to them. They commented to one another that everything was kept very well organized and clean. The guide went on to explain to Campbell and Yates that while everyone was free to live his life as he wished, under the circumstances of course, and to say whatever he wanted to say, there were fairly strict guidelines on conduct. The Administration did not tolerate what they called, "lack of dedication to purpose".

As they visited the Detention Center, they observed the guests as the inmates were called, busily engaged in various forms of work for the benefit of the community. The projects they were involved with were not make work projects. They had an immediate and direct benefit to the Association. Some of the guests had been observed out in the Zone removing graffiti from walls and buildings. Most had been placed on the walls and buildings well before the organization of the Administration but, some had been placed since. It was a serious crime to be caught painting graffiti on anything and the guests that were assigned this particular task were those either caught at it or caught at something else and suspected of having painted graffiti at other times. In any event, graffiti was becoming something of the past. The other tasks being performed by the inmates, included road repair, painting, appliance repair, cleaning, and other tasks that had to be done by someone anyway.

Yates commented to the guide that the men seemed to be in good humor and not sullen as he would expect them to be. The guide replied that all of the men were right where they wanted to be. This puzzled the two visitors and the guide went on to explain that everyone sentenced to the Detention Center had the choice of taking detention or leaving the Zone. No one wanted to leave the Zone. That included men and women that were facing long terms. Very severe crimes, on the other hand, such as murder or sedition would automatically involve exclusion from the Zone. The perpetrators had no choice in those cases and if they had, they would have stayed in the Zone. It was considered a death sentence to be ostracized and sent over to the mainland. Maybe in time that would change but being outside of the Zone without the protection of a well equipped and trained military unit was considered hazardous to one's health.

With the oil mission accomplished and fuel requirements apparently provided for, Stuart concentrated his time on the travel arrangements for the trip to Montana by the group and preparation of the North Farm area for the influx of settlers that would soon be going there. He had delegated most of the responsibility for planning the trip to trusted subordinates that were also making the trip, but he had very few people with experience to call upon for assistance with North Farm. All of what he called, the heavy hitters were making the trip to Montana and, in his view, the group going to North Farm were a rung or two below what he liked to work with. Nevertheless, he made up his mind to get the job done and find two or three men or women that he thought could handle responsibility. He spoke with Anders regarding who he might call upon and Anders was at a similar loss for suggestions, but Sarah overheard the discussion and came up with two people that she felt confident would be of considerable assistance and, in time, could take over the management of the new community. One of the people she was recommending was a woman that she worked with in the Intelligence Section and was not making the trip to Montana because her husband was an invalid and would not be able to handle the trip. As Sarah described her, the woman was a real mover and shaker that handled responsibility and had the temperament to deal with a large number of people. Furthermore, the staff in Intelligence had considered the woman a pleasure to work with. Stuart arranged to meet with her and after the meeting, agreed with Sarah's assessment. He put her to work immediately setting up the organizing staff for North Farm, scheduling organization meetings, and laying out tasks to those that would be running the show.

The other suggestion by Sarah for North Farm management was a bit of a surprise for Stuart, Jim McLeod, the Commissioner for Social Affairs. He had been doing an outstanding job for the Association in resolving disputes in the Zone and was very highly respected.

Carlos Moran arrived at the Marina on one of the Cuban cigarette boats accompanied by a small security detachment in a second boat. Carlos' boat came into the harbor just ahead of the first boat to return from the oil mission and consequently he was received rather hurriedly and sent off to his quarters to await an afternoon meeting with Stuart. It was close to six in the evening before Stuart knocked on the door to his assigned apartment unit and the two finally got together. Carlos was accompanied by two staff personnel who he introduced as being responsible for inventorying resources and facilities for the planned takeover by the Cuban garrison.

Upon being introduced, Stuart invited all three to have dinner with him in the Staff Dining Room where they could talk in private. The first matter that Stuart brought up was his conversation with Howard Stone , the leader of the Cocoa group. Stuart was anxious to get that situation resolved as time was running short for the expected visit to the area by Ricardo Ortega, the leader of the group that Monty Wyatt and his men had observed from the building basement in Cocoa. Stuart did not want to place any more of his men at risk in the fight between the two Cuban groups than he had to and with the help of Stones men, the task would be made easier. Carlos listened passively as Stuart explained the meeting that he had with Stone and the offer made by Stone to work with the Cuban National Socialists. When he had finished going over the conversation, Carlos thought a minute then said, "And what does Mr. Stone expect to get out of this arrangement?"

"Good question. I suggest you ask him. I believe that what he is after is to be left alone. How you handle that is up to you, but I would suggest that he does have a fairly sizeable group which I am sure your people could handle if need be, but it might make more sense to try to work with him and arrive at some sort of an amicable understanding. Don't you think that makes more sense?" Stuart passed the ball over into Carlos' court and Carlos smiled in return, recognizing the wisdom of what Stuart was saying.

The other two Cubans did not participate in the conversation or give any indication of their thoughts on the subject. Stuart was not totally convinced that their role was that of Supply Officers but for the time being, he would go along with the program. Carlos brought that topic to a close with the statement that he would have to communicate with his people as to how to handle the matter. Stuart suggested that he utilize the secure radio facilities that Sarah had made available to him for this purpose and that he would be provided every means available to protect the confidentiality of his messages. Carlos was aware that no matter what care was taken in that regard, Stuart would be privy to whatever he said over the so called secure net.

Nevertheless, most of what he would have to say back to his headquarters could be openly discussed with Stuart and the Association. As for the rest, code words had been prearranged before his departure from Vero so that confidential matters could be communicated back and forth without fear of detection.

Stuart next brought up the matter of dealing with the western Cuban force that was apparently about to arrive in the Cocoa area. Carlos assured him that the Cuban National Socialist troops were already moving into position to occupy ground to the west of Cocoa. They had their scouts farther out to the west monitoring the preparations and movements of the Ortega troops. Apparently Ortega was mobilizing a rather impressive array of men and equipment for the operation, including tanks and armored personnel carriers which did not overly concern Paco Morales as his men were fully prepared and trained to deal with such threats. Carlos went on to explain that Paco himself would be leading the operation in view of the size and strength of the Ortega force and that it may well be that Zone Defense Forces would not actually be involved in combat operations if present plans were successfully carried out. Carlos could give Stuart no details on the plans, obviously, but he said that he would keep him advised as the operation went forward and that Stuart was to continue to plan for and provide security for the bridge and beach areas.

As for the matter of Howard Stone , Carlos would immediately request a decision regarding Stone and would have a message to carry back to him hopefully the following day. The men continued discussing the transfer of Zone facilities well on into the night and in these discussions, the other two men did take an active role which made Stuart think, as he walked back to his dorm late at night, that maybe they were Supply Officers after all. He had to chuckle at how his attitude towards other people had changed over the years. Since the collapse of the government and the political high jinks of President Turner before and after the collapse, and that of all his phony, thieving staff, right down to the local government level, Stuart had stopped trusting anyone. Not a bad policy in this day and age, he thought, as he crawled into his bed to get some needed sleep.

One matter that Stuart had to take care of following his trip to Montana was the written proposal to be addressed to Matt Parker, who apparently ran the show in the Valley. The proposal, following the request of Parker, was to lay out the goals and intentions of the Association for their move to the Valley, particularly with reference to how they intended to benefit Valley residents with technical and educational assistance. The next morning Stuart met with the study group and explained in greater detail his discussions with the Valley representatives which led up to the request for the written statement. Irene Covington, as usual, asked most of the questions relating to what the people living in the Valley presently had with respect to industry, technology and education. Stuart spent most of the morning providing the details to the Group and then assigned them the task of laying out a White Paper on the Association, its organizational structure, short term and long term goals. It was the first task assigned to the Group that would delve into the core beliefs of each participant and as Stuart left the room, he was well aware that there would be sharp disagreements over how the finished product should read and he was not totally convinced that he would agree with it either, particularly if it bore the fingerprint of Irene Covington.

Stuart's instructions to the study group to restrict their remarks to what was in existence in the Control Zone could not apply to the organizational system that would be needed once they arrived. Bill Phillips, the study group leader, had to concede that point to Irene and Stuart was contacted for further direction with regard to how they should handle that issue. Stuart suggested that they come up with a suggestion for a temporary proposal for managing the day to day operation of the Valley pending a joint decision that would be made once the new arrivals were stabilized in their new surroundings. The temporary proposal would, of course, have to be jointly agreed upon by the leaders in Montana and the Association.

The arguments regarding the Temporary Management Structure, as the proposal was referred to, began immediately as soon as Stuart gave the go ahead to the study group. Irene vehemently insisted on a number of basics that had to be included in any such proposal. One was a system of representation of all residents by some means. Another was the right of the residents to participate through a voting mechanism. Again, sides were taken in these arguments and it was obvious that consensus was not possible without concessions by everyone. No one in the five members of the Group was able to articulate a position that was totally acceptable by the other four, or by even a majority of the group.

A majority did not accept absolute suffrage where all had votes, nor did a majority accept absolute representation in the management process. After what seemed like endless hours of argument, an agreement of sorts was finally worked out which no one was totally pleased with. The proposal would be that pending adoption of a permanent form of government among all residents of the Valley following the move, the Association would continue its present form of governance and the Valley people would do the same.

In addition, a council, comprised of seven members would be formed which would handle the general community duties of governance, including police, fire, water, sewer, road repair and other communal responsibilities that would relate to all residents regardless of whether they were old time valley residents or newcomers. The seven Council members would select one of their number to act as Community Manager to serve in an executive capacity as the directing agent of the Council. The Council would be elected based on cumulative voting which would guarantee representation by either involved group. Thus if the newcomer represented one third of the new population, they would be able to elect one-third of the council members if they so chose. The proposed voting requirements were age twenty-one, completion of some predetermined educational level and having conducted oneself in a productive manner. The last qualification would require further definition but was intended to encompass only individuals who were working productively either on their own behalf, on behalf of their family or on behalf of others in the community. Irene argued strongly against incorporation of the final requirement but, on this point, she was the only dissenting vote. After a week of hard fought negotiations, concessions and compromises, a final draft, as requested by Stuart, was submitted to him for approval. He made a few minor changes which did not affect the purpose or intent of the document and after Anders and Sarah had reviewed and approved the content, had it radio transmitted to Matt Parker in the Valley. Stuart attached a request to the message to Parker to reply at his earliest convenience in view of the time restraints they all faced.

Right now Stuart needed to turn his attention to two separate matters that he had been neglecting for the previous two days. His two separate groups of guests, Yates and Campbell and the Cubans. Any further delay could be interpreted as a definite lack of interest with respect to either party. He had Barnes give him a status report on what was happening with respect to Yates and Campbell. Barnes filled him in on what sites they had visited and the nature of the briefings they had received. It sounded as though their time had been well occupied and they should, by now, have a good idea of how the Association operated. Barnes gave Stuart his opinion that the two men seemed genuinely impressed by what they had seen and heard and, unless he was grossly mistaken, they would most likely come on board, assuming there was not a fly in the ointment somewhere. Stuart was not quite so sure they would join up as he thought one or the other may try to drive a bargain that could not be met. Time would tell. Stuart told Barnes to have the men come to his office and they would sit down and discuss where we go from here.

Yates and Campbell were at Stuart's office within the hour and after exchanging pleasantries which included an apology from Stuart regarding his absence from the scene, Stuart brought up the matter of their intentions regarding the invitation from Stuart and the others to join up with the Association. Yates did the talking for the two and opened by thanking Stuart for the offer to take them in. They were very impressed by what they had seen, particularly by the organization of the community and the spirit of good will that seemed to permeate everyone they had met. Yates went on, "If it was a mere matter of joining, that would be a nonissue. Our problem is the baggage that we are bringing which is our connection with the Federal Security Police and what might happen if they get the idea that we played some sort of game with them. We know where the very sizable stash of weapons is secreted. The FSP knows that we know that and they want those items very badly. They'll chew us up and spit us out in a heartbeat if they realize that we have crossed them. They do have the horsepower to do that and if you were to stand in the way, they would take care of your operation as well. They have a fairly long reach and they have probably two times as many men under arms as you have with some pretty good equipment."

Stuart listened quietly as Yates explained the problem and then responded. "I don't disagree with anything you have said, but there are a few other facts here that you gentlemen are not aware of. At least, I don't think you are aware of them and they might affect how you look at the situation." Stuart went on to explain to Yates and Campbell the plans for most of the residents of the Association to leave Florida for Montana and the intentions of some to remain in North Farm. Stuart questioned that the FSP's long arm would extend to Montana and if it did, they might have more to deal with than punishing two guys would be worth. "I really doubt they would take on the whole valley for you two fellows, charming as you are."

Yates only comment was, "Food for thought." Stuart then went on and explained that the Cubans would be taking over the Melbourne area and "There could well be considerable confusion about who took what or who did what to whom."

Both Yates and Campbell were clearly surprised by this news. They had figured something was going on with all of the travel preparations and figured a move of some sort was in the making, but the Cuban takeover came out of the blue. Stuart went on, "No one has to explain to your friends up in Georgia as to what exactly transpired or what munitions were taken from here. Furthermore, they would be well advised to stay the hell out of the way of Paco Morales and his troops. They are nobody to screw with and I assume the FSP is smart enough not to tackle a pit bull with their poodle, if you know what I mean." Yates just nodded in agreement. Stuart could tell he was convincing Yates that a decent cover story could be created. He was not too sure about Campbell, because Campbell had thus far neither said nor indicated anything.

Yates then queried Stuart regarding the Association's interest and intentions in the weapons cache that was hidden somewhere in or around the Control Zone. Stuart let him know that all of that would depend on what was there, how much of it was there and how much the Association could use of what arms or ammo was available. Yates explained the quantities and varieties of munitions that were supposedly stored and it was substantially over the needs of both the Montana and North Farm requirements combined. In his estimate of what would be required for

Montana, Stuart included weaponry well sufficient to also provide for original Valley residents who were presently very ill equipped.

At a lull in the conversation, while both Yates and Stuart were pondering where they went from here, Campbell spoke up for the first time. "Assuming that we deliver the weapons to you, that is telling you where they are, what's in it for us?" Stuart figured that Campbell might be the one to have a high level of self interest in this matter. Barnes had informed him of that possibility some time ago. Stuart was not about to bargain away something that might present complications in the future.

Stuart explained that there was nothing to be given in exchange other than they would be given the safe haven the Association provided and would be placed in positions in the Administration commensurate with their abilities, just like everyone else. Yates said nothing and Campbell only replied, "Interesting, we're going to have to talk about this. Maybe we can get together tomorrow some time."

Stuart stood up to indicate the meeting was over. "Fine. Let me know what you want to do. I'm easy to find. Right here in the office." The two men got up and left the office. Stuart thought that Yates appeared a bit irritated at Campbell. Possibly he had no interest in getting into a bargaining situation when they really were not in a very good position to do so.

Stuart had been right on target, closer than he possibly realized. The FSP did not know the actual location of the weapons cache and Yates figured that once they did know it, both Yates and Campbell would be excess baggage. When they left the office and were out of earshot, Yates asked Campbell, "Just what the hell did you think he was going to do?" Campbell shot back, "Listen we're holding four aces on this deal. They need the guns and we know where they are." Yates had thought this through beforehand and walked Campbell over towards the Marina. "Take a look at the troops and notice what they are armed with, all AR20s. State of the art. I haven't seen any troops that were not similarly equipped. I've also seen storage boxes on the tour that I had seen before and guess what they contained when I saw them the last time, ground to ground and ground to air missile launchers. There is no doubt these guys could use more weaponry, but they aren't hurting quite as badly as you seem to think. Not only that, but between you and me, I think we are too dead chickens, headed for the pot, just as soon as we let the boys in Georgia know where the goods are."

Campbell thought about that for a moment, apparently having arrived at the same conclusion some time previously. "Well, what do you want to do?"

The two men were walking towards the dormitory buildings, through an area that had been set up as a park. Some of the mothers were watching their children playing on the swings and did not pay any attention to the two men deep in conversation on the far side of the park. Yates stopped walking and, looking at Campbell, said "I want this. This is the closest thing to something I faintly remember when I was a kid, or God knows when, that I can think of. I am impressed. They have done a hell of a job. You can go to bed at night and not sleep with one eye open. There are no punks here that would just as soon put a bullet through your back as look at you. There are kids here. Look! Playing on swings. When the hell was the last time you saw that? Give 'em the fucking weapons. Screw Turner and the FSP They'd screw us in two seconds. Maybe one."

Campbell merely nodded and said "Yeh. I guess you' re right. Okay, we'll let him know tomorrow."

Yates said, "What's wrong with right now? We've got things to do before we bail out of my place and they also have a tight calendar. Let's role on this right now." Campbell agreed and the two headed back to Stuart's office. As they walked in, Stuart looked up and with a smile on his face, said "I thought you two gentlemen might be stopping by. What can I do for you?"

Yates chuckled and said, "You know damn well what you can do for us. Let's talk about what sort of jobs might be available these days."

The three men sat in Stuart's office for a number of hours laying out the details of their move into the structure of the Association. Yates had various supplies and equipment at his farm that he wanted to bring with him, assuming it could be transported to Montana and assuming Stuart had an interest in doing so. Yates also had three men that had worked the farm for him for a number of years and all three had prior military backgrounds that might be of value to the Association. Stuart assured him that they had room for anyone that wanted to join up with the Association and help carry the load. After all of the basics were covered, they went into the matter of the location of the weapons stores. They were buried under the concrete pad in front of one of the old hangars on the military airstrip. The concrete was three feet thick at that point and was going to be a problem to penetrate without the use of explosives which, of course, they couldn't use. Stuart suggested they get rolling on the excavation in the morning and after the exact location was marked out, Robert Thomas would be available to run them back to their farm for their men and equipment.

# Chapter Thirty

As Yates and Campbell were leaving his office, Stuart had his secretary get a message to Carlos Moran to meet with him at his earliest convenience. He needed to resolve the matter of Howard Stone and his group up at Cocoa immediately or that was going to fall through the developing cracks. The western Cuban force was expected within the next week or two and the people involved, including his own Defense Team members guarding the bridge area had to know what was going on. In less than ten minutes, Carlos was at his office door. Stuart waved him in and sat down. Stuart went right to the point. "Carlos, what is the decision on the Cocoa group? We have to know that now."

Carlos apologized for the delay in getting the response from Vero which was to work with Stone and to assure him that the Cubans had no great interest in Cocoa at the moment. That was the gist of the response and Carlos went on to say that, "If plans presently in effect are carried through, Mr. Stone will not see Ricardo Ortega's troops in Cocoa. The job will be done before they arrive."

Stuart nodded, understanding that Morales men would make their move to the west of Cocoa, probably in the cane fields. "Okay. Who deals with Mr. Stone?" Carlos responded that he would handle that and requested Stuart to set up a meeting as soon as possible. Stuart had his secretary get a message to Monty Wyatt to set up the meeting for the following morning.

With that matter at least apparently resolved, Stuart inquired of Carlos as to how his work on the turnover of the Zone was going. Carlos shrugged his shoulders and said, "As well as could be expected. You have done an excellent job of organizing very few resources. I would have preferred moving into a more productive area, but we can assume that lies across the water in Melbourne and to the west." Stuart agreed. He had his fill of trying to find food and water to provide for the residents. There were good crop lands to the west that could be utilized and Melbourne had a good natural harbor that could handle deep draft boats for shipment of materials and produce down to Miami. That would be of value to the Cubans and may have been of interest to the Association if the demographics of South Florida had been otherwise. South Florida was basically Cuban with only pockets of Caucasians here and there. People tended to flock with their own kind and South Florida was no different. Carlos told Stuart that the supply men that accompanied him had been busy inventorying storage space, housing availability, power equipment, water treatment equipment and, in general, all of those facilities and the equipment necessary to provide for a large group of people. Carlos also informed Stuart that he had been instructed to stay in the Zone pending the departure of the Association to act as the liaison for the C.N.S.P. with the Association. That was fine with Stuart and he had been about to suggest that to Carlos as matters came up constantly that needed some input or decision from the new tenants. Also, Stuart had been thinking that, from what Yates had to say about the weapons stored at the old base, an excess might be available to use as a bargaining chip to solve two concerns that he had been thinking about. The first was his underlying concern that they were not being set up by Morales and his troops. Stuart did not think so, but he was not naive.

The Association was hauling some pretty good equipment out of the area that they had managed to accumulate over the time they had operated the Zone and the Cubans might take a fancy to keeping it for themselves. The second concern that he had was the matter of security of his convoy once they left. Obviously the Cubans could not guarantee their security to Montana, but they could help by providing additional security probably well up into the panhandle of Florida. Stuart was most concerned with the FSP who had tentacles reaching throughout Georgia and down into parts of Florida. They might think twice about tangling with the Cubans. After he saw what was buried up at the base, he would discuss this further with Sarah and Anders.

Carlos had been working mostly with John Barnes and that seemed to be going fairly well, so Stuart told him to talk to John if he needed anything and if need be, he could see Stuart. Carlos thanked him and left the office.

Sarah came by just as Carlos was leaving and said that she had received a reply from Parker and everything was a go as far as they were concerned.

Stuart had not expected any problems, but, nevertheless, this was good news as he could check off one more hurdle to overcome in their departure from the Zone. "Good. Now we can get down to business. Sarah, I want you to work out a final departure calendar that gets us out of here on schedule and post it on the Boards. Give Carlos a hard copy so that he doesn't have to copy it off the Board. He is going to want the details so that he can move his people in right behind ours as they leave. Tell Barnes to bring me up to date on how we stand with the vehicles. How are we on parts and is he getting enough of the armor plating that we talked about for covering the tires and engines and shielding for passengers. Seems to me if we don't have that protection, those trucks are going to be very vulnerable. Robert Thomas said he knew where we could obtain the protective Marsden-Kevlar synthetic fiber material but someone has to fabricate it and install it. I want to know what the hell is going on with that. We have six weeks in which to do an awful lot of work and we'd better get rolling or the Cubans will throw us out." Sarah had been making notes as he talked and assured him that she would look into the matters personally. She also brought up the latest intelligence on the FSP that she had obtained from her sources in the Macon area and suggested that he come by Intelligence for a full briefing. He agreed but asked her to give him a quick rundown on what they were up to.

Sarah set her notes down and responded, "Quite a bit. I'll try to pick out the key points. Turner had been solidifying his base up there and more and more of the FSP personnel have been drifting in. They occupied the old Robins military base south of Macon as well as former military facilities in the Atlanta area. Their attention had been devoted during the past year or so to getting the Atlanta and Macon areas under control as the situation was one of total anarchy before they began the clean up. As a result, the people in Georgia generally welcomed them and probably still do. It will take some time before their new subjects realize how they operate. Turner has his cadre of opportunists with him at Warner Robbins and we have no reason to believe that they have changed in any respect. I should add that their clean up, particularly in the Atlanta area was very brutal. Many, many dead from what I am told."

Sarah continued, "I was also told from a source in the Tallahassee area that FSP patrols were coming through there and were appointing local groups to act on their behalf. So far the strength of such groups is not a significant factor but, in time it will be. The FSP is also active in getting roads opened up again, spoking out from Macon and Atlanta. They have made it known that anyone interfering with road traffic will be shot on sight. That also is very much welcomed by smaller communities and pockets of civilization which will presumably support the FSP in anything they want, at least for the time being. They are also refurbishing rail beds and have some trains running, at least now between Macon and Atlanta. As far as equipment is concerned, I can give you a better picture on that if you have some time and we can put together slides with the exact information that came into us, but until then, they possess an impressive number of armored vehicles and a few aircraft that appear to be flying fairly often. I thought virtually every plane in the country had been destroyed, and they probably were, with the exception of Frick's, but maybe they cannibalized enough parts and put a few back together."

Stuart interrupted with a question, "What kind of planes are we talking about?"

"Not the kind you would prefer. I am told these are ground support aircraft. Either former Army or Air Force." That was not welcome news to Stuart, nor was the information that the FSP's activities extended down into the Tallahassee area. The trip to Montana was going to have to pass very close to Tallahassee and he had been concerned about the area even without the presence of the FSP. "What other good news do you have this morning?"

Sarah smiled and replied, "Not a hell of a lot. Do you remember the militia and how popular they were? Well, they have been amazingly silent for the past few years which has surprised a lot of people, but apparently they were involved with establishing their own communities and solidifying their own bases of operation. I think that with the passage of time, they have accomplished these goals and are becoming more active. A number of such groups in the Georgia area, I know, have been working with the FSP as their area representative. I don't know how long that will last, probably only as long as the FSP needs their services. In any event, from what I am told, you have to sing the right song in Georgia or you are in trouble. Militia units across the country are, in general becoming more active and taking control of larger pieces of ground. Before this, it was smaller groups of armed bandits, trying to take whatever they could find. Now it is becoming more organized which is going to make our trip more difficult. I would say that in another year or two, without a sizeable military force backing us up, we would not be able to make the trip. The answer to providing us some relief might be in intelligence. There are numerous groups of varying sizes now operating around the country. They are all in competition for ground. Consequently they might well be played off against each other and if we know who and what we are dealing with, at least as much as we can, it just might save us from having to play hardball."

Stuart thought over what she had said and responded, "Sarah, I could not agree more. I don't know how much of your section you are devoting to that effort, but I would suggest that it take center stage, especially now when time is drawing short for our departure. Also, whatever you need to support an active, communications center and intelligence unit on the trip, take it. If you need any support from Anders or me, let me know. I agree. If we know who and what we are about to encounter, it can make all the difference in the world. Keep me posted on that and I would suggest you prepare special briefings for me, Anders and Ross Perry whenever you receive information that we should know."

In the morning, Stuart got a hold of Andy Moss and had him organize the men and equipment necessary to do the excavation at the old base. He also had Perry assign a security detail around the area to keep everyone at least a mile away from the excavation site, most particularly the Cuban visitors. Stuart did not want them to know what was going on at the base. Stuart also told Perry that he would be given all the weapons he wanted for protection of the convoy and to make sure there were gun ports for all passengers to utilize for defense. Perry could hardly believe this good news as weapons and ammo had always been in short supply.

Yates went with Moss to show him the area where they were going to have to do the digging and further, described the material they were going to have to dig through which included three feet of concrete hardened with one inch rebar reinforcement. Due to the nature of what was below the concrete, they could not use explosives to break through the concrete surface. It was going to be a tough digging job and after discussing the matter with Yates, Moss sent his men out to find the proper drilling equipment necessary to get through the concrete. He also sent one of the men to find Robert Thomas who was a specialist at hard to find items in the area because he doubted that really hard drill bits could be found anywhere around the beach area. His messenger returned some time later and assured him that Thomas knew where he could most likely find some but it was over on the mainland and that would require some assistance from Jack Nix and his people. Moss had to run that through Perry who gave the request an immediate thumbs up. Thomas was back in three or four hours with the required drills and bits. They had experienced no problems on their visit to the mainland as the area they had to visit was under the control of Howard Stone and Monty Wyatt was able to negotiate a clearance for them without any trouble. Thomas didn't know what that was about but figured something was in the works because Stones men, who were usually not very friendly, were most accommodating.

Carlos had been directed to Monty Wyatt for the setup of his meeting with Howard Stone. The meeting was held over on the Cocoa side of the bridge and Wyatt was not able to set up the appropriate equipment to determine what was being said between the two men. He was able to observe Stone following the meeting and apparently it had gone without any major problems as Stone was friendly and courteous with Carlos when they separated.

A request had been sent by way of Carlos back to the Morales Headquarters at Vero Beach for Association military observers to join the operation against the western Cubans. Carlos reported to Stuart that they had approved two observers and they would be met at Stone's Cocoa office the following morning by Morales troops. Stuart had Monty Wyatt select the men for the observer mission and was not surprised to hear Wyatt request that he be one of the two. Stuart did not like to put key people in high risk situations, but he also wanted a trained and experienced observer to report back as to how the Morales troops functioned in combat and the tactics that they appeared to favor. That information could be useful in times to come. Wyatt had one of his senior squad leaders accompany him and before they left, Stuart and Perry gave both men instructions on what they were to be looking for. Stuart also told them not to get involved in the action and to make it back safely so that they could get the information. Wyatt smiled as he assured Stuart that he had every intention of making it back safely.

Stuart was in his office early the next morning in time to wish Wyatt and his companion well on their mission with the Cubans. Both men had secured their combat gear from supply in the event that they found themselves a little too close to the action. Stuart again cautioned them to stay out of what was basically an intertribal matter that did not involve the Association and Stuart did not want to create any more enemies than they already had. Wyatt again assured him that they would take extra precautions to avoid trouble. After they had left, Carlos came into the office and requested the use of one of the empty buildings as an infirmary in the event that it was needed as a result of the anticipated military action.

Stuart saw no problem with that and also contacted John Barnes to be prepared to issue some medical supplies to the Cubans that were not part of the Contingency Kit. The Kit was an inventory of basic supply items that Stuart and Sarah had put together to represent the bare essentials needed to sustain the community for a three month period. Barnes shook his head with that request, advising Stuart that almost everything that he had in Supply was on the Contingency Kit list. He did have some blankets and, what he called hard goods that he could provide to Carlos. The available items included beds, items of furniture, some basic medical items such as bandages, sterilizing equipment, and various medical tools. Stuart also contacted the medical officer on duty in the dispensary and advised them to be prepared to provide emergency medical care should casualties start to come into the Zone.

Carlos was beginning to request more and more items from Stuart and the others in the Administration which was causing some friction with the staff. When Carlos came in for the third time on one of Stuart's busier mornings, he set aside what he was working on and told the Cuban to take a chair, they had to talk. Stuart told him that the staff was running in circles, working with very scarce resources, preparing for the move of hundreds of people to Montana as well as the move of hundreds to North Farm. They were not prepared to also support the move of the Cubans into the Zone. In the meantime, Stuart would try to help, if he could do so without adversely impacting the departure efforts of the Association. Stuart advised Carlos that empty buildings in the Zone would be made available to him for storage and a truck would be assigned to the Cubans for their use in bringing in equipment. One of the empty docks in the Marina would also be set aside and Morales people in Vero could ship items up to the Marina dock and Carlos and his men could then set it up in the assigned buildings. Stuart also authorized an additional cadre of Cubans to move into the Zone to help Carlos in loading and unloading the equipment. This appeared to satisfy Carlos as he said that was all that was hoped for and he would try to stay out of the way of the staff but that occasionally they did need a little something in order to do their job.

Two days after Monty Wyatt had departed to join the Cuban force in its mission against Ricardo Ortega's group of Western Cubans, Sarah came into Stuart's office with the news that the mission had been a success but that there were a fair number of casualties that needed immediate medical assistance. The senior Cuban officer on the mission was requesting the assistance of the Association in treating the men and was awaiting a reply. The medical staff was notified and within hours patients were arriving from the north. From the appearance of the wounded, it had apparently been a bruising battle, even for the victors. Stuart was thinking to himself that if these were the winners, what shape are the losers in. He told Perry that as soon as Monty Wyatt returned to report to him as to what had transpired. Shortly thereafter Wyatt did return to the Zone and came directly to Stuart's office. Stuart took the two men up to the Intelligence Section so that the staff people could interrogate them and Sarah could also hear their report.

Monty Wyatt was provided a map of the area to use in his report and when everyone was seated, he began by describing their meeting Morales' men at the headquarters of Howard Stone in Cocoa. Stone also had two men serving as observers and the four were guided on the mission by two of Morales' staff people. They were treated very well and politely by the Cubans. Before they left Stone's office, they were given a full briefing on how the mission was expected to be carried out. They were advised that they were not to speak to anyone for any purpose unless they first requested permission of their Cuban guides. Wyatt had no problem with that, understanding well the need for security. According to the plan, the Western Cuban force was to be ambushed to the west of Cocoa out in the marsh lands. The Western Cuban troops had to travel on the only road running west to east and either side of the road was heavy brush, tall sugar cane fields, or wetland. Cover would be excellent for Morales' men, provided they could handle the mosquitoes and bugs, and there was little if any question as to the route the intruders would be taking. As the Cuban briefer saw the anticipated layout of the two combatants, the situation appeared to favor Morales' force. According to scouts that were shadowing the intruding Cuban force, they should be in the target area within hours which would be around six that evening. Sunset was expected to be at around seven-thirty which would provide adequate visibility for the expected action.

The briefer advised the four observers that Morales men were already in position and were awaiting the arrival of Ricardo Ortega's company. The briefer then explained the route that Wyatt and the others would be taking to the observation point which was a plot of level ground approximately one mile from the expected area of combat. A bunker had been prepared for the men at the site and additional troops would be detailed to provide protection should the need arise. Following the briefing, all of the observers were thoroughly searched by the Cubans present and all weapons and ammunition were removed to be made available on their return. Wyatt protested giving up his AR20, but the Cubans advised him that they were taking absolutely no chances that someone would accidentally or otherwise, fire a rifle, warning the advancing force of trouble. With that, the observers and their guides left the safety of the Cocoa area and headed west. They were accompanied most of the way by a squad of Stone's men who left them as they entered the area now secured by Morales' troops.

There were a number of bunkers dug out around the observation point and the guide indicated the one that the observers were to occupy. Monty Wyatt commented to Stuart and the others in the room that, while the bunker was not very comfortable, it was very well constructed for its intended purpose. They did, indeed, have an unrestricted view of the anticipated field of combat and yet, were not visible to those coming from the west along the road.

Their guides then instructed them to remove all reflective devices, watches, buttons, whatever that might give away their position and for those that, for one reason or another could not be removed, could be painted over. With that final task being completed, the men made themselves as comfortable as they could. Mosquito lotion, which was in very short supply, was passed out by their hosts and eagerly applied by the observers. After four-thirty, complete silence was imposed on the observers and the Cubans with them. All eyes were now focused on the roadway and from their position, they could look down the length of the road to the west a distance of approximately three miles. Wyatt was very familiar with the road as he had traveled it many times in his youth and in his recent patrols. It was the main thoroughfare from Cocoa to Orlando and at one time was a four lane road. In recent years, the only use of the roadway was by well armed units of men and they only used one section of the road so that what had been the west bound lane was now totally overgrown. The remaining lane was a long, ribbon like stretch of road which, with its lack of use, was overgrown in parts, but one could still recognize it as a roadway. The brush, along what had been the sides of the road, now reached out into the remaining roadway and in places, formed a virtual canopy of foliage over the road. Wyatt related that as he looked down the roadway, he was wondering how he would bring a force of men down that exposed pathway in safety. He knew one thing, he wouldn't just drive down it with his men, humming a tune, which appeared to be what the Cubans were expecting.

After a long uncomfortable wait in the bunker, when Stone's men, in particular, were beginning to grumble and shift their positions frequently, searching for some relief from their cramped quarters, Wyatt thought he observed some movement at the far end of the roadway. The sun was beginning to set and Wyatt noted that according to his watch, the visitors were quite a bit behind schedule. On further thought, they may have planned to arrive in the vicinity of the Cocoa area in the dark of night rather than in the light of day. Monty Wyatt went on with his briefing to the rapt attention of his listeners. The first movement down the overgrown roadway was that of a single, all terrain, armored vehicle. No one on foot and no sign of any following traffic, on foot or motorized. Interesting Wyatt thought. At that point in time, he began to think that Ricardo Ortega may not be the fool that his Cuban brethren expected him to be. As the vehicle proceeded towards the east and came more into view, Wyatt recognized it as an all terrain, personnel carrier that was capable of transporting up to twenty fully armed foot soldiers. Everyone in the bunker was of one mind, what were Morales men going to do? They could easily knock out the single vehicle if they chose to do so, but in so doing, they would show their hand to the larger force to the west. As the vehicle came towards them, it became clear to Wyatt that the order had been passed to permit the vehicle to move through the ambush area. Wyatt learned later that the Cuban cadre at Howard Stone's headquarters were warned by radio of the approaching vehicle and ordered to make themselves scarce and Stone was instructed to play along with the visitors as though their arrival was according to plan.

Wyatt's next observation of activity confirmed in his own mind that Ricardo Ortega was indeed using his head. After approximately ten minutes, he observed the same vehicle now heading in the opposite direction, followed by its return only a few minutes after it disappeared in the west, presumably with a fresh load of troops. What was going on was now apparent. The Western Cubans, not totally trusting Stone, were taking steps to avoid just what was, in fact, planned for them. Morales men now had to decide how many men they were going to allow through the ambush area before they made their move. They could well find themselves in the wrong part of a vice if they allowed too many troops to get through. Their guide, who had been listening on his radio, told the observers that the troops were being dropped off at a bluff just outside of the town and were taking up positions, apparently awaiting the arrival of their comrades. As the vehicle came back down the road again, now with its fifth load of troops, Wyatt estimated that there would soon be one hundred or more of Ricardo Ortega's men dug into position between the observers bunker and Cocoa.

Wyatt did not find that comforting in view of the fact that his AR20 was somewhere back at Stone's headquarters. His future rested entirely with the Cuban squad around his bunker. He also realized at that point that his position was first on the list for an attack from the east by Ricardo Ortega's men that had already been dropped off.

It was now getting very dark as the sun had set over thirty minutes ago and were it not for the clatter of the personnel carriers treads upon the remains of the roadway, Wyatt would have difficulty knowing what was going on. He could faintly make out the movement of a shadow down towards the roadway and figured that was the vehicle. As he stared into the darkness, a brilliant light came out of the bush on his side of the road and left a bright trail as it sped towards the now visible personnel carrier. The explosion as it hit the vehicle lit up the entire area but the vehicle itself was obscured by the explosion. As the brilliant flash of the explosion died down, a reddish ball of flame erupted from the wreckage of the carrier and exploding small arms ammunition could be heard crackling through the roar of the fire. There was no sound of a human voice, scream or otherwise coming from the carrier and Wyatt assumed they had all been killed instantly by the massive explosion when the missile struck. A long period of silence ensued while both sides were apparently deciding what to do next.

It did not take Ricardo Ortega very long to decide as he had anticipated something like this occurring. What he did not know was who the culprit was. He had not trusted Stone and at first assumed that Stone was the cause of the problem and he could easily be disposed of. With that in mind, he launched anti-personnel rockets into the area which rained down on either side of the road in the vicinity of where the carrier had been struck. He then sent in his tanks with troops coming in behind to mop up any survivors of the rocket and tank assault. As the tanks came in, they raked either side of the road with cannon and machine gun fire. Morales men were well dug into their positions and stayed unexposed, not only to prevent being hit, but also to prevent detection from infra-red detection devices which they knew were being used.

As the Western Cubans made their way down the road, Wyatt watched the action taking place and realized that Ricardo Ortega was now the one making the mistake. He was assuming a much smaller force was awaiting him than in fact was there. He was doing what Morales men had wanted him to do in the first place. As Ricardo Ortega's men obliterated the road on either side with their massive firepower, their confidence grew and what appeared to be the entire force was now out on the roadway, firing everything they had into the darkness on both sides of the road. Wyatt figured there were undoubtedly casualties on the part of the Vero troops but they would be dwarfed by those of Ricardo Ortega's men when it came time to return fire. As the Western troops moved down the road to the east and were all now exposed to Morales massed troops up on the north side of the road, all hell broke loose. Wyatt was stunned at the mass of firepower generated by Morales. The entire sky lit up as the roadway exploded in a cloud of smoke, dust and debris. Flares were launched lighting up the entire roadway. Small arms, rocket, cannon, everything destructive that Wyatt had ever been familiar with rained down on the Western Cuban force. No one could survive such devastating firepower and as it turned out, apparently no one had. More flares lit up the night sky as the order was given to cease firing. There was no return fire from any of the wreckage or bodies littering the roadway. After a while a patrol was dispatched to check out the carnage. There was an occasional rifle shot heard which Wyatt figured was to dispatch some luckless Western Cuban who had somehow survived the murderous fire.

Attention was now directed to the troops that had been unloaded on the bluff overlooking the town of Cocoa. They too had been observing the action and awaiting orders that never came. Seeing the overpowering force that had obviously obliterated their comrades, the group of approximately eighty men lit out to the north in an attempt to save themselves. By this time, the cadre back at Cocoa had been alerted to their presence and was in position watching for them to make a move. When they did and they left their secured positions, they were likewise dispatched when, in the light of flares, they were hit with heavy cannon and machine gun fire. A few of the troops, seeing their situation was hopeless, could be seen in the light of the flares throwing down their weapons and waving that they were surrendering. They were shown no mercy and mowed down along with the rest. As the last shots were fired, the smell of burnt gunpowder and the smoke generated by the burning vehicles and explosions covered the entire countryside.

The burning rubber of the wheeled vehicles made breathing difficult and Wyatt had to hold a dampened cloth over his mouth in order to filter out some of the toxic fumes. As they came out of their bunker, Wyatt could see, in the light of the flares that were still being fired, that Morales men had, indeed, suffered a number of casualties. There were a number of dead that were buried on scene as the surviving casualties were being brought to the roadway for transport. Vehicles were brought in and the injured were being loaded into them to be taken for medical treatment. Wyatt was unaware at that point in time that the request had already gone to the Association for the use of medical facilities.

As he watched the wounded being loaded, Wyatt thought to himself that the operation may have succeeded, but it was very costly in troop loss. Most of the injured had come about in the initial barrage by Ricardo Ortega's men into the brush and that could have been prevented by better preparation and placement of positions. In Wyatt's mind the operation had been a somewhat bungled success. All of the observers were rapidly herded back to Stone's headquarters where they were returned their weapons and sent back to their respective departure points. That concluded Monty Wyatt's report of the operation and he then asked if anyone had questions. There were a number, particularly from Sarah's staff. How many men in Morales force, what types of weapons, did they appear well fed, clothed, equipped, how was their morale, and so forth. Wyatt answered their questions as well as he could and Stuart, observing that Wyatt was very tired from his two days in the bush, dismissed him so that he could get some rest.

# Chapter Thirty-One

While the operation to the west of Cocoa had been taking place and Carlos' attention was somewhat diverted from the Zone, Stuart took the opportunity to proceed with the excavation project at the airbase. Perry's security detail was positioned to keep any of the curious well back from the project area. Perry had also taken precautions not to make the enhanced security too visible as that would invite greater interest in what was taking place. The base was not what one would consider a high traffic area anyway, so the few people, mostly children, who did venture out onto the old base property could most likely be handled without drawing much attention. Heavy equipment was brought in and Campbell and Yates were on hand to advise the excavators as to the area where the digging should take place. It soon became apparent that the project was not going to go as quickly as everyone thought. Furthermore, clouds of dust were rising from the project due to the drilling and even though valuable fresh water was being poured on the drilling areas, the dust kept rising. The excavators could not use the endless supply of salt water for fear of damaging the weapons and ammunition under the concrete.

By the end of the first day, the drillers had penetrated the three feet of concrete in one small area. It took well into the second day before they had an opening large enough for the dirt machines to dig down to the environmentally protected container where the weapons were stored. The container was basically of synthetic construction with various layers of plastic sealing out all water and moisture. The diggers had been running into some water as they penetrated deeper into the earth but they were able to control the flow of seepage with pumps which were placed in the pit. Stuart and Perry had been concerned that with the high water table on the beach, salt water or a briny mixture of salt and fresh water could be damaging the goods but the protection afforded by the container appeared to be doing the job.

Workmen who entered a small opening in the container reported no sign of moisture anywhere. They also reported the dimensions of the interior of the container and the fact that it appeared to be completely filled with weapons and ammunition of various types. That information was passed onto Barnes so that he could make the necessary arrangements for transporting and storing the equipment in a secure area. Once the excavators had cleared off an area on the top of the container large enough to permit access with the equipment necessary to unload the weapons and ammunition, heavy hydraulic lifts, with pallets, were brought in by Barnes to remove the weapons and place them in waiting transport trucks.

As the project neared the point where the weapons were about to be transported, it began to get the attention of the residents. They had seen the dust rising to the north in the area of the base and now the heavy equipment was being taken to that general area. Carlos and his companions as well took notice of the activity and in time, Carlos inquired of Stuart as to what was going on up at the base. Stuart did not want to give a cover story to Carlos as he knew that eventually, Carlos and his associates would know what had taken place at the base and Stuart wanted to maintain a relationship of candor with the Cuban, if at all possible. On the other hand, he didn't want to tell him what was occurring so he, consequently, dismissed the inquiry with a shrug and a comment, some things we have to take care of. It was apparent to Carlos that Stuart had no intention of telling him what was going on and for the moment he accepted that fact. Carlos was fully aware that eventually he would find out what had occurred.

As the reports from the base came to Stuart's office, it became apparent that they had a huge arms cache on their hands. Barnes had a warehouse reserved for the weapons as the dig began and in time that was virtually filled to the ceiling with a wide variety of weapons and ammunition. There were literally thousands of crated, disassembled AR20 automatic rifles with approximately four thousand rounds of ammunition per rifle. There were also anti-armored vehicle and anti-aircraft hand held missiles by the hundreds, grenades with launchers, anti-personnel mines and a number of other weapons and support equipment. As the cases were being hauled out of the storage container and into the secured warehouse, Stuart sat down with Sarah and Anders and the three discussed just exactly what they were going to do with the huge arsenal they now possessed. All three unanimously decided without discussion that they would segregate a substantial store of weapons for their own use and for the use of their anticipated future population growth, by merger or otherwise. They would also do the same for the North Farm operation and in order to get a handle on the numbers of weapons and varieties that they should be thinking about, they called Perry in and, after filling him in on the quantities involved, delegated to him the responsibility of determining how many and what types should be set aside for their own uses. Perry was ecstatic with the concept of having an excess supply of state of the art military equipment at his disposal. Up to this point, rationing had been the name of the game and he had some units under his command that were using four or more different types of weapons. It was difficult to manage military operations when your men were working with dissimilar equipment.

After Perry had left, the other three continued their discussion regarding what to do with the excess. It was clear that they did not have the space available in the trucks to haul all of the weapons to Montana. They would have liked to do that, but it was out of the question. The only viable alternative left was to ship a large portion of the excess up to North Farm and re-secure it up there before they left for Montana. They could again bury the weapons in a remote area of North Farm and, again, environmentally protect it in a similar fashion to the manner in which it had been preserved before. In order to do that effectively, they would have to handle the shipment without the Cubans being the wiser or it would make North Farm a very attractive plum for them. The balance, they would store in the complex until they decided what to do with it.

With the discussion focusing in on North Farm, it was decided to bring

Jim McLeod into the conversation so that he would be privy to what was going on. He, of course, had no knowledge of the arms cache and was taken by surprise when Stuart brought him up to date on what had been going on up at the base. McLeod agreed with the concept that a sufficient number of rifles, ammunition and other weapons should be allocated to the North Farm operation. Stuart had not been totally sure that McLeod believed in the use of weaponry to ensure the safety of his community. A number of people in the Association were of the view that weapons were per se evil and Stuart had never sounded McLeod out on the subject. With McLeod being in general agreement with the scheme, Stuart then brought up the matter of secreting a fairly large shipment of the arms in North Farm. McLeod was not as enthusiastic about that, but after further discussion which centered around the alternatives, giving the excess to the Cubans or to the FSP, McLeod saw the light. Stuart advised McLeod that they would have to begin shipments immediately as that had to be done, in small shipments, without the knowledge of the Cubans. The cover for the shipments would be that they were goods going up to North Farm to provision the new area. That was, in fact, a very good cover as frequent shipments in large quantities were already going up there for that purpose. The problem again was, could Robert Thomas find a sufficient number of boats to do all the hauling that had to be done for North Farm with the added load of the weapons. He was already complaining about not having a sufficient number of boats to do the job.

Stuart then brought up the matter of using a portion of the arms cache to work a deal with the Cubans to provide security up through the Georgia area. From all the information that Sarah had provided thus far, it appeared that one of the higher threat areas that they would face on the journey to the northwest would be from their present site at Melbourne up through the southeast corner of Georgia and into Alabama. There was no way that they could avoid these areas without going around the northern part of Georgia and into Tennessee which would actually be more dangerous. Stuart wanted to work a deal with Morales whereby they provided a security detail of two hundred men or more with their own provisions and sustaining food and water supplies.

Monty Wyatt had informed them regarding the weapons that Morales men were using in the Cocoa operation and it appeared that they suffered from the same problem as other armed groups; they were using a variety of weapons, whatever they could obtain. Sarah and Anders listened attentively as Stuart laid out the groundwork for his proposal. He figured that Morales would be very willing to work a deal provided the price was right. Sarah asked the crucial question, just what is the right price. Stuart had considered that and suggested that they start with five hundred AR20 rifles and fifty thousand rounds of ammunition. If that didn't do it, which Stuart believed it would, they could raise the offer to eight hundred rifles. They did not want to make it appear that they had access to a much larger number or they might be creating a problem for their own security. One problem they would have to overcome was that they were going to have to secrete the weapons before the agreement was entered into with Morales which created a bit of a problem. The problem being that they were going to have to anticipate the number of weapons that would get Morales attention. Stuart thought five hundred would do it, but suggested that they secrete eight hundred weapons. At the end of the journey, Stuart would let them know where they could find them. If the agreement had been entered into for five hundred weapons, the Cubans would have a three hundred rifle bonus. Not letting them know where the weapons were until the bargain was carried out would afford the Association with some protection against a double cross from Morales. He would presumably not want to try anything with them without knowing how to get the payoff.

Hiding that many weapons under the prying eyes of Carlos and his companions would not be easy and the three sat and discussed how that would be accomplished for over an hour. Sarah suggested that the engineers could rig up a water tight container and it could be sunk with the weapons out in the Indian River after being hauled out there and dropped on one of the shipments up to North Farm. The boats were running back and forth to North Farm on a regular basis now and another boat pulling out of the Marina would not attract anyone's attention. The container could be secured to concrete block anchors that had previously been dropped in the river and used as buoy anchors for Thomas' boats. He could spare one or two for this purpose as his boats were out almost all the time anyway with the heavy shipping requirements for North Farm. Back in his office, Stuart pulled out his workbook on the Montana move and directed his attention to the matter of packing forty truck loads of people and equipment into fifteen tractor trailers.

Stuart felt like he was balancing ten bricks on the head of a pin. So far everything had been working out alright but he had no doubt that luck had played a part. Most of his time was spent running around the Zone, overseeing tasks related to the move, talking with supervisors and closely watching the time schedules. Arrangements had to be made for breaking down equipment that was to be taken to Montana, packing it for shipment and loading it on to specific assigned vehicles. He was thankful that they had competent people in the Association that he could rely on.

There was always the underlying question of how to handle the people question. The real problem came into being when it was determined that one member of a family was not in condition physically to handle the rigors of the trip. That could be due to a temporary problem such as pregnancy or a chronic illness that had depleted ones strength. The really heart breaking cases were those involving the pregnancy issue. Stuart's position had always been that they could not take people on the trip who were going to be a substantial burden to others. That was the broad measure that he used, personally, in deciding who was going to be permitted to go and who was not. As it turned out, there were only three cases of those that wanted to go that could be considered as medical problems due to pregnancy.

Stuart's first order regarding the women was that they were not allowed to take the trip and were assigned to North Farm. In all three cases, their husbands were solid, contributing members of the Association and they all, very much, wanted to make the trip to the northwest. Furthermore, they had numerous friends that were making the trip that wanted them to be part of the new community. As time went on, they generated a very vocal support group in their plea that pregnancy not be considered as prohibiting the opportunity for these young people to participate in the new life in Montana. Stuart could not ignore their pleas any longer, particularly when the volume had increased to a level where it was becoming a topic of conversation throughout the complex and he realized that something had to be done. Either a way had to be found to take the three cases or he had to somehow deflate the growing discontent with his control of who went and who didn't. Consequently, he called in the three family groups for a conference and sat them down in his office. He explained to them what the basic problem was. Space on vehicles was at a premium. They did plan on carrying a transportable medical care facility but that was planned to be used for emergencies only. There were bound to be accidents and there was always the possibility, better yet the probability, of armed combat with various lawless individuals or groups that they would run into on their trip. Facilities had to be available for any members of the Defense Force that may be injured in these encounters.

Stuart laid the problem in their hands and told them that if they had some reasonable solution to the matter of care and treatment for the mothers in the course of the journey to the northwest, Stuart would consider the suggestion. He also brought up the fact that making such a journey for a woman in the final stages of pregnancy was potentially life threatening and they were not going to have the level of medical care available to treat such cases while on the road. This care would conceivably not measure up to what these families would have were they to go to North Farm at the outset.

None of these arguments carried any weight with the listeners and they responded that Stuart was just coming up with possibilities that would most likely never occur. It appeared that the two sides were deadlocked and Stuart realized that something had to be done to arrive at a consensus one way or the other. Stuart and Anders had not yet resolved the matter of how the people going to the Northwest were going to be transported. This was still being worked out as the numbers of who was going and who wasn't was still up in the air.

It appeared that with proper organization, they would be able to transport four to five hundred people in the trucks with sleeping quarters set up for one hundred and fifty in tight bunk bed accommodations. This meant at least three shifts of sleepers in hot bunks with those awake, packed like sardines in the transport vans. They would have to stop every few hours to stretch and relieve themselves. They were going to have latrine facilities for only those people in the Dispensary facility and a very limited number elsewhere for the children and emergency cases. Everyone else was going to have to fend for themselves during the breaks. Stuart did set up a system to provide some organization for necessary relief breaks with Perry's men acting as monitors and directing the people to assigned outside facilities.

Stuart was pondering the accommodation problem as he sat talking with the families and he decided to concede one point that he figured he could live with. He said that he would provide bunk space for the women in the last trimester in the medical van and would allow the duty physician to handle the deliveries provided he was not in surgery handling combat injuries, but he said that was as far as he could go. The rest was up to them. The families huddled together and then suggested that they would provide all other care required in the course of the trip and would assume the fair share of work that the involved women would normally have been allocated. With that understanding, Stuart relented and allowed the women to make the trip on the further condition that any burden created by his allowing the women to go would be borne by the families. They all consented to this and he then had the family members present sign a statement promising to do what they had said they would do. Stuart also told them that if anyone did not honor his promise as made that day, he would personally see that they were offloaded regardless of where they were on the trip. All again assured him that there would be no problems. As they were filing out of the room, Stuart thought to himself, if it isn't one thing, it's another.

He knew that his giving in to this group would possibly create problems in other situations where people figured that they could get some community action to support their particular case. So be it, he thought. He figured if anyone made a solid case that appeared reasonable, he would make a concession just as he did in this case. There was no sense in laying down an iron clad rule that did not allow for reasonable exceptions. He had decided some time ago that he was not going to be the unreasoning bureaucrat who hid behind rules and regulations that in their absoluteness made no sense. Other requests for exceptions did come up in the following weeks and in some cases Stuart permitted the person or persons to make the trip provided others were willing to pick up the slack and handle the special problems created by the situation. In most, however, the problems created could not be alleviated through any reasonable means and, in these cases, Stuart had to refuse permission. In giving his decision in the disallowance cases, Stuart always suggested to the people involved that they consider this a temporary setback and that if they ever desired to join up with the Association in Montana, they would be permitted reentry and that there were others going to North Farm who intended to make the trip to the northwest, so they were not alone.

For the next few weeks before the planned departure date, Stuart was bombarded with special requests on items, supplies or equipment that people in the Association wanted to take to Montana or have delivered up to North Farm. He had more flexibility with North Farm as that was fairly close to the Control Zone and only involved additional shipments which were relatively safe to make. Robert Thomas had procured a larger tug which could be used for hauling some of the larger pieces of equipment such as generators, tractors and heavy machinery. Even Beth Sloan had pleaded with him to increase her storage allowance on the trucks for her educational equipment. About half of the teachers on her staff were going to North Farm and the other half to Montana which solved part of the problem as they also wanted the same supplies but more than half of the students were going to Montana and that made her argument stronger. Nevertheless, Stuart had to ignore her pleas as they were absolutely running out of room. Barnes had been able to add two more semi truck trailers to the fleet that Thomas had managed to locate in a warehouse on the mainland. They had to get those trucks into running condition in order to drive them up to Cocoa and, with Stones clearance, across the bridge and over to the Zone. Stone was being very cooperative since he had worked out an arrangement with Carlos, but again, Stuart was always cautious in his dealings with either party.

The Zone was a beehive of activity with the North Farm residents scurrying around doing their packing and hauling their goods to the docks for shipment on Thomas' boats. Stuart had not been up to North Farm as he had been too busy taking care of organizing the Montana move, but he had spoken frequently with McLeod who kept him apprised of what was happening up there. Sarah had also sent equipment up to North Farm, with technicians, some of whom intended to stay up there. In short order they had an operating communications center with most of the capability of the one in the Zone. The center was now manned on a twenty four hour basis and Sarah was in radio communication with North Farm whenever the need arose. Perry reported that the permanent party Defense Team for North Farm was up and operating and McLeod was confident that they could handle their immediate needs quite well. The only problems that they had encountered thus far were just local punks and thieves trying to break into their storage areas or steal equipment being used to put up the dorm buildings.

Stuart figured that when they were down to two weeks prior to the Montana departure date, they would begin hauling the residents up to North Farm. McLeod was fairly confident that by then they would have the basic community infrastructure established up there to handle the influx. Wells had been dug, water systems were being constructed and sewer drains were almost completed. By the time the first residents were to arrive, they would find all of the basic facilities, housing, water, sanitation and electric power available. It wouldn't be as comfortable as the Control Zone, by a long shot, but it would be livable. Stuart wished that he had the same support for their anticipated arrival in the northwest. As far as he knew, they were going to have to build their homes and facilities from scratch. What they did have going in their favor was the existing Valley community that they could possibly bargain with for assistance. North Farm only had a few small farms in their immediate vicinity and no one seemed to know if anyone even lived in them anymore. The North Farm area was fairly isolated from any large community and that was one of the reasons why it was selected. Large towns in Florida, or elsewhere, meant trouble and one was well advised to stay clear of them.

In the final week before the North Farm resident departure date, Stuart had already begun packing the trucks with various supplies and pieces of equipment to be used in Montana that they could temporarily do without while they were still in the Zone. They had secretly loaded the weapons in one of the trucks which had virtually filled it to the top. They had also been careful in loading the other vehicles to see that Carlos and his companions were elsewhere when equipment of value was disassembled and placed aboard the trucks. Stuart did not want to make his departure look overly expensive to the Cubans coming in to take over. He saw to it that the basic items of infrastructure that were necessary for life remained for the new residents, but his first responsibility was to see to the needs of his community in Montana. Life was going to be difficult enough for them in setting up their new homes.

It was also during this week that he called Carlos in to discuss the matter of providing a Cuban security force for their trip north. At first he merely made the request to see how that would go over, without any sweeteners offered. Carlos was his usual self. Without giving any indication of how he thought Morales would respond, he said he would pass the request on to his headquarters. Stuart then implied that they would be willing to pay for the assistance with some hard goods. With that Carlos perked up and asked what he had in mind. Stuart told him that if they would provide a cadre of two hundred self sustaining troops with their own vehicles and supplies to an area near Montgomery in the State of Alabama, that he would pay for their services with five hundred new, not out of the case, AR20 rifles with fifty thousand rounds of ammunition. Carlos eyes widened with this offer. He said nothing, but studied Stuart for a moment. He was obviously trying to figure out if Stuart was bluffing or if he really had the hard goods he was offering. "Where are the guns? I would like to see them before I contact my superiors."

Stuart only smiled and said, "You will see them when we are at the agreed destination point."

Carlos was a bit perplexed by this and asked what security they would have if the weapons were not delivered then. Stuart knew that would be a concern and told Carlos that his security was the two hundred armed troops that would be with the caravan. They would be a sufficient threat to the well being of the travelers to ensure that the deal was carried out.

"Interesting," was Carlos' only reply. "I will contact my office and let you know what they have to say." That concluded the meeting and Carlos departed.

# Chapter Thirty-Two

Sarah had informed Stuart the day before that the weapons had been placed in an absolutely water tight container sealed inside of another absolutely water tight container and anchored well below the surface, chained to one of the huge concrete block anchors used to secure larger vessels in the Banana River. She was positive that security had been tight and no one had observed the operation. It was carried out in the middle of the night when only the security force was around and she had also taken measures to see that Carlos, and all of his people, were elsewhere when the goods were taken to the pier, loaded into the container and pulled out to the anchorage site. He had expressed an increased level of interest in the old base facility, particularly since the excavation, and Sarah had arranged for him and his companions to stay overnight in what had been former housing for personnel on the base. She had Perry fix up quarters there and suggested to Carlos that he could use them while they were rehabilitating the parts of the base that they were interested in using. She had warned him; however, that he would not be able to reenter the residence compound until morning as security personnel did not permit people to stroll around the area after dark. He was also provided with security on the base and they were instructed to not let him depart until morning. Consequently, he was out of the picture so far as secreting the weapons for the Cubans was concerned.

Another matter that Stuart had to take care of was to provide transportation and security for Campbell and Yates to return to their home turf and pick up their men and equipment. There were still three men who had worked for the two for years who Campbell and Yates wanted to bring with them to Montana. They assured Stuart that the men would be valuable to the administration in that they were both excellent mechanics and could be of assistance to Barnes in getting the vehicles in good operating condition. The two men also wanted to pick up certain items of equipment for their future use and for that of the Association. They had radio gear, tools, portable generators, various weapons, agricultural equipment and other items that would come in handy in their new home. Lastly, they had their own personal gear that they wanted to bring. After discussing what they wanted transported, finding most of it of value to the Association, Stuart decided he had better have the tug with the barge stop by on its way back from North Farm and do the pickup. One of the smaller boats would not do the job and besides, they could then pick up Campbell's heavier equipment including two diesel tractors.

Campbell and Yates went with the tug on its way up to North Farm and were accompanied by a security team provided by Jack Nix to provide protection for the trek to the farm. Campbell figured that he could load all the items on his farm trailers and pull the load out with his tractors. He would also bring the five hundred gallon diesel fuel tank if they could figure out some way to lift it on to a trailer. They could worry about that when they got there. The weather was a bit rough for the trip, but the tug could handle it without too much difficulty. They were going to try to bring the barge up to the shoreline near the access road to Campbell's farm so that it could be loaded right there. The barge did not draw much water due to its great beam and length so it could handle great weight and not draw over three feet of depth. It would help if they could find a dock fairly close to the area of the farm in order to do the loading but if worse came to worse, they could load even the very heavy items right off the shoreline. They finally found one a few miles up the coast from their usual landing site which meant that they had to keep part of the security force there to protect the vessel.

The others took off on foot for the farm and after a long hike of two hours, they finally entered the grounds. Their men were very glad to see them and wondered what had kept them out so long. Campbell and Yates immediately sat the three down and briefed them on what had transpired.

The men were not aware of the buried weapons and that subject did not come up. Campbell explained the Montana move with its good points as he saw them as well as the bad points. He then asked if they wanted to come along with the two of them and their response was, "Might as well, nothing doing around here."

The three men did mention that there had been inquiries as to where Campbell and Yates were by a group of what looked like FSP men a few days prior. They were told that no one knew where they had gone to, but that they were expected to return shortly. The FSPs, or whoever they were, said they would be back. With that, Campbell and Yates eyed one another and suggested that they get to work, get loaded and get the "hell out of here."

The day after Stuart had spoken to Carlos, he was back with a response from Morales. Carlos came into his office and told him that Morales would do the deal, but he had to see the weapons first. Stuart told Carlos to have a chair and he would explain to him why that was not possible. They were not taking the weapons with them when they left; rather they had secreted them somewhere accessible to the Cubans and would notify them, when the deal had been completed, as to their exact location. Stuart could tell that Carlos was considering the possibility of locating the weapons prior to the departure of anyone and Stuart cut him short when he assured him that they would not be able to find the weapons without directions, so "don't waste your time looking for them, either before we leave or after."

Stuart made that comment with a smile and it drew a similar reaction from Carlos. Stuart went on, "Now if you want to see what a new AR20 looks like, fresh out of the case, which is what we have waiting for you, we can show you that but I think you are already very familiar with the weapon. But... if that's what you want, fine. In the meantime, tell Morales that we cannot comply with his request and tell him why. He has all the assurance that he needs that we will carry out our part of the bargain." Carlos nodded and replied that he would send off a message immediately.

The following day, Carlos returned and said that Morales was agreeable to doing the deal and that the troops would be arriving the following week from Vero. He requested housing for the men which was not a problem as the North Farm people were departing prior to the arrival of the troops and quarters would be available. Stuart reminded Carlos that the Cubans were going to have to provide their own vehicles for transporting the troops as well as food, fuel and maintenance support. Carlos assured him that those matters would be taken care of.

As he was about to leave, Stuart stopped him and told him not to worry about the delivery of the weapons. Stuart would personally ensure that the weapons were of new quality and that they would be in excellent condition at delivery or Stuart would see that they received five hundred of the Association's new AR20 rifles. Carlos was now more than curious as to where the supply of arms had come from, but Stuart was not about to provide that information. Carlos just stopped and looked at Stuart for a moment and then replied that he would pass that on.

Sarah also had the problem of buttoning up her own operation and getting it packed while maintaining an operating intelligence section. Part of her staff was already operating out of what was now the mobile intelligence van which was in its assigned caravan location spot with antennas bristling from its roof top and sides. All of the caravan vehicles were lined up in their respective order with large numbers fastened to their sides. The numbers were for the purpose of directing those responsible for doing the loading to put the right equipment on the right vehicle. When all vehicles were loaded, the numbers would be removed and camouflage paint would be applied to the tractors and trailers.

A number of the vehicles were being revamped on the interior to provide sleeping quarters, or kitchens or, in the case of the medical group, a complete operating room, medical supply storage area and sick room accommodations for whatever may lie ahead. Barnes also had his men working on the exteriors of all vehicles installing synthetic armor plating in some areas to protect people or certain items of equipment from small arms fire that could be encountered along the route.

Truck engine compartments were also protected with the synthetic sheets as were the tires on the tractors and the trailers. Barnes had high strength flaps laid over the cabs on the tractors to afford the drivers maximum protection. At the head of the caravan, heavily armored vehicles were lined up to clear the roadways of mines, debris, road blocks and any threat to the caravan that followed. There were also personnel carriers that Barnes had constructed in the past few months from various vehicle parts found in the Zone. Barnes had created the gun ports in the trailers that Stuart had requested so that all passengers capable of handling the AR20 would have a relatively safe location from which to view their attackers and fire their weapons. It was becoming very apparent that only a very heavily armed force or complete idiots would attack the convoy as it passed through their areas.

Barnes had also constructed a number of heavily armored two man, three wheeled escort vehicles that could be used to run from one end of the caravan to the other under fairly heavy small arms fire without damage to the vehicle or injury to the driver and gunner. The gunner sat on a special swivel chair, well protected and equipped with a light weight Gatling gun that could fire two thousand rounds a minute. The vehicle was highly maneuverable and could do a one hundred eighty degree turn in a ten foot wide roadway.

Barnes was very proud of his development of the armored motorcycle, but the modification that he was most proud of was the work that he had done on Hans Frick's airplane. Stuart had originally suggested that it would help a great deal if there was some way that they could utilize Frick's plane as a scout aircraft to check road conditions ahead of the caravan and also to provide reconnaissance in the event of threats from armed groups that they might run into. He had talked with Frick and he was agreeable to doing whatever had to be done, so long as his aircraft could be modified back to the condition it was in. With that understanding, Barnes said that he would give it some thought. The first problem that he had to overcome was the matter of transporting the aircraft. Frick would not be able to fly every day due to the unpredictable nature of weather and the caravan could not come to a grinding halt with every cloudy day. Consequently, if they were going to take the plane, it was going to have to be part of the caravan.

The immediate problem for Barnes was the wing span. He put the NASA engineers to work on the project and in time they presented him with the blue prints for modifying the wings of the aircraft to permit their easy removal and rapid replacement. This modification was presented to Frick who was not too happy about it until he went over the proposal with the aerospace engineer responsible. When they were done talking, Frick was of the opinion that the strength of the wing was actually increased. He gave his approval and the work began.

It was Barnes intention to build a ramp into one of the trailers and this could be used for aircraft storage and maintenance. He also built a small area in the rear for Frick to keep his personal gear, his bunk and a flight planning stall. This area gave Frick an amount of privacy the others did not have and he was very pleased to have that, as was Sarah who had been seen visiting Frick's private office on occasion. With the space he was getting, Frick was more than pleased with the changes to his plane. Barnes also discussed with Frick the possibility of installing flare launchers and rocket tubes on the underside of the wings. Frick was willing to do that as long as the aerospace engineer approved the work but he brought up the problem of how he was going to land his aircraft at night if he was up firing flares.

"How am I going to find a place to land?" Barnes had figured he would bring that up and had a ready answer. He had portable strobe lights that would provide a five thousand foot strip provided the road they were traveling on was sufficiently straight, wide enough and surfaced to act as a runway. Obviously if the road was not suitable for such night operations, the plane would not be launched. Again Frick was agreeable provided he first gave the strobes a test out at the base. They waited for an overcast, dark night and then gave it a try. Frick departed the area a short distance and then when he figured he was back over the base, he gave a call on the radio to turn on the strobes. He did an approach to the field and landed. As he climbed out of the plane, he shouted over to Barnes, "Better than any runway lights I've ever used."

Frick was a bit concerned that when the time came, would they work. Barnes assured him they would and that there was a backup power source if the primary failed for any reason. After the flare and rocket pods were installed and the wiring run up into the cockpit, Frick gave that modification a try and everything worked as planned. Sarah had taken steps to upgrade four thousand gallons of automobile grade fuel to the higher octane required for Frick's aircraft.

All of the fuel that had to be taken on the trip provided Barnes with his biggest head ache. Where was he going to store the fuel? He did not want to assign all of the fuel to one or two vehicles as that was too risky in the event one or the other was destroyed. Consequently, he decided to hang a number of fifty and one hundred gallon tanks below each trailer with additional armor plating to protect the contents from shrapnel or small arms fire. Even if they lost a truck or two, they should have sufficient fuel to handle the journey. Some of the NASA engineers then devised a system of packing the fuel tanks with synthetic foam which would prevent an explosion of the fuel if struck by bullets. The foam did not decrease the volume of fuel the tanks could hold but prevented the necessary fuel air mixture for an explosion.

Ross Perry was very concerned about the defenses that would be available to the caravan while it was underway. He got together with John Barnes and Jack Nix to discuss what they could do to protect the passengers and cargo they would be transporting in the caravan. Barnes suggested that his men could construct protected gun positions in the roofs of the trailers which could then be equipped with rocket launchers and smaller caliber automatic weapons. He would not be able to build platforms for larger weapons without major modifications to the vehicles. With the shortage of materials and time left before departure, that was out of the question.

Barnes was confident that he could equip each vehicle with armor protected weapons sites capable of handling ground to air and ground to ground missile and gun stations with room for a three man team. They would also have to have access to the intervehicular communication system that was already in place in the tractor cabs and extending it to the gun positions was not a major challenge.

Jack Nix had made a number of suggestions but had not been tasked to perform anything, which caused him to inquire, somewhat jokingly, as to what he was doing there. Perry assured him that he was there for a purpose. Nix and his team were to act as scouts on the trail. They were to check out suspected threat areas and, more or less, clear the way for the caravan. Barnes had two heavily armored, speedy, scout cars ready for this purpose and they could handle direct hits from anything up to the larger armor piercing missiles and artillery weapons which they did not expect to encounter unless they ran into a group such as the FSP or something like their Cuban friends. Hopefully they would avoid such groups in the course of their journey. As Nix's mission was explained to him, he jokingly inquired if they didn't have something a bit safer for him to do on the trip. There was little doubt that he had been assigned the riskiest task thus far. There were numerous ways to stop a heavily armored scout car without hitting it with cannon fire or dropping a bomb on it and Nix was well aware of that fact. Fortunately, many of Nix's men were the type that looked forward to combat. Two in particular were eagerly anticipating confrontation. Nix referred to these two young men as "Guns and Ammo". He would put them in the scout cars, the vehicles most likely to encounter trouble first. That was fine with them.

The final two weeks of residence in the Control Zone were filled with round the clock activity. Lights blazed around the caravan as loads were placed aboard and modifications to the trailers were done. Heavy lift equipment was brought in to assist in the modification as well as the loading. Tractor and trailer bodies were being spray painted with a dull green and brown camouflage and the large, bright numbers on the sides of the trailers were being replaced with a single small number on the back of the trailer. All administrative section leaders were busy seeing that their assigned storage space on the trailers was being utilized to the fullest so that they took the maximum amount of equipment and supplies that they would need in Montana.

The Cubans that were beginning to file into the Control Zone looked on in admiration at the well organized departure taking place before their eyes and Carlos, as well, commented to Stuart that he was impressed with what he was seeing. Particularly the weaponry that was being installed on the trailers and the support vehicles that were also well armed and defended with armor plating. He let Stuart know that when he first learned of their intentions to travel from Florida to Montana with tractor trailers, he had been very skeptical that they would ever make the trip alive. He based that on the stories that he had heard from small groups that had found their way down to Florida from the northern part of the country. Now that he was observing the preparations taking place before him, he conceded that they might possibly make it provided they did not run into some of the groups that are out there. Stuart just smiled at him and said, "Well, that's why we want you guys to come along with us at least part way."

The Cuban cadre that was going to accompany the caravan was now in position and Stuart had Perry, Barnes and Nix meet with the Cuban commander to ensure that they were all singing from the same song sheet along the route. Radio frequencies were exchanged as well as command and control issues, such as who had final authority. There was a considerable amount of discussion regarding this latter issue and understandably so. It was finally resolved that Perry would make the final decisions from the Command Post vehicle; however, any unit commander down to the squad level, would be able to take whatever steps were necessary to defend his men if they came under attack. Perry's concern, as had been discussed in the meeting with Nix, Barnes and Sarah, was that someone could precipitate a problem with a local group that could otherwise be avoided with good command and control. The Cuban Commander agreed with that point, not wishing to become involved in combat if it could be avoided. It was decided that the Cubans would bring up the rear of the caravan which, again, pleased the Cuban Commander. Perry wanted to have his own men on point so that he knew exactly what he was walking into and he did not want to have to rely on people that he did not know. The Cubans would only be called upon if the very existence of the caravan was threatened.

During the final two weeks, all of those going to North Farm were loaded on Robert Thomas' boats and driven to their new homes. Provisions were also sent together with supplies, personal items, generators, food supplies, and anything that was not going to Montana that was worth keeping. When inventory lists were reviewed by Anders and the others, they had nothing to be ashamed of with respect to the allocation for North Farm. That area was the recipient of a much larger portion of available food stuffs and hard goods than were going to Montana. There had been some friction over the allotment by the Administration to North Farm but when it became apparent that the caravan just did not have room for many of the items that they wanted to take, that issue died down. When the boats were loaded with the departing friends and neighbors, heading to their new home in northern Florida, it was a sad occasion for both those leaving and those waiting for their own departure to Montana.

Jim McLeod came back to the Zone from North Farm and accompanied the final boatload of residents north. Before departing, he met with Anders, Sarah and Stuart to discuss the move and their respective plans for the future. McLeod's final words before getting into Thomas' boat were, "Don't sell those trucks. We may need them on down the road."

Stuart assured him that they would be available whenever he was ready for the move. Stuart truly regretted that McLeod was not going to Montana with them, but he was hopeful that the day would come when he could make the trip. Stuart would do all he could to see that those in North Farm that wanted to join up with them would do so. Stuart, Anders and Sarah stood on the pier at the Marina until the boat carrying McLeod was out of sight heading out into the ocean for the trip north. Thomas was bringing a load of drivers and maintenance people back with him when he returned from North Farm as he was then going to turn what was transportable in the Marina facility, as well as boats and equipment, over to them for their use in northern Florida.

Thomas was not looking forward to parting with his boats, or his organization, as he had done an excellent job of fine tuning not only the boats, but also the men that drove and maintained them, into a smooth working organization. It was almost unheard of for one of the boats to have engine trouble on a mission. The engines were spotless and perfectly tuned. The Marina was likewise always clean, everything in its proper place and the Marina personnel always looking like they were expecting an inspection at any minute. Possibly they were. Thomas ran a tight ship and Stuart had developed a great deal of respect for the man. In the final days before turning over the keys of his boats to the men from North Farm, Stuart had made it a point to assure Thomas that he would receive equal or greater responsibility in Montana. He could tell that his words meant a great deal to Thomas as he was the kind of person who had to be involved in a challenging venture or he was not satisfied. Stuart was certain that there would be plenty of challenge to go around in the days and years ahead.

With just two days left before the departure date, the effort to get everything packed and loaded turned into a race against the clock. Work was still going on modifying the trailers as last minute loads were being placed on the vehicles. Food stuffs were the final category of goods to go on the trucks before the last item which were the residents making the trip to Montana.

Barnes had his people checking each tractor and trailer to see that they were ready for the trip. Fuel tanks were all topped off and diesel fuel in barrels was secured to the underside of the trailers protected by bullet proof mats hanging down on each side of the barrels. As final modification of the trailer gun positions was being accomplished, weapons and ammunition were being loaded into storage areas for the gunners. Perry also had each gun position equipped with night vision equipment and also had the vehicle

drivers practice night driving using the night vision equipment. In some
of the high threat areas that they would have to traverse on their way to
Montana, Perry thought it best to proceed through those areas under cover
of darkness. Vehicle assignments were passed out to the residents and their
personal items were weighed and loaded on the final day in the Zone.

Each passenger was allowed a limited amount of baggage which could
not exceed thirty pounds nor take up space over four feet square. Again
there were numerous requests for exceptions and Stuart turned that over
to Barnes as he was in charge of the vehicles. Barnes absolutely refused to
allow any exceptions as he was already over his weight and space limits.
He figured that if he stuck to his limits, there would always be some who
had less and he could use that space to handle the expected overage. As
the goods were loaded, his guess turned out to be accurate and it appeared
that they would be able to accommodate all passengers and baggage, but
with no room to spare.

The final night before departure, all traveling residents, and there were
still a few that had elected to stay in the Zone, were loaded and spent the
last night sleeping in the trailers. It was tight quarters, but it was apparent
after everyone was in for the night that they were ready to depart.

In the morning, the Cubans began to pour into the Zone by way of
their own boats coming into the Marina area and by personnel carriers
over the bridge from Cocoa. They had been on the road for two days from
Vero and they were a tired looking bunch. Carlos had room assignments
prepared for the Cuban security force that would be manning the Zone
during the takeover and the men, upon arriving, were immediately billeted
and disappeared into their quarters. Cuban Field Mess units arrived and
were busy setting up portable kitchens to feed the new arrivals. Stuart,
in turn, complimented Carlos on the work that he had apparently done to
prepare for the influx of troops.

As the public address system announced the final boarding call for those
traveling in the Caravan, Stuart met for the first time, face to face, with
Paco Morales, the leader of the Cuban National Socialist Party. Morales

was not a tall man, relatively short, not over five and a half feet tall, but he had the appearance of a man with boundless energy who was in excellent physical condition. When Carlos introduced Stuart to Morales, the Cuban leader gave a broad smile and extended his hand to warmly shake hands with Stuart. Between Morales' English and Stuart's Spanish, the two men were able to converse. Morales wished Stuart a safe trip and Stuart did the same for the Cubans and their stay in the Control Zone. Both men were eager to get about their separate tasks so the conversation did not extend beyond the pleasantries. Stuart was impressed with the Cuban. He seemed friendly, but alert and businesslike. As they parted, Stuart again wished him well and said that he appreciated the assistance of Morales in sending along the security force. Morales only commented that they were glad to help, but frankly, they needed the weapons. The two men parted and Stuart headed for the Command Post truck which was to be his assigned position during the trip.

As Stuart walked over to the vehicle, he observed Perry's Defense Forces in position on board vehicles and in bunkers around the area. During the final days while the Association staff and residents were busy getting their equipment packed and loaded, Ross Perry had placed his Defense Force on a state of high alert. His men were fully equipped with combat equipment, wearing their sharp new uniforms designed by Robert Thomas and were strategically located throughout the Zone in the event that their Cuban friends had bad intentions. Their departure from the Zone would be conducted in similar fashion with defensive positions vacated only when there was no further need of them. Sort of like rolling up a carpet as the last vehicle passed a certain point. Stuart and Perry had, likewise, briefed Howard Stone on their departure plans from the Zone. There was no sense in trying to surprise Stone and his people regarding the route as there was only one route across the bridge and through Cocoa in order to access the roads to the northwest.

Stuart wanted Stone to know that they would be coming across the bridge in full combat mode and that his people were to withdraw from the intended route so that there would be no mistaking anyone's intentions. Stone was agreeable with that, particularly when he began to get the drift on the degree of preparations Stuart and the others had made to provide for their defenses en route. Stuart wanted everyone, the Cubans and Stone, to understand that if any games were played during their departure, the price to pay would be very costly.

# Chapter Thirty-Three

The departure schedule called for the first vehicles to be crossing the bridge at ten in the morning. Nix's scout cars had proceeded ahead of the caravan and radioed back that Cocoa appeared clear for the trucks to proceed. By ten-thirty in the morning, the last vehicle passed out of the Zone and the caravan was moving to the west at a pace of thirty miles per hour. The men in the scout cars were kept very busy with frequent stops to clear debris from the roadway in advance of the trucks. After the caravan had gone a few miles west of Cocoa and then a few miles north on what had been highway 95, Nix radioed back to the Command Post that he needed more assistance on clearing the roadway as his men were becoming exhausted with the frequent stops to clear the road. Stuart decided to make some changes as he wanted Nix's men for security and not for road maintenance. They had an armored anti-mine vehicle strapped down on one of the trucks and after talking with Barnes, it was decided to attach a large plow blade to that vehicle and use it to clear the roads instead of the men. Barnes was confident that his mechanics could keep the vehicle running for extended periods without too much trouble. After that truck was put into use, the column proceeded smoothly until nightfall.

The road on which the caravan was proceeding to the north was formerly a four lane road, two northbound lanes and two southbound. The two southbound lanes now well overgrown, the two north bound lanes still passable at least in one lane, except for occasional debris or fallen trees. It was overgrown in spots, but the roadbed was still solid enough to handle the heavy vehicles. As the convoy made its way to the north, Stuart observed the roadway and surrounding terrain and realized that in another year or two, roads such as this would be totally overgrown with brush and other vegetation. From the appearance of this fairly well built roadway, he concluded that they would be required to use their heavy construction equipment before they finally reached their destination.

They only occasionally caught a glimpse of a human being until they came to within a few miles of Titusville. Anyone they did see took cover immediately upon seeing them as their visible armament presented a very menacing appearance. As they drove north, they saw pockets of humanity more often as was to be expected and those that did not seek cover stood looking at them with blank looks on their faces. They all were gaunt appearing and their clothing was in rags. Occasionally there was a woman clutching a child that appeared to be dying of starvation. Small groups of armed men were seen as the smaller communities came into view, but they did not make any threatening moves, most likely because they knew they would be outgunned by the weapons trained upon them.

Sarah had planned the route and was in constant radio communication with contacts in surrounding communities as well as with Nix's scout cars to determine if any changes in routing were advisable. Nix was maintaining a distance of approximately one mile ahead of the caravan, not wanting to get too far ahead which would place his men at great risk, yet far enough ahead to warn the caravan of danger. The thought was that if Nix ran into trouble, the caravan could extricate him unless it was a very large military force. It was Sarah's job to keep them out of territories known to be under the control of such groups. The plan was to go north to highway 44, then west and join up with the old Turnpike to go north again.

The intended route did not go through Orlando. All large cities were being avoided unless there was absolutely no other way to go. According to the travel plan currently being followed, they did not expect to have to go through any large city other than Tallahassee until they were well out of Florida. Hopefully, they would find more hospitable hosts in the west than they expected to find in the cities of the southeast.

Nix called back to the command post to verify the location of the turning point and after some discussion to decide if he was at the proper point, he made the turn to the west assuming that was 44. This was their first taste of the problem of identifying roads. There were no longer any signs posted on anything. Furthermore, some roads or what had been roads, were virtually unrecognizable as roads. Consequently, the old method of taking the third road to the right no longer applied. Also landmarks were not necessarily visible any longer. Airports were totally overgrown. Radio and water towers had been destroyed either out of vandalism or for scrap materials. Buildings with architectural significance were now overgrown pieces of wreckage. Some were burned to the ground, while others were bleak hulks with their doors and windows gone, portions of the buildings torn away or covered with debris and brush. Stuart had driven this road many times in the past and he was at a loss to recognize anything that he saw.

Sarah's staff was busy handling the navigation, using global positioning equipment to verify positions for turns and distance covered. If it was not for that equipment, Sarah told Stuart, they would not be able to find their way. The route that Sarah had planned on taking was to go well east of Orlando, moving to the north and then west on 44 when they were well clear of the city. They would then join up with what had been the old turnpike. Hopefully that was passable and Sarah did have some reports, although sketchy, indicating that those areas were passable. As they passed around to the north of Orlando, Nix observed a number of vehicles moving ahead of the caravan in the same direction. As time passed other vehicles joined those and it became apparent that they might have problems farther up the road. Sarah's staff studied the maps and saw that they had to pass over a small river a few miles ahead. That looked like a good spot for trouble and was probably where their new friends would be waiting for them. After a hurried consultation, it was decided to take an alternate route to the north, short of the river, and join up with the interstate farther up the road. Nix was told to continue in a westerly direction and just short of the bridge over the river, he was to reverse course and floor it to the turning point. Perry would leave a small force at the turning point to indicate the way and Nix would rejoin the caravan which would then be ahead of him moving north. He was not to exchange fire with anyone unless it was absolutely necessary for his own safety. The caravan found the new route slow going as it was covered with vegetation and difficult to follow. It was not the straight stretch of road the other one had been and was more like what they might expect in their future travels in northern Florida and Alabama.

As Nix proceeded to the west, now at a slower pace, he came over a rise, and observed the bridge about a half mile ahead of him. He slowed down further and when he was about a quarter mile from the river, he made a rapid turn and sped back to the east. The other scout car did the same and as they made their turn, a flurry of small arms fire struck the two vehicles. They were well protected and no one was injured as they sped off to the east. As the two scout cars drove to the east, they saw that they were now being followed by five or six automobiles, each loaded with a number of armed men. They were too far back to be a threat but with greater speed, they would be upon them shortly. Nix radioed his situation to Sarah and Perry authorized him to launch a missile at the first vehicle which he did and that stopped their pursuers in their tracks. The driver of the targeted vehicle spotted the missile coming towards them and tried to take evasive action by leaving the roadway and heading off into the brush, but the missile already had a lock on the car and it was too late. It was difficult to see what happened after that as the car was well into the brush when the missile struck and there was nothing visible other than smoke and flames. The other pursuers apparently did have a good look at their companions as they came to an abrupt stop and gave up the chase. Nix picked up Perry's men at the intersection and in a short period of time, was again at the head of the caravan scouting the route.

That evening as the caravan came upon the access road to what had been the Florida Turnpike; it was decided to call it a day as soon as a suitable stopping point could be located. There was an open area up the road, just a short distance after getting on what had been the turnpike, and Nix reported back that it would be suitable for a stopping point. There was no sign of anyone in the vicinity and the old parking area was still adequate for parking the trailers. Nix had his men stationed around the area with hand held radios to alert the caravan of any potential problems. They were soon relieved by sentry teams sent out by Perry who immediately began constructing temporary bunkers to serve the guards through the night. The cafeteria staff had been preparing food for the evening meal even while the caravan was still on the road. That was a bit difficult as the road bed was not that smooth and considerable care had to be taken not to drop the entire meal on the kitchen trailer floor. After everyone was fed, Anders made an announcement regarding the following day's schedule which would commence at five thirty in the morning. "Breakfast at six and everyone on the road again by seven."

Perry briefed the location of temporary toilet and shower facilities. The availability of shower baths was totally dependent upon water reserves which would have to be replenished from rain water or water sources encountered en route. Thus far, the water stores were adequate to allow each person one minute of a relatively weak spray of cold to lukewarm water timed and controlled by one of Perry's security staff. Even with that limitation on use, Anders was told that they would not be able to provide showers unless the water supply was replenished every five days.

After the evening announcements were completed, Anders put out the word to the Section leaders that there would be a staff meeting in the Command Post trailer in fifteen minutes. Much had been learned on the first day of travel that required changes in their procedures and Anders wished to discuss those changes with the section heads.

They had planned to be traveling at night during the course of their journey to Montana, but after seeing the actual condition of the roadway and the difficulty in navigating the course, night travel did not appear to be an option. Even with night vision goggles, it was extremely difficult to see where the road bed lay. More than once, Nix had driven off into a field thinking he was on the road. He had to be pulled out more than one time by his following scout car. On those occasions, he had placed markers on the roadway so that the trucks coming behind would not make the same mistake.

Perry then briefed everyone on the defensive preparations that were being implemented during their stopovers such as their present situation. There were approximately thirty men stationed around the area with night vision equipment and radios to alert the Command Post of trouble. There was a combat ready squad of twenty men, in radio contact with the CP who were roaming the area and another company of fifty men, fully equipped and ready to go, resting outside of the Command Post vehicle. The Cubans were bivouacked a short distance from the caravan and had their own defensive positions established. Perry saw to it that the Cuban commander was briefed on the sentry positions and security layout of the Association so that they did not run into one another during the course of the night.

At the conclusion of the meeting, Perry also discussed with Nix and Stuart, the run in with the locals in Orlando. Perry suggested that there should be a debrief anytime weapons were fired so that they could learn from the experience. Stuart totally agreed with that. Nix provided the details of the encounter and the three men then discussed whether or not alternative measures would have been better rather than the firing of the missile. Perry did not want to use their missile supply if other means would accomplish the same goal. Nix was firmly convinced that using the missile was the right thing to do as they did not know what weapons the following vehicles had available to them. The others agreed with his decision.

Stuart was supportive of the decision to use the missile but did bring up the possibility of using radio activated mines which Nix also had available which could be dropped and activated when the following vehicle was in position or within the area of probable damage. They had many more of the rather simply constructed mines than they had of the high tech missiles and that might be a better use of resources. Perry agreed but, in making his decision, he had been under the impression that the cars coming up on Nix were doing so at a pace that did not permit use of the mines. The matter was resolved with the unanimous agreement that in the future, missiles would only be used when absolutely necessary, but that decision should be left with the on scene commander, in this case Nix. The three men also agreed to continue these combat debriefing sessions in the future so that policies such as that adopted could be developed.

Their first night out on the road was relatively uneventful. There were a few contacts with intruders during the early morning hours, but upon being detected by sentries, they rapidly departed the area. Perry had passed out strict instructions that weapons were not to be fired unless they were fired upon. Anders had made it clear to Perry that they wanted to preserve their ammunition supply. Arrangements were also made to collect all fired shell casings for possible reloading. In addition, they wanted to avoid antagonizing any local insurgents. They would have problems enough with known armed groups they expected to encounter along the way and did not need to create any more. As for the passengers, they had handled the trip thus far fairly well. A few who were not used to being cooped up in darkened trailers became ill, but for the most part, they fared quite well. Games had been organized for children and during the day, while the trucks were underway, they were assigned to two trailers that were specially equipped to keep them occupied and out of harm's way. Kate Nolan, one of the teachers, was in charge of what they called the nursery trailers.

There were certain tasks which had to be taken care of both while the group was encamped for the night and also while they were underway. Anders staff had passed out assignments among the passengers for cleaning, cooking and other necessary activities and these assignments rotated among the passengers. That way, everyone had his or her turn at good jobs along with the bad. Everyone over the age of fifteen years of age was assigned to the work force and, as could be expected, most of the complaints came from the youngest that had other things on their minds.

The first morning on the road, everyone was ready for breakfast at six, lined up at the mess trailer for coffee, bread and cereal. Those assigned kitchen detail had the food prepared and ready to serve, so the scheduled seven o'clock departure time was met. The scout cars departed the camp site at exactly seven o'clock with the trucks close behind. As the caravan proceeded to the north, up the turnpike, the pace was slower than the previous day because the weather had turned and the heavy rain was causing problems on the road bed. Again, the roadway was totally overgrown in some areas and covered with grass and mud. The rain had turned the surface into a greasy, slippery mixture making control of the vehicles very difficult. Nix had to call a halt a number of times in order to repair impassable portions of the road. It was clear that very few vehicles had passed over the turnpike in the previous five or so years. The rain did have a beneficial side to it. Barnes had installed rain water collectors on the roofs of the trailers which fed into storage tanks below. Within two or three hours of heavy downpours, the caravan had replenished all water used to that point in the journey. This was not a surprise as Sarah had estimated that water shortages would not become a serious problem until the caravan entered the western states where rainfall was not as plentiful as it was in the southeast. When they entered that area, they would have to adopt very conservative rationing practices in order to extend their water resources to last to their destination. To provide water for the western dry areas Sarah had proposed cleaning and filling the diesel fuel 100 gallon tanks with rain water when available. As the trucks used the diesel fuel, the tanks were immediately converted to holding tanks for water that could at least be used for cleaning, showering and for drinking in an emergency.

Aside from the bad road conditions the first part of the trip north was uneventful. They were passing through an area that was virtually uninhabited even in better times as it was basically a grassy, wetland for miles either side of the roadway. When the turnpike connected with what had been Interstate Highway I-75, it was obvious that this roadway had been traveled more often. This was the road that ran from Tampa, on the coast, and moved on up through central Florida into Georgia. They again began to see small pockets of humanity along the roadway, huddled in makeshift shelters some distance from the road. These people made no threatening moves, only stared at them as their children gathered about them wondering who the travelers were.

Nix radioed back to the Command Post that a truck had been coming towards him on the road they were traveling, but had turned around and headed back to the north. Perry told him to keep an extra sharp eye out as they were going to be passing fairly close to Ocala and Sarah had no information on the situation in that town. When they were about five miles outside of Ocala, Perry had Nix and his companion scout car fall back to within a quarter mile of the caravan. All passengers were alerted to assume protected positions behind the armor plating and gun positions were double manned with additional troops. The troops in the transport vehicles were also placed on alert taking up positions at the gun ports in the plating surrounding their trailers. As they came within a mile or so of Ocala, Nix reported a fairly substantial barricade across the road. The plow as they now referred to the armored anti-mine vehicle was sent up to clear off the barricade. Nix and the other scout car had pulled up short of the barricade about a hundred yards.

As Nix was waiting for the arrival of the plow, he could see a vehicle approaching them from the other side of the barricade. As that vehicle came up to the barricade, two men jumped out and waved to Nix to approach. They did not appear to be armed and Nix drove on up to the barricade telling the other scout car to keep him covered. By this time the caravan had come to a stop about a quarter of a mile back. Jack Nix stepped out of the scout car and approached the two men. As he drew near them, he could see that they presented a very rough, unkempt appearance. They were the first to speak. "Just where the hell do you think you are going?" Nix had never been one for diplomacy and as he surveyed the two men in front of him, his immediate thoughts were directed to which one he should take out first. His more rational side then prevailed as he knew the safety of the caravan now rested on his shoulders and he didn't want to make a stupid move that would endanger his companions. Nix said nothing, just stared coldly at the two men. After a long pause that conveyed the message to the pair that this was not someone they should be screwing around with, Nix replied. "We are heading north and just passing through this area. We are not going to be causing anyone here any problems so you don't have to worry about that."

One of the two men laughed and slapped his companion on the shoulder. "He is not going to cause us any problems. That's awful sweet of you, mister. Maybe we might cause you problems."

Nix saw that being diplomatic was getting him nowhere. "OK guys. I don't know what you've got in that town over there, but we have enough guns and ammo to blow your ass completely out of Florida." Continuing now with a sweet smile on his face, Nix went on, "Now we don't want to do that and if you doubt what I have to say, come with me in my vehicle and I'll give you a tour. After the tour, I would suggest you run your ass back to your side of the fence and tell any friends of yours not to do anything stupid. Then we will drive along this road and not bother anyone, or," and Nix paused here, "we will not only blow your ass apart, we will stop and see what you have to offer. Now what do you want to do?"

The one who had spoken before looked at Nix and with a slightly less confident tone to his voice said, "Tough talk."

His companion seemed to have more sense and told him to "Shut up, Willie." Turning to Nix, "You don't have to give us a tour. I'll take your word for it. You move through and we won't bother you. C'mon, Willie, lets head back."

The two turned around and headed for their car. Nix went back to the scout car and radioed to Perry what had taken place.

The plow was brought up and in one swipe, the barricade was pushed over to the side of the road. All personnel stayed in their combat positions as the vehicles began to move north along the road and enter the outskirts of the town. This was the first town of any size they had encountered on the trip and it was the first time many of their passengers had a chance to catch a glimpse of what the world looked like outside of the Control Zone. The place was a mess, garbage and debris everywhere. There wasn't a sign of a building or home that was not virtually destroyed. Windows and doors gone. Exterior wood surfaces ripped off apparently for firewood. Groups of hungry, half clad men, women and children gathered in small clusters as they passed down the road. A number of the men were armed with a variety of weapons and as they passed through the town, Perry estimated the number of armed men he could see as not in excess of one hundred. They had been wise to back off from the caravan, but communities such as this still constituted a threat to the well being of those aboard the trucks as combat injuries would be a burden to be avoided.

When they were well out of town, a futile shot was fired at them by one of the armed men they had seen in the center of the town. They were too far away for the shot to cause any injury or damage but it was indicative of the sort of welcome they might expect from communities along the way. The larger cities were going to be a real problem. As they moved along the road to the north, they passed through a number of smaller communities and were fired on by disorganized pockets of armed men lying in the brush along the road. Perry passed the order to his troops to return the fire if they knew where it was coming from. It was only small arms fire which he did not consider a particular threat but he did not want to risk a freak shell penetrating a fuel tank or, worse yet, going through a gun port and killing or injuring someone.

Some of the passengers were complaining about constantly being cooped up behind the bullet proof screens in the body of the trailers. Barnes had installed benches on the roof of the trailers so that people could get a breath of fresh air every now and then and some of the passengers had seen them during the overnight stop and wanted to get up there and out of the foul air in the trailers. With the occasional small arms fire that they were experiencing, the Command Post would not allow anyone access to the roofs for fear of injuries or fatalities. After two days of being on the road with the complaints of being cooped up increasing by the minute, Anders decided that a noon rest stop should be built into the schedule. That set the travel schedule even farther behind as the caravan was already losing time with the poor road conditions.

The decision as to when to stop was left to Perry as they wanted to ensure that a relatively safe defensible site was chosen. Perry, in turn, discussed this with Nix who was better equipped with his scout car to check out the terrain. It was decided between he and Perry that if there was an old turnpike rest stop spotted at anytime between eleven a.m. and one p.m., that was where they would park unless there were other factors making it too risky. If the area on either side of the road was relatively open, affording open views to the gunners on the tops of the trailers, they could then stop in position and let the people out for a stretch while the kitchen staff dispensed a light lunch.

Anders passed the word that the caravan was stopping for forty five minutes to allow everyone to get something to eat, to stretch and to take a latrine break in areas secured by Perry's troops. With five minutes to go, the all aboard was shouted by the security force and the trucks were all moving at the scheduled time.

It was now apparent to all of the people in the caravan, whether staff, Defense Team or passengers that this trip was going to be no picnic. It was very uncomfortable sitting or trying to stretch out in the trailers while they were underway. The road bed was very rough and the constant jarring, swaying and jerking of the vehicles reminded some of what it must have been like traveling across the country in a covered wagon. There were a few people who could not seem to adjust to the motion of the trucks and were constantly sick, much to the added discomfort of their fellow passengers. The medics passed out motion sickness pills, but these seemed to do little good for the more serious cases.

At the staff meeting on the second evening, the caravan physician said that he was concerned about the well being of more than one passenger. Anders had no suggestion other than to provide the best care they could and if need be, they would have to drop them off with someone along the way. All in the meeting looked at one another as no one had seen anyone along the road that looked half way civilized. Anders, sensing what they were thinking, commented, "Sooner or later we are going to begin to run into people just like ourselves. They are around somewhere. They aren't all gone."

Sarah backed him up with, "They are out there. We're on the radio with them every day and we will be going through some areas where people with similar beliefs and goals as ours can be found. It is not all animals out there."

For the next two days, the trip continued much as it had before. It was starting to take on a routine with early morning departures, lunch stops, and travel until dusk and with small arms fire to contend with at almost any time. A further annoyance that some found to be particularly troublesome was how to deal with the growing numbers of beggars and pathetic creatures that they encountered along the roadway, begging for assistance, food, water or, in many cases, pleading with those in the passing vehicles to take their children or babes in arms as they had no food or water to give them. Tears streaming down the faces of gaunt mothers and fathers standing in the mud of the roadway, no shoes, obviously starving to death, clutching a half dead child in their arms, begging anyone that would listen to take the child. Some in the trailers tried to pass out bits of food that they had saved from lunch or breakfast and even pleaded with the Security troops to help this or that unfortunate soul who was obviously going to die without assistance from someone.

That evening at the camp debriefing, with everyone in the caravan present, Anders laid down the law that no food or water or other provisions would be provided to anyone outside of those in the caravan and if anyone violated that order, they would be evicted from the caravan. There would be no exceptions. They did not have enough food or water to handle their own needs as it was and they could not afford to give any away. There was some grumbling with this announcement especially from those who had seen the cases of food loaded onto the trailers back in the Control Zone. When Anders heard the grumbling coming from a number of those in attendance, he became very angry. "For those of you who may consider violating this order, I suggest you take a good look at the people you want to help because that is exactly what you and your children will look like if you are turned out of this caravan. For those of you that want to live and hopefully take on a better life than what we have witnessed in the past few days, do not violate this order. I will just leave it at that. The rest is up to you." There was no grumbling after that final comment.

At the staff meeting which followed the general meeting, Sarah announced that they had picked up messages on the radio relating to a large convoy of armed vehicles proceeding in a northerly direction up I-75. That had to be them and apparently someone in the Ocala area was announcing their presence. That was not good news as they were expecting to pass through the Tallahassee area in two or three days and that was considered to be very high risk by Sarah and Perry in particular. By Sarah because of the many negative reports that she had obtained regarding conditions in the Tallahassee area and by Perry because he considered it to be a highly vulnerable choke point. He had considered suggesting the beach road to the south of Tallahassee, but that would restrict their options even further than taking the old interstate which passed through the northern part of the city.

Tallahassee was considered to be basically a battle zone. There were a number of gangs contending for control of the city and all of them would look upon the caravan as sweet meat. It was entirely possible that they would even consider a temporary truce among themselves to take on the caravan. Another, greater threat than they posed was the presence of the FSP in the Macon area. That was less than three hundred miles to the north of their intended route and it was known that their tentacles did extend down into Tallahassee. Sarah indicated that one or more of the gangs contesting for power in that city were possibly allied with the FSP If the FSP had learned of the arms turnover by Yates and Campbell to the Association, it was highly probable that they could be waiting for them when they made their way to the west on old Interstate 10. Even if they did not know of the arms turnover, they may still be interested in whatever goods they might be carrying. Unfortunately, there was no other viable alternative route and they just had to ready their defenses and fight their way through the area if that became necessary.

Once they were to the west of Tallahassee, their options as to what route to take opened up but until then, their intended route could easily be predicted by anyone with knowledge of their final destination. The following day, their suspicions were confirmed when Sarah informed Anders, Stuart and Perry that her team had intercepted a message to the effect that the caravan was expected to turn to the west before Tallahassee. Someone had said something to someone that they should not have and it was now rather certain that they would be facing problems up the road. They were still quite a ways from Tallahassee and Stuart did not want to delay their arrival any longer as it would provide additional time for anyone to prepare for their entrance into the city. Unfortunately, the only viable highway ran through the highly populated northern part of the town. Stuart had Sarah radio back to the Cuban commander that they needed to meet and make plans for their entry. He had kept the Cuban advised regarding the information they were obtaining through Sarah's intelligence network so the Cuban commander was aware of the problem. Stuart also had Barnes prepare to off load Frick's airplane as he wanted to know if there was any activity to the north of their intended route which would indicate the presence of the FSP in force. If they were there, they were going to have to come up with plan B.

One of the scout cars brought the Cuban commander up to the Command Post and Stuart called for a temporary halt in the caravan. The passengers were permitted to off load and take care of their personal needs while the Command Post staff decided what they were going to do. Stuart also called for the off loading of Frick's aircraft as the weather conditions appeared favorable for an over flight of the Tallahassee area. Barnes had rigged up a video camera in the aircraft which produced a remarkable image on the screen in the CP. In order to have the necessary detail in the images to discern combat equipped troops, it was necessary that the aircraft be flown no higher than ten thousand feet over the area to be inspected. This could be very risky with the slow speed of the aircraft and Stuart could not afford to lose Frick or the airplane on this mission.

Stuart told Frick that if he was picking up any radar lock on signals on the modified radar detector that Barnes had installed in the aircraft, he was to leave the scene immediately. The same applied if Frick began to pick up flak of any type. Stuart doubted that they would encounter these problems because Sarah's intelligence reports indicated that the area was under the control of warring gangs of ruffians and not a well organized military Force. The question lingering in the background however was that involving the presence of the FSP They did have the equipment to bring Frick's plane down and they knew how to use it.

Stuart had the caravan open up a section of road, five thousand feet long, to serve as the runway and Barnes saw that the aircraft was fully loaded with flares, rockets and fuel. Frick walked the entire length of the runway, kicking aside rocks and debris that could damage his tires or be sucked up by the propeller. After viewing maps of the area and checking out the condition of his plane, particularly the sections where the wings had been reattached by Barnes' men, Frick started the aircraft and, turning it to the side so as not to blast the trucks with his prop wash, ran up the engines to check the power. Everything appeared normal and he pointed the aircraft down the road and pushed the throttle full forward as the aircraft accelerated over the rough surface. When he had gone about half of the distance available, he noted that he had sufficient airspeed for flight and pulled back on the stick. Frick hadn't flown for some time and it was exhilarating to feel the power of the aircraft and the enjoyment of flight over terrain that took on a different view as he climbed to altitude.

As his aircraft flew higher into the sky, Frick could now see both the east and west coast of Florida. He could make out Orlando to the south and what he assumed was Tallahassee to the northwest. The city was covered by a hazy brown layer of smog which cut down visibility somewhat. Frick flew over the caravan to check for any sign of unwanted visitors in the vicinity. Seeing none, he turned to the northwest towards Tallahassee. He checked his radio to see that he had contact with the CP and Stuart's voice came back loud and clear. Frick climbed up to ten thousand feet while radioing back to Stuart his observations concerning the condition of the road yet to be traveled to the city and also turned on his video monitor so that those in the CP could observe what he was talking about. There were occasional buildings along the route and he did observe small groups of people in the vicinity of the roadway, but nothing that appeared to be a particular threat. As he approached the city, he noted that there was some sort of activity down at a bridge site on their route of travel with a group of men doing some sort of construction. This was about a mile short of the major intersection that the convoy would be passing through.

Frick flew lower over the area and reported back to Stuart that they were making some sort of barricade across the road that comprised the entry lane for the bridge over I-10. When he circled back for another look, he saw that they were firing at him with small arms fire. He wasn't too concerned about that as he was too high for them to hit his plane with those weapons. When he told that to Stuart, Stuart immediately told him to climb even higher, to be safe, and move on to the city. Frick radioed back the GPS coordinates of the bridge activity and Sarah's staff plotted the position on the wall map in the Command Post. While Frick proceeded in the direction of the city and the intersection, Stuart, Perry, Sarah and the Cuban commander carefully studied the map. Frick then reported that there were numerous fires burning in the city and the smoke obscured his view somewhat but from what he could see, there were no military vehicles of any sort in sight. There were a number of civilian cars moving about the city and a fairly large group of people massing in the vicinity of the overpass on the interstate that the caravan intended to take. Frick passed the coordinates of this site back. He also said that many of the people were armed or appeared to be armed. He was not picking up any flak of any sort, nor had his fuzz buster activated. He estimated that there were two to three hundred men in the group and there did not appear to be any organization to the gathering. He said further that the city was a mess. Debris throughout the downtown area, with overturned burned out vehicles, and extensive areas in the city which were entirely burned out and blackened by fires that must have just burned out of control with no one attempting to put them out. Stuart told him that they could observe on the monitor much of what he was reporting, but to keep providing his descriptions.

Frick then turned his aircraft to the northeast to check for any activity coming down from Georgia. He flew over some small communities and saw people, but no sign of an organized military column of any sort. He noted that some of these communities appeared to be in much better shape than Tallahassee. He saw no one taking any shots at him and one person even waved. He dipped his wings in reply and then turned back towards the convoy to conserve fuel. Frick's landing back on the highway was rough but other than that, uneventful. He taxied the aircraft back to the trailer and Barnes crew was already unloading weapons as well as the video tape and dismantling the wings before he had come out of the cockpit.

They all again viewed his video tapes to get a better idea of what they were facing and they found that Frick's radio transmissions very accurately depicted what they were seeing on the screen. The Cuban commander suggested that he take his force and move around to the north of the city and come into the problem area as the caravan approached on the interstate. He stated that his tracked vehicles would have no problem negotiating the secondary roads that he would have to take in order to position himself in the vicinity of the overpass and furthermore, he added, his men were getting a little hungry for some activity. He added that the Association's trucks were far more vulnerable to small arms fire than his armored personnel carriers and if some of the trucks were disabled, they would all be parked here for some time.

What the Cuban Commander had to say made sense and Stuart was more than willing to accept the offer as he did agree that the trucks were vulnerable, even to small arms fire.

The Cuban commander estimated that he could be on the north side of the intersection by one hour before sunset which would be perfect although the caravan would have to drive some distance to the west of the city to be safe and that could mean driving after dark on the interstate. Barnes was very familiar with that section of road and was convinced that with the night vision goggles and proper use of the scout cars, they would be able to make their way to a safe stopping point. They would not have to contend with sharp curves, hills and other hazards once they were a few miles to the west of the city. Furthermore, the lead vehicles could use their lights for the occasional times when they were necessary.

Barnes had taped all of the headlights so that only a thin line of light emitted casting a beam no further than twenty feet in front of the truck. That would still attract some attention, but far less than if the lights were uncovered. The only other problem remaining was dealing with the barricade at the bridge. It could be more than the plow would handle. Perry suggested that they could use dynamite to remove it, but Stuart was against that as that also was a very scarce item. They would use the plow and manpower to pull it down. It was put up that way and it could be taken down that way. Barnes estimated that at the outside, the barricade would only hold them up no more than fifteen minutes. The caravan had a shorter route to go than the Cuban force and should have no problem taking care of the barricade and arriving at the overpass at the time targeted by the Cubans.

It was decided that the Cuban force would move in on the mob at the overpass at the targeted time with the caravan no more than a half a mile to the east of the overpass. The caravan was to keep moving to the west, the assumption being that the mob would be well occupied by the Cubans and would ignore the caravan passing by. Furthermore, the caravan gunners would be adding to the problem for the locals and if they were true to form for such rabble, they would be running in all directions to save their lives. The plan was then for the Cubans to fall in behind the caravan and provide a rear guard should anyone decide to give them any trouble. They all agreed it was a viable plan and they coordinated their watch settings to ensure they were on the same time. The Cuban Commander was driven back to his unit and Stuart had the caravan pull over to the side of the road to allow the Cuban vehicles to pass. They were an impressive force and by the looks of the smiles on the faces of the young men that could be seen, they were eagerly looking forward to some action.

When the Cubans had passed, the caravan proceeded towards the north, heading to I-10 and Tallahassee. Perry began briefing his company commanders on what to expect as they approached the city and Barnes prepared his men for the work of removing the barricade. He also tasked Perry for assistance from some of his troops should they be needed. As the trucks made their way along the highway, with the scout cars leading the pack, they occasionally came upon settlements, again with small groups of people staring vacantly at the passing scene. A lone beggar was on the roadway every now and then, with their hands out imploring those in the vehicles to give them some food or water. By now, the passengers in the trailers had gotten the message from Anders that nothing was to be passed out to the pathetic creatures along the road and nothing was. All along this route, as before, the passengers had to stay down below the protection of the bullet proof curtain which extended on the underside of the trailer and up four feet along the sides. Any movement in the trailer had to be conducted in a hunched over fashion to prevent exposure and the security force monitoring activity in the trailer saw to it that no one violated this practice. In this manner, the vehicles proceeded towards Tallahassee.

It was around five in the afternoon when Nix reported that they were coming upon the bridge over I-10. This bridge was only the entry point onto I-10 and the other bridge, across I-10, was where they expected most of the problems. There were some men in the area that appeared to be armed but they had scattered into the brush as the scout cars approached. Perry sent the plow up to check for mines while the scout cars fired short bursts into the brush to keep the snipers at bay. There was an occasional shot fired towards the plow, but the operator was well protected as were the engine and tires. A thin wisp of smoke rising from the snipers gun would give away his position which would immediately draw withering fire from the two scout cars. After the first few shots from the snipers, they quieted down.

The plow was able to remove the larger pieces of debris and push them off the road, but it became apparent that manpower was needed to clean up the area sufficiently for the vehicles to pass through. Perry sent some men out and also assigned a detail to check the bridge and ensure that it was not wired with explosives to be detonated by someone on the far side. The scout cars again sprayed the surrounding area as a number of men took up positions to provide cover for those detailed to the barricade and the bridge.

When the work was completed and no munitions were found on the bridge, the scout cars again fired a burst or two into the brush while the men ran back to their vehicles. All of the trucks crossed over the bridge and onto I-10 without incident and Perry ordered a slow down as they were only a few miles from the overpass and they had a half an hour to go before their scheduled arrival. As the time passed and they came closer to the city, they caught the smell before they saw anything they could associate with a town of any size. It was a combination of smells, including burning rubber, urine, rotting animals and it permeated everything. It entered the cabs of the vehicles and the trailer compartments where the passengers and troops were.

Most of the people in the caravan were familiar with the smell of smoke, burning tires, decaying garbage and refuse and knew what it was, but there was another offensive, somewhat sweet smell, but yet putrid and they did not know what that was until they were told that it was the smell of death. Apparently bodies had not been buried and were rotting out in the open. As the trucks moved farther along I-10 into the city and burned out buildings began to appear alongside the road, everyone on board, whether security force or resident passenger, became increasingly apprehensive about what might happen. Perry had everyone on full alert status with gun positions double manned with orders to fire on anyone that appeared to have a weapon or that could present a threat to the caravan. They were now receiving some sniper fire and all passengers were curled up in their compartments to present as small a target as possible. A number of the smaller children were crying as their mothers or fathers gathered them up and held them tight so that they would not be hit by the small arms fire.

The Defense Team manning gun positions and firing through the slit openings in the armor plate were returning fire from what appeared to be a very disorganized group of renegades firing at will for their own amusement. Nix reported that he was now approaching the major intersection where the Cubans should be coming from the north to meet the caravan which was moving west. He could now see the overpass and there was a large mass of humanity gathered about it waving weapons and hurling debris down on the roadway. They were obviously going to try to stop the caravan below the bridge and that presented a problem in that someone was going to have to clear it out of the way. Perry sent the plow forward again, still out of range of the guns blazing away at them from the vicinity of the overpass.

At that time there appeared to be something occurring just to the north of the bridge and hundreds of people in the mob directed their attention in that direction and simultaneously began scurrying like rats leaving a sinking ship as Cuban armored vehicles sped through the mob with automatic weapons blazing. Within a span of one or two minutes, the mob of two or three hundred people was wiped out. They fell by the tens and twenties as the Cuban force sped through their midst with every weapon on board in continuous fire. By the time the scout cars and the plow reached the overpass, there were only a few left who were dropping their weapons and holding up their arms in surrender. Again, as was witnessed in the Cuban Cocoa operation, the guns kept firing until there was not a single living soul left.

The caravan proceeded under the overpass, preceded by the plow removing debris, and on through the city while an eerie silence prevailed.

The only sound that could be heard now was that of the diesel engines of the trucks. No one in the caravan was talking. The passengers were in a state of shock, having for the first time witnessed the savagery of very one sided mortal combat. Many of the members of the Defense Team had been involved in gunfights of one form or another, but witnessing what had happened at the overpass made them all question whether or not there were any ethics involved when it came to war. Ethics involved acting according to principles, but when you no longer had a governing society, who then would establish the principles under which people lived and related with one another.

Very clearly the Cuban force had a different understanding of what was right or wrong in a combat situation than did most of the people in the caravan. They spoke about it during the remainder of the day as they made their way to the west but after hours of further discussion, on the road and later in the campground, there still remained many unresolved issues as to what was right and wrong in time of war. There was even argument as to whether or not their present situation was war which would justify more severe impositions on the rights of others than would lesser forms of social dysfunction.

One lesson that everyone in the caravan did learn was that they were many times more fortunate than the poor souls they had seen over the past few days. They had food, shelter, protection and a governing body that was somewhat autocratic, but generally fair. Many had not given much thought to that before leaving on the journey to Montana and as time went on, they were becoming much more appreciative of their situation than they had been when they were in the safety of the Control Zone, protected from what was going on elsewhere.

Stuart and the others in the Command Post also discussed the incident at the overpass but while he did not defend what had taken place, he suggested that they should be looking at the situation from the point of view of the Cubans, because they were the ones that were going to have to return through this very same area in the near future. What were they to do? They obviously could not take prisoners and if they had let the mob run away, they would be a much greater threat on their return trip. "Their lives were at stake," Stuart argued. "Not ours. We will be well away from this area in another day or so. We have nothing to worry about from these people who would have killed every one of us for no good reason. I think we have a great deal to be thankful for to the Cubans. They were the ones that put themselves at risk for our benefit. They volunteered to do the mission. We might have done it differently. Maybe, maybe not. Who knows how men react when the firing starts." The others did not comment one way or another. It was a troubling issue and one that would come up again. Most everyone that was in the room was aware of that.

That evening at the campground when Anders was making his announcements, he felt that he had to bring the matter up, although he would have preferred not to. He did not want to do anything that would create dissension among the group and he was aware that there were many differing opinions concerning how the Cuban force acted. He said that he was thankful for the assistance of the Cubans and explained how they had volunteered to do the mission. There were a few comments from the audience on that statement and Anders pointed to the hecklers and suggested that the next time they were to meet an armed group of semi human renegades that the hecklers could be sent out to handle the mission and do it in a much nicer fashion. That made them quiet down. He told all assembled that many of them undoubtedly owed their lives to the Cubans that night and they should be thankful. "We are not here to pick apart how they went about their task. We may have done it differently, but that doesn't necessarily make it the right way. We are here. We are alive. We have our vehicles and supplies and that is what counts. If anyone thinks that is not what counts, step forward and explain to me what does." When no one did, Anders just said, "Good. That's the end of it. No more discussion on that topic while we are on the road. Get some sleep, same schedule tomorrow." Everyone dispersed and headed to their respective trailers for some sleep after a very exciting day.

The following morning after the caravan was again moving to the west on Interstate 10, Anders called a staff meeting for Stuart, Sarah, and Perry. He had Sarah proceed with her latest intelligence reports, included in which was a statement on conditions in and around Montgomery, Alabama. Apparently renegades were in control of the city and were well organized under a Black leader, one Richard Johnston. Stuart found that interesting as most Blacks had adopted Muslim names in the last twenty or so years. Johnston had a fairly well trained force and his area of activity extended down to and including the former Army Base at Fort Rucker. That was not that far from their present position and what had been their intended route of travel.

Sarah suggested that they proceed farther to the west on I-10 before turning to the northwest and avoid all cities of any size by taking state highways rather than the old Interstates. She added that there were a few areas that they could stop at between their present position and the Little Rock, Arkansas area that were in the hands of groups that she believed would be friendly with the exception of the city itself. It was possible that they might even restock food and water supplies, but she had no hard data to base that on. In any event, hopefully the passengers could rest up for a day or two before continuing the journey. The continuous jolting when underway and the poor sleeping conditions were causing some morale and health problems. Somewhat longer stops along the way might be very beneficial for mind and body.

Anders commented that they had enough slack built into their schedule to allow for such stops and, as far as he was concerned, Sarah's proposed route sounded good to him. They then discussed the agreement with the Cubans which was to be with them all the way to Montgomery. Sarah suggested that when they reached the Montgomery to Mobile highway and crossed it on their way west, the Cubans could be released. Everyone hated to see them go, but they all agreed that would be a fair solution. Stuart said that he would discuss it with the Cuban Commander that evening over at their campground. He saw no reason why they would object as the proposal would cut off about two hundred miles from their trip.

Sarah then continued the briefing with what was known about conditions on their new route. There were many blank spots in the route for which she had no information whatsoever, other than general demographic data from before the collapse of the government. Most of the ground to be covered in the next few days was farming country with an occasional small residential community to pass through. Sarah suggested that these communities were of the type that they should expect the least trouble from. She did caution, however, that little was known about them and they would have to prepare for the worst until they were assured otherwise.

That evening, Stuart talked with the Cuban commander about releasing them from the agreement when they reached the Mobile highway. That was agreeable with him as he was eager to return to Florida. The next two days went by with only minor problems. Two of the trucks required maintenance. One of the dual tires on a trailer developed a leak and went flat while the other truck had an engine problem that brought the entire caravan to a halt. While the mechanics worked on the engine, Barnes had another team changing out the tire. The passengers took advantage of the stop and some took a swim and bath in a nearby lake under the protection of the security force. They were traveling in a relatively uninhabited area that was heavily overgrown with trees, brush and vines that covered everything making it difficult to see beyond a distance of thirty feet in any direction. It was very doubtful that anyone knew they were in the vicinity.

The work on the trucks took over two hours and by the time it was completed, everyone was ready to get back on the road. The weather on this particular afternoon was hot and humid but with the ventilation windows, it was cooler to ride in the trucks with some breeze than it was to sit outside in the hot sun. Mosquitoes were a problem as well and Stuart had Barnes pass out lotion for the use of the passengers and security force. That helped considerably, but they were still a nuisance. On the evening of the second day, as they proceeded in a northwesterly direction on a rather narrow state highway, they came around a curve and Nix reported what appeared to be an intersecting four lane highway leading down to the southwest. Sarah checked the coordinates and concluded that they had arrived at the Mobile Highway.

It was late in the day, so Anders instructed Nix to scout around for a campsite while Stuart radioed to the Cuban commander that they had arrived at his turn around point. The Cubans responded that they would spend the night there as well which was appreciated by Stuart as he was not looking forward to losing the added protection of the Cuban force. While they were awaiting Nix's report on a suitable campsite, Perry brought up to Stuart and Anders the suggestion that they should create a small separate company of men to serve as a quick reaction tactical squad to replace the service the Cubans had provided. Perry had been impressed with the Cubans in the overpass operation and felt that the caravan would very well have a need for a mobile tactical unit for diversionary actions in the future. They all agreed that had it not been for the Cuban attack on the overpass from north of the interstate, the caravan would have sustained casualties and may well have come to a stop by reason of damage to vehicles. Stuart questioned Perry as to how they could be mobile when they had no armored personnel carriers. Perry had been thinking about that and suggested that the two scout cars which were sufficiently armored and equipped with automatic weapons could carry up to eight combat equipped personnel apiece and there were in addition two small utility trucks that could be modified by Barnes to carry an additional twenty men. There was also a two and a half ton truck carrying supplies that was already covered with material protecting the engine, tires and interior from small arms fire and that could be modified to carry an additional thirty combat troops. That would give them sixty to seventy troops that they could rapidly deploy for flanking maneuvers or to handle threats that could not be dealt with by the unwieldy, ponderous caravan.

It made sense to Stuart and the only concern that Anders had was how the supplies presently in the trucks could be carried elsewhere. They had used up some of their food stuffs which amounted to approximately the load of one of the utility trucks so that helped to solve the problem. They would just have to cram the other supplies into already tight spots in the remaining vehicles. Stuart was also questioning turning over Nix's scout cars to Perry. They had been kept quite busy on the trip thus far and were proving to be very handy as they were at this very moment, searching out a camp site. Perry had a ready answer for that. They would stay with Nix and he would lead the tactical group. The scout cars would continue to function as they had been and would take on the additional assignment as the need dictated. That would appeal to Nix as well as he had been seeking a more active role should trouble develop, so there was little chance he would object to that proposal.

Stuart later discussed Perry's suggestion with Nix and he enthusiastically supported the plan. Nix had always considered the basic heavily armed, but ponderous, caravan concept as particularly vulnerable due to its lack of flexible response. The Flying Squad, as Nix labeled the new unit, would provide the flexibility that they sorely needed.

Stuart told Barnes to get to work on the modification just as soon as he could so that the Flying Squad would be up and operating quickly. Barnes had a mobile workshop that he had been setting up at every encampment to handle minor maintenance needs and he immediately proceeded to expand this facility to handle the new assignment. By the time the camp was set up that evening, Barnes had gathered the necessary materials together and was already working on the first vehicle. Stuart considered himself very fortunate to have a fellow like Barnes in charge of supply and maintenance. He hardly ever complained about anything, other than a shortage of good power tools and always did the job that was asked of him.

On the final night that the Cubans were encamped with them before their departure back to Florida, the command post received a call from one of the sentry outposts that there was a man and a young boy walking down the road towards their position. Stuart was present in the room when the call came in and he told the sentries to escort the pair to the CP. Within fifteen minutes, the man and boy, apparently his son, were standing outside the

Command Post trailer accompanied by one of the security guards. Stuart and Sarah brought the two into the conference room in the CP vehicle and gave them some water and biscuits. The two, who appeared to be emaciated and in poor health, quickly devoured the food that was offered them,.

Stuart had one of the staff people order up two trays of food for the two as he wished to find out what was going on in this part of the country. After he had something to eat, the man perked up considerably and explained that he and his son had been wandering around for the past month since they had been driven out of their home outside of Montgomery by roving bands of renegades. They had barely escaped with their lives and were only saved by the cries and screams of neighbors who were attacked first. They had lived in Montgomery in prior times and the man explained that he had been an electrician for the city for years.

When the collapse came, anarchy reigned and for the first few months, or even the first year, while it was very dangerous to be about, it was possible for a person with the support of a few armed neighbors to keep the wolves away from the door. Everyone had guns and when darkness fell, it was necessary to barricade oneself in your home with someone awake at all times. With neighbors doing the same thing, it was possible to survive the attacks of small, roving bands of thugs that would just as soon kill you as look at you. In time, however, the thugs were becoming more organized, more powerful, and better equipped.

It became apparent to the man that he had to get his family out while there was still time to do so. His neighbors disagreed, believing it was safer to stay where they were. There were always rumors afloat that the United States Army was coming, or some other country, such as China, was coming to rescue them from their plight. But as he well knew, those were only rumors. He decided that he would go on his own. It was not safe to leave your somewhat protected immediate neighborhood in the daytime so he packed up what little food he had remaining and, in the dark of night, took up what he thought would be the safest route out of the city.

He figured that he would head south into the farming country where he might find food and shelter. At that time he was accompanied by his wife, daughter and son.

They were almost out of the city when they were spotted by five drugged up bastards with automatic weapons. He told his family to run for it and he would try to hold them off with his own weapon, a six shot revolver. He did slow them down, but they fired a burst at his wife and children, knocking down his wife and daughter. His son then ran back to him and luckily escaped another hail of bullets. He watched as "These damned animals ran over and blew the brains out of his wife and daughter." There was nothing he could do but to try to save himself and his son. While they were ripping their victim's clothes off looking for valuables, he was able to escape into the night with his son. They made their way out of the city that night and when dawn came, they were in heavily wooded country south of Montgomery and safe, at least for the moment.

That was about one month ago and they had been wandering ever since. They had a few close calls but nothing like what they were experiencing in the Montgomery area. Stuart took the man over to the wall map and had him give a general explanation of where he had been since leaving Montgomery. His route of travel was of interest to Stuart as the caravan was going to take a route very close to the areas the man had passed through, with the exception of the Montgomery area. The man told Stuart that most of the people that he came in contact with once he was outside of the city were friendly. Very afraid for their own well being and short of food supplies, but willing to help if they possibly could.

As the conversation between the man, Sarah and Stuart continued, the boy had fallen asleep in a corner of the trailer and Sarah told one of her staff people to take him to a cot in the dispensary so that he could sleep in some comfort for a change. As they continued talking, Stuart was impressed by the character of their visitor and found him to be an intelligent person with skills that they could probably use in their group. After a while, when they took a break and the man was escorted out for a visit to the latrine,

Stuart suggested to Sarah that they consider letting the man and his son join their caravan. Sarah totally agreed as she had the same impression concerning the two as did Stuart. When the man returned, Stuart told him that he could spend the night in their camp if he so desired. The offer was eagerly accepted as the man had spent the past month trying to sleep with one eye open at all times except for the few nights he was with family groups that he could somewhat trust. When he had been escorted out of the CP by the security guard, Stuart and Sarah met with Anders and discussed the possibility of an addition to their group. Anders was not enthusiastic about adding additional mouths to feed when their supplies were already being severely tasked, but he had always respected the judgment of Stuart and Sarah and he wasn't about to go against it on this occasion. Stuart told Sarah that he would talk with the two in the morning and offer them room in the caravan if they wanted it.

The following morning the Cubans departed, heading back to Florida. Before they left, the Commander came by the Command Post to get the location of the arms cache which he had to radio back to the Control Zone before departing. Within a half an hour, he informed Stuart that the cache had been located and they were in the process of retrieving it. Stuart told him that they had left an additional three hundred AR20s so Morales should be pleased. He also told him that if there was any problem with any of the weapons by reason of salt water damage or whatever; to call him on the radio frequency for the Association and replacements would be provided. With that assurance, the Cubans loaded their vehicles and turned around for the long trip home.

As everyone was packing up for another day on the road, Stuart had the two guests brought to him in the Command Post. They had been fed breakfast at the food trailer and were very thankful for the treatment they had received. They were in the process of thanking Stuart when he informed them that there was a possibility that they could stay with the caravan if John Barnes could use the type of electrical experience the man had to offer. The father's eyes lit up with excitement at being told of the possibility of joining a group of people that appeared to honor and respect the basic values of a civilized society. It had been a long time since he had been with people such as he had met in the caravan. He was also very aware of how scarce food was and how carefully people guarded what little supplies they had available. He was well aware of the fact that he had nothing to bring to the table except for his skills and thus far, they had not been of interest to anyone. He was at a loss for words before he blurted out, "Yes, my god, yes. We'll do whatever we have to in order to travel with your people. My god, we're out here with absolutely nothing."

Stuart interrupted the man, calling to Barnes who was just coming into the CP, "John, talk to this fellow and see if he can be of assistance to us." Barnes had been briefed by Sarah so he was aware of what was going on. He had a serious need for anyone with knowledge of electricity as most of his maintenance problems involved that area of expertise. Stuart introduced the man to John Barnes and then apologized as he had never gotten his name or that of his son. Names were exchanged and Barnes took the man to a corner of the conference room to find out the depth of his knowledge and experience. In the meantime, his son was out meeting some of the other children in the caravan and it was obvious that he would have no trouble fitting in with everyone. Barnes sat and talked with the fellow for over an hour and at the end of the interview, Barnes went up to Stuart and just said, "Hire this guy." That was enough for Stuart who then let Del Sutton and his son Andy know that they were welcome to stay provided they abided by the rules and policies of the Association. With that in mind, he had Sutton go through an extensive briefing by the intelligence section on how the Association operated and what was expected of everyone. Stuart had no doubt that Sutton would fit in quite nicely.

As the caravan departed the campground, Stuart was a bit more wary about everyone's security now that the Cuban force had departed. Barnes had said that the modification on the vehicles would be completed by the following morning, with his mechanics, now including Sutton, working all night long. Some of the work could be performed while the caravan was underway, but very little. Most of the work required the involved vehicles to be elevated on blocks and that had to be done while the caravan was camped for the night. According to Sarah's reports, they expected to be traveling in low risk areas for at least the following two days.

In the second day after the Cubans had departed, the caravan came up on a small town in western Alabama. As they were about to enter the town, they were stopped by a group of armed men who wanted to know who they were and where they were going. In these situations, Nix would radio back to the Command Post and Stuart or Sarah would come up and do the talking. In this case Stuart came forward, driven on one of the three wheeled vehicles Barnes had constructed. The men were all armed with a variety of weapons and did not appear threatening, but they clearly meant business. They had no intention of permitting the caravan to enter the town until they were sure the visitors meant no harm.

The spokesman for the men informed Stuart that the people in the town knew they were on the road, had been forewarned and were well armed should there be any trouble. He pointed to some of the obvious fortifications that had been constructed in the town to make sure that the visitors knew he was not bluffing. From where he was standing, Stuart could see that the town was adequately protected and guarded by a large number of people bearing arms. Stuart told the men that the caravan only wished to pass through the town and would like to replenish water supplies if that was possible and would also like to purchase some food supplies if they had them available. If neither was available, that was understandable. Stuart explained that they had women and children in the caravan, where they were from and where they were going.

The spokesman said nothing for some time after Stuart had finished his explanation and only stood, holding his weapon and studied the caravan. He focused in on the gun emplacements on the trailers as well as the automatic weapons on the scout cars. He did not seem to be overly intimidated by what he saw. Turning his attention back to Stuart, he took a long look at him before he asked him, "Any blacks in your group?"

Stuart only responded, "We have some."

Hooking the butt of his rifle in his trouser belt with the barrel pointing up, the spokesman took a drag on his cigarette, blew out the smoke and said, "You can stop and fill your water tanks at the well. We have plenty of that. I will see where we stand on grain and corn. We should have plenty of that too. But you keep those blacks out of sight. We've had some problems around here and feelings are running pretty high. Ya hear? I'm not shitting you about that. You let those blacks be seen and I don't care how many automatic weapons you might have, you are going to have more trouble than you want. Do you clearly understand that?" The last words were enunciated slowly and, to Stuart, most clearly.

Stuart said, "Understood. They won't be seen. We'll need a few minutes to take care of that. Do we follow you into town or what?"

The spokesman flipped his cigarette butt and replied, "We'll wait. You follow us into town when you're ready. Don't take too long. We have other things to do, you know."

Stuart returned to the CP and told Sarah to see that every black person in the caravan was totally out of sight until they were well on the other side of this town. That might be several hours as there was a possibility that they would be taking on water and food. Sarah raised her eyebrows at the request, but said that she would take care of it. There were only four blacks in the caravan other than Perry, but wherever they were, they were not in sight while the trucks were parked in the town square. Stuart asked where Perry was and Sarah told him that he was getting a cup of coffee in the chuck wagon as everyone labeled the truck with the food service function. Stuart walked back to the chuck wagon, found Perry and sat beside him at the counter.

"Ross, I've got a problem." Stuart explained the situation and before he had laid it all out, Perry held up his hand and said, "No sweat. I understand. Don't worry about it. Let me know when I can come out of here. Hell, I'll have another sandwich."

Water tanks were refilled at the city well and they were able to buy grain, eggs, corn and vegetables. Not as much as they wanted, but much more than they had expected. They made the buy with gold which was first inspected by the town jeweler who confirmed it was the real thing. The townsfolk were friendly, but they were nervous with all of the armored vehicles, bristling with guns, sitting in the center of their town.

Stuart could tell that there had been some fighting in the vicinity as there were bullet holes in some of the buildings and one or two of the homes had been destroyed by fire. Bunkers had been built around the outskirts of the town and barbed wire installed around the perimeter. The bunkers were all occupied while the caravan was in the town and Stuart estimated that another hundred or two hundred men under arms were in positions around the square in the event of trouble. Stuart could not blame the local citizenry for being careful about their presence and he instructed Perry to keep his armed troops out of sight while he sent word to the passengers not to leave the immediate vicinity of the caravan. They were not in the town over a few hours while they took on their supplies and paid for their purchases. After they had loaded everyone onto the caravan, Stuart let the leader of the guard detail that had been with him since arrival at the outskirts of the town know that the caravan was ready to depart.

They were escorted out of town by the same men who preceded them a mile or so down the road and then waved them on. They had not been the friendliest group Stuart had ever run into, but he knew they would not be the least friendly that he would encounter on his journey to Montana. He had no complaints with the way he had been treated as their water tanks were refilled and they had taken on a good supply of fresh vegetables.

While supplies were being loaded in the town, Stuart had spoken with his escort about conditions in the surrounding areas. According to the escort, most of their problems involved small bands of opportunists who would try to penetrate the security of their village to steal food, weapons or anything of value. Occasionally they would succeed, but as time went on, the townsfolk became wiser in such matters and were able to keep them out.

Stuart passed on to his escort the information that he had on Richard Johnston. The escort advised him that Johnston was well known in the area. One of those encounters with Johnston's group occurred in the early morning hours two weeks prior when twenty or so in a patrol unit overran a sentry post and held a corner of the village for the better part of a day while they emptied out the contents of a storeroom and brutally killed a number of the townsfolk that they had managed to capture. Everyone in the town was now very frightened that they would not be able to hold off the next attack and there were many who were for going elsewhere, but they did not know where to go.

# Chapter Thirty-Four

In many parts of the Deep South, as elsewhere in the country, the anarchy resulting from the disintegration of the government had turned into a race war. In the larger metropolitan areas, with the predominantly black populations, the white residential areas were soon overrun with killings and atrocities being common place. In the rural areas, there was not the same tendency for the anarchy to develop into a racial conflict. Stuart, Sarah, Anders and Perry discussed why that was so and the general consensus was that it was because the two races were not as separated in their daily lives in the small towns as they were in the larger cities.

That evening at the general briefing conducted immediately after everyone was fed, Stuart explained his actions concerning hiding the Blacks in their group. Stuart did not argue the issue or apologize. He merely stated his position that he would do whatever it took to save lives in the group.

While Stuart and the others were talking in the CP, Barnes came and announced that the Flying Squad vehicles were all modified and ready to go and also commented that Del Sutton was "One hell of a find. He's not only an electrician but he also did all of the work installing the radios in vehicles so that they could communicate with one another as well as with the CP." Stuart was glad to hear that. He had stuck his neck out by taking the lead with Sutton and was well aware that it could have gone the other way. Sutton had come by more than once to thank him for taking him and his son on board.

Nix was pleased with the modification of the vehicles and his new responsibilities. Navigators were assigned to each vehicle to handle all road and off road navigation utilizing night vision equipment and global positioning equipment as well as detail maps provided by Sarah. The men underwent extensive training with this equipment, in the vehicles, in off road situations, until they had achieved a level of familiarity which would enable them to serve in their assigned roles. Tactical procedures were developed for various combat scenarios that the crews might be expected to encounter as well as procedures for extraction of crews who were pinned down by hostile fire with damaged vehicles. Nix had the assistance of members of the tactics team in preparing his men and Perry loaned him three of his best tactics men for permanent assignment to the group.

Fortunately, this portion of the trip was relatively problem free except for the usual mechanical issues with the trucks. They had spare engines for most of the trucks, including both the larger tractors and the smaller utility vehicles. They also had the equipment that would permit them to do a quick engine or tire change so that it was not necessary to bring the caravan to a halt for an extended period of time. Barnes had facilities in the maintenance trailer to perform engine overhauls while the caravan was underway. In this way, spare engines were always available for quick changes and in one day they had to change out two engines from tractors and they were still able to cover planned mileage.

As they proceeded up through the back roads of Alabama, their major problem was the poor condition of the roadway. These were narrow, poorly surfaced roads to begin with and time, misuse and lack of repair had taken its toll. In some cases it was virtually impossible to determine where the road went as vegetation covered everything. The road bed itself was overgrown with grass, weeds and brush which, on occasion, was so thick as to require someone to physically determine which way it went. Most of the roads still had at least narrow pathways still visible and that enabled the drivers to proceed.

They saw very few people during these days however they knew that the people saw them because they drove by homes and shelters that were obviously occupied. The people who lived in them had apparently fled when they heard the vehicles coming. They did have occasion to speak with a few people who did not see or hear them coming until it was too late to run. From the information they received, there were no organized armed groups in the area other than the Johnston thugs over in the Montgomery area and their roving packs hadn't been around for some time. The people they spoke with were all living on their own, trying to find what food they could from hunting, fishing and small parcels of crop land that were off the beaten track. There did not seem to be any organized activity of any sort among the people in the area. It was each man for himself.

As the caravan was about to enter into the State of Mississippi from the west central part of Alabama, they were making good time when they were met by a group of people carrying belongings and traveling on foot in the opposite direction. Some tried to take cover in the heavy brush on either side of the road, but Nix was upon the main part of the group before they had a chance to unload their bundles and run. When they saw that Nix was apparently not going to harm their companions, those in the brush came out and joined the main body. They told Nix that they had farms a few miles down the road and that they had fled as they were told that Johnston's men were coming from the west and heading to Montgomery. They would be there before nightfall. Nix was told that there were fifty to a hundred men involved and anyone that came in contact with that bunch was slaughtered.

The caravan came to a stop while the Command Post staff interviewed some of the group and decided what to do. Sarah, Stuart and Perry studied the map and concluded that Johnston's men more than likely were coming from the west on old highway 80 which ran from Meridian to Montgomery. The road the caravan was following intersected that road in the vicinity of Demopolis, Alabama, some ten miles to the north of their present position. Based on the distance the caravan was from the intersection, it would be difficult to pass through the area and avoid meeting the renegades.

The three entered into a discussion on the alternatives involved. Sarah was of the opinion that even if they were able to go through the area ahead of them, that fact would be made known to Johnston's men shortly thereafter and that could lead to trouble. Perry was leaning towards setting up an ambush along the road. He figured that they could take out most, if not all of their force before they had a chance to react. The third alternative was to sit where they were and hope the men did not take the road to the south where they were. There was also the chance that Johnston's men would get word of the caravan's presence in the area from someone who had seen them along the road.

After further discussions and more study of the map, it was decided that the least risky action, provided it worked, would be to set up an ambush and catch the unit on the open road. If that was done, it was decided that the main body of the caravan with a minimal security force would be secreted a few miles to the south of the intersection and the Defense Team would position itself along Highway eighty just to the west of a bridge that would be mined in advance of the column.

Remembering Captain Wyatt's report of the Cuban Cocoa operation, Ross Perry suggested that if the column was strung out, that the first few vehicles or troops should be allowed to pass over the bridge before it was blown so that the main body would be in the target area. Nix was then to be stationed a mile or so down the road to the east of the bridge to take out the early birds. Perry did not want anyone getting out to contact their cohorts for assistance. After the attack, everyone, including the caravan, would reassemble in the small crossroads village of Forkland, north of Demopolis. They would have to watch out for stragglers from the conflict who could be anywhere along the road. Sarah laid out the map and showed the back roads that they should take to get into position for the attack on the highway while Barnes was busy seeing that missiles and heavy weapons were loaded on vehicles for transport to the site of the ambush.

According to the information from the Refugees, they had at least two full hours before the renegades would be in the vicinity and that was about how long it would take Perry to position his men. In the following two hours, using the Flying Squad vehicles, they shuttled men and materials up to the site where Perry, Andy Moss and Monty Wyatt were busy positioning the men, seeing that they were adequately dug in and camouflaged. Approximately one hundred men with automatic weapons and missile launchers for armored vehicles were positioned along a line on the south side of Highway eighty. Nix was situated further to the east to hit any troops that managed to get across the bridge before it was blown. No one was to fire until the signal was given by Perry. Perry had a scout in position a mile up the road to give the alert by radio when he saw the column heading their way. The scout would also provide Perry with force numbers, equipment and to report on the type and number of any rolling stock involved. That was the term used to describe tanks or armored vehicles of any kind.

The Defense Team was in position in the brush along the road as was the Flying Squad farther down the road. The column was expected any minute but the minutes dragged by without any word from the scout. Perry ran a radio check every now and then to ensure they were in contact and found that everything was working properly. As the sun began to set in the west, Perry and the others were getting anxious about the wisdom of their plan. About that time, the scout radioed back that there was movement on down the road. His next report to Perry who was on scene at the ambush site was very disconcerting. The message was also received back in the Command Post on their equipment. Stuart, Sarah and others were at that time in the Command Post trailer positioned with the rest of the caravan some two miles to the south of the road in a wooded area. At that time, they were protected by a small security team that functioned more as sentries than as protectors.

The scout reported that he could not determine the total number of troops, but they were a hell of a lot more than fifty or a hundred. He reported that they were being transported in what appeared to be duce and a half's, or two and a half ton trucks, and there was an endless stream of them coming. He had approximately twenty trucks in sight that appeared to be loaded with at least twenty to thirty troops each. There were also what appeared to be armored vehicles, but he could not tell whether they were personnel carriers or weapons platforms.

At that point, Perry cut him off and told the CP that he was pulling his men back while there was still time. Perry radioed the Defense Team that they had only minutes to evacuate the area before they would be spotted. The operation turned into a rout with some of the men leaving some equipment in the camouflaged bunkers. Hopefully they would be able to pick it up later. The scout up the road was advised of the fallback and told to conceal himself and under no circumstances to put the caravan at risk. That meant that he was to go down fighting rather than be captured alive. Units were literally running through the brush and trees to the pickup point with some already waiting for the vehicles to arrive. Back at the Command Post, some of the mid level commanders had taken charge of preparing perimeter defensive positions and wishing they were in a better spot for holding back a force that was two or more times larger than their own.

Not wanting to alert the column to their presence, Perry had those troops that had not yet been picked up, run back to the caravan site. He was afraid that someone would hear or see the activity on the dirt road leading down to the encampment and alert those in the column. The scout continued with his radio transmissions although he had withdrawn to a safer vantage point. He estimated the total column strength at around one thousand men and they appeared to be armed with a variety of weapons including some heavy tractored weapons that could cause real damage. The men in the column appeared to be a mixed bag of renegades and in two of the vehicles there were what appeared to be men and women prisoners, under guard, and in chains. Most of the troops in the vehicles were black but a sizeable number were white, which came as a surprise to Stuart and the others in the CP.

When all of the Defense Team was in position around the caravan and still digging their bunkers, ever deeper and with more protection, the staff was hurriedly meeting in the Command Post. It was clear that they had made a serious error in judgment in their decision to engage in a military action against a force that they had little if any information on. They all agreed to that but decided to forestall any further discussion on that subject until they had extricated themselves from their present situation.

Perry sent a team of scouts to points about a mile south of the intersection to provide warning of any movement in their direction. He also maintained radio contact with the single scout who was still monitoring the column. When the end of the column finally passed by, it was just getting dark. From his last view of the vehicles, it appeared that they were going to proceed to the east in the direction of Montgomery without stopping for the night.

After another hour of nervously awaiting any report from the scouts, it appeared that for the moment, they had literally dodged the bullet. Perry did not want to send Nix or anyone out to pick up the scout who was some distance up the road, so he advised him to find shelter for the night and they would send vehicles out to pick him up in the morning. The other scouts were told to maintain their positions and they would be relieved in a few hours by replacements. In the meantime, all Defense Team commanders reported to the Command Post for a live and learn session. It was agreed that there had been no reason why they could not have sent the aircraft out to check out the situation early on. That way they would have known what they were facing. It was further agreed that in the future, they would use the airplane at least every other day, weather permitting, to scout areas that they intended to be traveling through. The caravan only covered an average of one hundred miles per day and Frick could check that out in an hour of flight.

They had all been lucky on the journey thus far and apparently their good fortune had made them a bit over confident. They would not let that happen again. They were undoubtedly going to run into situations that they could not avoid. There was no sense in creating situations that they could avoid. Anders told them all to get some rest but that they were not totally out of the woods just yet and he told Perry to keep up a high state of readiness until they were well out of this area. This instruction was not necessary as Perry already had half of the force on perimeter duty with the other half resting.

The next few days as the caravan proceeded to the northwest, through Mississippi and into Arkansas, they proceeded with the utmost caution, running patrols and flying reconnaissance missions whenever possible. After a few days of this, Sarah informed the staff that if they kept up their currently slow pace with the frequency of flight operations they were presently using, they would be out of aviation fuel well before they reached their destination. It was decided to shift the responsibility for obtaining area information more to Nix's patrols and less to Frick's aerial reconnaissance. The product would not be as informative, but that was the price they would have to pay.

It was on one of these extended patrols some twenty miles ahead of the column that Nix and his Flying Squad ran into a group of insurgents and sustained the first combat injuries of the journey. They had proceeded ahead of the caravan, bypassing larger villages and talking with anyone that would speak with them. Nix had been told of the presence of a small organized group with a long time Militia background that was located some distance away. He avoided the area and was checking out other routes around the area when he drove directly into the middle of what appeared to be one of their patrols.

The patrol was taken completely by surprise and had apparently either stopped to rest or to have something to eat. Half of the men in the group were asleep and no warning of the approaching vehicles was given until they were in their midst. There were approximately twenty men in the patrol and they were all well equipped with automatic weapons. Nix was in the lead vehicle and came around a bend in the road, driving right into their campsite. His driver came to an immediate stop and that was when the firing began. The other vehicles behind Nix driven by Guns and Ammo drove into their defensive positions and set up a withering hail of bullets into the Militia position. At the same time, they were receiving automatic weapons fire from the encampment and now also from the other side of the road where some of the Militia men had taken up positions. Nix's vehicle was literally shot to pieces, but he and some of the men were able to run to a ditch that ran alongside the road. The second in command in the squad took over and called for vehicles to come across a field and pour fire into the second source of gunfire. As they did, a missile or shell blew up the first vehicle as it entered the field. By this time, Defense Team members had offloaded from the duce and a half and had circled around to the back of the encampment. They charged in on the Militia members from the rear and were able to unload a clip or two before their position was determined by any in the camp. In a matter of seconds they had neutralized the threat and were able to drive off the force on the other side of the road.

Scouts confirmed that the Militia survivors had departed the area and the Flying Squad then began assessing the damage that they had sustained. Two were killed in Nix's vehicle and seven in the one struck by the missile, including Richard Chastain, Kate Nolan's problem student. They also had a number of injured men, some severely including both Guns and Ammo and a number with minor injuries. They had also lost two vehicles in the incident. It was a very costly reconnaissance mission and one that could hopefully be avoided in the future.

They loaded their dead and injured into the remaining vehicles and headed back to the caravan. They also picked up all of the weapons of their dead and wounded as well as the weapons left by the Militia members. They had radioed their situation to the Command Post so that by the time they arrived, the Medical Trailer was fully staffed and ready to render assistance. Nix and his assistants reported to the Command Post for a debriefing. It was a sad day for the men and women in the caravan as a number of families were tragically affected by the loss. Kate Nolan was particularly grieved as she had grown fond of Richard Chastain who had made such a turnaround in his personal life since first appearing before the Judge back in the Zone. Kate, like everyone in the caravan, had friends or relatives that were counted among the casualties in the conflict.

The Command Post Staff discussed the recon mission at great length, trying to figure out what went wrong and how they could avoid such losses in the future. The only other possibility was to run single vehicles ahead of the Flying Squad, but that would invite attack by relatively small groups that presently let the vehicles pass unharmed, seeing how many of them there were in their squad. After hours of discussing the operation, it was decided to proceed as before and to accept the fact that every now and then, losses may be incurred. For the time being, they were down two vehicles and a number of well trained men. Anders suggested that they keep their eyes open for replacements in both categories. They had seen a number of repairable vehicles along the road and there could well be more.

The effect of the losses incurred in the operation on the caravan passengers was even more profound. Up to this point, there was a bit of a picnic atmosphere connected with their journey to the northwest. They were well protected while they had been living in the Zone and thus far, they had been shielded from the more brutal aspects of the new society they now lived in. The fact that people that they were in intimate contact with just a few hours ago, were now dead, killed protecting them from attack, brought home to them that they were living in a different world.

Back in the Command Post after the evening briefing, Stuart questioned whether the Militia unit they had come in contact with would visit them along the road again. Sarah did not believe so based on the reports of Nix and his commanders. It was the general consensus of those men that they had seriously crippled the unit and Sarah did not have any reports of a sizeable Militia group in the area. She had fairly good contacts that triangulated the area where the trouble occurred and none reported any groups over thirty to fifty members operating in the vicinity.

The staff continued to discuss that day's mission as well as the failed ambush mission well on into the night. Again, they concluded it was part of the risk of the journey that had to be accepted.

Del Sutton came to Stuart the following day with a suggestion that he had been thinking about since the loss of the men in the Flying Squad. He had relatives that lived up in Arkansas, in the very western most part of the Ozark region which was sparsely populated. A number of them had gathered there when everything went to hell, and as far as he knew, they were still there. He thought that some of them might be interested in filling in some of the gaps from the losses in the squad and they were all good with guns and also were excellent tradesmen, at plumbing, electrical, or whatever they were called upon to do. Sutton didn't know if the route of the caravan was going to go near that area or not, but if it was, he could take off and visit with them to see if they were interested. That was, if the Association wanted to take on more people. Stuart told him that he would take it up at the staff meeting that evening as there had been some talk about taking on a few more people.

Stuart did bring Suttons suggestion up to Sarah and Anders and they readily agreed that if the people would be good additions to their group and could be expected to contribute then the Association would be interested.

Within a few days, the caravan would be within range of the area in question and Stuart was advised to have Sutton precede the caravan and meet with his relatives. They had room for as many as ten people provided at least six were men who could be trained to serve in the Defense Team and the others had skills or talents useful to the organization. Stuart discussed this with Sutton who assured him that he would be pleased with the men and women involved if they were in fact interested in joining the caravan. Stuart had Nix assign five men to travel with him for protection as well as for their skills in being able to travel, undetected, through hostile territory. When all arrangements for Sutton's departure had been made, Stuart advised Anders and final approval was given. The men were provided with rations for ten days and they took off on foot for the Ozark region, some fifty miles to the north. They were told the GPS coordinates of where the caravan would be encamped in six days waiting for their return.

Frick was continuing his aerial reconnaissance of the planned routes although the frequency and duration of his flights had been reduced and were supplanted by more frequent mobile patrols. In areas that were questionable or suspect of being potential threats to the caravan, the mobile patrols utilized their radios to communicate with Frick in his aircraft when both assets were operating. In that fashion, they could not only get his input in what might lie ahead for them on the road, but they could also call upon him for tactical support if the need should arise. They did have use of his services on one occasion when they ran into heavy automatic fire which they were unable to suppress. Frick unloaded a number of rockets at the target after being given the GPS coordinates by Nix and was able to knock out what turned out to be a lone gunman in a well protected bunker overlooking the roadway. It was a strange situation in that there was no radio gear found in the bunker and Nix could not understand why a person operating on his own would engage a far superior force for no apparent reason. It was just one of many bizarre incidents that the caravan encountered while on the road.

Receiving hostile fire was not particularly unusual for the Flying Squad or for the caravan and it was always difficult to determine the strength of the attacking force as everyone knew that it could be a single deranged individual or a sizeable, well equipped group. There was no shortage of weapons in the country as it appeared everyone they encountered was equipped with a gun of one type or another.

One problem that had begun to occur as the caravan moved to the west was that of the former Reservation Native Americans who were rather suddenly cut off from their monthly allotments and benefits when the government began to collapse. Many of these people found themselves in a difficult world of limited means with little or no skills to provide for themselves. This was a problem not unique to former Reservation Indians but was particularly acute in the areas of the Reservations where they constituted the majority population. They had limited or no experience in providing for themselves due to the practice of the government acting as their caretaker and provider. Some of these former reservation bred Indians now became professional thieves and targeted anyone that had property or assets that they could use or sell. They would lay in wait until the caravan paused for the night and then when it appeared most were asleep, they would sneak into the caravan encampment and carry off anything available, weapons, food, clothing or other supplies.

After this became recognized as a recurring problem, Stuart and Anders passed the word that night time visitors, Indian or otherwise, were to be shot on sight. The night time sentries killed a number of them but that did not end the problem. In time some of these intruders were captured and the problem then became what to do with them. They could not be imprisoned and releasing them only invited them back. Consequently it was decided that they would forfeit anything of value on their person and would be given one firmly applied lash with the leather whip on the bare back the first time they were captured and told that they would receive twenty lashes if they were a repeat offender. That did seem to produce the desired results as very few came back a second or third time.

It did not take Irene Covington long to raise a ruckus about the barbaric mistreatment of the night time thieves and a demand that the whippings cease immediately. There were discussions and arguments among the leadership and the members but the leadership stuck to their guns and refused to change the policy. As the word spread among the western communities and reservation lands that this particular caravan was not one to be played with, the frequency of theft decreased to an almost manageable level.

A little over a week had expired since Sutton and his security team had left the caravan. The population of the caravan had increased by ten men and women that returned with Sutton when the caravan met him at the assigned pickup point in Arkansas. The new members were well qualified to join the ranks as each one was skilled in a craft or trade that would be of considerable benefit to the Association. Most were experienced in the building trades, carpentry, plumbing and related fields while the women that came with the group were knowledgeable in the fields of medicine, education, and home skills such as spinning, weaving, natural food preservation, and other lost arts of the modern world so necessary in the present situation.

As the days turned into weeks on the road, the caravan slowly made its way across the country through the southeast and Midwest, on into the plains leading to the foothills of the Rocky Mountains. They continued to have problems with people shooting at them or putting up road blocks in an attempt to stall their progress and make them a more vulnerable target for attack. They also encountered friendly groups of people who were trying to survive the anarchy that reigned across the country. As they met these people and discussed their respective situations and experiences, they concluded that while matters were difficult, they were not without hope.

There appeared to be a trend towards organization that was occurring across the country. Not on a national level, but certainly on a local area level where more people were realizing the benefits of joining together with their neighbors in forming communal organizations for the purpose, not only of, mutual defense but also for the purpose of building communal infrastructure needed for their survival.

Development of water and food sources, medical care facilities, production of materials needed for housing, clothing, and the other necessities of life were primarily responsible for bringing the people together. The caravan was encountering very few people, particularly as they entered the west, that were trying to go it alone. Maybe the ones that had tried and failed were no longer around. In any event, there were hopeful signs that possibly a growth of a national spirit, however dim, was in the making.

An immediate problem faced by the caravan staff was what to do about the increasing shortage of potable water. They had stopped using their good water source for washing or personal hygiene and had restricted such activities to water stored in former fuel tanks and water sources they encountered along the route, such as lakes, rivers and streams. They were able to obtain supplies of drinking water when they were in eastern Nebraska, but that was the last that they expected to receive until they reached their destination unless some unexpected source turned up. They considered that very unlikely based on what was known about their intended route through western Nebraska, Wyoming and into Montana.

Anders figured that with strict rationing, they would have enough water but he, along with the others, was worried that if one of the trailers was destroyed by an attack and the water it carried was lost, they could have a real problem. They had already lost some of their water supply through damage to the water barrels by small arms fire. They could not afford to lose anymore. Fuel supplies, on the other hand, seemed to be holding out quite well. Frick was monitoring his supply of aviation fuel very carefully, but the diesel fuel for the vehicles was proving to be more than adequate.

As the caravan moved west, they were encountering less hostility than what they had experienced in the eastern half of the country. This was due in part to the fact that the population in the western half was nowhere near as dense as in the east. It was also due to a different attitude on the part of the people living in the west. They were more hospitable by nature than their eastern brethren and less hostile to strangers entering their territory. That did not mean they were naive or less vigilant rather that they would find out who the new people were before they fired their guns at them.

It was also easier for the caravan to protect itself once it was in the western plains. You could see for a considerable distance while on the road and anyone that meant to harm you was visible for a long ways off before they had a chance to do any damage. In the rolling hills and thick vegetation of Alabama, you didn't know what was fifty feet away from the road as it was totally hidden by brush. That was very different from the topography of the land they were passing through in the west. Nix did not even run ahead of the caravan out there. They could look down the road five or ten miles and see what was ahead. That would not always be the case on their way west as the mountains would present numerous ambush sites, but for the time being, they enjoyed the protection the wide open spaces afforded them.

Throughout the trip, the study group had met in their assigned trailer where they had their boxes of books and materials. They used the time afforded by the journey to continue their reading of philosophical theories relating to the broad area of governance and to discuss their separate concepts of what constituted good management of a society. There were only five people in the group but each had his or her own idea of what was the most effective, progressive way to govern a group of people. Irene Covington stuck to the classic liberal approach that more government was better and that less government was dangerous as lending itself to authoritarian rule.

The others all tended towards the more conservative approach to government and constantly hurled the history of failed socialist governments at Irene. She, in turn, always had a reason why the particular government had failed and it was never by reason of its liberal approach. Again, on this issue as well as most others, it was Irene against the other four led by Bill Phillips. It was he who had argued most articulately against her in the submission of the government plan for the new community to be established in the Valley and it was his argument that had prevailed in that discussion with the exception of the right to vote issue which had been left a bit broader than he would have liked. In the many days spent in the close confines of the trailer with extensive reading followed by in depth discussions which went to the very roots of the beliefs of the participants, it was not hard to understand why animosities occasionally developed.

During the journey of the caravan to the west, other administrative functions of the Association were carried on although under somewhat adverse circumstances. Beth Sloan continued her school system in space assigned for that purpose in the trailers. The students listened to lecturing teachers while the vehicles were on the road and learned to handle occasional interruptions in their studies as a result of mechanical difficulties with the vehicles or the need to seek shelter when the caravan came under hostile fire. In this fashion, the students were well occupied and this helped to control the problem of supervising the young people while the vehicles were on the road. There were occasions during the encampments when some of the boys and girls would wander out of the protected areas but fortunately none of these trips into the bush turned out badly. When these incidents were brought to the attention of the Staff, Stuart had thought back on his own youth and figured that he would have been guilty of the same transgressions.

The court system also continued to function as necessary. The workload was considerably reduced while the people were underway, primarily due to the reduced interaction among the members. They just did not have the opportunity to become problems for one another when they were separated for most of the day in their own individual areas and at night were basically under heavy guard in an armed camp.

There was an occasional incident or two that did require judicial intervention. One involved a fight between two of the men in camp one evening. Apparently one of the men accused the other of having stolen something from his personal items located in the trailer. The accused person took considerable offence at the allegation that he was a thief and struck out at his accuser. That was where he made his mistake. Both men were brought before the duty Judge and made to account for their separate actions. The accuser was ordered to present all evidence that he had that the other man was the guilty party. After his explanation of the basis for his complaint, it was clear that he had very little to go on. The Judge chastised him for that and warned him that if it happened again, he would be punished for his unsubstantiated complaint. The other man, who had taken physical retribution on his accuser was chastised and given a sentence compelling him to provide additional hours of service in the evening encampments for a period of one week. That would afford him the opportunity to think over his transgressions and not repeat them in the future.

Another incident that created a stir in the community of members was the age old problem of one man's wife becoming interested in another woman's husband and vice versa. It seems that virtually everyone in the caravan was aware of what was going on with the exception of the staff and the spouses of the involved parties. Both individuals had been meeting secretly in the bush during the encampments until they were discovered by a vigilant sentry when their social activity in the restricted area of the camp aroused his curiosity. They were brought before Perry in the Command

Post and when he realized what he was dealing with, he had Stuart come in to handle the situation. Both parties had children and the potential fallout from the incident was great. Stuart sought to handle the matter without creating additional difficulty for everyone if that was at all possible. He told both individuals that if the relationship continued while the caravan was en route, they would both be evicted from the caravan as their behavior could threaten the tranquility of the group. Furthermore, when they arrived in Montana, the policy guidelines proposed by the study group and presently under consideration by the leadership could well apply. That seemed to take care of the problem for the time being as both parties were deathly afraid of being banished from the protection of the Association. They also received a more in depth briefing by Stuart on the proposed policy guidelines involving divorce and adultery. He made it very clear to them that the guidelines had been approved for submission to the membership by the staff and pursuant to those proposed guidelines, if eventually approved, they would have to have the permission of their spouses to have a divorce. That could be appealed to a special commission chaired by McLeod. Furthermore, that if they persisted in committing adultery in the future, without a divorce, that they were subjecting themselves to severe punishment and that they might consider the repercussions of their actions while they were completing their journey to Montana.

The proposed criminal laws and policy guidelines were printed up while the caravan was en route and distributed to the Association members at the encampment meeting. There was a great deal of discussion involving the proposals over the course of the next week or two at the end of which time period, Stuart held discussions where everyone had an opportunity to comment on the proposed measures. There were, as could be expected, many suggestions for change but, in general, the substantive aspects of the proposed laws and guidelines were acceptable to the vast majority of the members.

With that response, the staff announced that they had been adopted in their entirety and would apply from that day forward. The study group informed Stuart that they would next tackle the difficult areas of criminal procedure and the rules of evidence which would present more difficulty for them than had the previous assignment. Stuart, knowing the makeup of the group and their diverse philosophical views, just wished them well in their task.

One of the problems that communal living created for the members of the Association that was particularly exacerbated by the journey to the west was that parents in the caravan were becoming less involved with their children. It was institutional living to the maximum. Parents had little to do with the day to day care of their own children. Food was provided by the kitchen staff, recreation by the personnel responsible for the children during encampments, protection was handled by the Defense Team, transportation by Barnes people and virtually nothing by the parents. A few of the parents had complained to Stuart about their lack of direct participation in these matters with their own children and Stuart passed on the complaint to Anders and Sarah. They did come up with a plan to allocate an hour in the evening for family time, but after a few days of that and seeing children running around unattended and at risk brought an end to that solution. It was decided that the encampments were risky places to be and it was best under the circumstances to see that all of the children were closely monitored so that they did not wander off outside of the protected environs of the camp.

In the last year before the departure of the caravan to the west, Stuart's life had changed considerably. Before then, he had always had time to take a break, even for a short period of time, to dwell on matters other than Association business. As time had passed, he became more and more involved in the society that he, and the others in the staff, were trying to create. His leadership role in these activities likewise evolved from one of a supporting staff person to the number two man in the organization and eventually to the person in charge. He accepted his increased responsibility without thought or hesitation and only after these changes had well taken place, did he realize in his own mind what was happening. It had become like an obsession with him and with respect to the journey to the west, he sometimes thought of himself as Moses leading the Israelites out of Egypt.

Stuart could not explain the reason for his zealous commitment to this project and could not tell when it had taken such a grip on his life. He only knew that from his waking moment in the morning to his last thought at night, he was totally wrapped up in seeing this task through to its final success. He had thought many times about what the goal of his efforts was as his thoughts for the future seemed to go out into a vast unknown. To Stuart, there was nothing definite anymore in the world as it now existed. He had vague thoughts about what might happen after they did set up a community in the Valley. He had considered what they might become involved with after that, including the possibility of uniting other similar communities with theirs to form a stronger organization. What if they were able to do that, then what? He would have to talk with Parker at length as to what his thoughts for the future were. On a number of occasions, he had talked with Anders about this and found that Anders had similar views to his own.

Stuart had always enjoyed working with Anders as the two were very similar in their outlook. Sarah had blended into the mix quite well also. She had different opinions from theirs on a number of issues, probably because she was a woman, among other reasons, but she had a talent for maneuvering them into seeing the wisdom of her suggestions. She was very smooth about that and if she had not been, there would have been problems as both Stuart and Anders had their egos. Their egos did not get in the way, like Perry's occasionally did, but they were present and those in the Administration staff were well aware of that fact. But it was this total involvement with his work that was slowly changing Stuart's view of society in general. He knew it was happening, as did those working with him, but no one seemed overly concerned about it. Stuart was becoming more authoritarian in his view of society in general and viewed the people in his charge as ones in need of guidance and control. They no longer possessed the right to determine most of their own actions. That now became the province of Stuart and his staff. Otherwise chaos could and most likely would result. Not only Anders but also Robert Thomas strongly supported this view. Everyone had been working long hours to see to the success of their immediate goal which was to journey safely to Montana and they appeared to support Stuart's style of leadership. Other matters could be resolved later when they were safely situated in Montana.

As the caravan began its climb in the foothills of western Nebraska, the strain on the vehicles began to show. After a day or two of climbing to the higher altitudes, the breakdowns began to occur requiring frequent maintenance stops and slowing down the progress of the journey. Barnes staff was overworked trying to keep the equipment in operating condition and if it had not been for the assistance of Sutton and his extended family from Arkansas, the delays would have been much longer.

The caravan had found a number of communal groups along the way that provided safe stopping points and they took advantage of this hospitality to take care of their maintenance needs. Stuart commented to Sarah that the farther west they had gone, the more conservative were the groups that they encountered. Sarah agreed and noted that more and more were religious based rather than the predominantly secular communities that they had found existing in the east. The reception by these communities had generally been favorable but there had been one or two contacts that were less than pleasant.

In the western part of Nebraska, as the trucks were beginning their ascent into the foothills on the eastern side of the Rocky Mountains, they entered the outskirts of a small town and were stopped at a barricaded checkpoint by a number of armed guards. They were questioned in the usual fashion with where are you going, how many people do you have with you, any diseases, and with the customary instructions, you cannot stop in the town, weapons will be put out of sight as you go through the town and so forth. The Administration staff was well familiar with the concerns of groups trying to ensure their own safety and they had no problem with complying with these requests. As they came up to the barricade, Nix assured the guards that the caravan would be observing the normal requests and that their intent was only to pass through. He did inquire if they would be able to refill water tanks or to purchase food, but coming as no surprise, these requests were denied. Nix was then told that if they carried any alcohol, drugs or non-Christians, they would have to bypass the town on a series of country roads which could be taken, adding some five additional miles to the journey. Nix was a bit taken back by this requirement, as he had never heard it before, but not wishing to put extra miles on everyone and especially on unsurfaced roads, he assured the guard that they had none of the above. That unfortunately did not satisfy the guard who was standing holding his automatic rifle at Nix. The guard then informed Nix that it would be necessary to search all of the vehicles to ensure that they were in compliance with the requirements of Pastor David.

With this, Nix began to lose his composure and without clearing his following comments with the Command Post and after taking a long look at the town occupied by Pastor David, He told the guard that his leader, Pastor Anders, did not allow such inspections, particularly into the holy places and that it would be best if they just allowed them to peaceably pass through. With this the guard became a bit flustered and said that he would have to confer with his superiors. He left the other security man in charge of the barricade and departed, on foot for the town, a distance of a mile or more away from where the caravan was stopped.

During the respite, Nix advised the Command Post as to the problem that he was encountering. They found his manner of dealing with the guard most appropriate as they were all becoming tired of trying to pacify these small town dictators who were making life difficult for travelers along the road. They had already run into some of these groups that wanted to tax the caravan for permission to pass through. On one or two occasions when it appeared wise to comply, they had done so but in the other cases, they were able to negotiate their way through without any great difficulty. Looking at this town from the somewhat distant vantage point of the caravan, it was Nix's estimation that there were not a hundred or more people living in the town and he questioned that they would be able to raise much of a ruckus if the Association told them to get the hell out of their way, we were coming through.

The caravan sat, stopped on the roadway in the hot sun for over an hour before they observed, in the distance, the lone guard walking towards them, apparently with further word from Pastor David. Stuart had gone forward to talk with the guard in the event that clearance to pass through the town was not obtained. When the guard came up to the two men, he informed them that Pastor David wished for Pastor Anders to make his request directly to him. It was obvious to Stuart that this long distance negotiation was going nowhere and he agreed with Nix's appraisal of the military might of this community.

Stuart took over the negotiations. "Look, we're tired of screwing around. We only wish to pass through your town, without stopping, now we were going to put all of our hardware away as you requested, but you have managed to piss off Pastor Anders. Let me also tell you that it is Pastor Anders policy to collect contributions for the church in every town we pass through but he is resting right now but I don't know for how long. If we sit here any longer, he is going to be up and around and looking at your little village like a fox looks at a hen. Now in exactly thirty minutes, we are starting up our vehicles and we are coming through your town and you will see our weapons because they are going to pointed directly at all of you and if anyone gives us any trouble, you tell Pastor David that we will blow his fucking town to pieces. Have you got that?"

The guard was clearly taken aback by Stuart's angry statement but made no move to pass the message on. Stuart paused waiting for the appropriate response and, not seeing it, pursued the matter further, "Look, asshole, I said to go tell Pastor David what I had to say. Now either you get your ass moving right now or we will just drive right over your fat ass and go to town right now. Now move." With that, the guard got the message and took off at a rapid pace back to town. Stuart passed the word by his hand held radio that they were moving forward in thirty minutes and that Perry should have all troops manning combat stations and ready to move, at the sign of trouble. As he was putting his radio away, Nix commented that, "I don't know why you had to walk all the way up here. I could have handled that myself. That's the way I like to do business." Stuart laughed because he knew Nix was ribbing him a bit for Stuart's previous criticism of how Nix handled such matters.

When the clocks had gone exactly another thirty minutes, the engines on all of the vehicles were started. The lone sentry manning the barricade appeared confused as to what to do and Nix politely suggested that he raise the arm of the barricade or he would drive right through it. He also suggested to the sentry that he not try anything with his automatic rifle because if he did, he would gain another forty or fifty pounds of lead. He did not have to repeat his request to raise the gate as the sentry saw the futility of trying to stop him. The trucks proceeded through the barricade and set up a fairly rapid speed as they progressed towards the town. There was no sign of the sentry that had gone in to talk with Pastor David. As they entered the town, there was no one in sight but all in the caravan knew that they were being observed by every living human being in the town. Perry's men were fully armed, manning the gun ports and machine gun stations on the top of the trailers, fully ready to return fire should anyone be foolish enough to fire upon them.

They passed through the town without incident and were on the outskirts on the other side before a few ineffective shots were fired at them. The Defense Team, under instructions from Perry, did not bother to return the fire. No damage was done to vehicles and no injuries to people and getting back at Pastor David was not worth wasting ammunition. There were other incidents somewhat similar to this that had occurred on their trip west which were the topic of conversations around the campfires in the evenings. There were many humorous comments about Pastor David and Anders was addressed as Pastor for many days following the incident described. Stuart had a new found respect from the men in the Defense

Team. He had always been well liked by the men on the force but they had been a bit disillusioned by the number of times they had been restrained by the staff from dealing with pompous, arrogant, blowhards in the fashion that they would have preferred. In this case, they would have enjoyed entering the town with guns blazing and giving this arrogant jerk a lesson but most of them realized that one person injured would be too high a cost when there was little, if anything, to be gained.

As the caravan moved on towards the mountain areas, Sarah advised Stuart and Anders that her staff had received reports that a sizeable portion of the State of Wyoming was a restricted area. When asked what that meant, Sarah informed the two that an area of land in the center of the state containing approximately ten thousand square miles was under the control of a loose organization of very wealthy people from around the country who had seen the collapse coming and bought up this land. They had then stockpiled it with virtually unlimited quantities of food and resources for their own survival and set up a security force that rivaled any others known to exist in the country, including the FSP. From all reports that she had obtained, they were not involved in any aggressive actions towards their immediate neighbors, but they were absolutely off limits to anyone attempting to enter their lands. They were very well equipped with state of the art military equipment and also had a number of aircraft that they used for patrol but were also capable of serving as tactical support.

The principals involved in the organization were a combination of former entertainment industry figures, business entrepreneurs and some associates of President Turner who were able to move secreted government assets and funds to the area before the collapse. Apparently any ties that had previously existed with Turner no longer existed and had been replaced by friction between the two groups. Turner, it is said, was angered by the transfer of, what he considered his personal treasure, to the Wyoming area. Sarah opined that the day might come when Turner decides that he is going to go out west and reclaim the goods that he had stolen from the American people. For the time being, that was not something to worry about as the

Hollywood crowd, as Sarah referred to the group involved, was better equipped militarily than Turner, although that was likely to change in the not too distant future. Anders inquired, "So what does this mean for us?"

Sarah replied, "Not a hell of a lot as far as we can tell, other than the fact that we have to avoid the area because we are not going to be able to use the roads through their territory." Sarah then referred to a map of the area and showed Stuart and Anders the designated restricted area and the route that her staff recommended that they take north through the State of Wyoming.

The alternate route took them through more rugged terrain, but it avoided any large cities and should be relatively hazard free. The only concern that Sarah had was that some of the roads were through narrow canyons and she could not get any reliable information on the condition of the roads or possible threats in those areas. They could well find themselves in the road building business so they might give that some thought. Stuart commented, "Just what we need. It's the one thing we haven't tried yet."

As they entered the high country, the nights were becoming significantly cooler and for the first time, they had to stop the caravan when a late day thunderstorm dropped freezing rain and sleet on the road that they were traveling on. This came as a surprise to everyone as they had assumed that summertime travel would be free of such road hazards. They did not have to wait long for the slippery surface to melt and they were soon on their way but it was a lesson for all the drivers to be alert for slippery roads, particularly through the passes and on the downhill portions of their journey, especially in the high country. There were no sanding trucks out to help them along the way and they could see themselves and their vehicle going over the side of a mountain cliff if they were not careful.

Barnes held a meeting with all of the drivers and discussed tactics for getting out of dangerous situations should any of the drivers find themselves in over their heads. He didn't have to try to gain their attention. They were all ready to listen to his advice and that of drivers who had extensive experience in mountain driving. Nix was instructed to warn the drivers of icy roads that he came across in his vehicle which preceded the main body of the convoy.

Barnes had installed heaters in the trailers that were used for transporting passengers or where people worked during the journey so they were fairly comfortable even though the temperature would get down below freezing in the high mountain passes when they were encamped for the night. As a result, there were some shortages which were becoming very evident at this point in the trip. Good cold weather clothing was scarce and people were making do by layering various articles of clothing in an attempt to stay warm. The heaters provided decent heat, but they were not perfect and their heat was not dispersed evenly through the trailers. Consequently, some were too warm while others in the trailers were not warm enough.

A number of the people were coming down with respiratory problems brought about by the severe temperature changes during the day, inadequate clothing and the high altitudes. Some of the older people who were not in good physical condition were experiencing altitude sickness. Light headedness, shortness of breath and fatigue. The dispensary doctors could not do much about these problems, other than to advise rest. They would have the people drink more water, but that was now being severely rationed. They had not been able to refill their water tanks for weeks and there was some question as to whether or not they would be able to do so before they reached their destination. They had taken some water on from the collectors on the trailer roofs, but not enough for their needs. They were down to a quart a day per person for all purposes and that was considered inadequate by the medical staff but there was nothing they could do about it. After a couple of weeks of minimal water rationing, they came into the vicinity of a fairly large lake from which they refilled a few of the tanks, not wishing to contaminate all tanks as the water was tested and found not to be potable. The bacteria level exceeded acceptable amounts but they did consider it safe for washing and other cleaning purposes, provided it was first boiled. Food was also becoming extremely scarce and Stuart suggested that Perry send some of his better shooters out into the mountains during their stopovers to try to get elk, deer or bear.

The elk were now beginning to come down from the high country, particularly during the hours of darkness and Perry's men were having some success. One problem for the hunters was that Denver and other large cities were only a few hundred miles away and many people had fled to these mountains and were attempting to live off of the wild life just as the people in the caravan. That was what had polluted the lake they drew the water from. Consequently the elk and deer populations had been decimated and it was a lucky day when one of Perry's men even got off a shot. Nevertheless, the caravan hunters were better equipped with longer range weapons than most of the independent hunters and they had a better chance of bagging the game so that every night, one or more was bringing in fresh elk or deer meat. Bear meat was another matter. It was very rare for someone to even see a bear, much less get a shot at one.

As the caravan approached the restricted area that Sarah had briefed them on, they decided that it would be best to run Nix's Flying Squad well ahead of the other vehicles so that they didn't find that they were on a narrow canyon road, forced to turn around but unable to do so. They also had Frick check out a number of bridges that they would have to cross on the alternate routes for the same purpose. It would be very difficult to impossible to back the tractor trailers over a long distance without expecting some very serious problems. They did not want to find themselves in that situation if they could prevent it.

Frick returned from his reconnaissance mission with his report that all bridges were up, but he could not tell what their condition was. He did note that one, in particular, appeared to be constructed of wood pilings and it should be inspected before any of the heavier vehicles tried to cross over it. He also reported sighting a number of encampments along the route. The largest being a group of around fifty people. He said it appeared that they had set up fairly permanent appearing shelters, some canvas covered and some constructed from materials gathered from the site. No one had fired upon him, but he did see a number of the men on the ground carrying weapons. What that meant, he was not able to say. There were one or two smaller communities along the road that appeared to be intact and there were people walking around the streets. These communities all had barricades on the road at either end of the town and he could see that they were manned.

When Frick had completed his report, Stuart looked at the other staff members and just commented, "More of the same." They all nodded in agreement. There did not appear to be any insurmountable hazards along the route, they would just have to continue to be careful. His comment about the possibility that the wooden bridge might be a problem drew some attention and Anders had his secretary see that the NASA engineers were aware that they might be called upon to give an opinion as to the strength of a wooden bridge. Something they had not been requested to do up to this point in time.

The caravan proceeded on the alternate route with Nix taking a substantial lead and maintaining radio contact. He had his entire Flying Squad with him in the event that he encountered unfriendly people along the way. He did pass a number of the encampments that Frick had mentioned and the appearance of his well armed and protected squad was apparently sufficient to deter any hostile action on their part. When he came up on the larger encampment, he confirmed by radio that there were in excess of fifty people there, probably closer to a hundred or more with at least fifty unfriendly looking men bearing arms. As he came into view of the group, they came down the mountain side obviously with the intention of stopping the vehicles but upon seeing how many there were and how well armed they were, the men came to a halt and lowered their guns.

Nix pulled up in front of what appeared to be the leader of the group to sound him out on what the caravan might expect when they entered the area. Nix had all of his men at their gun stations in the event of trouble but told them not to point their weapons at anyone lest they provoke a response. Nix took the offensive with the apparent leader of the group and said, "Look, there is a large group of well armed troops coming through here in trucks in about an hour. I just want you to know that they are friendly. They won't be stopping and they won't bother you, so don't be concerned. Just wanted you to know that. I know how things are out here. You have any questions?"

The man paused for a moment, being somewhat taken aback. He had obviously expected a bit more respect, seeing as how his group was the occupier of the land they were passing through. "Yeh, yeh. Okay. No problem."

Nix then asked him how the road was ahead of them and he was told that their group was headed in the same direction so he couldn't help him on that point. This brought the conversation to an end and Nix wished him well and moved on up the road. Nix sent a report back to the Command Post as to what they might expect and to be on the alert, but again, not to provoke as they looked like the type that might fire their weapons if they saw someone aiming a gun at them.

Nix crossed the two concrete bridges and had his men conduct a brief inspection of the supports to determine if they were adequate and undamaged and finding they were, they proceeded on the route. When they came to the wooden bridge, Nix could easily see why Frick had been concerned. It was obviously very old and some of the pilings were built right into the river which ran under the bridge. Some of them were obviously rotted by their having been sunk in water for so many years and a number of the support braces had become detached at one end or another rendering them totally useless.

Nix ran some of his vehicles across to test the bridge while his men were below observing the effect on the structure. They reported they could see bending and twisting of primary structure taking place and strongly advised that additional support would have to be built before the loaded transports would be able to come across and even then it would be risky. Nix radioed this information back together with his comment that under no circumstances should any passengers or troops be in trailers that were taken across the bridge.

The Command Post immediately set about preparing for the bridge repair and Barnes was tasked to come up with equipment that would be needed for that purpose. He advised Sarah that he had the tools and some of the supporting metal brackets but that they would have to pick up the timbers to be used in beefing up the structure. Sarah radioed to Nix to gather the lumber from the surrounding area and have it there when they arrived, if possible, so that they were not delayed any longer than necessary.

When the caravan of trucks did pull up at the bridge, having had no problems whatever with the large encampment down the road, Nix had a number of sizeable logs pulled out of the surrounding hillside for the use of Barnes people to strengthen the bridge. The engineers crawled all through the underside of the bridge determining what type of support was needed and where. When they were done examining the structure, they gathered around Barnes and told him what was needed. Their instructions for repair were more extensive than anyone had anticipated and seeing as how it was past mid day, Stuart decided that they should unload the vehicles and camp for the night at the bridge site. That way the men working on the project could go about their work without being unduly rushed. The last thing they needed was for a tractor trailer to go plunging into the river, destroying the bridge with half of the caravan on one side and half on the other.

Stuart advised the engineers that with the extra time now available for repair that if they were to err, do it on the extra strength side and not the other way around. They agreed with this and told Barnes to add some more supports around the center of the structure where some of the primary beams appeared to be very weathered and questionable. Barnes needed extra help with getting the logs trimmed down and into position for the workers to install so Perry assigned twenty of his men to the project.

Within three or four hours the work was completed and the engineers agreed that it should be able to hold the heaviest of the vehicles provided some of the materials were first unloaded and carried across separately. There was no problem getting the passengers and troops to leave the vehicles and walk across as no one wanted to be in a vehicle crossing what appeared to be a very questionable bridge structure. After all of the vehicles were safely across the bridge, they set up their encampment on the mountain slope alongside the road. It was a heavily wooded area both above and below the roadway which ran alongside the slope and consequently it was difficult to provide complete security for the long string of trucks making up the convoy. Sentries patrolled the length of the parked vehicles but as they discovered the following morning, visitors had come by during the night and taken some of their food stocks and other goods from one of the supply trucks. Stuart figured that it was the group that they had passed on down the road as some of the guards had spotted men up on the mountain observing their work on the bridge. The loss was not particularly serious as they had not been able to make off with a large quantity of supplies.

While they were camped, Stuart had Sarah make radio contact with the Valley headquarters and advise them of their position. Stuart figured that they were approximately a week or more from the Valley provided they did not run into any unforeseen obstacles in their travels. Parker was not in the Valley Office when the call was made, but he was there when the Valley Office returned the call about an hour later. Fortunately Stuart was in the Command Post when the call came in so he was able to speak directly to his counterpart in Montana.

Parker told Stuart that they were preparing for the arrival of the Association by gathering up food stuffs and supplies that they knew would be needed by the weary travelers. Parker also indicated that while fall weather was in the air, it should still be fairly comfortable for the following month or two to allow the new residents time to prepare for winter. Stuart commented that the Association members would have to undergo psychological counseling in order to handle winter, but he was sure they would adjust to it in time. He did request that Parker pass the word that the Florida residents could use any spare winter clothing that might be available as that was the one item that was in severe shortage. He also mentioned that they were very low on food and potable water supplies and Parker assured him that Valley stockpiles were more than adequate to handle the need. Parker also mentioned that they had been having problems with an increasing frequency of intrusions over the past month or two and they were looking forward to the security resources of the Association.

Stuart responded that the Defense Team had acquired considerable experience during the days and weeks of the trek to the northwest and were now quite able to handle most any group operating around the northwest. That was a great relief to Parker as that had always been his number one concern in the Valley. They had all the other bases covered there except for the matter of security. They lacked the trained personnel and were very short of good equipment. Their guards were using a collection of different hunting rifles with very limited stocks of ammunition. They had little if any communication equipment for their security force and no missiles to repel armored vehicles were they to show up or other modern items such as night vision equipment or hand held navigation computers.

The Valley residents had a definite need for the resources of the Association just as severe as the Association's need for what they had. It was definitely a marriage of necessity for both parties and fortunately for all concerned, most everyone realized it. Parker suggested that they send a patrol out to guide them in the final few days, but Stuart thought that was too risky for the Valley Security Force. It was unnecessary and there were too many 'unfriendlies' out there for a small patrol to contend with. The caravan was better protected and would most likely intimidate such people that were between them and the Valley as they had intimidated those they had passed along the road.

As they drew closer to the destination, the mood of the travelers in the caravan improved considerably. There was less criticism of the day to day decisions coming from the Command Post and less griping about the rationing of food and water. Everyone figured that they would be able to have enough of both within the next few days. Stuart did speak with them almost every night during the evening camp briefing that the really hard work was about to start. Summer was about over and winter was not that far away. They had to literally build a town in the next two months that would shield them from the fury of a harsh Montana winter. He also brought out the fact that the cold season in the northwest lasted for quite a bit of the year and that everyone should prepare themselves mentally for the depression that could result from day after day of ice cold weather and heavy snow. Warm clothing was a matter of considerable concern for Stuart, as he had mentioned to Matt Parker, and he had Barnes see what he could do to alleviate that very serious need.

Barnes, working with the NASA engineers did some experimenting with canvas from the trailers and using synthetic linings and packing materials for insulation came up with a parka design that was comfortable and retained body heat at very low temperatures. They stripped as much of the canvas off of vehicles as they could, now that they were short of their destination, and Barnes set aside some space in the maintenance trailer to begin fabricating the parkas. Using some of the passengers for assistance, Barnes was able to turn out twenty parkas a day and figured that when they were settled in the Valley, he could turn out five times that number, especially with the extra canvas that would then be available from the trucks. As the parkas were completed, they were distributed first to the men out in the field performing sentry duty as the nights were cooling down to at or near the freezing mark, particularly in the high mountain country. Barnes was proud of his product and had his staff begin working on making gloves and coveralls as they would also be needed in the cold temperatures of their new home. Within a day or two, he was showing Stuart and Sarah the prototype for both and Stuart had to compliment Barnes on his new found talent.

The caravan was slowed down an additional day of travel due to the condition of roads in the narrow canyons. They had to stop many times and clear boulders and debris from the roadway that had come off of overhangs or steep slopes. Mud slides were another problem where heavy rains had washed sand and dirt down the slope onto the roadway. The vehicles in the caravan appeared to be the first to pass over this road in a very long time.

There were travelers along the road, but they were either moving on foot or horseback. Stuart spoke with a number of them who were only intent on making their way north with a minimum of difficulty. Most of those that he spoke with were from the metropolitan areas in the southwest, including Denver and Albuquerque. After the collapse, the southern border with Mexico was open for anyone who wished to cross and at first there was a flood of people streaming north to find better living conditions.

That was a mistake as by that time anarchy and chaos existed throughout the southwest and it was every person for himself when it came to finding food and shelter. Conditions were no better in what had been the southwestern United States than they were in Mexico. Not finding what they were looking for in Arizona, Texas and Southern California, the influx of people coming in from Mexico moved north primarily into New Mexico, Colorado, and southern Utah. Their migration north in California came to an abrupt halt just south of the San Francisco area where they were forcibly stopped by armed citizens. How long they would remain stopped there was another question as there were many sizeable Hispanic settlements to the north, even up in Oregon and Washington.

The Mormons were quite well organized in Utah and prevented the further migration to the north, except for the lower third of the state, but the other states were already populated heavily by Hispanics and while not enthusiastically received, the new arrivals were not prevented from coming. The Mexican American communities in the southwest immediately following the collapse had become united in at least one respect. They all wanted a Mexican-Hispanic controlled southwest. They had been militant before the collapse, believing fervently that the area had belonged to them historically and that it was rightfully theirs to begin with. When there was no national government to prevent them from taking over what they saw as rightfully theirs, they immediately filled the void and took over local, county and state government offices.

There were numerous rivalries among the separate groups involved that resulted in much bloodshed until after a period of time, a few militant, well led, organizations emerged in control of vast areas of the southwest. There was further fighting between these large, powerful, organizations, but it was sporadic as each was busily involved in consolidating the gains they had made and were not interested in expanding their territories just yet. As a consequence of this somewhat alien culture in control of the land, and partly due to force, most of the whites living in the southwest had migrated north to more hospitable areas and these were the people that Stuart and the others in the caravan were seeing along the roads of Wyoming and up into Montana. These people had lost everything they had and were moving north in the hopes of beginning a new life in a less hostile environment. There were pockets of white enclaves still existing in the southwest, but it was the opinion of the emigrants that this was a temporary situation at best as the Mexicans would tolerate their presence only if the whites accepted the fact that they were there as guests and not as owners of the land.

Surprisingly there was not a great deal of bitterness on the part of the emigrants. Most of the southwest was primarily Hispanic since the early years of the century and the Mexican Americans had controlled local government for many years. The only difference was that the former control was under the auspices of what was left of the American Constitution which the post collapse leaders totally ignored once the power of government was in their hands.

Many of the emigrants that they met along the road wanted to join up with the caravan and they had all appearances of being good candidates for membership, but Stuart did not consider himself authorized to accept any additional members over the number that he had told Parker he would be bringing. He was short approximately fifty from the number anticipated and as he neared the destination, he did take in some of the families that he had met along the road. The Staff participated in the interview process and all those that were allowed to join were skilled in some craft or trade that was considered particularly valuable to the Association. Three medical doctors, a number of university professors with both scientific and arts backgrounds, two biologists, a chemist and others with very specific expertise were taken in. It was truly a buyer's market and Stuart was making the best of it.

Stuart had announced at the encampment briefing that they expected to enter the pass leading into the Valley by noon on the following day. It was close to noon on his watch when Nix announced over the radio to the Command Post that the Valley entry barricades were in sight. A loud cheer went up in the Command Post on receiving that report and everyone rejoiced that they had arrived at their destination safely. They had lost some members in the course of the journey but their preparation for the trip and the caution exercised throughout the many days and weeks of crossing the country had paid off. Furthermore they had learned a great deal about what was going on in the country and about their own possibilities and limitations.

The trip had been a confidence builder for not only the leadership of the Association but also for the members. They had seen the plight of others in the country that were not organized or had not taken the necessary steps to preserve and protect their very limited resources. There was a renewed interest in the structure of their own group and where they were going to go as a group once they were resettled in the new land.

By the time the caravan came to a stop at the entry gate, Parker and a delegation from the Valley were on hand to greet them on their arrival. Stuart introduced Matt Parker to Anders, Sarah and the others while Frick renewed friendships with a number of the men whom he had spent time with during his brief stay. The passengers looked on silently at their hosts and new neighbors, visibly curious as to what kind of people they were and how they would all get along once they were settled there.

After the introductions, Matt Parker told Stuart to bring everyone on into town so that they could have something to eat and rest up after their long trip. Parker had a temporary settlement constructed on the river site that Stuart and the townspeople had agreed would be the new home for the Association residents. A well had been dug that would handle the needs of the community and privies were installed and ready for use. A large tent kitchen was also fully equipped and ready to turn out the evening meal for the weary travelers. Anders was overwhelmed at the hospitality accorded to the group and was a bit embarrassed at what they were bringing to the table in return. The Valley needed the technical and scientific skills the Association had to offer but mostly needed the ability to defend itself from the marauding bands that were threatening its very existence. The size and strength of these roving bands of thugs had been growing in recent months and the arrival of the caravan with its sizeable Defense Team and advanced weaponry was none too soon.

As the caravan entered the town of Riverton, all of the people in the Valley must have been there as both sides of the road were packed with men, women and children for the last mile leading into town. Sarah commented that she hoped someone was watching the Valley entry points because the crowd seemed to exceed the population figures that she had been given. Obviously the people living in the Valley were as curious of the new arrivals as anyone was. They stood along the side of the road and waved as the trucks rolled in, but their welcome displayed a certain amount of controlled enthusiasm, limited by their concern that these new arrivals would not be more trouble than they were worth.

People in the west, particularly in the mountain country, had heard for many years of the excesses of the people living on the east and west coasts of the United States. They feared that by opening their doors to people from those areas, they were endangering not only their cherished life styles, but also the morals and positive goal orientation of their children. Stuart had been made aware of this concern when he visited the Valley and he was very sympathetic with respect to their concern. In his briefings along the way to the northwest, Stuart had harped on this one issue almost nightly. The Association would not tolerate any behavioral problems among any of the residents regardless of how valuable or necessary the person involved might be for the Association. If someone did not straighten out a problem that was an embarrassment to the Association or an irritant to the Valley residents after being warned once, the next message they received would be an order to leave the community and the Valley.

After they arrived in the center of Riverton, they were treated to food and drink by the townspeople. There were welcoming speeches by Matt Parker and others representing the Valley residents and there were administrative matters to cover such as facilities available for water supplies, food supplies and the other requisite needs of the newcomers. Anders took the microphone and thanked all of the people of the Valley who had obviously contributed food and other supplies to the welcoming ceremony. He assured all of those listening that the members of the Association looked forward to making a significant contribution to the well being of the residents of the Valley and that the Defense Team would be meeting with the Valley Security Force to ensure that the entire length of the Valley was a protected sanctuary for its residents. With that announcement, a cheer went up from the Valley residents, particularly those in the outlying areas. It was clear that the need for increased security in the Valley had been a matter of concern for everyone.

Stuart took the podium and briefly thanked Matt Parker and others that he had worked with in bringing the two groups together and he then introduced the staff of the Association so that their counterparts in the Valley would be able to recognize them and know their area of responsibility. Stuart assured all that he was very confident that they would be able to work together amicably and that their cooperative efforts would combine to achieve a much greater success than if they each tried to go it alone. "Our separate resources complement each other and fill a corresponding void in our organizations. Together we can move a lot farther a lot faster than we ever could apart." Stuart told them that there was a great deal of work to be done in the future for the success of our community. That brought a resounding cheer from both groups as the Valley people were clearly enjoying what they were hearing from their new neighbors. After the speeches, food was served for a very hungry group of travelers who had been living on limited rations for weeks. Music was provided by a group that had played together in the Valley for years and this was very much appreciated by the newcomers who had been required to restrict all noise levels while they were encamped for fear it would inhibit the efforts of sentries to hear as well as see any sign of intrusion.

The following morning, bright and early, Anders, Stuart, Sarah and the other staff members met with Matt Parker and his associates to lay out plans for constructing the necessary community buildings. People were going to have to continue living and working out of the trailers until adequate shelters were constructed. Barnes went over the equipment that he had available for the work that had to be done and while it was an impressive list, there were some voids. Parker introduced Barnes to his counterpart at the meeting and the two met separately to see what was available in the Valley shops to help meet the shortfall. Perry was teamed up with the head of Security for the Valley after each gave a short briefing on the resources available to each group. It was clear following Perry's part of the briefing that the Association was providing virtually all of the defensive resources that would comprise the new Valley Defense Team.

Sarah had no counterpart for her area of expertise and Matt Parker and his associates found her work very interesting. Up to that point in time, their source of outside information came from the occasional renegade that they captured attempting to steal from their storerooms. That information was always highly suspect, so they were particularly hungry for news about what was happening around the country. When Sarah realized the low level of current knowledge possessed by the Valley residents, she suggested that a daily news briefing be provided by her staff in the high school auditorium for anyone interested. That was enthusiastically received by Parker and the others and they suggested that if possible, they would appreciate it if that could commence immediately. Sarah assured them that it could and she looked over at Anders for approval. He nodded in agreement and with that, she motioned to her staff to get the briefing prepared.

Matt Parker announced to the meeting that they had a ready supply of lumber, insulation and other building materials ready in the warehouse sufficient to put up fifty single room ten by twenty buildings. Parker figured that with the short time before really cold weather hit that if construction began within the following day or two, the buildings could be completed before the first snow fall. Stuart assured him that everyone in the Association was ready to lift a hammer and he, further, thanked him for having the materials ready for their use. In time, Stuart said, they would be repaid. Parker replied that he never had any doubt about that. By that afternoon, materials had been delivered to the construction site and footings were being dug. Stuart had told Barnes to combine at least three of the single units into one large structure for the administration building. He told him to also use the lumber for four buildings and make two larger buildings out of that for a machine shop and the other for a utility building. He suggested the other single unit buildings be divided by a wall across the narrow section so that more families could be accommodated.

Stuart found Robert Thomas and put him to work on a project that would require his talents. Matt Parker met Stuart and Thomas at the tent being used by the Admin Staff and the three drove to a large warehouse on the outskirts of town that was filled with farm tractors, of varying ages, most of which were in need of maintenance or parts replacement. The machines had been donated by the farmers in the Valley for the use of the newcomers. There were also dozens of other pieces of farm equipment, cultivators, balers, wheat threshers, seed broadcasters, corn planters and virtually every piece of equipment needed for modern farming. Parker looked at the two men and said, "There it is. It's all yours but somebody is going to have to do some work to get them back in shape." Stuart looked over at Thomas who was already beginning to examine an old diesel tractor that had a layer of dust on it. "It'll run but it's going to take a bit of doing all right."

Parker gave the warehouse keys to Stuart who again told him how much he appreciated his help. Parker made no reply and the three then headed back to the building site. Stuart told Robert Thomas that he was going to be running the farm operation and that was probably the biggest challenge that anyone had to handle but he knew that Thomas was the right man for the job. He had the mechanical know how and the drive to get the job done. He would be given whatever help was available whenever he needed it. Thomas told Stuart that the first thing he needed was a base of operation and he managed to talk Stuart into assigning two of the new structures for the use of the "Ag Department". He also said that he wanted his old team back that had been assigned to him when he ran the marina. There were a number of good diesel mechanics there and he could certainly use them now. Stuart agreed and told him to give him the names and they would be reassigned. Some were now working for Barnes and now that they had safely arrived in the Valley, those men could be reassigned for the farm operation. He also needed the tools that he had turned over to Barnes when they left the Control Zone and Stuart told him to deal directly with Barnes on that unless he had problems, in which case he should get back to Stuart.

His new assignment gave Thomas a real 'shot in the arm'. He had been wondering just where he was going to fit into in the new community and was thinking that possibly he had made a mistake by leaving Florida, but the job just given to him by Stuart was right up his alley and he was looking forward to it. As he looked over the vast plains of the valley and the thousands of acres that had been assigned to the Association as crop land, he envisioned his men on tractors developing the land the same way they had built up the marina operation back in the Control Zone. They turned virtually nothing into an effective resource using materials scrounged and fabricated into useful building blocks for a valuable asset. They could do the same with this project and the fact that there was little time in which to accomplish the task was all the more appealing to Robert Thomas. If it had been easy, he would not have enjoyed the assignment. Stuart brought up the assignment at the evening staff briefing and told Barnes to provide as much help as possible.

Thomas contacted John Barnes after the meeting to make sure that there were no hard feelings about the transfer of men and equipment to

Thomas. Barnes looked at him and laughed. "I was scared shitless I was going to get that one. You are going to need all the help you can get and I'll do whatever I can to give you a hand. I don't need more than two or three diesel guys now anyway and I have enough to keep me busy for the next ten years. No problem Mac." Barnes had all of Thomas' tools loaded into one of the trucks and added a number of other machine tools that he could spare from his current projects.

The men all liked Barnes, but Robert Thomas held a special magnetism for them. It might have been his cavalier approach to problems. It seemed like the more difficult the problem, the more humor Thomas would find in the situation. The men liked that attitude as it was contagious and in time, back at the Marina, they never thought of any problem or challenge as insurmountable.

By the morning of the next day, Thomas was back in style with the vehicles assigned to him running back and forth between the home site and the warehouse with smiling men hanging on to the materials, tools and machinery being transported. One thing Stuart liked about Thomas was that once he was given an assignment, he hardly ever heard from him again. Thomas did not like to report to anyone and was a bit of an empire builder which had bothered Stuart at first. But as time had passed, Stuart realized that Thomas was a "results guy". He delivered on the bottom line provided you did not bother him too much in the process. Stuart liked the style.

In the days and weeks before the caravan had arrived in the Valley, Sarah had concentrated all available time of her staff on gathering as much data as possible regarding the land areas surrounding the Valley. She wanted to know who was living there and how they were coming along since the collapse of the government so that she could be aware of any possible threats they might present. There were organized groups in other parts of Montana, on either side of the Valley, that were active on the radio net and they ran the gamut of political beliefs. Many were religious based but most were formed out of mere necessity, which was the overpowering need of people to come together for their mutual aid and protection. The religious based communities were, again, a varied lot. Some were set up on the lines of social communes where no one owned any private property, rather everything belonged to the group. Others, also with a pronounced religious overtone, believed more in prayer than in any form of organized governance.

All claimed to be armed with a collection of weapons for their own self defense. In Sarah's opinion, with very few exceptions, these smaller groups were what she would label as 'on the fringe', politically. She did not hold out much hope that these groups would be in the proper frame of mind to enter any form of informal organization for some time to come. That was her opinion following extended discussions between her staff and representatives of those groups over the radio net. They all wanted to "Go it alone" without any interference from someone trying to tell them what to do.

The largest organized group south of their future home site was what she had labeled, "Hollywood." That being the collection of surviving super wealthies that had taken refuge in the restricted area of Wyoming that the caravan had to bypass. Their territory encompassed hundreds of square miles but their population numbers were minimal. While few in number in comparison with other land masses, their armed strength was impressive. Sarah had been in contact with their communications staff and had become fairly friendly with her counterpart in that organization. When Sarah explained where they were going and provided a description of their group, the Hollywood communicator suggested that they might be interested in discussing some sort of trade agreement in the future. They were very interested in building up their food supplies, of which they were beginning to become concerned, and it was their understanding that the area Sarah was moving to was a bread basket for grain crops. Sarah confirmed that the Valley was rich in wheat, barley, corn, oats and rye as well as beef and dairy products. That was why they had selected the area.

Hollywood, on the other hand, was short on those foodstuffs but did have access to all varieties of petroleum products as they had numerous wells pumping in their territory and the crude oil they were pumping was so pure that they were getting thirty gallons of aviation and automobile quality fuel from every barrel of crude. That was an unheard of recovery rate and the other byproducts were of superior grade as well. The lamp oils and heating oils were of an excellent quality but all of this did them little good if they were not able to put it to use or trade it for the products that they were lacking.

The Hollywood organizers had been trading with the Mormons in Utah for the basic necessities that they lacked and thus far, that had kept them afloat, without digging into their sizeable reserves. They were interested in finding other sources for food stuffs so that they were not totally dependent upon the Mormons who had also managed to develop their own petroleum sources but to a much more limited extent. Apparently the Mormons had not yet refined their techniques to the level where they did not need to deal with Hollywood any longer as they were still interested in bargaining.

Sarah's Hollywood confidant suggested that the major concern of the Mormons in Utah might possibly be their geographic position, being just to the west and north of the expansionist Hispanic groups in Colorado and Arizona. The Mormons had their own defense force which was very efficient and well led, but they lacked the necessary hardware to repel a substantial modern force. The Mormons had discussed a mutual defense pact but thus far that had not gone beyond the introductory discussion phase. Sarah found that very interesting and suggested to Stuart that it might be something very worthwhile to pursue in the not too distant future. If they were able to work together with two other well organized groups of considerable size, regardless of how dissimilar in political or personal philosophy, it might bode well for all. Stuart agreed and told Sarah to maintain contact and when matters had settled down a bit more at the new home site, it would be something to look into.

Within days of having arrived at the Valley, the Association was operating out of a temporary tent office in the area designated as the town center. The staff had named the new community Goodland as the land and other natural resources in the vicinity appeared to be even more bountiful than they had hoped. Barnes was in the process of beginning to lay out and construct an electric power plant, harnessing the energy created by the rapidly flowing river which ran along the banks of the community. He was also assigning staff to construct water irrigation lines running from the river out into the crop lands for the dry times of the year. They were virtually assured to have substantial yields with the rich black earth and the unlimited water available for growing the crops. The water in the river flowed from a spring inside the valley, being supplemented from the mountain run off so there was little, if any, danger of either someone upstream taking over the water supply or of water pollutants from outside sources contaminating this valuable resource. The chemists had already checked the water both from the river and from the well that had been dug for their benefit and both were free of contaminants.

Within days, Robert Thomas had a number of diesel tractors available for pulling flat bed trailers around for the use of those building the homes in Goodland. All of the people of the Association, down to the age of twelve had been assigned a task in the construction of the town. It was a beehive of activity and most of the people took to the task with enthusiasm. As in all projects, however, there were a few who were not interested in the task at hand and some of these had come to Stuart to inform him that now that they were in Montana, they were going to depart for other areas in the northwest. Either they had relatives in nearby communities or they just wanted to go it alone. Stuart discussed these requests with Anders and Sarah and the three concluded that anyone that wanted to leave had a right to do so and it would not be a great loss to the Association as the group interested in joining up with them were still camped south of the Valley entry point.

Stuart had spoken to Parker about the people wanting in, giving an estimate of their number and telling him of their various areas of expertise. Parker had not committed to granting them permission to enter, but he had not refused it either. He was going to bring it up with his associates and see what they had to say. He did tell Stuart that the original number authorized for entry with the Association still stood and if there were vacancies there, that should be no problem. Stuart could tell from the conversation that there were some in the Valley who were not totally enthused about turning their land over to strangers and that was very understandable. After granting permission to those wishing to leave the Association, Stuart went out to the encampment outside of the Valley entry gate and spoke with the men leading that group. He advised them that he had room for fifteen people and suggested that the leadership make the selection, keeping in mind that they would then be interviewed by the Association. Stuart further advised the men as to the qualifications that the Association looked for in granting permission to join. They wanted skills and not problems. Stuart also gave them a brief summary of how the Association functioned, its court system and the rules and regulations that it operated under. He did not want anyone coming in and then becoming disgruntled after they learned how matters were handled. The men in the leadership group assured him that those submitted would be thoroughly briefed as their small group had been functioning using the same basic management principles.

Upon arrival at the new town site, Perry had met with Nix, Andy Moss and the men who had been handling Valley security prior to their arrival. Moss requested a briefing from the ranchers that were providing the security and it didn't take very long to realize that there was no organization of any consequence in existence and that one was sorely needed. The frequency of incursions had been increasing dramatically, primarily at the northern end of the Valley which was closest to a few larger communities. The farmers up in that area had taken to building their own bunkers and banding together to fend off the increasingly aggressive attacks. They had captured a few of the renegades trying to overrun their defenses and they all seemed to be coming from small gangs of opportunists operating independently and moving around the countryside looking for a possible target. Some of those captured mentioned that there were larger groups in the making with some of the stronger groups taking over the leadership of the small groups and merging the people in with their own so the risk of intrusion was obviously going to increase.

It was decided at the meeting that a permanent cadre had to be stationed at the northern post as well as at the southern entry point that could more carefully observe when the intrusions were taking place. These posts would be equipped with high tech detection devices and good communications gear so that they would be able to radio back to the Command Post under all weather conditions and get help if that was needed. Nix was to maintain his Flying Squad and the vehicles they used in their operation as a rapid response force.

Perry assigned Moss the uncomfortable assignment of training the men in the force to operate in the high mountain country so that if need be, they could repel a substantial force trying to come across the mountains. For emphasis, he added, "Even in the dead of winter". Perry said that he would assign the brunt of the Defense Force to assist in the construction project which had to be completed before the snow came, but that they would be ready to move on a moment's notice should they be needed. The ranchers sitting in on the meeting were clearly relieved to hand the reins over to men who obviously had the skills and experience to deal with such matters this would allow the ranchers to get back to what they knew best and that was ranching. They also had a much elevated level of confidence that their ranches and livestock would be safer with these men in charge of their security. When they passed the word to their friends and neighbors, some of the friction that had existed from Parkers demands laid upon them for land, tools, food and other supplies disappeared. Perry, furthermore in an effort to let everyone know they were around, had Nix run his patrols up and down the length of the Valley, checking on the well being of the ranchers in the more remote areas. When these people saw that they were well protected by people who knew what they were doing, the attitudes on the streets of Riverton were much more positive than even the initial welcome.

Pursuant to Stuart's request, Perry also had a security team stationed down at the encampment of volunteers that were outside the environs of the Valley. Stuart wanted that group to stay in the area as he was quite sure that in time he would be able to incorporate them into their community. The technical and professional skill level in that group was unusually high and Stuart did not want to lose the benefit of their knowledge and experience. He also had food supplies and warm clothing sent down there when that eventually became available to him.

During the trip out to the west, Mark Campbell and Roy Yates had been assigned to Ross Perry's Defense Team and he put them to work with the Tactics Team reviewing intelligence data provided by Sarah. The two men were very adept at reading between the lines of reports and pointing out potential trouble spots along the route. They were the ones that had suggested creating the Flying Squad for advance reconnaissance rather than relying on the complete defenses of the caravan to handle every situation. It was true that the Flying Squad had incurred some heavy losses but who was to say that the losses would not have been heavier if the full caravan had wandered into the center of the well armed group of insurgents. There is little doubt that fighting would have broken out anyway and certainly many people would have been killed or injured. Both Campbell and Yates had approached their assignments with enthusiasm and energy and Perry found them to be valuable assets in his organization.

When the Association had reached its destination, Perry suggested that the two stay on with the Defense Team and Stuart said that was fine with him if the two men agreed. He called them in while Perry was there and posed the question directly to them. They both replied that they were probably better qualified to work in the area of community security than anything else and they did like their work so that settled the matter.

Both men also inquired if Stuart had any information on what the FSP was up to and if there were any further inquiries regarding their whereabouts. Stuart could tell that they were still concerned about their own safety following the arms deal and he assured them that he would talk to Sarah about it, but he assumed that in view of no comments regarding that matter coming from her, she must not have heard anything. He would get back to them just as soon as he had any information.

Later that afternoon, Stuart did discuss the matter with Sarah and she admitted that she was a bit worried because the last message received from North Farm, which stated that the FSP was inquiring about the two, was in fact the last message received. That was unusual and she was wondering what was going on down there. She had made inquiries of her contacts in Jacksonville and elsewhere and they had no specific information but they had heard that the FSP was moving about northern Florida in force. This was a change from when the Association had left the area as at that time they restricted their activities to the Georgia area. It was possible that a sizeable force had gone down to find out what happened to their associates, Campbell and Yates and the weapons cache. North Farm had adequate weapons with which to defend itself from a fairly strong attack but they lacked the experience and, more seriously, as a group, they lacked the interest and drive necessary to organize and operate an effective defense force. Furthermore if the FSP learned of the weapons at North Farm they would be able to track where the missing weapons most likely had gone.

Too many of the people that had elected to go to North Farm did so primarily because they weren't willing to undergo the hardship of the cross country trek to the northwest. That weakness of character carried over to all other aspects of their community and, as Stuart saw it, was potentially the fatal flaw in their achieving success. Stuart would not be surprised if they didn't make it as a group or were overcome by another group of equal or even smaller size and strength.

Sarah contacted Carlos Moran and inquired about the people up in North Farm and Carlos had heard there was fighting up there, but he had no further information and their patrols no longer went up there per an agreement made between Paco Morales and the FSP whereby the two parties would stay separated at the Tampa-Melbourne line and not interfere with one another. Sarah just commented, "Interesting" and wished Carlos and his people well. Carlos did the same and that ended the conversation.

During the two months following the arrival of the caravan in Montana, all of the Association members, with the exception of the few that had left, were busily involved with constructing their homes and support structures in anticipation of the approaching winter months. Barnes had increased the size of the clothing shop and within weeks, everyone who needed a warm parka, hat and gloves was provided for. In anticipation of the snow that was expected almost daily, Barnes had detailed a number of his people to make boots and snow shoes. He now had access to fleece that was provided to him by Parker when it became known that they were making parkas for the residents and were very short of insulating materials.

The Valley had extensive flocks of sheep and their storage bins were filled with fleece that had been sheared in the spring for which there was no longer a viable market. The quality of the wool in the Valley was excellent coming from a combination of hardy, cold weather, Merino sheep, known for the fine texture of their wool. The breed combination produced wool that, in previous times, had been sought after for its lightness, moisture absorbing and insulating qualities.

During this building phase when vast quantities of resources were being transferred from Valley suppliers and warehouses to the building of Goodland, as well as the feeding and clothing of its inhabitants, no one in the Valley appeared to be keeping any records of the transfer of these valuable materials. When Stuart learned that there was no record keeping taking place, he had Sarah take the responsibility for recording all such transactions so that the account books could be balanced at some future time when the people of Goodland were settled and producing on their own. He also called together the key people who were most knowledgeable in communications, engineering and the sciences to begin a study of how the Valley was utilizing its resources and how it's very basic local government was providing municipal services to the community.

There were people in the Association who were intimately familiar with advanced techniques for providing basic infrastructure needs, such as water and sewer, for communities. Others were expert in management systems and communications as well as various other fields that could be of assistance in bringing the Valley leadership up to speed in carrying out their civic responsibilities. Stuart also cautioned them not to take a patronizing approach in dealing with the residents. He had observed some from the Association acting in that manner and it was tempting for one to take that approach upon observing the backward condition of some of the Valley practices. If the people in the Valley thought for a minute that they were being talked down to, they would back off and no changes would ever be made. In some cases, he told them, it might be best to let them just observe how we do things and let them decide if they want to do it the easy and least wasteful way or if they want to continue doing what they have always done.

In an attempt to begin the payback for all of the goods and services provided to the Association, Stuart had Barnes begin repairing the roads, beginning with the north south road that ran the length of the Valley. It had not been touched for years, ever since the Montana Highway Department had last worked on it and it was now barely passable without a four wheeled vehicle or horse drawn cart. There were a large number of automobiles in the Valley but with the fuel shortage, very few were operating. This caused more of a problem than just reducing the frequency of trips to town. Field work involving tractors had been cut back considerably and farming was the life blood of the Valley. Farm products of foodstuffs, wool and beef were the principal commodities of the Valley and if they were ever to regain markets for their goods, they had to be able to produce in large quantities. Sarah had further conversations with her contacts in Hollywood and, in time, with the assistance of Stuart, agreements, between the two groups, were entered into for the trade of specific quantities of food and wool for petroleum. Stuart made an agreement with Parker whereby Parker provided the desired products and Stuart handled the delivery down to Wyoming and back.

In return, the petroleum would be divided between the two communities on the basis of their respective populations. It was further agreed between the Valley residents and the Association that if either group needed immediate deliveries, Parker would deliver the necessary product and Stuart would provide the transportation and security. The distance between the two protected areas was only three hundred miles, but the larger problem was the lack of vehicles necessary for transporting the petroleum. There were two tanker trucks available in the Valley, but at least five were needed to transport the desired quantity of petroleum or much more frequent trips would have to be made.

Sarah was able to locate three vehicles that the Mormons had and these could be run into the Wyoming safe zone without any trouble as the Mormons controlled all the land up to the Hollywood property. Sarah made the arrangement with the Mormons on an open ended agreement whereby they could request them back at any time or in the alternative, the Association could be tasked at some future date to be of assistance to the Mormons. Stuart inquired as to just what that meant and Sarah only raised an eyebrow, commenting, "we'll see". Stuart made the final arrangements with Parker for the goods needed in the exchange and had Perry take care of providing the necessary security force for the delivery. Barnes provided the vehicles and Nix was assigned as the mission commander on the trip to Wyoming. By the following morning, the trucks were loaded with foodstuffs and bales of fleece and were ready to depart. Stuart was anxiously checking the weather with Sarah as there were two mountain passes to be traversed and at this time of year that could present problems.

All of the trucks were equipped with chains which had to be procured from Parker and the plow that had come in so handy on the trip to Montana from Florida was loaded on one of the flatbed trucks in the event it had to be used to break trail.

By ten in the morning the last vehicle had departed and again, it was an impressive sight with gunners manning their positions atop the vehicles and well armed scout cars leading the caravan. The only difference between this lineup of vehicles and the trip from Florida was the number of trucks involved. This time there were only five including the two fuel trucks compared to the much larger number that had come to the northwest. As they disappeared from view, Stuart commented to Sarah that he hoped the weather would hold out so that they could get back with the petroleum before winter hit with its full fury.

The day had commenced in clear sunlight, but even now it had turned overcast with cold blustery winds coming over the snow capped mountains which ran the length of the valley on both sides. Sarah's briefing that morning included the latest observations from contacts in the Seattle area as well as from up in Alaska. Both areas were experiencing stormy weather which did not bode well for Montana. Fortunately, the distance involved in the trip to the Wyoming territory was less than three hundred miles and the caravan should be there by that evening, barring unforeseen problems. The three fuel trucks were also to be delivered to Hollywood by the Mormons at the same time and hopefully, the caravan would be back by the evening of the following day.

Stuart was heartened by the entire transaction because it was the first time that the Association had been able to negotiate and come to an agreement with two other well organized groups. He looked at the arrangement as the possible first step in a mutual defense pact involving three organizations with somewhat similar goals. He had many questions as to whether the three groups were, in fact, sufficiently similar with respect to their philosophies and goals but from information provided by Sarah the other two organizations were efficiently run, well armed, were not aggressively seeking to dominate others and were reputed to deal with outsiders in a civil manner. That was a good starting point as far as Stuart was concerned and even if they were not able to agree on all issues, they should be able to cooperate on some to their mutual benefit. They could worry about the finer points at some future date. Stuart discussed these matters with Sarah and Anders in their private meetings and the other two were of like mind that further contacts should be made for the purpose of establishing mutual assistance pacts, particularly at this time when conditions in the country were so unstable.

From Sarah's intelligence information, it appeared that the Federal Security Police organization had extended its reach to an area bounded on the north by the northern borders of Kentucky and Virginia, on the west by the Mississippi River, the south by the Gulf and the east by the Atlantic. They also controlled the northern part of Florida to the Melbourne-Orlando Tampa line. The Cubans had the area to the south of that line. It was obvious that the FSP was making rapid strides in its expansionist policy.

The information that Sarah was receiving indicated that they were rapidly growing in strength as they took over smaller, well armed groups who then acted as their local agents, adopting their methods and following their leadership. The very few that tried to maintain their own leadership organization were very brutally treated, dispossessed of their territory and resettled in labor camps in Mississippi. The FSP had amassed extensive territorial acquisitions in recent months and it was Sarah's opinion that they would be fairly quiet for some time as they consolidated their gains. After that, they could become a problem for the west and that was what communities such as the Valley had to prepare to deal with. From all appearances, the goal of the FSP was to recapture the entire country under the leadership of the former bureaucratic gang that destroyed the last vestiges of a democratic America. Should they again gain control, there would no longer be any attempt to pretend to follow democratic principles.

The FSP was operated as a virtual dictatorship under the guidance of a small cadre of former government opportunists, led by Turner. They were going to be difficult to stop in their quest for control because they possessed a substantial arsenal of weapons, men and materials that they had secreted in various locations prior to the collapse. They had tactical aircraft, helicopters, armored vehicles and abundant supplies of ammunition, fuel and men to do the job. It would take a well organized group with strong resolve and a certain amount of hardware to stop them. The Cubans posed that threat to the FSP in the south of Florida and at present there was no force in existence in the west that could stop them. To their north lay the industrial belt of the Great Lakes. At this point in time, the FSP had no designs for expansion there as it was a region lying in deep decay with social strife to the extreme under the virtual control of various Muslim groups operating under the dictates of Sharia Law. It was questionable if it was worth the effort to take over and that was what was holding the FSP back at this point.

As Stuart, Anders and Sarah discussed these matters, the three concluded that they had to expedite their organizational efforts and the place to begin was right there in the Valley. Stuart agreed that he would meet with Parker the following day to begin the task of setting up an effective organization for administering the affairs of all Valley residents. They would need that before they could begin to enter into mutual assistance pacts with their neighbors.

The next morning, Stuart met with Matt Parker in the Riverton administration building which consisted of a small office, occupied sparingly by Parker or whoever else was handling some Valley problem that called for a solution, and a larger room that was used as a meeting room for various purposes. There was no staff assistance and all problems were resolved by bringing the participants together and coming to some form of agreement. Everything was done verbally and no records were kept, but that was how the Valley residents preferred to do business. They were a very independent group of people that believed in little or no government.

As Stuart sat down in the sparsely furnished, small office with Parker, he was fully aware of the fact that to bring an efficiently run government organization to this community was going to be an uphill fight. He also realized that if he failed to do so, their future might well be in jeopardy. Parker made some small talk on the weather and other unimportant matters and then opened the conversation with, "What's on your mind today Stuart?"

Stuart had brought some charts with him that Sarah had prepared to bring Parker up to date on what was occurring around the country. He briefed Parker on the situation on the west coast and worked his way across the country to the territory controlled by the FSP and their expansionist policies. Stuart then gave Parker a brief description of their present situation with respect to defensive equipment and personnel together with some of the known information on Hollywood and the Mormons who could be considered possible allies in the event of moves by the Hispanics in the south and west or by the FSP in the east. While he went through the facts and figures, Parker listened without comment. When Stuart had finished with the briefing on the current state of affairs around the country, Parker looked at him and shrugged his shoulders, commenting, "So, what do you have in mind?"

Stuart leaned back in his chair and proceeded to go into detail with what he, Anders and Sarah had concluded was needed in order to prepare for what Stuart saw as the inevitable attempt, not too far in the future, by either or both, the FSP and Hispanic forces from moving in on their territory. He considered the FSP as the more likely threat as the Hispanics had thus far not made any moves on areas in which they either had no substantial historical claim or in which they were not the majority population. Those characteristics did not apply to the Mormon controlled territory, Hollywood or to Montana. Assuming the most likely scenario, which was an expansionist move by the FSP to take over the west, Stuart, Anders and Sarah had assumed that was very likely within the next five years. He based that on the assumption that to wait any longer would make it more difficult for the FSP to succeed in their rather obvious goals.

Parker interjected and suggested that if all of that was true, possibly the Hispanics would be a more likely first target for the FSP due to the extensive natural resources in the areas under their control. Stuart had considered that and was of the opinion that at some future date, there would be a conflict between the two but that the FSP would first go after the easier target and that was the entire west above the Denver-San Francisco line. "That is us. After they get that and solidify that area, then they may look to the south of that line. Only then could you be assured of an active role by the Hispanics in countering the FSP A little late for our benefit."

Parker nodded, agreeing with Stuart's logic. "OK, what do you suggest we do about all of this?" Stuart laid his charts down and collected his thoughts before proceeding. "The first thing we have to do is to set up an organization here in the valley that can act on behalf of everyone, Valley residents and Association members, in an expeditious and effective manner. We do not have that now. We in the Administration of our Association can speak for our members. I don't see a similar executive body for your Valley residents. We should set up a governing entity for all that can deal quickly with rapidly developing problems. We can't run up and down the length of this valley trying to gather a consensus on potentially life threatening issues that will be coming up in the future. There must be a recognized, full time leadership that can communicate with our neighbors and enter into trade and defense agreements with them when the times for such agreements are ripe. Not a month later when opportunities may have been missed. You and I worked a very good arrangement on the fuel, if we get it back before it snows, but how many of those can you and I work in the future before you are accused of acting without authority by some farmer up on the north end of the Valley."

Parker nodded. He had thought of this at the time of the fuel for food trade and had been criticized by a number of the farmers for giving away their food stuffs from the warehouses. Some of the farmers were quite happy plowing their fields with mules, a practice that had grown in popularity following the shortage of fuel for tractors. The farmers were able to sustain their families quite comfortably with what they were able to raise on their farms and still have some left over to trade in the village for other materials that they needed.

Parker was fully aware that Valley production was now only a fraction of what it had been prior to the collapse and without fuel for tractors and other machinery, they would never be in a position to enter into substantial trading agreements with their neighbors. Parker agreed with Stuart's basic premise but the problem that he faced was the independent nature of the people. "Stuart, I agree with you and you don't know what I went through to get some level of cooperation on the food trade. The biggest problem that we face is the total lack of interest in these people in setting up some form of government to tell them what they can and cannot do. I don't know how you would ever get them to accept government after what the last one did to all of us."

# Chapter Thirty-Five

Seeing his opening, Stuart proceeded with the real purpose of his meeting with Parker this morning. "Matt, we have to take a firm hand with this. You and I." Stuart had thought long and hard about this before coming to Parker's office. He knew exactly what he wanted for government. He wanted absolute power to do what needed to be done but he would have to be careful about how he achieved that. "We have a proposed temporary governing body that thus far is only in the formative stage and has not had a chance to function and that is the Council of Seven proposal whose seats we have not yet filled. Suffice it to say that I would incorporate the same concept in a more permanent governing body. In other words, that we have a representative council to handle the matters that the Council of Seven was to handle, which were primarily local problems. Civic issues primarily: water, sewage, public facilities, recreation and so forth. The major economic and political issues would continue to be handled as they have in the past, by you for your group and me for my group. We can continue to call it the Council of Seven and have them elected by all residents. Very democratic, which is what many of them are crying for. Now either your people or my people would be out voted in electing the membership of that Council but the Council would not be involved with defense, governmental negotiations with outside groups or agricultural issues. Those issues, you and I would handle. There is no way in hell that my people are going to turn an excellent Defense organization over to someone who hasn't the experience or know how with that sort of thing anymore than your people would turn over the farming responsibility to my bunch of beach dwellers."

Stuart continued, "I would suggest that those areas of responsibility, negotiating with outside organizations, defense and farming, stay with their respective organizations. I would suggest that we have the experience and know how in dealing with outside entities, potential allies as well as potential enemies because defense is an essential element in those negotiations. That you, likewise, have complete freedom to manage and structure your agriculture operation. That a unanimous vote of the Council of Seven be required to veto any decision of either group with respect to those areas of responsibility that are the specific responsibility of that group. Otherwise, all other matters would be handled by a majority vote of the Council and that the Council President would act as the executive authority on all general community matters. That way, cumulative voting, guaranteeing representation in the Council of Association members, being in the minority, would prevent any interference in the exclusive responsibility for farming or for defense and outside relationships unless it clearly called for interference. Matters such as the food-fuel trade would be handled by the Association but would require a majority decision of the Council to release the food and accept the trade."

Stuart went on. "This is a less than perfect form of governing body, but it is a starting point for, what I recognize as, a very independent minded group of people, who are slightly in the majority at present, and who are going to balk at any suggestion for government period. I am fully aware of what you have had to say on that point and am willing to start out slowly in this matter. Now, one additional problem we have is that we have a significant part of our group full time engaged in defense matters, intelligence gathering and other activities which benefit everyone, including the Valley residents. We need some support in the way of food stuffs and other basic materials needed for our livelihood which we are losing because our people are busy in these other tasks. I know this smacks of taxes, but we have to have this or we are going to have to pull our people away from a Defense Team and put them to work out in the fields and that benefits no one. I don't know what quantities we are talking about here, but Sarah can gin those up for your consideration. I would assume that the Council could deal with that matter later. Now, I suggest we get rolling on this immediately. We can print up informational flyers that lay out the basics of the governing plan and a time and place for public discussion. The people should also be informed that a decision will be made following the discussion meeting. Also, and I think it is key; we must lead the people to water on this matter."

Stuart said this slowly to emphasize the point that the issues should not be thrown to the mob for solution. Rather, those attending the meeting should be guided, as much as possible, towards the sought after goals that Stuart and Parker had discussed. Stuart had followed that policy with the Association and then the Alliance and learned the hard way that people preferred to be led and that the average person wanted government solutions provided by others who had given them more thought.

Stuart was of the opinion that the average person did not want to concern himself with the structural aspects of government. They only wished to complain if it became intrusive or presented some particular hardship to them. It was the job of those governing the group to create and manage the government, hopefully avoiding the pitfalls that could awaken the sleeping beast of the governed. Clearly any system of government included interference with personal freedoms. That was the difficulty in setting one up in the Valley at this time and in order to gain support with the majority of the residents, the proposal would have to minimize interference with those to be governed. Stuart's plan would appear to do that while permitting considerable freedom of action on the part of those responsible for defense and negotiations with other organized groups of people.

Stuart could see that he was making some headway with Matt Parker in the form of government he foresaw. "Pending further development of the organization, you and your staff would continue to be in charge of the agricultural programs and my staff would be in charge of defense and extra-territorial policies and negotiations. The Council of Seven would be basically an advisory group with veto power only when voting unanimously. They would have no veto power over operational decisions, only policy decisions. In other words, they couldn't tell you how many acres to plant but they could veto your decision on who could vote. You would deal with problems arising from your people and I would do the same. I think you and I could resolve problems that came from our group that affected the other group."

The two men continued talking for the better part of the morning and before leaving, Stuart said, "There is one other matter we need to resolve immediately. We need a Valley police force that has jurisdiction over both Goodland and Riverton. I suggest we have Perry work with your police chief and have the two of them work out the staffing and operational aspects. Is that agreeable with you?"

"I agree, Stuart. I have been thinking of that for some time as well. Have Perry make the contact. If any problems develop, you and I can handle them ourselves. OK?"

"Agreed, Matt."

As they were leaving, Parker said that he would see to it that the flyers were printed up just as soon as the two men agreed upon the wording of the announcement. Stuart returned to his office and drafted up a proposal which Parker made some minor changes to and following Stuart's review and approval sent to the printer. The meeting was scheduled in the local theater building the following week.

During the week after which the flyers had gone out, the weather had held so that the five fuel carrying trucks had made the trip over the mountain passes with a minimum of difficulty. Nix had to use the plow at the first pass as there was a good three feet of snow on the road that wound its way over the top and there were some scary moments on the way down the other side of the mountain due to a thin layer of clear ice that covered the roadway. Nix reported to the Command Post upon his arrival and commented about the new surroundings. Barnes had put the construction of the administrative building, including the Command Post, on the priority list and it was virtually finished by the time Nix returned. The Command Post was laid out and constructed according to instructions from Sarah and it was now equipped with permanent projection and display screens which were much better arranged for viewers and briefing personnel than the prior facility at Bayside.

In the days preceding the meeting of all Valley residents to discuss the need for a community organization, Stuart and Parker had spent considerable time working out the format and the presentation. It was decided that Matt Parker would lead off the meeting with a general overview of what it was they hoped to accomplish. All of those in attendance had access to a somewhat detailed written plan for the proposed organization so there were no surprises for anyone as to what was going to be discussed and what the purpose of the meeting was. Both Stuart and Parker anticipated a difficult time in convincing the long time, independent residents of the Valley that they should let others make decisions that could possibly affect them in some fashion.

Stuart had brought Anders up to speed on his talks with Parker and Anders suggested that he continue the negotiations. Anders was in total agreement with the governmental plan worked out by Stuart. Anders was also beginning to slow down in his involvement and was quite pleased to see Stuart taking over.

Prior to the meeting, Stuart held a closed door meeting with a select group of staff which included Thomas, Perry, Moss, Nix and a number of the Defense Team leaders. After the meeting, the group was close mouthed as to what was discussed and merely dispersed to their separate work areas.

# Chapter Thirty-Six

On the evening of the meeting, the theater was filled with both Valley and Association people to the point where it was standing room only in the aisles. Fortunately it had turned cold with a strong north wind and the lightly heated building was relatively comfortable with all of the people crammed inside.

The room was set up with a podium for the speaker, a large screen set up behind the speaker with two flags, one on either side of the screen. One on the left side of the rostrum was apparently the state flag of Montana and the one on the right was a new flag with one blue sword surrounded by a flaming wreath on a field of yellow surrounded by a field of green. To say the least it was a dramatic appearing flag with the greatly contrasted colors. As the residents began filing into the room and taking their seats, the conversations were obviously directed at the new flag.

Matt Parker took the podium and immediately addressed what was on everyone's mind. He explained that as most of the Riverton residents were aware, the flag to his left was the Montana flag and the flag to his right was a proposed flag for the new territory temporarily named WestPac. "Very impressive, don't you think?" Most of the Riverton residents present were not quite sure what to think of the flag or if they even wanted a new flag for their community.

Stuart had Robert Thomas come up with the flag concept as he wanted to let all residents know right from the get go that this was a new beginning for everyone. He expected it to be a bit of a shocker but was willing to gamble that it would have the results he hoped for. Robert Thomas considered it an excellent idea and also had some of the security force in his newly designed uniforms assisting people to their chairs and guarding the doors. The uniforms were also a topic of conversation with gold shoulder boards that displayed the rank of the wearer offsetting the dark blue blouse and trousers. It was an impressive uniform that conveyed the message that these perfectly attired and trimmed troops were professionals to be respected.

Matt Parker began to go over the format of the meeting and as he began to explain the need for a community organization that would encompass both the old time residents and the newcomers, a chorus of grumbling spread throughout the large room. Parker was a man of patience, but he could not stand discourtesy and he slammed his fist on the podium and told those who had provided the audible dissent that he expected to be heard and he expected the same courtesy for those that would follow. He further suggested that what was being discussed would possibly determine their very survival in the next few years to come and that everyone had better start paying attention if they had any interest in that sort of thing. He then told those that had no intention of contributing something positive to the discussion to take this opportunity to "get the hell out of the theater". A few did stand up and walk out of the room as Parker mumbled into the microphone for all to hear, "Good riddance."

Matt Parker first introduced Sarah Taves and explained who she was and what her responsibilities had been with the Association. Her credentials were definitely impressive to anyone that had any knowledge of the world, but the room did contain a significant number who were of the opinion that women did not belong in positions of responsibility. As she took the podium there was a light patter of polite applause from the Valley residents and an enthusiastic welcome from the Association members. Sarah had a series of very impressive slides prepared with supporting data showing what was occurring in the rest of the country. She explained what was known with respect to the areas of the country controlled by the FSP, by the Hispanic organizations, the Blacks, Muslims and by the smaller renegade groups around the country. She also described some of the other groups scattered around the country that were very similar in ethnic makeup and aspirations to what they had in the Valley. Sarah finished this part of the briefing with a description of what was known about the Mormon and Hollywood communities and the fact that there had been trade of food and materials for fuel supplies for those who were not aware of that fact. By the time Sarah completed her portion of the briefing, the audience was very attentive, leaning forward in their seats and studying the charts and data that Sarah was using in her presentation.

Following Sarah was Stuart who was also supplied with a number of charts, graphs and slides showing the relative armed strength of the groups around the country. Much of the data was based on data gleaned from Sarah's intelligence section but even though the figures were estimates, they were considered quite reliable. Stuart then presented data showing approximate numbers of men and materials available for the defense of the Valley should it come under attack from outsiders. The disparity between the relative strength of the large organizations of the FSP, the Hispanics and the Blacks compared to what was available in the Valley was shocking to many in the audience.

As matters stood, it was obvious that the valley residents were presently at the mercy of any of the larger organizations should they choose to attack. Stuart then went on to impress upon the listeners that if they took the proper steps now to protect themselves they had hope. It was essential that they begin immediately to organize first themselves and then their military Alliances. Well protected bunkers should be constructed at the north and south choke points of the Valley. Likewise, the airport defenses needed to be built. Stuart referred to these as minimal defensive moves. More effective would be Alliances with their neighbors. If they were able to enter into a defensive pact with Hollywood and the Mormons in Utah, at a minimum, they could present a formidable force that would make an adversary think twice about attacking them. They should then reach out to other smaller organizations in Montana, and elsewhere in the west, to unite them and bring them together in a coalition forming a united wall against threats coming from the east.

Stuart finished his portion of the briefing with short and concise statements to the effect that the threats to their security from the east were certain to materialize within the next five years and that if they took the right steps now, they stood at least a fair chance of withstanding the threats. When he finished, you could hear a pin drop in the theater and it was clear that all present had taken his words seriously.

Concluding the program was Matt Parker who told the people that he firmly believed that they had to prepare now for what appeared to be a very perilous future. The first step in that preparation was to set up the community governing structure that was laid out in the information packets. He argued briefly for the plan, which he stressed, retained in the original Valley residents, control over the agricultural program and he also pointed out that the Council of Seven was elected by all residents so that they would have a say in what decisions were made in the Council and by the Council President. Parker again explained cumulative voting whereby each voter would cast seven votes and he could distribute his votes among all candidates as he saw fit. He acknowledged that the purpose of that voting system was to give to both groups in the Valley, the new and old residents, the power to elect some members to the Council of Seven. Without cumulative voting, it was likely that one or the other group would fill all seats on the Council. He also explained that under the proposal, the Goodland Association would handle relationships with outside entities as well as defense and security matters. The Valley had historically stayed away from associating with outside communities so for most in the theater there was no great loss giving up that particular area of responsibility. He then suggested a voice vote in favor of the proposed Council of Seven organization. The ayes carried the evening although there were a few loudly shouted nays which made it clear that the vote was not unanimous. Matt Parker then adjourned the meeting and joined Sarah, Anders and Stuart to map out the election process to fill the seven seats of the Council and the Council would elect the president. That election process would occur the following evening.

For the Council of Seven candidates from the Goodland Association, the executive council selected the names of Anders, Sarah, Thomas and Stuart as those to be submitted. According to the computations provided by Sarah, with all of the eligible voters in the Association casting their ballots, three were guaranteed under cumulative voting to be elected to the council. Every person could cast seven votes and they were told to cast one for each Association candidate and one for the three persons they most preferred out of the four.

When the flyers were sent out in the Valley describing the proposed justice system for the Valley residents, the arguments pro and con began. Everyone in the valley was talking about the new rules and were wondering if all of this regulation of their lives was a good or bad thing. Many were irate about the proposal and others were enthusiastically in favor. Matt Parker was no longer as confident as he had been that the proposal would pass without any difficulty and as the crowds of people flocked to the auditorium, the arguments in favor and against continued with voices raised in anger either attacking or defending the idea. Most of the residents of Riverton were clearly for the proposal but many in the outlying areas did not like the idea of someone having authority over their lives. They had survived on their own for generations in secluded ranches in the Valley and saw no reason why they could not continue to take care of themselves in the future. As the meeting progressed, again chaired by Matt Parker, the candidates for the Council of Seven seats were introduced. There were ten candidates from the Valley, including Matt Parker and four from the Association. As each was introduced, loud cheers came from either side, depending upon who was being presented.

Matt Parker then addressed the matter of the proposal for a justice system for all residents of the Valley. He explained that it was in fact modeled after the Association system which he had been observing for some time. He told the audience that he had been impressed by what he saw and believed that the time had come in the valley for adoption of the same or a similar system. "If in time, we find that it needs changes that are more in line with our way of life, we will make those changes."

Stuart took over the microphone and began explaining the judicial system. As he did so, grumbling was heard among the Riverton residents which became loud enough to interfere with his presentation. Stuart knew what was bothering the dissidents in the crowd and after a while, he set aside his notes and looking directly at those who were obviously not in agreement with what he had to say, he continued. "Now look, before I go on further, I think it is essential that we all understand a few basics about living together. There is no way in hell that all of the people living in this valley, Riverton, Goodland, the outlying ranches, all of us, can go on without some structure, some minimal understanding of what is expected of everyone, yes, some rules and regulations. If we don't have that, there is no way in hell that we can progress as a community and grow and develop into the kind of society that we all would like to have at some time in the future."

Stuart now had the attention of all in the hall. This was the first time that Stuart had brought up the proposal for a unified government structure that would encompass the entire valley, including Goodland and the original Valley residents. He had not even discussed this in advance with Matt Parker who would have preferred that he had, although he was not against the concept. Stuart went on to explain all of the major points and characteristics of the judicial system, how it would function, where, how punishment would be carried out, where the Rules of Conduct would be posted, and how some of the more severe crimes would be punished. When Stuart had finished, he had carried his points successfully to most everyone in the theater.

Matt Parker announced that all of the ballots would be tallied by those candidates that had been presented that evening. The results would be posted the following afternoon at the Riverton community building and the Goodland administration building.

The next day, after the ballots were counted, the results showed that the three Goodland Association candidates were easily elected to the Council of Seven and Stuart had been elected President by reason of being selected by a vast majority of the votes. Matt Parker and two other valley men filled the remaining seats. Surprisingly, the Florida group held three of the seats and the Presidency. The voters had also voted in favor of the judicial system by an overwhelming majority. Stuart's election brought up the question of could he serve as a member of the Council and also as president. That question became the first matter handled by the Council and it was the general consensus that he could not hold both posts and consequently another person had to be selected. In fairness to the representation on the Council of the Association members, Thomas, Sarah and Anders were allowed to select a replacement to serve as the seventh member. The following day, they submitted the name of Irene Covington who had been very put out that she had not been a candidate from the start. Stuart was not overly happy about having her on the Council, but, beyond a doubt, she was the most civic minded person in the Association and did represent a growing body of people residing in Goodland who were of like mind politically. Stuart asked her if she would be able to handle all of her tasks that she was presently involved with or if the new assignment was going to be too much for her.

Irene responded, "You've got to be kidding, Stuart. If you think you can talk me out of this one, you've got another guess coming. I want to be right there looking over your shoulder." Irene said that with a smile on her face, but Stuart knew that she was deadly serious.

The Council of Seven was in operation within days of the election and with the adoption of the judicial system, they had their work cut out for them. Judges had to be appointed, facilities created, procedures drafted and agreed upon and various other tasks had to be accomplished, all involved in getting the system up and running. Needless to say, Irene was right in the middle of every decision pushing her old style liberal philosophy. Fortunately for the other council members, Irene's interest in restricting the power of the police and protecting the rights of the citizens was generally not in line with the attitudes of the others. No one wanted to give the law enforcers any more power than they absolutely needed to carry out their work. On the other hand, there were arguments between Irene and the others over the protections to be afforded those that did come under the power of the new judicial system. She proposed adoption of many of the rights available under the old criminal justice system before the collapse. Everyone else on the council was generally opposed to those measures and that was the end of it. No one supported Irene's rights policies.

Barnes was called in by the council and assigned the task of handling the construction projects. Already there was a growing merger of responsibility and operations taking place between the Association community and the Valley residents. Stuart was very satisfied with the way matters had progressed and Matt Parker was pleased as well. They were bringing their two groups together and they were developing into a well knit community of people with common goals. There were community events that were now sponsored for and by everyone in the valley rather than by the Riverton residents or the people of Goodland. The school systems were soon merged so that students in the valley could attend Beth's schools.

The Association had an excess of well trained teachers and professionals to staff a school system twice the size of the one operating in Goodland and it was a shame to waste their talents when the valley was so short of properly trained teachers. Furthermore the school buildings in Riverton were much better suited to their intended purpose than the makeshift buildings in Goodland. Consequently, all students and faculty above the fourth class were moved over to Riverton to continue the educational process. This was a boon to Barnes who needed more room for his manufacturing operations. The distance between the two communities was not over a mile and consequently students in the fifth class and above could easily handle it without the need for transportation.

Other community services were combined where it appeared beneficial to both groups to do so. The medical facilities of the Association were very limited while at the same time Goodland had an excess of trained physicians and technicians. Their shortage in facilities and excess in staff was a perfect mix for the excess facilities and lack of staff on the part of the valley. There were some civic functions that each community was handling without difficulty but they were still combined pursuant to orders from the Council of Seven following studies that determined there would be efficiencies gained by bringing the two offices together. That is what happened with respect to the public utility offices of both townships that were responsible for electric, water and sewer services. When those offices were brought together, it was found that the combined staff could be cut by one third freeing up people to work in other areas where they were needed.

As far as the Association Administration was concerned, most of their functions had been transferred over to the Council of Seven. The intelligence and defense sections operated without oversight by the council as they were kept separate for the Association pursuant to the original merger agreement as was the agricultural responsibility which was solely controlled by the Valley farmers.

Other community activities were coming into being as a result of the influx of talent from the new arrivals in the valley. A theater group was started and plays were being performed in the Riverton Theater by actors from not only Goodland but also from up and down the length of the valley. A newspaper was being published in Riverton and that was a major cause of concern for many in the valley. The issue of freedom of the press, which had been a basic principle in the former so called democratic system, had been twisted around to become a shield for those using the national media for their own purposes. The print and television media in the years prior to the collapse, while claiming independence, were under the thumb of interests closely aligned with the government and this became a powerful tool of the bureaucrats in controlling the masses. Even up to the final days of the national government, the media was issuing bulletins, writing articles and presenting programs showing the government as the great benefactor, protecting the people's interests and working for the common good. Clearly the concept of freedom of the press had been misused to the great detriment of the American people. When it should have been criticizing the crimes of the bureaucracy and pointing out the excesses, waste and corruption that existed in both government and the business world, it was silent.

In the years preceding the collapse, there had been a steady flow of people between the media/entertainment world and the national government with actors and actresses, television personalities and others with power and influence, created by their constant presence before the cameras, moving into political positions. Using these willing dupes to publicize and carry the message that everything was going along just fine enabled the bureaucrats to prolong their wasteful practices adding to the severity of the eventual decline and final collapse of the government.

At the last moment, when it became apparent to even the most fervent believer that the United States of America was a hollow giant living on printed money, with inflation out of control, debt that could never in anyone's lifetime be paid off and virtually zero gross national product, those that had raped the national wealth completed their final act of theft by hauling their stolen treasures off to safe havens either in the mountains of the west or to Caribbean islands protected by their private security forces.

A very few were not able to carry out their escape and were caught by enraged mobs as they attempted to haul their loot to safety. Unfortunately, most did affect their escape as they were more informed on what was really occurring than the public that was being fed their propaganda through the medium of the so called free press. It was for this reason that when the newspaper began publication in the office in Riverton that many in the valley were questioning what to do about it.

The issue of free speech and freedom of the press became the hot topic among everyone in the Valley including not only the Association members who were acutely aware of the power of the press, but also the farmers, ranchers and residents of Riverton who were not oblivious to how the media had been manipulated by the government in years past. At first word of the publication of a local paper went unnoticed with most people assuming that local news was of interest to all and the newspaper would provide a forum for distributing matters of interest to the people living in the valley.

The controversy developed when some of the more conservative elements in the Goodland community began revisiting the excesses of the former national media and suggesting that controls be imposed right from the start before matters got out of hand. At first, most of the people in the valley, including those living in Riverton and Goodland were either unconcerned or generally believed in the concept of allowing people to speak their mind on any topic and in time, the truth would prevail. Anders, Stuart and Sarah observed the storm developing over this issue and their first thought was to let it run its course and in time it would just die out.

As time passed, it became clear that the controversy would not die out. Under the former government, a mutual admiration society was informally established between the Hollywood elite, the media and the Washington bureaucracy. You couldn't turn on a television set without a major network or cable station playing homage to President Turner. The president usually had his face plastered on the TV screen whenever it was turned on. The adulation for this fraud of a president was unexcelled. Success achieved through hard work, self discipline, abiding by a moral standard, respect for the existence of a supreme being, all were the subject of a barrage of humor based attacks in the national media. Unfortunately, with the virtual destruction of formal education in the country, the ability of the average person to see through the constant assaults on long held beliefs gradually eroded to the point where there was very little respect left on a national level for the old tried and true concepts of 'duty, honor, country'.

The media would possibly not have been successful in carrying out their assault on long held traditions and principles of virtue were it not for the corresponding decline in the existence of a middle class in the United States. This was the result primarily of the rapid growth of the bureaucracy and the toll it placed upon the national economy for its support and expansion. From the end of the twentieth century to 2020, the labor force employed by the national government, together with state and local governments grew to two thirds of all working Americans. The tax burden on those trying to engage in lawful production of goods and services was overwhelming and in the first years of the twenty first century, those fleeing lawful self employment accelerated to the point where the only so called businesses existing in the year 2017 were the huge multinational conglomerates that were closely allied with the government.

The demographics of the United States suffered a profound change in the fifty-five years from 1970 to 2025. The nation, over time, became populated by a small group of super wealthy individuals who were in control of the nation's wealth producing resources and the vast majority of Americans lived from day to day in conditions reminiscent of life a thousand years before. Food and housing were rationed. Medical care was virtually unheard of. In the earlier years of this transition into national poverty, the government had pretended to be the answer to all things.

The population under the barrage of propaganda from the media and the entertainment community fell under the spell that all of their troubles would be taken care of by Washington. Just let Washington take care of you was the message. Don't try to take care of yourself because you are incapable of doing that. In time, Americans were incapable of even thinking of handling their problems themselves. The independent nature that had always been in the psyche of Americans was nowhere to be found and all eyes were turned to Washington for food, housing, medical care, education, and all other needs of a civilized society. Of course, when conditions deteriorated to that level, there was no one left to do the work of creating the products, services, food and materials needed to support all of those demanding the necessities of life. It all came to a crashing end and the prominent part that the media and so called freedom of the press played in this charade were much on the minds of the people questioning whether a small, local newspaper should be able to function without some controls.

The study group, now comprised of four men and no women, after Irene's departure for the Council of Seven, took the matter under advisement and went into seclusion in their library and conference room that Barnes had built for them. Even though the four men were of a generally conservative persuasion that did not mean that they could readily agree on matters affecting personal liberties. Freedom of speech and of the press had always been a somewhat vague concept in that people did not attempt to define it in their own minds unless an issue presented itself which affected them directly. For most people, this meant that they would never be faced with having to decide whether or not there were limits to the concept or if it was an absolute right that no man could restrict. Obviously, historically, most, if not all governing bodies had restricted the right of free speech in one respect or another.

The problem for the study group in analyzing the problem arose when the publication aspect entered the picture. If the tools required for mass dissemination of information were in the possession of only a small segment of a community then, the study group, concluded certain controls were not only authorized, but were necessary for the protection of the entire community.

Having decided that controls were needed in the case at hand, the study group then began the task of deciding what controls should be applied and to what extent. The first step that had to be taken was to establish standards of free speech.

The task of the group was formidable. They had to come up with definitions of restraint of speech which permitted criticism of the governing agency but which prohibited the publisher from becoming a tool of the government. The study group came up with a solution to the problem which even they concluded would have to grow with the times and be subject to further modification. The solution proposed was that any mass producer of information for dissemination throughout the community was required to obtain a license from a committee to be established and any published information relating to political or governmental matters was restricted to a recitation of the facts involved. There could be no arguments raised in favor of or against any matter involving politics or governance. There would be no editorializing of such matters.

Any publication relating to political or governmental matters had to include all relevant facts at issue in the matter and a failure to present the view of the facts as seen by all major players in such matters could result in the loss of the individual's right to publish. The committee to be established would be comprised of three persons voted by the eligible voters of the Valley, using cumulative voting to protect minority interests, and they would make all decisions as to whether or not the publication was in compliance with the regulation. No one could be eligible to serve on the committee if they held a government office or were connected in any way with an information publishing agency. It was the intent of the study group that the regulation would apply to all forms of media publication, print, speech, radio, film or video. All other prior restraints in effect under the former constitution were adopted and continued in force. When the group had concluded their deliberations, they submitted their proposal to Stuart who, in turn, passed out copies to Matt Parker, Sarah, Anders and the executive council for review.

It was clear to all that the proposal was a marked change from what limits on speech had been permitted in the country in former times. No longer would newspaper publishers be able to present one sided arguments in favor of or opposed to governmental actions. All relevant facts relating to such actions would have to be laid out or the publisher would be subject to loss of his or her right to publish in the future.

No radio or television newscaster would be able to select out the facts which supported his or her personal political philosophy, rather on such matters, they had to present the facts both pro and con. It was not the intent of the study group to stifle dissent, as they made clear in the cover letter on their proposal. An information publisher would be permitted to lay out the facts which presented an argument for the reader or listener to form in his own mind that a particular government action was overreaching or improper. The publisher would still be able to present information that he or she considered particularly newsworthy involving politics or government in such a fashion as to draw the reader's attention to the topic by placement, repetition, and other such tactics.

The result sought by the group from the adoption of the regulation was that readers, listeners, or viewers would form their own conclusions on matters relating to their government from all of the facts and not from a selected few combined with glossy arguments. As a final suggestion and one that struck at the core of the problem, the study group proposed that ownership of the instruments of dissemination of information be limited to one per entity so that, for example, a newspaper publisher would not be able to acquire another newspaper or radio station.

The old concept of news services operating in a network system to pass their political philosophies around the country could no longer be legal, at least under the law existing in the valley. A further restraint was adopted by the Council to the effect that so called "editorial comment", when allowed with prior council approval, was restricted to the editorial page followed by counter arguments in opposition and a violation of that prohibition could cause loss of license. The Council of Seven adopted the proposal on a vote of six to one abstention, with Irene Covington being the sole holdout.

In the first spring following the arrival of the Association members, the Valley farmers came to Riverton to teach the new residents the art of raising crops and handling livestock including cattle, horses, sheep and other farm stock. Courses were conducted as were workshops where the farmers would show the residents when, where and how to plant. In return, the residents of Goodland had something to offer the farmers with respect to agriculture. The farmers had done their work in the same manner for years and change was not in their nature.

The residents of Goodland were prone to question why farm practices were carried out in a certain fashion and in many instances came up with suggestions for performing the task in a more efficient manner. This was particularly true with respect to the issue of mass production of farm products. The team assembled by Robert Thomas to handle farm production in Goodland was of the opinion that all farm lands should be cultivated, planted and cropped as a single unit. This suggestion ran into the independent nature of the Valley farmers but was adopted after extensive discussions were concluded by an agreement between the Goodland agricultural group and the Valley farmers that a farm board would be appointed to determine the usage of farm land in the valley. A certain percentage for grain crops, pasture, etc. The land subject to the agreement would be allocated its yearly crop assignment which would coincide with a similar assignment for adjoining land.

In that manner large tracts of land could be prepared at the same time even though they extended over a number of separately owned plots of land. Costs for land preparation, established by the board, were allocated and paid out of farm production. At the close of the first year when this was tried, the small farmers realized that their overall costs of production decreased considerably while their product yields increased. As confidence in the system grew even the holdouts, of which there had been a few joined the program.

As farming techniques continued to be improved, the success of the program was reflected in the bountiful crops taken from the lands. The grain bins and storerooms were filled with crops and it became very clear to all that the entire valley was capable of producing far more than it would ever need to sustain itself. Sarah had continued her negotiations with interests throughout Montana and Idaho and had entered into a number of agreements with neighboring communities to transfer excess food to them in return for goods and materials in short supply in the Valley.

Robert Thomas had, likewise, been busy traveling throughout the region, meeting contacts established by Sarah and negotiating transfers of food in trade for other materials. As time progressed, trade between the four states expanded to the extent that more efficient means of transporting goods and services between those participating became an ever increasing need. Security problems involving attacks on convoys engaged in the trade had been frequent in the earlier time period, but this was handled summarily and effectively by Ross Perry sending units out to track down and exterminate the culprits. As word of the swift reprisals levied upon those who attempted to interfere with trade went out among the various communities, the problem soon disappeared.

With the development of extensive trade extending from Wyoming, Utah, Montana and Idaho, interest developed among all participants in furthering the relationship to include better transportation systems and mutual defense pacts.

There were vast numbers of rail cars and engines lying dormant in deserted rail yards that could be called into service provided the rail beds were repaired. This was a vast undertaking as in many places, the ties and tracks had been ripped out to provide fuel or for the construction of housing throughout the four state region.

A four state conference of those interested in resolving some of these problems was called and scheduled for the following summer at Riverton. Sarah, Stuart and the others involved in Valley management had a large conference center constructed for the purpose and saw to it that comfortable accommodations were available for those attending. Approximately two hundred participants came from various communities in the four state area and some from beyond. The agenda was limited to trade matters and protection of trade routes although it was clear that the interests of most attending extended beyond these matters. Sarah and Stuart were the principal organizers of the conference and it was their intent to limit the initial formal contact to objectives that were obviously needed by all and were attainable. They could build on their first success at a later date. The first task was to repair the rail beds and bring them up to operable condition. Security for the accomplishment of this task was a concurrent requirement.

Rail lines were mapped out and communities were assigned the responsibility for repairing the track running through their areas. They were also responsible for providing security, not only for the work crews, but also for the tracks when the work was completed. At the same time, rail yards were reactivated to bring the locomotives and rail cars up to operating condition. As before, diesel fuels remained in short supply and production of operating refineries was increased to meet the expected need. Clearly something was going to have to be done in the not too distant future to provide the necessary fuels for sustained operations.

Negotiations were begun with powers in the southern Hispanic areas to explore potential sources of large quantities of petroleum products for the forecast increased need. Communications facilities in Sarah's offices soon became overloaded and additional radio equipment was brought in to meet the need. In some areas of the four state area telephone lines had been reinstalled and this alleviated some of the need for radio communications. Eventually computer network services began to appear and become available.

More and more communities wished to become a part of what appeared to be a successful enterprise intent upon improving the standard of living of those participating in the still somewhat informal Confederation. As the work was being accomplished, the growth of interest in the four state community was developing so quickly that it was beginning to task Association assets beyond their limits. Sarah and Stuart anticipated the problem and had Barnes construct a much larger administrative facility for the purpose of dealing with the added responsibilities. Additional staff was brought in and trained to handle the increased work load.

Ross Perry became the senior security official in what was loosely being referred to as The Confederation. Robert Thomas assumed the far more challenging post of overseeing the economic trade between the communities in the four state area than his former task serving as a traveling salesman. He was supported by a team of economists, geologists, farmers, businessmen and statisticians who directed, facilitated, and encouraged trade throughout the region. Some areas were rich in resources that had never been exploited. Others were attempting to develop or manufacture products that were not in as great a need as others that they could be producing. Trade bulletins were published and disseminated among participants to inform them of what was needed and where.

This was a period of immense growth of community spirit among the involved participants in the informal Confederation which now extended beyond the four state area. Interest now reached into areas of California, Oregon, Washington and pockets of Nevada. Idaho, Utah and Wyoming were beginning to participate with greater interest daily. This interest in organizing with others was spurred on to a great degree by the growing realization that unaffiliated groups would not be able to fend off challenges to their independence by themselves nor would they be able to develop economically and socially without the advantages Confederation brought.

The FSP had been increasingly active in their military operations in parts of the west and seemed to be concentrating their activities for the most part in the Nebraska and Colorado area. Their patrols had been growing in strength and aggressiveness as they continued to test the resolve of the Hispanic forces in control of these areas. Pitched battles involving mechanized units had occurred even in the vicinity of Denver.

A new threat had been added with the introduction of helicopter assault units of FSP troops being air landed to the rear of defending Hispanic lines resulting in great numbers of casualties for the defenders. The Hispanic military force was not known for its use of sophisticated equipment and consequently they had no defenses available to counter the airborne assaults. As these increased in frequency with amazing success for the FSP forces, it appeared that the fall of the Denver and Colorado Springs areas was imminent. A plea for assistance was received by the Alliance communications center from the beleaguered Colorado defenders.

This drew a quick response from the Valley officials as it could open the door to greatly improved relations with their neighbors to the south for the purpose of obtaining critical resources not available in large quantities in the northwest such as petroleum. Barnes had a sizeable inventory of ground to air missiles that had been brought up from Florida and furthermore had set up a munitions shop capable of producing replacements for those used up in combat. That shop had recently been activated for the purpose of building up inventories of weapons that it was anticipated would be needed in the not too distant future when the FSP focused on their territories.

Stuart had Ross Perry respond to the communication from the Hispanics and instructed Perry to set up a meeting between Stuart and the leader of the Hispanic force in the Southwest region. Stuart did not want to be talking to someone that could not be of assistance to the Valley for the return of the favors. Perry had no difficulty getting the message across that the negotiations were to be handled at the highest level.

A meeting was set up in the Denver area and according to the Hispanics, the sooner the better as the situation was critical. Hans Frick was contacted to have the aircraft ready for an immediate flight south and Sarah ran a check of the weather which appeared to be favorable for a flight departing the following morning.

Barnes was instructed to prepare fifty heat seeking missiles for shipment by air and to have them ready to load in Frick's plane the following evening in anticipation of a deal between the two organizations. Stuart departed in the morning and was sitting across from Louis Donley, the military leader in charge of all forces in the southwestern United States by noon. The two men exchanged pleasantries while Stuart suppressed his curiosity as to his counterpart's background. He appeared to be Hispanic but his name did not fit his identity. Donley explained that generations back, there had been a union of blood lines between his Mexican ancestors and an American trapper by the name of Donley. The two chatted amicably for a few minutes and then Donley got down to the business of what help he needed from the Association.

Their defenses were sorely in need of anti air weaponry. They had suffered considerable casualties in defending the eastern perimeter and they anticipated greatly increased assaults in the coming summer months. It was clear that the FSP intended to retake the southwest for the resources that it had to offer. Stuart responded that there was little doubt but that the FSP intended to attempt to retake the entire country and that the southwest was only the first target.

Donley agreed with that assessment and suggested that the northwestern and southwestern organizations should work together for their mutual protection. Stuart did not jump at that invitation immediately because he was not yet convinced as to what Donley's intentions were once the FSP threat was removed, if it ever was to be removed. The Mormons had been complaining of incursions into their territory by Hispanic units operating in southern Utah. The Wyoming settlements had likewise been under periodic attack by forces to the south although they were not entirely certain as to their affiliation.

Stuart decided to speak frankly to Donley about the problems that had been reported to him. He laid out the complaints and the concerns of the residents of Wyoming and Utah with respect to the alleged incursions. He also brought out the fact that there had been problems in the western parts of Utah with what appeared to be organized units coming in from Nevada. Stuart went on to explain that his associates would be interested in working out a mutual defense pact with their southern neighbors as there was strength in numbers but they wanted to be certain that they were not merely arming forces that would be attempting to move on them in the future. His associates also wanted an immediate withdrawal of all forces encroaching on lands in the former states of Utah and Wyoming. Donley sat back with this demand and appeared to be measuring Stuart as one would a newly found adversary.

Stuart went on, knowing that he had Donley about where he wanted him in this conversation. He explained that the Valley had ample supplies of sophisticated weaponry and was, further, capable of fabricating vast quantities of replacements for what they had. They were in possession of the materials and the know how to fabricate and develop improvements to state of the art military hardware. They also had ample numbers of trained military personnel guiding their troops in action. With these statements, Donley could not suppress his increased interest in what Stuart had to say. Stuart continued, "You may wonder why we have an interest in such equipment. We learned long ago that in order to survive in the present condition this country is in, you'd damn well better be well prepared to defend yourself against anybody else in the playground. We think we are about at that point now. We are going to be a hell of a lot stronger in the months to come for a number of reasons, but we are in very good shape now."

Stuart wanted Donley to know that the Valley was not as concerned with his potential threat as it was concerned about what the FSP could do. Having made the Valley position fairly clear, and knowing the great need the Hispanic forces had for the military hardware, he forced Donley to come to terms with the following statement. "You know what the concerns of my associates are. They are eager to work with you, but they want your assistance in bringing peace to their border areas. Why don't you think over what I have had to say and let us know what you can do for us in that respect?"

Stuart knew full well that Donley was not going to let him out of there without an agreement that provided the Hispanics with the weaponry they needed. Stuart then added an item that had been a major problem for the Association from day one, fuel.

The resources for fuel production were mostly located in the southwest under the control of the Hispanics. Stuart explained to Donley that the Association had other sources for fuel but the day would come when increased needs would become more difficult to satisfy and the Hispanics would be called upon to provide the supply. Stuart wanted an understanding that the need would be met by the Hispanics and that Association technicians were available to help in the production of fuel resources.

Donley was silent for a moment and then smiled. "You are a very good negotiator, Stuart. You know full well that we will take the steps you have requested that we take. Frankly, I was not aware of the border activities that you have mentioned, but suffice it to say that they will stop even though they may not be troops affiliated with our forces. I will see that they stop. As for fuel, we presently have a much larger supply than we will ever need. We will want to talk with you about trade agreements as we have some shortages, particularly food and water, that continue to plague us that we feel you could help us with. But first things first. Let's get down to business. We need missiles for the helicopters. We are doing fairly well in other areas, but we are very vulnerable to the air assaults. We could also use military tactics instructors if you have that available. Again, remember Stuart that if they succeed in driving us out of Colorado or farther west, they will be right after you next."

Stuart nodded in agreement and commented, "That's why I'm here. You need us right now and, I agree, we may need you in the near future. We will work with you with the understanding that we may be calling upon you in the future. Is that a deal?"

Donley smiled, reaching across the table and grasped Stuart's hand. "You've got a deal. Let me assure you, we have no interest in any land to the north of Colorado. We have the southwest only because it was primarily Hispanic. We are not hungry for territory and I am assuming that you are of a like mind." Stuart agreed, stating that they had no territorial ambitions for the southwest but that they were looking to the west from Utah to the ocean for future expansion. Anything to the south of that, they would stay away from.

Donley went over to the wall map and drew a line from the southern border of Utah west to the water and, looking at Stuart, said, "It's a deal. We have some interests that may extend a bit above that line, here and there, depending upon the people living in those areas, but that should not be a problem. We can iron out the exact line in the future."

Stuart looked at the line which appeared to bisect San Francisco and stated that his people needed the seaport and consequently considered that city to be in their area of interest. Donley thought for a moment but in view of his immediate need, conceded the California city to Stuart. The Hispanics had sufficient seaports in southern California and could do quite well without San Francisco.

Having accomplished a great deal in their meeting, the two men relaxed, had a drink and engaged in small talk while Frick readied the aircraft for the trip back. Stuart assured Donley that barring mechanical problems the first transport of ground to air missiles would arrive the following evening. Frick had been locating other aircraft in the Confederation area and had a number of them serviced and available to haul the materials needed by Donley's forces. Stuart would also send instructors along with the shipment to train personnel in handling and operating the sophisticated equipment. Names of contact personnel were traded for the implementation of the other aspects of the agreements between the two men and Stuart and Donley then parted on very friendly terms. It had been a very successful mission from Stuart's point of view and as he relaxed in the warmth of the cockpit, the monotonous hum of the engine soon put him fast asleep. It seemed that he had just gotten in the plane when Frick woke him up to prepare for the landing back at the now lighted strip in the Valley.

# Chapter Thirty-Seven

Stuart was met at the strip by Parker, Sarah, Thomas and Anders. They all returned to the conference room in the new administration building while Stuart briefed them on his meeting with Donley. They were all pleased with how the discussion had progressed and then Stuart laid out to them his further discussions regarding territorial expansion. When he took the ink marker and ran it across the wall map and circled all states to the north and west of the southern border of Utah to the ocean line, they all sat in amazement at what he had been able to accomplish. Territorial expansion had not been a hot topic among the Valley administrators, but it had been a matter of some interest in the minds of all. They all knew that for their continued security and economic well being, they would have to have access to the ocean ports and the resources available in regions to the west and north. Stuart had accomplished a coup that went well beyond their most favorable expectations.

Having entered into this agreement with Donley, it now became important for them to solidify their gains. If they made no moves to encompass the new territories, they would in time lose the benefit of the verbal agreement with the only other major power in the west. This same thought crossed the minds of the three as they listened to Stuart go over the agreement with Donley. All three posed the same question almost simultaneously. "How do you propose we go about this?"

Stuart had been thinking about this for some time and eagerly responded to their question. "We now have an informal understanding with four northwestern states and some areas beyond. Obviously we have to immediately begin to formalize this agreement and create a functioning government that effectively controls this area. We have to vastly increase our defense force from the people living in this area so that we can withstand any attacks from the FSP or others. We are next on the calendar as far as the FSP is concerned. Make no mistake about that. We have no time to waste. We must convince our new associates of this fact as well as the parties in Utah and Wyoming. At the same time we have to begin expanding our area of interest out to the west to encompass Nevada, northern California, Oregon and Washington. We already have interested parties in those territories expressing interest in our organization. We can feed on those groups and move out to other groups bringing them into the network. Robert, that is an area where we need your services. Sarah, that is where you are most effective with your organization. This is a tremendous task that we face and we must waste no time in carrying it out. We have to prioritize our resources to accomplish this purpose. It is not something that we can put off for the distant future."

Matt Parker broke the silence that followed. "What sort of a timetable do you have in mind for this?"

Stuart thought for a moment before responding. "That may depend upon a number of factors that we do not control such as what the FSP may have in store for this region. If we continue on our present track, with the success that we've been having thus far, I would hope to have a united Confederation representing all of the states in the circle I just drew operating within less than five years. These people across the country are thirsting for stability, protection and an improved standard of living. That has to be the message that we send to them. We must get an operating radio station functioning within the next month or two that will provide reception over the entire land area we are talking about. We should be spreading our message of hope and freedom to every person out there and then we must deliver the goods. The sooner the better. We have to also be aware that the FSP may try to undercut us in this task. They are already operating powerful radio stations that send their messages out across the country. They are offering virtually the same thing. The only difference is that once they take over an area, the residents find themselves virtually enslaved to the former bureaucratic masters who ran this country into the ground." As the meeting ended, the four went their separate ways deep in thought over the events that had occurred and the changes they would be facing in the not too distant future.

In the past year or two, Stuart had been propelled to the forefront in the management and administration of Valley politics. Anders favored the increased responsibilities for Stuart and took an active role in seeing to it that Stuart became the recognized leader in the Valley. Anders was getting on in years and was quite content to concentrate his activities on the task that he knew best and that was local government management. Anders oversaw the day to day functioning of the community of Goodland and also assisted, when asked, with respect to the same tasks with respect to Riverton and the Valley. He had no personal ambitions to move up higher in Valley government and absolutely no interest in anything outside of the Valley. Stuart on the other hand, since having a taste of the leadership role, first in Goodland and now as the preeminent political figure in the Valley, was fitting quite comfortably into his new position. He had for some time been envisioning an expanded area of influence that extended well beyond the four state area that was just now beginning to take form as a unified organization. He could see the day when the entire northwest was united under an umbrella organization with its own defense force in a stable, developing society with a healthy economy.

As he thought about the structure of the new government that he envisioned, he became more and more certain as time passed that a strong central government form was essential particularly in these perilous times. He knew that it would be difficult to achieve that goal in view of the universal dislike of people across the country for any form of organized government. That was part of the residue the former national government left following the collapse. The Confederation of the four states was taking shape at this time primarily due to the overwhelming need of the residents for food, shelter and protection. Stuart knew that when those needs were met, it would become much more difficult to obtain the cooperation of these people for the many tasks that lay ahead.

Consequently, Stuart reasoned that massive organization must precede or coincide with responding to their needs. Expecting the mass of the population to respond to rational arguments once they were well fed, housed and protected was a naive concept. As he imagined all of the various possibilities that the future held in store for him and those around him, he became more and more convinced that time was of the essence. He knew that there would be roadblocks placed in his way by well meaning people, but he would have to convince the majority of the wisdom of his intentions and in the end, if he were successful, he would have the support of virtually everyone.

In his few spare moments, Stuart thought about how to achieve his goals. He had now concluded that without reservation, he was going to be the person making the difficult decisions in the new Confederation that he envisioned. He knew he had the vision to create the new society to replace the United States of America in the west and he would not make the same mistakes others had made that led to the downfall of that political system. Parker, Anders and Sarah were all talented associates but Robert Thomas held beliefs regarding effective government quite similar to Stuart's. Neither he nor Thomas was overly impressed by the benefits of a democratic system. He could use Thomas' talents in gaining first the cooperation of the western populations and later governmental control of their territories. That would have to be done carefully but he knew it could be done.

As Stuart's concepts of a unified government structure whirled around in his head, particularly after his visit to Denver and his discussions with Donley, he began laying out his plans to make it all come true. He had to first formalize the very sketchy structure of the four state Confederation. He wanted to make that a success as that would be the drawing card for the states to the west and north. The people living in those states had to see that he and his organization were capable of doing the job. The job being to provide food, housing and protection to the vast majority of the people living in those areas that were presently living on scarce rations, in unheated shelters and fearing for their very lives from assaults by renegades. Although Stuart was the President of the Council of Seven, he did not feel comfortable in pursuing his ambitious goals through that governmental structure. He had always considered it somewhat of a window dressing for the real leadership group in the Valley that consisted of himself, Sarah, Perry, Robert Thomas and a few others. He would look to this group to work with him in moving his plans ahead. With that in mind, he set up a meeting with Parker, Sarah, Perry and Robert Thomas to expedite organization of the Confederation and to begin gathering information for expansion to the west.

The five sat down around the table in the conference room shortly after Stuart's return from the Denver trip. After they were all seated, Stuart explained his fears that the FSP would be moving on them within the not too distant future, depending upon what happened down in the Denver area. He explained to the others that he and Perry had detailed a cadre of tactics instructors to assist and train Donley's men in defensive tactics and also in the use of the sophisticated equipment that Frick had been hauling down to Denver in his planes.

Stuart was of the opinion that whether the FSP was successful or not in its attempts to overrun the Denver, Colorado Springs area was of little or no consequence with respect to FSP plans for Utah, Wyoming, and Montana. They would be coming this way whether they were successful in Colorado or not. "We will either be a follow-on or alternative target. A target in either event." He then went on to explain how imperative it was that they formalize the organization of the four states into a Confederation. He expounded on the need for a strong central government that could react quickly to emergencies and that could dictate policy and speak on behalf of all residents of the four states so that there could be effective negotiations with other groups throughout the country. Sarah agreed that formal organization was a necessity but stated that they needed a formal charter of organization that all would agree with and at this point in time, such a charter did not exist. Stuart agreed. They needed to draft a proposed charter, schedule a conference of representatives from the four state area and get the charter adopted.

At the same time, two other campaigns had to be carried out to guarantee the success of formalizing the conference. The other four at the table leaned forward, intently interested in what Stuart was considering that would guarantee the desired result of a solidly unified four state Confederation. "Perry, you must begin now to organize a four state defense force. Sarah, can provide you with the names of the principals in the larger communities and the people who run their security forces. Utilize those people. Make them part of the operation and bring them all together under a unified force with the operations control center right here in your headquarters. We will need an effective fighting force on a much larger scale than we have here in the Valley and unless all of those people are organized, we don't stand a chance against the FSP. Perry, get Barnes and the others involved in weapons manufacturing and development rolling so that they will be ready when the time comes. Anything you need to accomplish that purpose, let me know and I will see to it that you receive it." Perry's eyes widened as he absorbed the import of Stuart's words. He had always harbored ambitions that went well beyond the tasks assigned to him thus far and he was not only surprised at the extent of the responsibility assigned to him, but he was extremely pleased as well. Visions of being the military commander of all western forces flashed before his eyes.

Perry began to speak, but Stuart raised his hands signaling for him to wait. Stuart went on. "Mac, you are the super salesman of this effort. You control the purse strings of the economy now functioning in the four state area. You have the keys to the warehouses where scarce food stuffs and hard goods are stored. If we are having any problems in any areas of the region where people are not cooperating in our effort to organize the Confederation, we will expect you to respond accordingly. We face a couple of problem areas that are going to have to be handled more carefully. They are the Mormons in Utah and Hollywood in Wyoming. We will organize without them if they do not choose to join up. Hollywood may well participate because they are not as self sufficient as the Mormons. In time, if we are successful in what we are trying to do, they will have to come into the group because we will have all the marbles. Regardless, Sarah and I will draft the charter and we will have it ready within the next week. That is how fast I want to get rolling on this business. We will call a conference for two weeks from tomorrow that will take place right here. There will be some hold outs who will not participate and we can deal with them later after we have the organization set up. We are never going to achieve one hundred percent support, but I will settle for ninety nine. One more thing. This conversation is confidential. Matt Parker and I will deal with notice to the Council of Seven. I still have to make my report to them regarding my meeting with Donley. I am sure that Matt and I can convince them of how critical it is to expedite the organization of the Confederation, particularly if I expand on the FSP assaults on Donley's forces."

The Council of Seven meeting was scheduled for the evening following Stuart's meeting with Sarah and the others. All of the members were present, including Irene Covington, and they were all eager to hear about Stuart's meeting with the Hispanic leader. After preliminary matters were covered, Stuart gave his report on what had taken place in his meeting with Donley. He emphasized the frequency and severity of the assaults on the eastern suburbs of Denver by the FSP patrols and the severe losses experienced by Donley's men in repelling the attacks. He also explained that certain defensive materials as well as a small cadre of instructors had been sent to the Denver area for the purpose of providing support for Hispanic troops.

He downplayed the agreement that he had entered into with Donley regarding their respective territorial interest areas. He thought it better to lay out his thoughts on expansion west for a later time. Stuart dwelt at length on the movements of FSP forces in the west, including complaints received from the Wyoming settlements of insurgents operating in their area. He did not provide the information that he had been given by the Hollywood settlement that the insurgents were believed to be members of

Donley's forces and not FSP He needed to raise the level of concern of the Council members for the threat from the FSP in order to get their consent for his intentions with respect to the organization of the Confederation. He did not like to be two faced with people that he respected very much, but he knew that if organization of the Confederation was delayed until the FSP was knocking at the door, it would be too late.

Sarah listened passively to Stuart's presentation but could not suppress a smile at his baiting the members to ask him for a solution. She was beginning to admire his newfound ability to guide the local populace into pushing him in the direction of his intended goals. He went on, "We have to organize and we have to mobilize. Not only in the Valley because that would not be enough. We have to convince our associates throughout the west that we need to come together and combine our efforts so that we can repel these bandits when they choose to make their strike. We have to do that now. Not next week or next month. That could be too late."

All of the members with the exception of Sarah and Irene Covington were listening intently to Stuart's words. Sarah knew where all of this was headed but Irene did not. Irene was wondering just what Stuart was up to and what his real intentions were, particularly with respect to the proposed organization. She had, like everyone else, been aware of the increased contacts with the residents of the surrounding states and the commercial agreements which were bringing all of these people closer together in an informal relationship. Irene had also considered the possibility that at some time in the future, there might be an agreement of sorts among at least the four states most frequently mentioned. But, this talk from Stuart came as a surprise to her. His passion for repelling a threat which had not yet shown itself anywhere on their borders seemed a bit out of context, although she was aware that she was not as privy to security information as she would like to be. She had some doubts as to what was going on, but she could not quite put her finger on it. She also noticed that Sarah had been sitting through the presentation quite impassively, which was not her style when matters of import were being discussed.

As she thought about what was transpiring, Stuart was going on with his intention to bring their neighbors together for a conference and hopefully to arrive at an agreement to formalize their relationship. "We need to be able to act as a unit to handle whatever threats are presented to us by our very aggressive eastern neighbors. We need to convince our new friends of this need and convince them that their very future lies in our ability to act as a group, quickly and effectively and furthermore to be able to enter into economic agreements with other neighbors who wish us no ill."

As Stuart went on, it became apparent to Irene that Stuart obviously had in mind a larger, structured form of government than presently existed in the valley. This became more and more apparent as he continued to talk of the need for effective leadership of the peace loving people of the four state region. Stuart was not simply referring to some sort of consensus among pockets of residents spread throughout the region. He was clearly laying out the need for an organization that would literally run the show for all of the people living in the four state region.

Finally Irene could hold herself back no longer. "Pardon me, Stuart, but you speak of bringing the people of the four state region together under some sort of an umbrella organization. Just what sort of structure have you been thinking about that would serve this purpose?"

Stuart knew he would have trouble with Irene and was expecting some form of reaction from her. He looked directly at her and responded as if he actually welcomed her question. "Irene, we need a charter that establishes a representative government for the four state region. They are already looking to us for leadership in trade matters as well as defensive support. We need to move now to formalize a relationship with these people while they continue to look up to us for guidance. We are presently their acting government. We must take the steps to become the center of government for these four states in substance and form, not only for their own good but for ours as well. Now, Irene, you are probably wondering what sort of government I am thinking about. I will tell you that I believe we need a fairly strong central government in order to accomplish what needs to be done."

Stuart was speaking to Irene as to what "his" intentions were. He emphasized what "he" intended in the proposed government expressly for the purpose of letting Irene know that "he" was going to run that show and she might as well understand that from the opening gun. Irene questioned Stuart as to whether such a proposed draft of the articles of Confederation had been drafted and if so, when could the Council members see it. Stuart responded that he and Sarah were in the process of drafting the charter at that time and when it was completed it would be distributed to all for review and comment. His answer made it clear that Stuart did not intend to submit it to the Council for approval before sending it out to the four state regions prior to the conference. No one other than Irene appeared to take offense at that as Stuart was held in the highest esteem by most everyone in the Valley and they thoroughly trusted his judgment on such matters.

During the days preceding the announced four state convention, Stuart was extremely busy preparing for the event and persuading some of those reluctant to make the journey that the times necessitated their personal sacrifices. Sarah and her communications staff were working virtually around the clock sending out messages and carrying out a publicity campaign for the forthcoming meeting. Dispatches were sent out hourly, particularly to those uncommitted regarding the battle reports coming out of Colorado. The FSP was increasing their activities in the Denver and Colorado Springs area, but nowhere near the level that was being reported from the Valley Command Post. Sarah had some misgivings about sending out the exaggerated reports, but Stuart convinced her that a certain amount of puffing was justified if it produced the desired result of a solid Confederation. He harkened back to the days of World War II when President Roosevelt used far more puffery to get the whole hearted support of the American people behind the war effort. No one held that against him. Sarah thought about that for a moment and said, "Well, I suppose you are right." She had more problems with his request to send the same reports to the Valley newspaper, but in the end acquiesced.

A week or so before the meeting, when Perry's instructors were producing results for Louis Donley's Hispanic forces in the Denver area, Stuart had Sarah set up a meeting by radio between Donley and himself. When the Hispanic leader was connected to the secure radio frequency, Stuart expressed his hope that the support that had been sent was producing the desired results. Donley responded enthusiastically that their losses had been cut drastically by reason of their new found ability to defend against the aerial assaults. Stuart told him that he was pleased and to let him know if he needed more help.

Stuart and Sarah had also been busy drafting up the wording of the charter that they had to transmit to the attendees at least five days prior to the meeting in order to give the recipients time to review the document and travel to the conference center in the Valley. Protected routes of travel were also sent out to the participants where Barnes had stationed security forces to safeguard the travelers. Likewise, all operable trucks in the Valley suitable for the purpose were sent out to preplanned pickup stations to provide rides for those desiring transportation to the meeting. Stuart wanted everything to go as smoothly as possible as he was aware that if the conference was well managed, it would make a significant difference with respect to how the attendees voted on the crucial charter issue. As a last resort, he had a very private conversation with Robert Thomas and gave him a list of names of prominent holdouts that Stuart demanded Thomas produce at the meeting.

Stuart's last instructions to Thomas before he boarded Frick's plane for the face to face visits with the men on the list was, "I don't care how you do it, just make damn sure they are here and they are in the right mood."

Thomas only smiled and said, "Plan on it. They will be here and they will support the program." This sort of assignment was what Thomas relished. He had lived most of his life playing hardball and he had missed it over the past few years. Maybe as he liked to say, "Times were a changing."

In drafting the proposed charter, Stuart had to resolve some basic conflicts. He wanted to end up with a form of government that had the necessary power to do what had to be done. On the other hand, he was fully aware that there were going to be many at the conference, if not a majority, that did not want to transfer power over their daily lives to a central authority. He concluded that he was going to have to gamble that, by way of persuasion, reasoning or even the application of pressure of one sort or another, he was going to get them to sign on to his plan.

There was no sense in presenting them with a document that they would immediately agree to because that would not serve the purpose that he had in mind. Stuart firmly believed that their survival in the next few years depended upon a form of government that could act quickly and decisively in response to both internal and external challenges. That required a charter that has some teeth in it.

His confidence in the wisdom of people in general and their ability to handle the personal responsibilities that a true democracy entails had diminished after years of observing the lack of interest people had in such matters. He was beginning to believe that if you provided the majority of them three meals a day, a warm bed to sleep in and a comfortable pair of shoes, they would do what you wanted them to do. Not all of them were like Irene Covington or Sarah or Anders, or for that matter, himself who cherished personal freedom above all else. Stuart's beliefs in government had evolved from pursuing a goal of pure democracy to something between a very limited democracy and a somewhat benevolent autocratic rule. He continued to believe that people should be provided input into the decisions that affected their daily lives but that right or privilege should have a price tag on it. Not everyone that could pull the voting machine handle should have the unlimited right to pull it. They had to first demonstrate a qualification which he had not yet defined in his own mind. It was this confusion that was leading him to take steps that he would not have taken in the past to achieve the goals that he had set forth.

His beliefs in governance had now evolved to a point where it was now justified to use some subterfuge to accomplish what in the end would be good for the community. A few years before, he would not have done that. It did bother him somewhat to exaggerate reports of FSP activities but he suppressed the minor discomfort it caused by concentrating on the good effects of his tactics which were to expedite the unification of the west. Unless the people were brought together under a well led, umbrella organization, they were doomed. How that was accomplished, he reasoned, was far less important than the good that would result. He had wanted to talk with Anders about all of this but had hesitated because he was still a bit confused as to where these changes were taking him. When he had a better grip on the concepts that he was formulating, he would sit down with his long time friend to get his views.

As he worked on the document with Sarah, he adopted the tried and true, basic, democratic structures that history had proven to be most acceptable to the broad mass of people in most civilized societies, the bicameral legislature with a fairly strong executive department. He made a few changes that caught the attention of Sarah. The chief executive, or president, was elected by the legislature and the first legislature would consist of those attending the conference. Stuart explained that the legislative election of the president was, in fact, the forerunner of popular elections in the former national government. The legislature, in turn would serve for a period of five years and then be reelected by the general qualified electors in the population. These for the moment were undefined.

Under the proposal, the president was to serve as the chief executive officer of the government and further was provided emergency powers to guide the Confederation in times of important national interest. The emergency powers provision had a time limitation of ninety days, but there was no limit on the number of times a year they could be acted upon. The legislature could override the president's activation of emergency powers, but it would take a four fifths vote to do so. Under the Powers provision, the president had sole command of the defense team and all agencies of the executive department without oversight by the legislature.

As Stuart envisioned, if he ran the conference in as successful a fashion as he had in mind, he was virtually guaranteed to be elected president and could serve without interruption for a period of at least five years. By that time, he would either have succeeded with his plans to recreate a northwest national government or he would have failed and he would be forced out of office. He did not consider the latter alternative very likely. He was on a roll and he did not intend to fail. Sarah questioned that the delegates would permit the transfer of such broad powers to the president under the proposed charter. Stuart agreed that it was going to be a hard sell, but it was worth the try. He had a few other thoughts in mind that might assist in getting the delegates to sign on the dotted line.

The day before the scheduled conference, Robert Thomas returned to the Valley and reported to Stuart regarding his contacts with conference holdouts. He had great success with everyone on the list other than the Idaho militia groups who not only had no interest in attending, but were generally hostile to Thomas while he was visiting their areas. He could report that there did not appear to be any collusion between the five or six separate groups that he contacted which was a good sign for future negotiations. As Thomas said, "They just wanted to be left alone." He had also observed that they appeared to be very well armed and their encampments were well protected and security in the area seemed to be very tight. Thomas also observed that they were very self sufficient in their restricted communities with some farming operations in the immediate vicinity and he also noticed what appeared to be machine shops in the headquarters areas that were busily engaged in turning out metal products of one type or another. He could not determine exactly what they were producing. Their housing areas were well kept and the people that he saw were polite but not overly friendly. The staff was distinctly not friendly to his offers of assistance if they joined the Confederation.

When Thomas completed his report to Sarah, Stuart and Ross Perry, Stuart only commented, "We'll talk with them further down the road." He then directed his attention to the forthcoming conference and matters that he wanted their assistance on to make it a success. He directed Thomas to continue his work of ensuring the cooperation and specifically the votes of representatives from the outlying areas. He tasked Sarah to maintain an ongoing tally of the expected voting outcome so that Robert and others managing the conference could deal with damage control on a timely basis. As for Perry, Stuart told him to wait as he dismissed the others from the meeting. When they were alone, Stuart told him that he wanted the conference hall packed with as many supporters of Stuart's program as he could squeeze into the hall. He wanted them sprinkled around the hall to generate enthusiastic applause during Stuart's speech, particularly when it dealt with Confederation concepts. Perry assured him that it would be the most enthusiastic audience that he had ever spoken in front of.

When Perry had gone, Stuart called Barnes in to make sure that all arrangements for the care and comfort of the attendees was taken care of. He wanted to show the conferees the biggest bash that they had seen since the collapse of the nation. Many of those attending were undoubtedly former bureaucrats acting at the local, state and, in some cases, national level and they were, for the most part, familiar with well run, comfortable, government conferences. Stuart wanted them to know that he was quite capable of filling any shoes that they might be familiar with.

Stuart had a long standing low regard for bureaucrats, regardless of what level of government they were functioning at, and he was going to have to suppress that in order for the conference to be a success.

Once he had the charter approved, he could then deal with them in the language they understood. A little power to this one and a little material well being to that one and he could control the entire lot of them. That was why he was not too concerned with getting his way once the structure of the charter was established. He had been careful to maneuver and select the representative list from that vast body of people in communities of any size who had devoted their lives to directing the lives of others. For the most part, they were people without professions, trades or skills other than what might be related to government operations. Almost without exception, Stuart figured, they were people with goals limited to increasing the size of their office staff or a larger share of the available resources by way of budgetary allowances or material goods. People like that were easily manipulated. They were prone to compromise.

The ones that he would have to concern himself about were those with philosophical beliefs because they seldom compromised and could be a real thorn in his side. If he ran into them and their beliefs were counter to his, he would have to undercut their authority, bypass them or in some fashion neutralize their opposition. He would deal with that problem as and when it surfaced.

As the day of the conference drew nearer and attendees began to arrive in Riverton, Stuart's confidence was increasing. Sarah was reporting fairly broad support for the Confederation concept but was not quite as optimistic with respect to support for the charter itself. As Stuart had anticipated, there was a general reluctance on the part of most attendees to give up their independence. They wanted the benefits of Confederation, but they did not want to make the sacrifices that were necessary. He would have to deal with that in his speech and in the arm twisting before the vote. He planned to present the charter for approval shortly after the speech while the attendees were relaxing after the hearty dinner and ample supplies of wine. He wanted to get them while they were still impressed with the way the conference was being handled and at the same time, not make too much of a big deal over the long term effects of signing the charter on behalf of their constituents. In his speech, he would try to give the impression that signing the charter was the less important feature of the conference when compared to the various committee meetings that would follow in the days after the dinner.

Copies of the charter had been distributed to the new local newspaper and to those active in Valley government. Copies were also posted on the bulletin boards located throughout the length of the Valley for all residents to read. The reaction of the average resident in the Valley was that it didn't seem to be anything particularly different from the present administration and most everyone was quite content with the way things had gone, so, in general, it was basically a non-issue. As for the Council of Seven, there was some comment that they should have had more of a role in the preparation of the charter but Stuart handled that with an explanation that most of the Confederation activities thus far had been handled out of the old Association and the Council had enough to do in handling Valley matters without taking on the added duties inherent in organization of the Confederation. This seemed to satisfy all except for Irene Covington who saw in the charter a clear attempt by Stuart, and those working with him, to propel themselves to a much higher level of government to the exclusion of those active in Valley administrative matters. She had no problem with what appeared to be an ambitious move on Stuart's part, but she saw no one of her political standing moving to the Confederation level that would dampen the conservative thinking of Stuart and those around him. She had high regard for Sarah, but she also was aware that Sarah held many philosophical opinions in common with Stuart. Not quite as conservative as Stuart but too close for Irene's comfort.

There was one part of Stuart's master plan that was vulnerable to attack from Irene and that was the issue of who were the representatives in the Confederation from the Valley. Stuart had planned on handling that matter himself and did not select anyone from Riverton, outlying ranch lands or Goodland to participate as representatives in the new assembly. That was a mistake on Stuart's part because when Irene made an issue of the lack of representation at the Council of Seven meeting, she had no difficulty in convincing the Council members that the Valley deserved the same right of representation as any other population group in the four state area. Furthermore, she did such a fine job of convincing the other members of the need for representation that they appointed her and one of the ranchers, Frank Potter to be the Valley representatives. Potter was conservative in his view of government in that he believed in a strong executive but was a 'died in the wool' individualist who was of the opinion that he did not need anyone to tell him how to live his life. In some respects his beliefs were contradictory, but to him it all made sense. Stuart was not present at the Council meeting when the issue was discussed and was informed of the

Council action appointing the two on the following day. He was furious at the thought that Irene would be a participant but realized that it was too late to turn back the clock and appoint others to the post. He had been so busy organizing the meeting, drafting the charter and preparing for the Conference that he had neglected his own back yard. He resigned himself to the fact that he would have to live with this mistake.

As soon as Irene had been given the credentials to represent the Valley at the Conference, she immediately began moving about the conferees who were already arriving at the conference center. Room assignments, schedules and conference materials were being passed out in the arrival building and a reception area had been set up for the conferees to pass their time before and during the scheduled events. This was an excellent place for Irene to spend her time and meet the attendees as they came to the center. Whenever she could, she would gather together small groups of representatives and discuss various aspects of the charter. She had a number of complaints concerning the structure of the document and, in particular, she was of the opinion that far too much power was granted to the executive department and specifically to the president.

The people that she spoke with listened attentively as she pointed out the various clauses that transferred power from the legislative body to the executive and silently considered her suggestions for rewording the charter to ensure that the president's authority was subject to oversight.

Robert Thomas and his staff were very busy doing their best to influence the outcome of major voting issues and, in particular, the vote for the adoption of the charter. Thomas' argument for support of the charter as written was very persuasive; particularly when he made it clear to whomever he was discussing the issue that their cooperation would bode well with respect to their future dealings with the proposed administration. Robert Thomas was very effective in his talks with the delegates. He was not overbearing and certainly not threatening but at the conclusion of his contact, it was very clear to the listener that their cooperation would not only be appreciated, it would eventually be rewarded.

Robert Thomas shared Stuart's opinion of the majority of the delegates and the two men, in these last days before the meeting, discussed the general makeup of those in attendance. They all shared the bureaucrat's common belief, you scratch my back and I'll scratch yours. The two men found it amusing as they discussed various ways of convincing this or that delegate to support their cause. Thomas, in particular, took delight in these conversations as he had always been an outsider, in constant conflict with government agencies right up to the final days before the collapse. He harbored a deep seated hatred for what he viewed as their two faced natures, pretending to act for the common good of the represented people while taking money or other benefits from people who needed to have a favor done for them. That continued to be their primary weakness and Stuart intended to use that against them to gain the power that he believed he needed to do what had to be done. Thomas did not discuss this with anyone other than Stuart as he questioned that the others would understand that the times dictated forceful actions.

Stuart was aware of what Irene was up to and counseled Thomas to pay particular attention to those who appeared to be siding with her arguments. He could not stop her from meeting with the other delegates and in his meetings with her, he made only joking references to her attempts to change the charter as drafted. He, in fact, wished her well and suggested that this is what makes a democracy work. Irene was a bit baffled by his attitude and could not quite make out how he really felt about what she was doing but she was too busy with her conversion efforts to worry about it. She was aware that Robert Thomas, and others working with him, were busy conversing with the delegates but she could never get close enough to hear what was being said. She did notice a certain coldness on the part of those that she believed she had won over to her side after they spoke with Thomas and she concluded that whatever he was saying was having some sort of an effect.

The evening of the opening of the conference, virtually all of those that had been invited to attend as delegates were present. There were over two hundred attendees and all were busily involved in conversations with one another over Confederation proposals, charter provisions or other issues. Barnes had done a great job in preparing the banquet hall for the opening speech by Stuart. The room was laid out in three separate levels. The main floor, where the delegates and guests would be seated around fifty separate dining tables, occupying most of the floor space. Ample room was left at all tables for Perry's people to sit. In the front of the hall, there was an elevated section where the new Confederation organizers were seated. Ornate chairs for these dignitaries all faced the assembled delegates. Rising above the center of the leadership section was a magnificently carved wooden podium for the speaker. The backdrop of curtains and highlighting of the podium were very impressive and with the lowering of house lights created an almost mystical focus on the person occupying the dais. Flanked on either side of the leadership section would be twenty of Perry's finest troops wearing the new formal dress black uniform with polished leather boots. Behind them, Thomas had installed a row of brilliantly colored flags of the WestPac Confederation, the blue sword, surrounded by a red wreath in a field of green. Stuart had laid out the entire design for the interior of the hall with the sole thought in mind that he wanted every single delegate in the room to know who was in charge.

As for who would occupy the leadership section besides himself, Stuart had handpicked the people that would fill those chairs: Sarah, Ross Perry, Robert Thomas, Barnes, Jack Nix, Matt Parker and Anders. All were formally attired per Stuart's instructions and were advised to assume a very businesslike appearance at all times. Parker and Anders had been added purely as a matter of courtesy in view of their prior contributions to the Valley and the Association.

The role of Anders and Parker in the expanding government, particularly with respect to the Confederation was virtually nil. The focus of Anders' attention remained with the original community of Goodland where he continued to serve in a mayoral capacity. He was quite willing to turn over all vestiges of authority to Stuart as he knew that the tasks that lay ahead called for a much younger man than himself.

Shortly after the proposed charter had been distributed in the Valley on the bulletin boards and a copy had been sent to the newspaper for publication, articles began to appear in the paper criticizing certain clauses in the charter. The editor of the paper was known to be a confidant of Irene Covington and, like most of the people engaged in that profession, a person of liberal views. The editor was particularly concerned with the extensive grant of power to the president and this was the core value of the proposed charter as far as Stuart was concerned.

After Stuart had read the first two articles that were published, he called Robert Thomas into his office. Stuart had smelled trouble with the newspaper from the day of its inception but there was little he could do to stop it as the community was always hungry for news. Furthermore, he could not censor the publication. He did not have the authority to do so and if he tried, he would create a hailstorm of controversy. There were other ways to deal with the editor to make him more amenable to the changes that Stuart sought that might work. He suggested to Thomas that he call on the editor and try to make him see the good that could come to everyone if the charter was adopted by the representatives from the four states.

The tenuous political situation of the country demanded strong countermeasures and when the country was stabilized, then more power could be returned to the people. Stuart suggested to Thomas that he let the editor know that if he was more sympathetic to the goals as the Administration saw them, his patience and understanding would be rewarded. As a final plum, Thomas was to let him know that a Confederation wide radio station was in the works and he could be a significant part of that project. In reality, Stuart had no intention of letting the publisher or anyone else participate in the editorial content of that proposal. He intended to use that to disseminate his message once the Confederation was established. There were a few other newspapers now operating around the four state region, but thus far none of the others had taken a stand for or against the charter. Stuart had been careful not to send them a copy which only went to the selected delegate list.

Thomas did make contact with the editor using as a ruse the difficulty that he, Thomas, was having in obtaining the printers ink needed by the publisher. Robert Thomas informed the editor that the available supplies were being grabbed up by others closer to the source and that he was having an increasingly difficult time in being able to meet the requirements of the Valley publisher. This was of great concern to the editor who dropped what he was doing and cordially invited Thomas to join him in his office so that they could discuss the matter further. There had been problems in the past so this subject was not new to either man. Thomas explained how he was trying to work tradeoffs on other scarce commodities so that he could take care of the special needs of his friend, the editor. For this the editor was extremely thankful.

When Thomas figured that he had the hook securely buried, he brought up the subject of the articles critical of the proposed charter. The editor sat back in his chair with a guilty look on his face as Thomas laid out the many effects of his criticism, including the possibility that it made his obtaining the scarce printers ink even more difficult. Thomas spoke to the editor, not on behalf of Stuart and the Administration, but, as he said, from his own beliefs that the charter was the best thing for the future peace and development of all people in the region. "True it gave a wide grant of power to the president, but we all know who that would be, it would be Stuart and who could criticize what he was trying to do for everyone in the Valley and the four state region."

The editor listened passively, without comment, as Thomas went on with the plans that Stuart had for bringing stability back to the region and improving the quality of life for all of the people. As a final comment, he mentioned the possibility of the radio station which the engineers were currently working on. He did not specifically state that the editor would be brought in on the project, but he dangled the thought out there that, "They would be needing people with knowledge of journalism." By the time the conversation ended, Robert Thomas was fairly confident that the editor was now in their camp, at least for the time being.

On the day of the conference, Stuart had a final staff meeting with the key people in his inner circle to make last minute plans for the evening banquet and introductory speeches. He wanted to ensure that the program would succeed in gaining the necessary support to accomplish two essential objectives. The first to propel him to the top spot in the administration of the Confederation. He assumed at this point that creation of the Confederation was 'a given'. Sarah had kept him informed daily of the positions of the various delegates on that matter. The second essential objective that was key to his plan to create a strong central government for the Confederation was the adoption of the charter. This was a tougher issue as many of the delegates present were questioning whether or not they should surrender their autonomy to an organization that, while impressive in what they were doing, was still somewhat of an unknown entity. They would also have to return home to their own communities and convince them that what they had voted for was in their best interests.

Stuart figured that he would have to target the charter as the primary goal and if he was successful in getting that passed, the presidency would fall in place.

In the meeting, he directed Sarah's efforts to keeping him informed on an hourly basis as to the status of the charter issue. Robert Thomas had redoubled his efforts to convince those delegates that were on the fence on the issue to come over to their side. There were a number of delegates firmly against adoption of the charter and time was not wasted on them but they were not ignored either, as Stuart did not want them to leave the Confederation if the charter was adopted. He assigned some of his people to meet, on an individual basis, with these people to assure them that virtually all aspects of their autonomy would be respected and that the impositions on their lives would be minimal. Furthermore, what they would gain in trade agreements, political and economic stability would dwarf any negatives.

As people were filing into the Assembly Hall for the dinner and speeches, Stuart received a last minute briefing from Sarah. The charter issue appeared to be evenly split among the delegates, with a slight majority in favor of adoption, but even that was questionable. As they all took their seats, there was loud chatter filling the hall as they continued to argue the pros and cons of various aspects of the Confederation and charter proposals. Perry had arranged for musicians to play as the dinner guests continued their lively conversation and waiters moved through the hall filling and refilling wine glasses with scarce supplies obtained by Thomas in his travels through the west.

As Stuart looked through the curtain through which he would enter the hall, he noted the smiles on the faces of the delegates and their continual back slapping which reminded him of the well fed bureaucratic opportunists that he had observed at political rallies in the past. He had a great dislike for these people, but right now he needed their assistance and he was going to do his utmost to get it. He also noted Perry's men sprinkled throughout the hall, appearing to all in attendance as just other unknown delegates from some other part of the country. He also observed Irene Covington, while not engaged in conversation, was studying the makeup of the audience and stopping her scan occasionally as she homed in on one of Perry's men in the crowd. She could put two and two together and he would hear about this tomorrow.

The delegates were given ample time to enjoy the classical music flowing from the orchestra that Perry had assembled for this purpose and also to enjoy quantities of scarce wine that seemed to flow endlessly from carafes filled and refilled by the waiters. The dinner that followed was without doubt the finest any of the delegates had experienced in years. A true western game dinner with wild fowl, elk and deer with broiled trout for those with a milder appetite. Throughout the dinner, the wine continued to flow so that by the time plates had been scraped clean the laughter mixed with loud conversation created a deafening noise throughout the building. Stuart nodded to Robert Thomas who gave the cue to the orchestra leader that it was time.

# Chapter Thirty-Eight

The classical music ceased and a gradually increasing drum roll and dimming of the lights told everyone in the room that the program was about to begin. Spotlight beams circled the now darkened room while the drum beat picked up in tempo and as the beams converged simultaneously on the curtain to the side of the stage, out stepped Robert Thomas, resplendent in black tuxedo. Thomas gave a big smile to the now cheering throng and responded to the accolade with both arms raised in a victory symbol which brought out even more cheers and clapping from the now standing crowd. Robert Thomas waved to those in the audience that he could recognize through the glare of the spotlights now bearing down on the podium where he stood waiting for the room to quiet. When it did, he waited for the silence to linger a moment or two, before he shouted, "Is everyone having a good time?" This brought the crowd again to their feet, clapping and stamping their feet as they shouted back that they were having the best time they had enjoyed in years. Again waiting for the noise to die down and again for the silence to linger, Thomas arranged his notes for his introductory remarks. Stuart had selected Thomas to do the introductions as he was the one most of the delegates were familiar with and also because he was the super salesman of the key staff people. He was to be what Stuart considered the "warm up act" for what was to follow.

Thomas began with some inoffensive, humorous comments relating to certain delegates in the crowd which again brought the guests to their feet, clapping and shouting comments at the targets of his humor. He then introduced the guests of honor, Parker, Anders, Sarah, Perry, Barnes and Nix, all people that the delegates had either met or had heard of since the Confederation was first discussed. After the introductions, Thomas took on a serious tone as he went into the history of the Association and their

successful exodus from Florida to the Valley. He spoke glowingly of the
work of Anders, Sarah, Perry and those responsible for the tremendous
organization of the Association and what their efforts had produced, an
outstanding educational system, decent medical care for everyone, food
and clothing for those without, security and protection that was unsurpassed
by any other organization of like size. He then spoke of the one person in
the Association who had the dream of recreating a nation, of rebuilding an
economy that stretched across the land, of bringing educational benefits
to everyone across the country, of providing protection from renegades
and bandits to everyone, whether they lived in metropolitan areas or in
the hidden mountain recesses. As he listed the goals of this yet unnamed
person, the clapping and cheering grew with each accolade and with that he
increased the tempo of his praises so that he was soon shouting them to the
now standing, cheering crowd who knew that he was referring to Stuart.
When he had the crowd to a fever pitch, Robert Thomas turned towards the
curtain at the side of the stage and holding his arm outstretched, raised his
voice, shouting into the microphone to override the thunderous roar from
the delegates, "The man who envisioned this Confederation, our friend,
our leader, Stuart Martin." Amid circling spotlights and a crescendo of
drum beats, spotlights now focused on the curtain behind the podium,
Stuart stepped out, took a step forward and raised his arm in a salute to
the cheering throng. He then began walking towards the podium, amid the
deafening applause, and waving to the delegates but carrying himself with
the restraint befitting the office that he was seeking to hold.

Stuart stood erect at the podium, staring out over the assembled mass
of delegates who were on their feet, loudly cheering him and continuing
their clapping for what seemed an interminable length of time. He was
not smiling. He stood straight and tall with a businesslike appearance.
Turning to gaze at the crowd on his left; maintaining his stern appearance,
then to the right. Finally, he raised his arms signaling for everyone to be
seated so that the program could continue. On cue, Perry's men continued
standing, clapping and cheering, as did the others in the hall, until, one

by one, everyone took their seat. It was a resounding ovation that he had received and now as a hush fell over the audience and the lights were again dimmed except for those illuminating the podium, Stuart maintained his all business pose, looking over the crowd, with one hand on his hip, the other resting on the lectern, wearing the expression of a parent looking down at an errant child. He stepped back and stood a foot or so back from the podium. He kept this aloof attitude until you could hear a pin drop in the hall. He then brought his hand down forcefully on the surface of the lectern with a loud clap which focused the complete attention of everyone on what he was about to say. "There are some who question the need for a Confederation. Some people are willing to accept crime running rampant in their communities, poverty, starvation, lack of medical care, closed schools, and conquest by armed troops intent upon enslaving masses of people." Stuart paused a moment, stepped back, hand on one hip staring angrily at the audience, then again approached the podium as before. "I am not willing to accept that. Nor are any of the honored guests here on the stage with me willing to accept that." Again the applause was deafening. After it subsided, he continued. "I trust that none of you are willing to accept that and that is why you are here tonight." Again, on cue from Perry, his men sitting around the room all rose in unison shouting, "No, we will never accept that." Soon the entire room was again standing and chanting, "No, never again."

After everyone had again quieted down, Stuart went on with his speech explaining his plan for the Confederation, which he now referred to by its title, WestPac. He envisioned WestPac as eventually including all of the western states. Not just the four states that were represented in this assembly. He called out the names of each of the additional states and slapped the lectern with his fist after each name, "Washington." The crowd erupted in screaming and applause. Then "Oregon". The same response. "Nevada... and California, San Francisco to the northern border." The applause and cheering went on for minutes until he again raised his arms to bring quiet. He did not explain what was to happen to the lower part of the State of California. He told the delegates that the first goal of the Confederation was to establish political and economic stability in the original four state region. "Upon adoption of the charter, Defense Team Forces would be moving out among the member states to suppress all criminal elements so that citizens could again walk their streets without fear of attack by lawless individuals or groups. Your wives and daughters will be able to walk to stores, and schools and to visit friends without fear of molestation or assault."

This announcement brought lengthy applause and loud cheering from those assembled. Next, he pointed to Robert Thomas and informed the delegates that Thomas and his economic council were already organizing business interests in the four state region preparing trade agreements among them for the transfer of scarce resources from one area to another. He pointed to Matt Parker and informed the delegates that Parker's grain bins were filled to overflowing with food that would be going out to Confederation members as soon as the charter was signed. That was a hook that Stuart knew would get their attention as virtually everyone in the west was short of adequate food supplies. He then looked back at a beaming Robert Thomas and said, "I have another announcement that should be of considerable interest to all of you. Robert Thomas has succeeded in arranging for large segments of North Dakota, South Dakota and Saskatchewan to join the Confederation. For those of you not too familiar with the geography involved, that area produces more grain crops than virtually any other section of equal size on this continent. In return, we have entered into an agreement guaranteeing the security of those areas."

The delegates were shocked at the announcement which was truly monumental. They had all harbored varying degrees of doubt about the Confederation concept but had shown up at the conference primarily to see what benefits they might obtain from this ambitious group in the Valley of Montana. Seeing the Valley operation in action, enjoying the hospitality afforded them, and witnessing firsthand what the Confederation leaders had in mind for their future, converted them on the spot. After Stuart saw in the glazed eyes of those assembled that he had them where he wanted them, he turned his attention to the sacrifices that all would be required to make in order to turn this dream into a success.

The land of plenty that he envisioned would not come without the hard work of everyone in the Confederation. Not just the delegates present, but all of the citizens back in their respective areas. Crops needed to be planted, factories manned, supplies delivered, markets operated and managed. Economic Council members would be visiting areas and laying out plans to turn dreams into reality. All of these activities required rapid communication systems, transportation resources and above all, a safe and secure environment, be it the work place, the farm, the rail track line or the roadway from one town to another. "Agreements are right now taking shape to meet all of the energy needs that we must fill in order to accomplish our goals: Fuel for our tractors, for our diesel engines, to supply our ever growing aircraft fleet, for our military vehicles. We have made agreements to provide all of our needs for energy for the foreseeable future."

The crowd was on its feet, shouting cheering, stamping their feet in enthusiastic reaction to Stuart's words. "All that precious fuel that is essential and primary in carrying out our objectives. In your meetings commencing tomorrow, we will lay out our proposed Judicial Code of Conduct which needs to be adopted and disseminated among the citizens of the Confederation so that they will know what is expected of them. Renegades striking fear into the people of this Confederation must either change their ways immediately or suffer the consequences."

Again, this produced long and loud cheering among those assembled. That was one problem that all citizens had endured for far too long and was another hook that Stuart knew would provide impetus for the less popular clauses of the proposed charter. All through his speech, Stuart emphasized the seriousness of the business at hand by his somewhat somber demeanor. He did not try to humor his audience, nor did he cater to their sympathies in any way. He was all business and spoke to them as would a teacher to his students. After delivering a statement calling on them to dig deeper into their well of personal sacrifices for the goal of the Confederation, he would stand back from the podium, again with his left hand on his hip and slowly run his gaze over the assembly as if to ask each one in the room if they were man enough to participate in this venture. He would then stride forward to the dais, placing both hands on the lectern, leaning his body forward and, in rapid fire, with firm voice, call upon them for even more sacrifices. The audience was spell bound by the speaker. Even those on the former Association staff had never seen Stuart mesmerize an audience as he was this one. His dedication to this cause had taken over his entire being. He gave every bit of energy that he possessed to his plan for the organization and development of the west. He looked at WestPac as the rebirth of a national entity encompassing the western states and portions of Canada. He knew the people in the communities across that vast land hungered for what he wanted to create and he was the person that was going to deliver it to them.

The final topic of his speech before the assembly dealt with the adoption of the charter. There was a slight tempering of enthusiasm when he brought up the charter and when he noted that, he stepped back from the podium with both hands to his hips and a reproachful look on his face to chastise the errant members who were not totally accepting of the concept. By this time, he had control of virtually everyone in the audience and the look was enough to quiet any comments coming from the dissenters. He went on with his explanation of the need for the charter in a strong, firm voice, leaning forward, hands on the podium, jaw thrust out and sweeping his eyes across the room, first assuring them that he knew they were sophisticated enough politically to understand the need, at this particular time, for centralized authority in the new Confederation government. "After all, what is the best form of government a society can have?" Stuart paused for a moment to let the question sink in. "Is it not the form that delivers the most good in the most efficient fashion?" Shouting at the audience, demanding they agree with him. "Is it not the form that elevates the most qualified people to the top administrative positions based on skill, experience and record of accomplishments rather than how he or she smiles, or how many hands they shake, or babies they kiss? Do you believe that pure democracy is the one and only governmental system for a civilized nation to have?" This in a lowered tone calling for a negative response. Then louder, shouting. "History does not support that assumption. Democracies are the exception and not the rule historically."

"Furthermore, let me ask you to name one that has ever survived. I will tell you that as an ideal, democracy is a beautiful concept, but in reality it contains the seeds of its own destruction. You have all seen that happen at first hand. In order to sustain the democratic system, the masses that support the leadership must be promised more and more benefits, and over time there are no more benefits that can be promised because, by then, everyone knows they can no longer be delivered. Then the masses turn against their leaders as well as those who have provided the goods and services that they had received free of charge for so long. The result is anarchy." A pause, then shouting. "Is that what you want? You should know because that is what you have had since the collapse of the former government. I believe that the answer to what is the finest form of government is not pure democracy but a system that takes the finer points from the democratic concept and merges it with a more executive centered form. Let us think in terms of an autocracy for a moment. For many that term may bring up dreaded images, but ask yourselves why that is? Among the many benefits of an autocracy is that it is the most efficient form of government. Needless delay in resolving problems is avoided. Prompt response in the face of crisis is provided. Other benefits flow but there are deficiencies in an autocratic form of government that a democracy avoids. There is no benefit of counsel provided by a legislative body in a pure autocracy. Furthermore, there is no participation of the electorate in an autocracy which creates a society separated into two groups, the governed and the governors. It may be the most efficient, but it is not a perfect form of government by a long shot. Now, let us look at the proposed charter." Stuart then explained a few of the more significant provisions of the charter and pointed out that their effect was to combine the benefits of a democratic form of government with the efficiencies of the autocracy. He gave those holdouts favoring the democratic style of government another straw to grasp with his statement that, "As our society evolves and stability returns to our nation, more and more of the power of governance may be returned to the electorate who demonstrate the requisite sense of responsibility to handle that power." It was clear by that statement that Stuart's position was that the right to cast a ballot, when eventually granted, was not unlimited. That certain criteria would be placed on the citizen's right to participate at the ballot box based on education, property, accomplishment or other qualifying factors.

Towards the end of his speech, Stuart drew attention to the basic causes that led to the collapse of the former government. Factors which still existed and needed to be repaired in the country at large before it could again assume an acceptable level of social development. He pointed out first the well known cause of the collapse which was the hunger of the masses of people for more benefits with less work. A hunger met by more and more empty promises by a leadership hell bent on continuing itself in office at any cost, even the ruination of the country. He spoke about the lack of principle and absence of discipline, not on the part of the leadership because such people are always around, ready to take advantage of others, but on the lack of morality and personal responsibility on the part of the masses. "Unless the citizens of this union exercise self discipline in their daily lives and regain a basic morality and respect for duty, honor, country, we will never realize our dream of a stable, united, developing nation. To meet this need, we will institute an educational program in our schools which will teach our young people moral principles based on the religious beliefs of their own families. They will also learn to respect the principles that history has taught all of us that produce growing, strong, nations in the world and they will be expected to abide by those principles in their daily lives. We will not tolerate slackers, usurpers, hooligans or disrupters in our new society." The men and women in the hall were again cheering loudly. All present knew that the irreligious, nonsectarian policies of the former government were largely at fault for the disintegration of moral principles that enabled people such as President Turner to lead the nation to ruin.

The cheers began in the back of the hall and spread slowly to encompass everyone in the room. Delegates, staff, Perry's men and virtually everyone in the room, shouting, "Stuart Martin for President." The chant continued for minutes with loud clapping, stamping of feet and increased to such an extent that Barnes was concerned whether or not the windows in the building could handle the noise and vibration. Stuart, for the first time in his speech, smiled down at the delegates and raised his arms for them to again take their seats. He did not respond to their appeal but told them that in the next few days, they would have an opportunity to select the person they thought most able to guide the Confederation and he hoped that "They would provide that President with the tools that he needs to get the job done, and the tool that will do that is the proposed charter." With a wave and amid thunderous applause, Stuart left the stage and proceeded to his office in the company of Robert Thomas, Sarah and Perry. Stuart's passion for the Confederation and its future expansion was contagious and Thomas found himself becoming excited at the notion that he could become an integral part of this commendable undertaking.

The day following the Conference, Stuart had Sarah come over to his office and told her to bring Robert Thomas up to date on what was going on in the west. He then told Sarah that Robert Thomas was going to be the emissary for the Confederation in dealing with the western most states, Washington, Oregon, Northern California and Nevada and to see that he was fully educated on what was known about the leaders and communities in that area. Stuart realized it was a great responsibility that he was handing to his friend on top of his other duties, but one that was in very capable hands.

When Stuart finally had a few minutes to think about how Confederation matters were progressing, he closed his office door and sat back in his chair. This past week had been very fruitful. The Conference had gone virtually as planned. The delegates were quite willing to sign on to full membership in the Confederation and had overwhelmingly elected him to the Presidency but matters slowed down a bit with adoption of the charter. Irene Covington had been working overtime to weaken the authority given to the President, but with Robert Thomas working in the background among the delegates and assuring them that their cooperation in approving the charter would be appreciated by the Administration, it finally passed by a fairly safe margin.

There were a few holdouts and Stuart took the time to meet with them after the vote to reassure them that granting extensive powers to the president would not result in a misuse of that power. "I'm not a fool," he told them, "I am fully aware that if I don't have the support of the masses of people that reside within the boundaries of the Confederation, that I won't be around for long. I intend to gain that support and yours as well. The wording on a piece of paper is far less meaningful than the actions of the leader of a government. I suggest you concentrate on what I do for this Confederation and not on what people say that I might do." When the meeting was concluded, virtually every holdout on adopting the charter had been won over.

Even before the delegates had left the Valley, Stuart had his program in operation to solidify the gains he had achieved in the conference. There was little doubt in his mind that the delegates had little, if any, power over the people in their districts. Most of them were nominal figureheads that were nothing more than carryovers from the previous government. They continued to occupy state and county offices but did little more than pretend to represent a government that no longer existed. Some of the delegates were men of action that did have power and influence over communities or organized groups of citizens. Stuart would search out and use these people to rebuild the society that he envisioned, provided that he could find them. There was a tremendous amount of rebuilding that was necessary to reestablish a functioning government throughout the area encompassed by the Confederation. Representatives that would act as go betweens from the administration office in the Valley to the communities had to be appointed or recognized so that communication lines from the president to the citizen would be effectively operating.

# Chapter Thirty-Nine

S tuart knew that time could not be wasted in getting his message out to the individual citizen or he would lose the momentum gained as a result of the conference. He called a meeting of his staff, Sarah, Perry, Thomas, Nix, Barnes, Anders and Parker. He laid out specific areas each one was to tackle immediately. Sarah was already taken care of with her focus on the target western states. As for Perry, Stuart wanted a growth in the troop levels to ten thousand by the end of the following year. He wanted troops to look sharp in new military uniforms and to present an appearance of professionalism as they moved out into the western regions. "They must be disciplined and respectful and if they can't handle that, throw them out. I want our military to be an organization our citizens would want their sons and daughters to join. Sarah, work up a memo announcing compulsory military service for all citizens over the age of eighteen for a two year period." Barnes was to oversee research and development of new weapons and replacement of existing weapons as well as housing issues for the larger troop numbers. Parker was to assist him in this endeavor. "Anders, I know you have been more than busy but would you take on the responsibility of establishing a unit of currency and financial structure for Westpac? Find people who are financially literate and setup a fund structure. Right now everyone barters and that will only hinder progress."

Stuart then ordered Perry to assemble every available member of the Defense Force and fan out across the region to present a show of force by the new administration and also to clear the way for a special team of Administration Representatives to visit as many communities as possible to brief them on the political organization of the Confederation and explain the benefits and responsibilities that membership entailed. These representatives were to report back with the reactions that they were encountering as soon as possible so that the Administration could react to developing problems. Stuart knew that there would be problems and it was essential to know the extent and severity as soon as they arose.

The ability to get the Administration's message out to the individual citizen was key to the future success of the Confederation. In order to accomplish this, Stuart called Sarah in and told her that they had to have a radio station up and operating within the month. Furthermore, the station had to have sufficient power to reach all corners of the new Confederation and furthermore that she had an additional month to extend its range throughout the west to cover the target states that Robert Thomas would be working. In preparation for the time when the station would be operating, he assigned Robert Thomas to the task of developing a news and information service that would spread the Confederation's message of peace and plenty to every single individual in the west twenty four hours a day. Everyone had radios that were lying useless in storage bins or garages as virtually every radio station in the country had been silenced years before. A few continued to operate, but they were for the most part, short range, community stations passing out local news.

Sarah searched her personnel inventory records on members with special skills and knowledge of radio propagation and came up with a number of men and women that were suited for the project. Within three days of Stuart's giving her the assignment, she was back in his office with a promise that the station would be operating within two to three weeks. Barnes already had workmen building the tower. It would not yet look like a radio station, but it would be operating while the finishing touches were applied.

Stuart also met with Perry to discuss the obvious need for the vastly increased Defense Force now that the Confederation was a reality. In order to cover the greatly increased land mass with a number of satellite bases, Perry estimated that he would need between five and ten thousand men and women under arms. The Association had the weapons that would be needed, but they had only a small fraction of the manpower needs that would have to be met. Clearly, the new members of the Confederation would have to be called upon to contribute men and materials to the security force that would be needed not only to police the region, but also to defend it from external threats. Stuart told Perry that whatever he needed for the project he would have but Stuart expected to see large formations of troops training immediately. There was some discussion regarding the draft provision calling for military service for every young man and woman to serve in the Defense Force. Many suggested an alternative community service if such alternative positions were available. Stuart was amenable to that and put Sarah in charge of that project.

Stuart instructed Perry to use his regular troops as recruiters while they were out in the field, with incentives if necessary, to bring in the required personnel. Barnes was tasked to mass produce the uniforms and equipment that the anticipated force would require and Moss was instructed to prepare a training base for the volunteers in the northern end of the Valley where they could receive their initial indoctrination and field exercises.

All of these activities placed a tremendous strain on the operations and resources of the Association staff as well as certain Valley personnel. Stuart met with Matt Parker and explained the greatly increased need for services and materials which the expanded Confederation population entailed. Parker was sympathetic as he could see that the new organization would severely tax the available manpower and resources of the Association. In answer to Stuart's request, Parker turned over a number of storage bins loaded with grain, wool and leather products to Stuart so that Barnes could meet the increased demands. He also came up with volunteers skilled in the various crafts that would be needed to develop the supplies and equipment the new Confederation would need. Within days, Barnes had converted all available building space to the fabrication of equipment and clothing for the new troops which were already beginning to stream into Goodland for assignment to the training base which was now under construction.

The following months were a period of frenzied activity for the staff that Stuart had assembled to assist him in turning ideas into reality. His first objective that needed to be accomplished within the first month was to get the word out to all of the residents of the newly annexed territories that they were now citizens of WestPac and that there were certain benefits and responsibilities associated with that status. If Stuart had his way, the rules and regulations would have been published first and the very limited advantages explained much later. Sarah and Robert Thomas prevailed upon him to go slow with informing the populace that their unrestrained freedom was about to end. Everyone was aware that without stability and order in the communities, there would be no economic or social progress but public safety did not come without a price. After heated arguments, Stuart was persuaded to make the first contact of WestPac with the outlying communities a goodwill mission, bringing food and medical supplies to areas that were in greatest need. Perry's Defense Teams that were departing for all areas of the Confederation were accompanied by mobile medical clinics, supplies of pharmaceuticals, and grain trucks fully loaded for distribution to outlying areas. Stuart also had Beth Sloan prepare and staff training buses that would accompany the troops and bring a taste of WestPac schooling to outlying communities.

When Stuart was assured that the convoys had sufficiently shown the flag throughout the land mass encompassed by the Confederation, he had Robert Thomas print up thousands of flyers explaining the new government and the rules that would be applied on all communities to bring an end to civil unrest. Curfews would be applied and criminal acts such as looting and assault would be severely punished. Stuart had Frick flying twelve hours a day dropping masses of leaflets on the larger communities and townships first and later also covering the small hamlets and farm groups. After giving the populace a few days to consider what the leaflets had to say, messages were sent to the Defense Teams operating around the region to clamp down hard on any signs of civil unrest or criminal behavior.

While these actions were taking place, Sarah had the radio station up and operating and the Voice of WestPac was being transmitted across the original target region and on into the states to the west. The message was one of hope, building a new society where everyone would be engaged in productive employment and there would again be sufficient material goods to feed and clothe everyone. Schools were being organized based on the three basic skills of reading, writing and Arithmetic and in addition two courses, one entitled American History and the other Moral Principles. Interspersed with the messages going out over The Voice of WestPac were those concerning the many benefits to be realized by the citizens becoming part of this growing and developing political organization. All people that were not already working in some acceptable capacity were expected to report to their county offices, now manned by Conference Delegates, for assignment to work details. In return, they would receive food, clothing and housing if necessary. The Voice of WestPac broadcast the various locations of the county offices throughout the four state region as well as those parts of the Dakotas and Saskatchewan encompassed by the Confederation.

Perry's troops were instructed to ensure that the offices were open and functioning the requisite number of hours and if not, they were to take over the offices and run them themselves. They were also authorized to appropriate buildings and materials necessary to carry out the mandate. The first projects assigned to the work crews were to repair the infrastructure such as roads, bridges, rail lines, communications lines, water and sewer facilities and other projects necessary for the public welfare. There was no shortage of work that needed to be done. Furthermore, Stuart passed out the message that slackers were to be rounded up and placed in penal work details, under guard, until they had demonstrated a greater willingness to work for the new society. Perry's troops were authorized to arrest any young man or woman that was suspected of not being employed in meaningful labor on behalf of their community or on behalf of Westpac or the military.

After the first month or two, there was little doubt on the part of any of the citizens of the region that this new government meant business. At first the citizens tended to ignore what was said in the leaflets and their lives continued on much as they had before the conference ever took place. In time, they began to see the uniformed force in greater numbers moving about their communities. Some of the locals chose to challenge the Defense Team members who were carrying out the humanitarian assignments initially given. Perry, not waiting for word from Stuart, passed an order to swiftly respond to any insults or challenges to any member of the force. Local bullies soon learned that they were dealing with a cadre of experienced soldiers who knew how to handle such matters. As a result, the insults and challenges ceased and local citizens who used to fear the local toughs were once again walking the streets.

During these first few months, before the training camps were turning out sufficient numbers of new Defense Team members, there was far too much policing required in all regions of the Confederation for Perry's men to handle. Consequently, Perry instructed the county officials to deputize marshals to patrol the streets and highways. Most of these new marshals were previously members of the police force or sheriff's office so they had the experience necessary to do the job. They also had the benefit of the new rules and regulations and didn't have to spend hours after an arrest ensuring the civil liberties of the offender. If they needed support, Perry's troops were immediately sent to assist.

Some of the more power hungry obviously took advantage of the situation, but for the most part there were few, if any, problems with overzealous law enforcement. Perry also had his men ensure that community jails provided adequate, food, housing and supervision and that any sign of ill treatment was corrected immediately. The word from the Valley was to make sure that the image of the new government of WestPac was favorably received by the new citizens. There would be troubles enough without infuriating the citizenry with roughshod tactics.

The extension of authority into all regions of the Confederation did not go without problems. Convoys were halted frequently as they passed through the countryside by various armed groups espousing one philosophy or another. These semi organized gangs varied in number from fifty to three hundred members. Fortunately, most were very ill equipped with respect to military hardware. They had a multiplicity of weaponry, from shotguns to deer rifles with very few semi automatic assault rifles thrown in. They would normally stop the convoys on the only road leading to wherever the convoys were headed and demand payment of taxes for the local government.

Perry instructed all of the convoy commanders to first attempt to negotiate with the leaders, explaining who they were, the size of their organization, particularly the Defense Force and suggesting that the leader of the group become the local representative for WestPac. If this was successful, the local leader was then provided a thorough briefing on his duties and responsibilities with emphasis on his obligations to abide by all Confederation rules. This very often brought a negative response, but by this time he was basically in the custody of the Defense Team and had no alternative but to accept. He and his key people were then invited to attend an organizational meeting at one of the retraining centers where they were basically reprogrammed to function according to the rules and regulations of WestPac. Perry figured correctly that these renegade leaders were running their gangs because of their leadership abilities and if these could be harnessed in a productive way, the Confederation would benefit. The retraining centers were set up around the region and were quickly filled to overflowing as Perry's men extended their influence to the far corners of the region. As the camps were being set up, an urgent call had gone from Perry back to the Valley administration office for clericals, support staff and program managers to immediately come and provide assistance to the understaffed Defense Team members trying to set up the program. Stuart created a new organization called "WestPac Corp" modeled after the Peace Corp. These were young men and women who agreed to serve two years in outlying areas organizing the citizens into the WestPac mold. This relieved the load on the military much to the satisfaction of Perry who was becoming overloaded with responsibilities.

There were some renegade groups that were not interested in even meeting with the convoy commanders that were trying to pass through their districts. Once an aggressive stand against the convoy had been taken by a force of renegades, it was Perry's policy to attack in force and destroy all vestiges of resistance including their bunkers, headquarters, and all weaponry that could inflict harm or injury on WestPac forces.

By this time, Frick was operating a small fleet of ground support aircraft quite capable of decimating a fairly large force. If Perry considered an attacking force to be sufficiently sizeable, he would call in Frick's air arm and the battle would be short lived. The surviving leaders were then rounded up and, depending upon their attitude, sent either to a retraining center or a penal facility. The remaining survivors were then assigned to work details to clean up the local area. Small units of Defense Team members were stationed in the area for a period of time to ensure that peace was maintained and to see that local law abiding citizens were again placed in positions of authority.

There were a few areas in the region encompassed by the Confederation that were avoided by the WestPac Defense Force. Hollywood and Mormon controlled zones were bypassed. There was also an extensive area of northern Idaho controlled by a number of militia groups, apparently operating in concert that was left untouched. It was Stuart's opinion regarding these areas of the west that they would eventually see the light and join the Confederation.

During the following two years, there was relative quiet along the eastern borders of territories controlled by the Confederation as their neighbors appeared to be busy unifying and strengthening their own positions. The FSP continued their somewhat sporadic attacks in the Colorado area but only occasionally ran their patrols up into western Nebraska through the Scottsbluff area and into southeastern Wyoming. Confederation forces were stationed in that area and were in sufficient strength to rebuff the smaller patrol units without incurring casualties. There were some touchy confrontations between the Confederation Defense Forces and Hollywood patrol units who were likewise concerned about FSP incursions. Finally an agreement was worked out where Hollywood observers were allowed to accompany Confederation units operating in Southeastern Wyoming so that Hollywood was fully apprised concerning threats to their own territory. The land areas of the Dakotas and Saskatchewan that had elected to join the Confederation were relatively quiet during this period of time.

During this period of rebuilding, the Voice of WestPac continued its twenty four hour campaign touting the glories of the new Confederation and the benefits that were flowing to the new citizens. There was little if any voiced opposition to the programs and policies of the new government because any media publication or radio station had to first be licensed and licenses were only granted to those supporting the Confederation goals. Robert Thomas was in charge of the new Department of Information that controlled such matters and was responsible for the content of the Voice of WestPac as well as the newly organized newspaper, The Word of WestPac. Both of these sources of information had as their primary goal the building of a national consensus. Thomas' sales abilities paid off as the new citizenry enthusiastically fell into line supporting the Confederation and their new president, Stuart Martin.

Running the new Department of Information allowed Thomas' imagination full reign in coming up with new ideas to bring the citizenry in full support of the administration. He was a believer in symbolism and pageantry as tools to motivate the populace. He was the designer of the new national flag which was an upright sword centered in a flaming wreath. The new national colors of the flag were red, black and yellow and the nations flags were soon flying in great abundance throughout the Confederation territories. Courses on 'National Goals' were incorporated in the school system for all levels and while some people took offense at this, most approved because the goals were all commendable. There was really little basis for criticizing a program that stressed duty to God, family and country. Honor in all things and obedience to the lawful rules and regulations of the community. Children over the age of twelve were organized into youth camps during the summer time where patriotic goals and individual responsibility were stressed. Irene Covington, among others, was greatly alarmed at the power the national government was assuming over the citizenry, but she was unable to obtain much support for her position. As a result of the new policies, stability and peace as well as economic growth had taken over the Confederation like wild fire. There was little, if any, criminal activity anywhere in the new nation and when it was discovered it was quickly stamped out. The citizenry enthusiastically supported the government and its new policies. While the government appeared to be all powerful, there was a corresponding protection of individual freedoms so long as they did not impede upon government policy. There was complete freedom of movement and individual enterprise. So long as a citizen was actively pursuing an individual vocation, the government did not interfere with him or her. If the citizen chose to slack off and not assist in nation building, then he would have a problem.

The new Department of Education managed by Beth Sloan had established its tentacles throughout the Confederation territories and established government schools within reach of every citizen. Course materials were strictly monitored, focusing on the basic courses in the early years with add on courses such as history and the other sciences brought in as the students progressed. Every student by the time they reached the eighth grade level was expected to have a sound foundation in the classics and a solid understanding of mathematics through higher algebra. If they could not demonstrate an acceptable level of ability with respect to these subjects, their formal education ended and they were sent to technical schools to learn the trades. These students were not looked upon as failures, rather they were treated as individuals with interests in areas other than formal education and those interests were equally in demand with those of their former classmates. For those going on after the basic formal education, four more years followed with a heavy content of literature, the sciences, mathematics, and history. Beyond those four years, students who exhibited superior ability combined with sufficient interest were allowed to attend professional schools in the areas of their choosing, assuming vacancies in those programs existed. These schools of higher learning were devoted to turning out medical doctors, biologists, chemists, engineers, and social scientists. There were no law schools as such although the area of study was somewhat encompassed in the history programs. The teachers and professors in the undergraduate and graduate programs were carefully monitored to prevent left leaning politics from entering the curriculum. Stuart had brought that up and advised Beth Sloan to ensure that there was not a rebirth of the plague that seriously damaged the American educational system.

In the three years following the adoption of the Confederation and election to the Presidency, Stuart did not have enough time in the day to do everything that he wanted. Consequently he was working longer and longer hours to the point where Sarah and others around him were concerned for his physical and mental well being. He was obsessed with extending his western borders to the Pacific and recreating an economically and militarily strong union that could withstand threats from any quarter.

His closest confidants were Robert Thomas, Ross Perry and Sarah Taves, in that order. He had the utmost confidence in the policies of Thomas which were designed to bring him the maximum amount of support from the citizens of the territory. Thomas had a knack for finding the weak underbelly of any opposition leaders in the region and turning them into strong advocates for the president. Thomas already had developed a frenzied adoration of the masses towards their President to the point where very few spoke out publicly against Stuart for fear of reprisal, not from the government, but from the people.

Shortly after the region was somewhat stabilized, Thomas had organized rallies in all of the major cities across the land controlled by the Confederation for the purpose of bringing the people in close contact with their President. At first Stuart balked at these appearances because he considered them a waste of time. All were organized by Thomas along basically the same lines. The speeches were preceded by extensive pageantry. military parades, hundreds of flag bearers carrying the Nation's new flag, hundreds of well armed Defense Force personnel, crisply attired in their parade uniforms, bearing shining weapons and marching to martial music in perfect coordination with their arms swinging to exactly the same angle and their shiny black leather boots striking the pavement as one. The halls or open pavilions where the speeches would be delivered were again festooned with flags and if at night, by flags, banners and torches, creating a mystical effect on the thousands of attentive listeners. Stuart would be presented to the audiences only after the pageantry and music had attained its greatest affect on the crowd. He would be introduced in god like terms by, none other than Robert Thomas himself who had developed a special talent for raising the crowd to the appropriate emotional height.

Stuart, as well, learned how to control and move an audience. He had learned a great deal since the time he first spoke to the delegates at the first conference at the Bayside complex, but in these visits around the new Nation, he studied the most effective techniques and when he found them to be successful, he incorporated them in his delivery. He learned which postures to use at what point in the speech, when to pause, when to look stern, when angry, when considerate. He became a master of his own abilities and used them to the maximum.

Even Thomas, who had considered himself to be an excellent speaker, commented that Stuart could control a crowd like no one he had ever known. After speaking before cheering throngs of adoring citizens on a number of occasions and seeing the benefits that were achieved with the enhanced enthusiasm and participation of the citizenry in pursuing the Nation's goals, Stuart told Thomas to continue what he was doing.

Perry had likewise been extremely successful in developing what had been an effective, but small, military organization into a force to be reckoned with by anyone in the country. After three years, he had a regular force of ten thousand men with a part time reserve compliment of an additional twenty thousand men and women. Assignments of women in the regular active Defense Force were restricted but women were allowed to participate in Reserve units. In the event of a national emergency requiring the activation of all Reserve units, women were allowed to participate in all areas of military activity following additional training. The greatest impetus to the military buildup which resulted in the much larger force was the implementation of the national service obligation imposed upon the nation's youth. Everyone, young men and women, had to devote two years following their eighteenth birthday to either military service or alternative national service. Women were restricted to national service or to non-combat related military service activities and some men also elected to serve in the national service if slots remained available. After the two year period of required service, all young men had to serve an additional six years in the Reserve. Women could elect to serve in the Reserve, but were not required to do so.

In the years since Frick had first landed his aircraft at the Valley airport, the Confederation had located and refurbished a number of planes and helicopters. Frick continued to be in charge of the aviation component of the Confederation although he was now reporting to Perry rather than to Stuart directly. The aviation wing, due to its potential military value, was no longer considered as just a very rapid form of transportation. Included in the inventory of aircraft now possessed were a number of military ground support aircraft, a few fighter aircraft as well as assault helicopters that had been located in storage areas following the expansion of Confederation territory. Frick seemed to handle the transition quite well although he sometimes complained to Sarah about his loss of independence. One problem that he did not have was that there was no shortage of pilots as these came out of the woodwork when it became known that slots in the new Defense Team air unit were available.

During this period of heightened activity for all of the Association members, Sarah and Frick were married in a ceremony performed in the administration building and officiated by a Lutheran Minister, a long time resident of Riverton. It was as formal a ceremony as Sarah could generate under the very limited circumstances they were living under. Parker had seen to it that Sarah had a very lovely wedding dress provided by one of the Montana residents and Frick was outfitted in a tuxedo apparently on loan from Parker. There were bridesmaids, flowers, candles and the usual finishing touches of an antebellum wedding. The Minister was similarly outfitted as was the Best Man who it turned out was Stuart. A reception was held after the ceremony and it was attended by virtually everyone in Riverton and Goodland. The entire event was a success.

One concern of Perry's with respect to the aviation component was their vulnerability to sophisticated weaponry. For this purpose he had Sarah create a weapons research unit comprised of various engineering specialists to review, research and develop countermeasures to preclude the losses that they had been able to impose upon the air attacks of the FSP in the Colorado area. He also suggested that research and development continue in missile technology which had been allowed to languish since the space centers in Florida, Alabama and California had been shut down. Sarah had her staff review records, contact the involved people and within days research groups were organizing their people and addressing the task at hand.

Stuart and Robert Thomas spent many long hours in the evenings discussing their respective philosophies of government when other office personnel had long since left for their homes. While Stuart's methods of pursuing goals had evolved over time, his basic distrust of people in official government positions had not changed. He considered the classic bureaucrat as the enemy of the people and he was constantly on the lookout for people in his own organization that appeared to become too comfortable in their roles. As of late, he had begun thinking of himself in many respects as a messiah, who by good fortune or otherwise had been given the mission of guiding the people of the Confederation to a better life and ridding the land of those intent upon enslaving or taking advantage of those not able to defend themselves.

While his growing power over the citizens of the Nation was a subject of some criticism throughout the region, in his own mind, he valued personal freedoms as much as anyone. As he continued to extend the length and scope of his powers throughout the region, he did so solely for the purpose of gaining the tools necessary for achieving the benefits of freedom and economic prosperity for all of the citizens of the new Confederation. He had no qualms about the extent of his own personal powers as the President because he had no intention of misusing those powers, certainly not for his own good. He had no lust for material goods whatsoever and in fact had discarded what few worldly possessions he owned over the past two years because they were in the way of his higher goals. He spent virtually his entire time in his office. Food was brought to him and he had even taken to sleeping in the office for the few hours every night that he rested. The cot that he slept on was the same type as that provided to recruits in the training camp. For his personal clothing, he limited himself to a simple blouse and trousers made from the soft hides of deer. He wore an inexpensive watch that he had worn since he escaped from the mainland years before in a hail of bullets. His only item of decorative attire was a simple sterling bolo with a turquoise stone on a leather thong around his neck which with his deer skin clothing gave him a unique appearance to go along with his simple life style.

Barnes had suggested that he could build a comfortable bed for him, but Stuart had insisted that the issue cot would be perfectly adequate. He had likewise become Spartan in his personal tastes, eating lightly of simple foods and choosing Spartan attire unless he was performing before one of Thomas' arranged tours when he allowed Thomas to choose the suitable dress for the occasion. He was totally committed to improving the life of the people that were looking to him for direction and he had no intention whatsoever of letting them down.

He had also become almost ruthless in his treatment of administration personnel who demonstrated a lack of commitment to the task at hand. He had learned to tolerate staff that did not have the depth of devotion to the cause that he did but if he discovered someone abusing a position of trust, they were banished to the outer limits of the Confederation to perform menial labor. He was particularly intolerant of any form of theft or dishonesty on the part of Administration Staff. He looked upon them as trustees of the future of the citizens in their care. As his demands for perfection increased, the tensions among the staff likewise increased but for the most part, the personnel closest to him shared his views on the responsibilities of those in command.

With respect to Robert Thomas, Stuart was very ambivalent, particularly when compared to his treatment of other staff people. He had always known that Robert Thomas was a complex personality. Many good features and some that were not. Robert Thomas was not just an opportunist, which he was, but he was also dedicated to the goals that Stuart held so dear. Thomas did believe in what Stuart was trying to do and he was going to do his level best to see that he succeeded, one way or another. In some respects he saw in Stuart an honesty that he envied because he had never possessed it himself. All of his life he had lied and stolen with impunity. If lying provided an easy way out of a difficult situation or if it afforded a way to obtain an advantage, he could look anyone in the eye and come up with the necessary story.

In working with Stuart over the years, he had learned that there was one person that he would not lie to and that was Stuart. That did not mean that he did not continue his lifelong character flaw with everyone else. Stuart was fully aware of Thomas' habit of embellishing the truth when it served his purposes and in this respect, his treatment of Thomas was unique. Stuart tolerated Thomas' flaws because Thomas was so effective in the performance of his job. He was solely responsible for the success of the Department of Information which was the primary causal factor in the progress and achievements of the Confederation. Stuart knew that and so did Robert Thomas.

Stuart did suspect on occasion that Thomas possibly harbored some thoughts that he could run the government even better than Stuart. He based that on small bits of evidence that would crop up from time to time, never significant enough to create a conflict, yet they were there. Thomas had made the move to bring in the Dakota and Saskatchewan territories without first discussing it with Stuart. Had he brought it up beforehand, Stuart likely would have hesitated to include the Canadian territory for fear of antagonizing neighbors to the north. Such matters never bothered Robert Thomas unless there would be some unfavorable reaction to deal with and that did not seem to be the case. Likewise, Thomas had been pressing Stuart to move, militarily, into the western most states of Washington, Oregon, Nevada and Northern California without further delay before other organizations took over. Stuart intended to do so, but not just yet. He was conferring with Sarah on this issue and Sarah was cautioning him to go slow as the entire territory would most likely eventually come over voluntarily without the necessity of any use of arms. Sarah also saw no organizations developing that would pose a threat to the intentions of the Confederation in that region for some time to come. Stuart had always been cautious about the use of military might to obtain additional territory. He would do so if it was absolutely necessary but if other, peaceful, means were available, he would avoid military conflict.

On many other issues, Stuart did heed Robert Thomas' suggestions and opinions. He was by far the most influential staff person in the Administration other than Stuart and many of the Staff catered to his wishes for that reason. The power that Thomas achieved by reason of his ability to influence Stuart was a matter of concern for both Sarah and Stuart's long time friend and associate, Anders. Sarah was very involved in all of the programs put into effect in the Confederation. She provided the intelligence data that preceded virtually every move the Administration made in the region and she evaluated the effects of policies after they had been placed into operation. Consequently, no one was more versed on being able to measure the success or failure of Confederation leadership than she. By reason of her function in the organization, she was constantly involved with one project or another with Stuart, Robert Thomas or both.

Over time, since the inception of the Confederation, she had observed the changes taking place in Stuart. While she saw his growing fascination with power and what it could accomplish that logic and reasoning could not, she also was aware that his basic beliefs in honest government and personal responsibility remained as they were when they had first met. Consequently, while she questioned some of his policies, her loyalty remained steadfast.

With respect to Robert Thomas, her opinion was quite different. She saw in him the potential for problems. Stuart could handle him and use his many good points, but without the guidance and restraint provided by Stuart, Robert Thomas could become a manipulator on a massive scale. He was already the uncrowned second-in-command of the Confederation and was wielding influence throughout the region, particularly with the petty bureaucrats running county and district offices in the far flung corners of the Confederation. Sarah was aware that behind the scenes deals were being conducted between Thomas and some of these Confederation underlings, but thus far they had as their purpose, enhancing some worthy goal of the Confederation. She was curious as to when they would begin enhancing goals more directly benefiting Robert Thomas and some of his cronies.

Sarah had confided her views to Anders on a number of occasions. Anders was not one to criticize other people in the Administration and in recent years, with his advancing age, he had withdrawn more and more from active leadership roles. He was quite content to oversee the day-to-day operations of the community of Goodland. He had seen enough action in his day and worried about too many people and problems in the past to take on another concern, that being Robert Thomas. Anders was more focused on Stuart's general health and well being. He had observed his friend and fellow organizer burn the midnight oil, night after night in his office working on Confederation matters, getting less and less rest in the process. Anders also had some misgivings about the extensive transfer of power to the President that began with the adoption of the charter and continued to increase by way of executive decrees ever since.

Both Anders and Stuart had always favored a strong executive management style but in the past they had also seen the need for the participation of the citizenry for two main reasons. The first being that it involved the citizens in their own government and made them more active participants in effecting social and economic progress. This was good for the community as a whole. The second benefit of citizen participation in government was that it provided a forum for the shaping of ideas that could be implemented by the leadership. This was probably the root cause of the rapid growth and development of the United States of America during its early years before citizen participation was replaced by growing involvement of wealthy special interests and further cut off by the barrier of bureaucratic road blocks.

Anders had brought up with Stuart the fact that the Confederation structure could benefit from the more active participation of a legislative body. It was not absolutely necessary at the start that such a body have oversight powers over the President but the counsel and wisdom from such a body would be beneficial. Stuart had agreed, but replied that the time was just not right to have the Confederation delegates take a more active role. As soon as the Nation was stabilized and the other western states were brought into the fold, then Stuart would agree to open the doors of the Confederation government to everyone that wished to participate. Anders did not comment further, but he was aware that leadership that did not see the need for including the governed in the decision making process during the formative period, very seldom adopted such a policy later.

Fortunately for the Confederation, he saw in Stuart a leader that would use the powers given to him for the good of the Nation. There would undoubtedly be some mistakes, errors of judgment and accidental misuse of unlimited power, but by and large, Anders had no doubt, the benefits of Stuart's running the show would well outweigh the negatives.

Irene Covington had been effectively shuffled to the background ever since the Confederation Conference. During the banquet, which she had attended as a delegate, she sat in stunned silence as she observed what she later referred to as "The takeover of the assembly's future government." She lessened her involvement with her study group post to ensure her position in what she understood would be the nucleus of the new power bloc only to discover, as she sat among delegates at the banquet, that Stuart and his select deputies were taking a different road to power. A path that did not include anyone that was then sitting on the Council of Seven that governed Valley politics. Irene had studied the proposed charter until she had virtually every word memorized. In her opinion it was loaded with loopholes that would allow the future President of the Confederation unlimited power under a number of easily fabricated circumstances.

As she sat in the banquet hall while Stuart spoke to the mesmerized throng, she looked about her at the applauding delegates and noted that for the most part, they appeared to be a well fed group that did not seem to bear the marks of hunger and hardship that characterized virtually all of the people she had seen on her trip west. She then realized that the presence of the other delegates that she was observing was as carefully orchestrated as were all other aspects of the Confederation Conference. Stuart and Robert Thomas had done a superb job of manipulating the future of this new organization and Irene had little chance of altering the present course of events at this late date. She looked for a sign of disapproval on the face of Anders or Sarah who were seated at the head table. Neither seemed to be bothered by what was taking place and that further depressed Irene as they were two people that she had believed she could count on for a voice of reason with Stuart. Irene had always thought Stuart to be more interested in a political system with a strong executive than she thought wise but what she was seeing taking form as she listened to the speeches was a system of One Man, One Vote with Stuart holding the only vote.

Stuart's plan to extend WestPac to the west coast appeared to become reality when Robert Thomas briefed the Administration on the results of his negotiations with the leaders of the western states, Washington, Oregon and Northern California. Thomas first explained that the people of those states are very independent and, while desirous of many of the benefits that our Confederation citizens have, many of their citizens find it difficult to give up their independence. Nevertheless, virtually all of the leaders of the large population centers, with a very few exceptions, were willing to join the Confederation. Thomas added that in his view, once the major cities are on board, the outlying areas would come as well. Thomas commented that, "When they see how well their neighbors are living, we'll have a hard time keeping them out."

Stuart gave the green light to Thomas and advised the Association staff to provide him whatever he needed to bring the Confederation's boundaries to the western limits of the continent. His final comment, "Have Perry make a show of force from San Francisco up to Vancouver so that everyone out there will know we mean business."

Robert Thomas went to work immediately in finalizing the unification of the western states into WestPac. He did bring Perry in to provide security when and where it was needed and also for promotional purposes to bring his impressive cadre of finely attired troops and 'show the flag'. In general, the extension of WestPac out to the Pacific Ocean went quite smoothly, with little if any problems anywhere. There were pockets of passive resistance encountered from time to time, but these generally involved small groups and did not pose a threat to the new government in any respect nor did they interfere with travel or the shipments of food and much needed materials into the newly adopted communities.

What was really occurring in the days and months before and after the western states became a part of WestPac was that everyone in the Administration was becoming increasingly concerned about the health of Stuart. He was literally working himself to death in his efforts to organize the west and strengthen it economically and militarily. Stuart knew that they were going to have to fight for their very survival at some point in the future with either or both the FSP and the growing threat of the Muslim force which controlled the northern tier of states from New York to Chicago. The north central states presently acted as a buffer to the Muslims, at least for the moment, and thus far, the FSP seemed to be concentrating on the southwest, obviously interested in the petroleum and other rich mineral resources in that area. Sooner or later one or both of these groups would target the Northwest and WestPac would then have to be ready for the fight of its life.

Stuart went over the military strength reports daily with Perry and Sarah. He was keenly interested in research and development progress with respect to new weapons to fight the huge arsenal in the possession of the FSP. WestPac was particularly vulnerable to air and missile attacks and the N.A.S.A. group that Sarah had organized pursuant to Stuart's request to come up with a solution was making progress, but according to Sarah, they were still a few years away from having the equipment in the field. Stuart told her to redouble her efforts and, "See what you can find in the Seattle area now that they are on board. They have to have aerospace people out there that we could use." Sarah had already discussed that with Robert Thomas who confirmed Stuart's comment and a number of the men and women that had worked for the aerospace companies of the Seattle area were very interested but insisted on doing their work in Seattle "Where most of the resources are located." Sarah had no problem with that and suggested to the engineers in the Valley that, "They should consider moving the entire operation to the west coast, if in fact better progress could be made out there."

After extensive discussions and visits on the part of both scientific groups to Washington and to the Valley, it was decided that the technical resources on the west coast greatly exceeded those available in the Valley. A convoy was prepared for transporting the scientists, engineers and technicians together with their materials, lab facilities and supplies to the new aerospace facility in the former Boeing plant on the south side of Seattle. Within a matter of days the trucks were loaded and on their way to the new facility. With that significant move of talent and resources from the Valley, Stuart saw the writing on the wall that the center of operations and administration of WestPac was likewise going to have to move farther west to a more central location in the new nation.

Robert Thomas inundated the airwaves over the Voice of WestPac with news of the West Coast states joining the Confederation. He also made changes to the regular programming by including educational segments explaining the policies and regulations of the new government. Interspersed with the growing list of rules they had to abide by, were included glowing descriptions of the many benefits that they were now entitled to receive, such as free education, medical care and a guarantee of adequate food and housing. The population at large welcomed the new administration.

Within months of WestPac extending its borders to the Pacific Ocean, Stuart issued an order to move the Westpac Administration offices to Portland, Oregon. This did not come as a great surprise to anyone as more and more of the administrations activities were now being conducted out of west coast offices and the Valley lacked not only technical resources possessed in abundance by the larger West Coast cities, but also the transportation and communications networks so essential for the expanding size of the new nation. The move to Portland was not without its detractors. The Portland area had not been an enthusiastic supporter of the WestPac charter with its strong executive management program. The area seemed to be continuing its long time reputation as a hotbed of liberal thought which ran counter to Stuart's philosophy but he assumed that with the new military might of Perry's forces backing up the new government and the fact that there were side benefits and opportunities for the Portland region, he would, in time, gain the support of the populace.

All in the Administration were working long hours with their increased responsibilities. Perry was busy setting up the training camps for the new recruits brought in under the compulsory military service regulation imposed on the Western States. Barnes was tasked to the maximum with orders for food stuffs, materials for rebuilding community infrastructure, clothing requirements, tools and everything the new territories had been doing without for so long. Robert Thomas, as well, was burning the midnight oil setting up new trade agreements, transfers of scarce natural resources from an area of abundance to one of shortage, and shifting labor forces from areas of no or low employment to rapidly growing communities that were in need of skilled and unskilled labor. But no one was working himself beyond the limits of his physical being as was Stuart.

He had been run down before the demands of the new territories were placed on him and with the Administration's move to Portland, he was taxing his remaining reserves.

# Chapter Forty

Tragedy struck shortly before Stuart was to give a speech in Seattle at the new aerospace facility. As he approached the podium to the rousing ovation generated by Robert Thomas, he collapsed and struck his head on the step leading up to the makeshift podium. He never regained consciousness and passed away that evening in what had been the University of Washington Hospital in Seattle. The Nation was stunned as the news came over the Voice of WestPac radio. The image of Stuart among the residents of the new nation had been molded into a living icon through the masterful manipulation of the public mind by Robert Thomas.

Immediately following Stuart's death, Robert Thomas brought all of his talents into play to make Stuart's passing the vehicle for the elevation of Thomas to the Presidency. While Stuart was still alive in the hospital in Seattle, although comatose, Robert Thomas was already speeding to the Portland offices to take charge of the propaganda campaign that he intended would propel himself into the highest office of the Nation. Others in the Administration were numb struck at the loss of Stuart who had been the absolute figurehead of the Confederation and the guiding spirit since the days at Bayside. They were all truly absorbed in their sorrow at the loss of their friend and leader.

Robert Thomas immediately took charge of the Administration offices in Portland and no one questioned his right to do so or the authority that he manifested as their thoughts were elsewhere. Furthermore, Robert Thomas was generally viewed, particularly by staff in the West, as the person most qualified to take over the organization. Ross Perry never questioned Robert Thomas' right to lead the group in Stuart's absence. No one, that is, except for Irene Covington harbored any negative thoughts about Robert Thomas' ambitions . Irene had been operating behind the scenes

464

with her new Democratic Party movement in Portland. She made sure that she was not listed as an officer of the new organization as that would bring a quick reaction from Thomas' henchmen in the Administration. Nevertheless, she ran the show and virtually everyone knew it, but no one could prove it to support a charge that she was conducting a counter government campaign while still a delegate to the Confederation from the Valley. Irene immediately tried to contact Sarah and Anders as she saw what Robert Thomas was trying to do. It was absolutely necessary that the officers of the Administration unite to stop what was obviously a takeover attempt by the ambitious Thomas. Unfortunately, neither person could be located as they were somewhere in the Seattle area and with the flurry of communications activity by reason of the tragic loss of Stuart, she was not able to find them.

Robert Thomas, knowing full well what she was up to, made sure that what radio and phone facilities were available were all classified for restricted use only pursuant to his "National Emergency Decree" requiring special approval for the use of all scarce resources. In the Voice of WestPac broadcasts that were beamed across the land, Robert Thomas' voice assuring the citizens that he was in charge and not to panic brought comfort to most who listened. To most of the citizens, it was natural, in this time of emergency that a person such as Robert Thomas would move into the number one position in the government. The citizens were not aware of the fact that Robert Thomas had used all of the powers at his command to create just that impression.

Irene was finally able to make contact with Anders and Sarah who rushed back to Riverton to assist in frustrating Robert Thomas' plans. As soon as she had returned to her former offices, Sarah began taking stock of the situation. Robert Thomas was operating out of Portland with the staff set up there by Stuart. They apparently were directing their loyalty to Thomas as no one had yet challenged his position as the heir apparent to Stuart in running WestPac. Sarah pressed for the immediate appointment of Anders as the new President of WestPac to make others in the Nation aware of the fact that not everyone was in favor of Thomas taking over. Anders after some pressure, agreed to take the post in order to stop what he saw as an attempt by Thomas to establish his own Northwestern Empire. Using the radio facilities in the Riverton Command Post, the news of Anders appointment by the Council of Seven was sent out across the airwaves. At the same time, communiqués were sent to all military units that the Riverton offices of the Council of Seven were running the show temporarily. That message was sent out under the signatures of Anders, Sarah, Matt Parker and the other members of the Council. They were names that were held in high regard by virtually everyone in the Confederation. At the same time, contact was made with Robert Thomas' office in Portland and a conference call was established between Thomas, Sarah, Ross Perry and Anders. Robert Thomas was informed that he would be facing stiff resistance in his takeover attempt and that many of the units of the Defense Force were already reporting their allegiance to the Council of Seven.

Monty Wyatt was temporarily in charge of the forces loyal to the Council but Anders made it clear to Ross Perry on the other end of the line that he would again be in charge of the Force provided he returned to Riverton immediately. Anders came up with a face saving move for Robert Thomas when he suggested that Thomas could again assume the position of Director of Economics for the new government without fear of any retribution for his attempt to move into Stuart's job. There were some in the Riverton group that were of the opinion that Thomas should be summarily punished for his out of control ambitions but that could lead to further trouble in trying to solidify relationships across the communities of the Nation. There were many citizens and businesses in outlying areas that were loyal to Thomas and punishing him could turn him into a martyr.

Anders saw all of that as he made the proposal to Thomas and pressed the issue until Thomas said that he would consider it. Anders gave him one hour to make up his mind and told him that they would reestablish contact at that time to get the decisions of both he and Ross Perry as to what their intentions were. During that hour it was obvious to all involved that Robert Thomas and Perry would be assessing their relative positions in order to arrive at a decision regarding Anders' proposal.

In the ensuing hour, Sarah had her counterparts in the Mormon country and in Hollywood send communiqués to Thomas' Portland offices recognizing Riverton as the temporary Administrative Office and Anders as the interim President pending approval by the Westpac Council. Messages also came to Thomas informing him that the Seattle, San Francisco and other key organizations were remaining loyal to the Riverton Administration.

When contact was again made with the Portland office of Robert Thomas, the decision was made. He would revert to his former assignment as Director of Economics and would remain in charge of the Information Office which ran the Voice of Westpac and the Word of Westpac. Ross Perry would continue as the Commander of the Defense Force but loyal to Anders Jensen as the new President of WestPac. Word of these assignments was immediately sent out by both Riverton and the Portland offices and the attempted coup was over.

In the following year, the Council of Seven consolidated their position as the guiding force of Westpac. Anders Jensen resigned his position as President of Westpac after the situation was stabilized and following an election by the WestPac representatives, Sarah Taves assumed the position of President and vigorously took over the many challenging duties of the post. In time, she had consolidated the WestPac organization envisioned and set up by Stuart. She also began introducing a more democratic representative participation in the governance of WestPac including expanded powers of the legislative body to provide oversight responsibility.

Irene Covington had assumed her new post in the Administration as First Assistant to the President and was beginning to see the democratic organization that she had first envisioned. Irene was heavily involved in seeing that the draft of the new WestPac constitution modeled after the United States Constitution was adopted by the Legislature.

Irene had also succeeded in frustrating the attempts of some to set up administrative agencies with regulatory power that she firmly believed had eventually led to the growth of bureaucracy and the downfall of the former government. She was very focused on seeing that the leadership of WestPac did not again fall prey to the ambitions of some in the administration with goals of their own.

Robert Thomas saw that he had made his takeover attempt too early in the process and should have waited for a more opportune moment. He also saw that he had to gain the confidence of Sarah Taves and without it, he would never be in charge of WestPac. He still retained a substantial following in all areas controlled by WestPac and made it a point to massage those relationships continuously. While outwardly supportive of Sarah, Anders and Parker, Thomas held the leaders of WestPac in disdain as naive, sophomoric staff-qualified administrators. He knew the organization needed the dynamic personality of a visionary and he knew just who that person was.

Thomas continued his efforts to raise economic standards throughout WestPac and to spread the word for WestPac with frequent references to himself. Perry's military responsibilities soon took over his time, energy and thoughts while still retaining considerable loyalty to Robert Thomas. The security of WestPac was further enhanced by a series of successful military actions in the east that apparently frustrated at least the temporary ambitions of the FSP with respect to a takeover of the western states. There was much work yet to be done in reestablishing a successful working democratic government in the western states but from all appearances, WestPac was alive and well.

After matters had settled down considerably since the passing of Stuart Martin a few months earlier, Robert Thomas and Ross Perry sat down for their first meeting following the leadership fracas that had occurred following Stuart's death. Thomas had been trying to set up the meeting for some time as he wanted an understanding with Perry as to what the future had in store for both men. Perry had also wanted to get together with Thomas but had been heavily involved in reorganization matters in

Riverton with the new leadership and wanted to be a bit careful about appearances, especially those involving meetings with Thomas.

With Robert Thomas' heavy involvement in organizing the western areas of WestPac, it became necessary for the two of them to meet and everyone was well aware of that fact. The meeting took place in the privacy of Thomas' office in Portland and when the two men were alone, they greeted one another warmly and it was apparent to each man that their relationship was as solid as it had been earlier.

"Ross, great to see you. This has been a frustrating experience for both of us. I hope you are bearing up having to report to the Riverton staff. I like them personally but they really don't replace Stuart. He knew how to deal with people and how to control territory and these people just don't."

"Robert, I totally agree. Stuart's death was so damn sudden that we just didn't have time to get organized. Such is life. I am for pursuing the same goals we had before but we have to be a bit careful as to how we go about it."

"Yes, we have to line up the people we can count on that are in Riverton as well as here in Portland and when we are ready, we will make our move. You have the Defense Teams and I assume you have good support there. Some holdouts but I would think you generally have the troops on your side. How about Monty Wyatt? I always liked that guy but he was apparently backing Anders and Sarah. Do you have him on your team or not?"

"I think Monty could be convinced to side with us if we can convince him that it would be for the good of the organization which I firmly believe it would be. I just don't think Sarah, Anders and the rest of them are prepared or qualified to deal with the problems that we are going to face in the future and I think Monty, being a smart guy, sees that as well. I will work on that. I will move him up to my staff where I can have time to spend with him. John Barnes will be with us again after some talking to. Nix is a fighter and he can be brought over. He supported Sarah but that was primarily due to the fact he had always supported her. I don't know about Frick seeing as how he is married to Sarah. I think he will go where the power is. He is not stupid."

"Ross, let us do this. I have similar work to do with the admin types that I generally interface with. My Western political clients are generally in my camp as I have been the one working with them since day one. We are going to continue to have problems with Irene Covington. She is the perpetual pain in the rear and that is not going to stop. Sarah is not stupid and she may be convinced that the task at hand requires someone who knows how to play hardball. She knows that is my game so maybe we can convert her. I hope so. I like Sarah a lot. Smart, hardworking, politically savvy. Anders is another good guy but he is, frankly, a bit over the hill now and no longer a major player. Let's keep working and check in periodically to see how we are doing. I think we can make some progress here. What do you think?"

"I totally agree. We rang the bell a little bit too early. Other great leaders have done that in the past as well but after periods of frustration and reflection, regrouped and succeeded, so we are not exactly in bad company."

Thomas laughed, "Yes, as long as we don't try to invade someone that has more marbles in the box than we have, we should do quite well."

"I'll have to remember that. I think we'll do OK. All we need is time to organize."

"I firmly agree. Let's get it done."

The two men shook hands and promised to meet at least monthly with progress reports. They were confident they would be in charge of WestPac, it was only a matter of time.

# Acknowledgements

I wish to thank John McClure of Signalman Publishing for his able assistance in getting *Searching for America* published and Duncan Long for his great artwork on the cover. Their assistance and words of encouragement are greatly appreciated.

# About the Author

R. Thomas Roe is a retired trial attorney residing along the ocean in Florida. He also has a home in the mountains of Colorado where he usually spends the summers. Mr. Roe is a graduate of St. Thomas University and William Mitchell College of Law, both in St. Paul, Minnesota. He has written other fiction novels, *The Gaelic Letters*, winner of a Royal Palm Literary Award in Fiction/Suspense and *Palm Beach Gold*, a crime fiction novel. Mr. Roe enjoys reading and writing as well as mountain biking when at his home in Colorado.

www.ingramcontent.com/pod-product-compliance
Lightning Source LLC
Chambersburg PA
CBHW030926020726
47498CB00001B/130